RED HORSE
AND OTHER
SUPERNATURAL TALES OF THE SAGE

BRIAN KEITH DAY

Inquiries and Book Orders should be addressed to:

Great Writers Media
Email: info@greatwritersmedia.com
Phone: 877-600-5469

ISBN: 978-1-960605-32-0 (sc)
ISBN: 978-1-960605-33-7 (ebk)

INTRODUCTION

This is an anthology of four short stories and a novella that I have written. The following paragraphs are brief descriptions of the origins of these stories. I send these gossamer children of mine out into the world to prove or disprove their own merit. They claim literary adulthood now. Reader, judge them now at your own discretion, with no allowances for the shortcomings of their childhood or the inadequate rearing of the madman who brought them forth.

Good for the Gander came into my head one day when I was traveling through a local golf and real estate development community for the well-to-do. This was soon after the economy collapsed in 2009. Many of the large MacMansions were closed up and for sale. I thought how interesting it would be if those houses became haunted. This story had a will of its own and an agenda of its own. In the writing of it, many things sprang from the keyboard that I did not expect.

She Wore a Yellow Ribbon was inspired by a Ray Bradbury story about a cemetery down in Mexico where the naturally arid climate dried the bodies, and the locals put them on display.

Red Horse came into being from various incidences that have been relayed to me in my daily employment in the

Sheridan, Wyoming area. I meant for this to be a short story that would be a simple, fun, experiment for me. It kind of got out of hand.

The Gold of Deadwood had its roots in my first visit to Deadwood, South Dakota with my wife. We dropped into a casino at random to drop our token, five dollar, offering to the gambling gods. The casino was filled with elderly people, gambling as I have described in the story. I found the setting extremely surreal. I have researched the history of Deadwood over the years for various reasons. The fact that it has a network of abandoned mine tunnels under its streets added to the fodder for another story. I have kept the action in the story fast paced and to the fact, much as I imagine the pace of life moves in Deadwood.

Tom Sniffty is not specifically a western tale, although Wyoming is mentioned briefly. I felt that it was a good story to finish the anthology. I always felt that we needed a good story for November, and Thanksgiving was just not lending itself to the supernatural very well. The calendar seemed to have a big gap from Halloween to Christmas to fill concerning the imaginations of children. To my knowledge, I had never heard of the European traditions of Krampus before I wrote this story. I could have possibly read about the Old World's scary, animalistic, boogey man long ago in my childhood and thus have regurgitated him into this story subconsciously. Picasso claimed that he had never seen African masks before he created his Cubist figures. Other artists and authors have claimed similar things about their works which seem to copy a previous reality. Where my Krampus came from is a mystery to me and should not detract from a good story.

Brian Keith Day

CONTENTS

GOOD FOR
THE GANDER

"Piffffttt!" spat the Gamo Whisper air rifle, and the Canadian goose lurched sideways as the tiny pellet walloped into her breast. "Filthy goose! Serves her right," Bernard thought to himself, "Now gather yourself up and flap off to some other pond to die."

He had made the mistake of shooting the first one in the head, several fowl murders ago. That first goose had honked and hissed a terrible racket in its death throws, finally flopping down the bank of the Seventh Hole water hazard behind Bernard's backyard and into the water. Bernard had hastily left his house in the Elkhorn Golf Resort to exit the scene of his crime. Returning a half hour before dusk, he had waded out into the chilly, brackish, water in a pair of old tennis shoes to retrieve the corpse. The next day, he had hauled his own garbage in the back of his Escalade to the Buffalo city landfill for the first time, along with the double-bagged, dead, goose. From then on, he shot them in the breast with the lethal, silent, little, gun so that they would fly off to die elsewhere. No more goose droppings would besmear his back lawn, and a lot less of it would spoil his golf game in the future on the rest of the Elkhorn Golf Complex.

Bernard propped the air rifle in the corner of the kitchen and cranked the window closed to the morning chill. He slid the glass door to the rear patio open, picked a foundling golf ball from the bucket by the grill, and hurled it at the pair of geese. Wobbling up to speed for lift off, the wounded bird flapped her wings frantically and managed to get airborne, probably for the last time. Her mate followed after, honking encouragement. The birds turned to rise up the slope of the Elkhorn development. "Good riddance to you," Bernard mumbled, as he watched them angle around the top of the hill, "Serves you right for freeloading here all winter. You should have flown south like the rest of the proper geese."

Not so long ago, lawn mowers had hummed across the green grass and golf carts had whirred around the fairways of the Elkhorn at any time of day. Expensive automobiles had woven their way up and down the curving roads laced between the multi-million dollar homes. Lights had winked on in the facades of glass at dusk, making the hills resemble gigantic Christmas trees.

But, since the sub-prime mortgage crash in September, Christmas was over in the Elkhorn. "For Sale" signs had sprung from the ground like toad stools in a cemetery. The plague of insolvency had struck the new rich down in their golf shoes. Vacated homes stared out with cold, black, glass eye panes, their forgotten-monument expressions saying, "I told you so." Now, the goose couple would have their choice of any silent pond or abandoned back yard to say their final farewell in.

Marie had loved to watch the geese. She had put out goose seed, specially formulated by the local feed store, for them, and they had strolled right up to the glass doors on the patio, painting the bricks with their excrement. For Marie, Bernard had pretended delight in their proximity - washed their stinking, gray, slime away with the hose without complaint. After all, Marie's fading life hadn't held many pleasures for her. Her pain had waxed and waned like cloud shadows on a windy, spring, day. Powerful narcotics had muddled her reality from nightmare, through lucidness, into giddy intoxication. When she had sat still and focused on the waterfowl at the rear widows, Bernard had been able to remember her in the healthy bloom of youth.

Finally, narcotics could no longer hold the pain at bay. A sightless, wide-eyed, banshee writhed in the chair where Bernard's shining Marie had rested and laughed away the incidental discomfort of dying, only hours before. At his desperate call, the ambulance had strolled casually into the Elkhorn and down Bernard's driveway, without any flashing lights or sirens, as if it had long ago scheduled the hour of her departure. Within a week she was dead, leaving Bernard alone to answer to the hungry geese. But he had no answer to give them, so they mocked his love as futile against Almighty Cancer with their ceaseless honking.

In desperation, he had taken the remaining goose grain to a pond on the far side of the development, but still they had returned to his patio every morning to honk for Marie. When he had finally stormed out at them, flailing his arms and shouting vile new curses that he had not uttered since he was a teenager, their beady eyes had accused him of her death. He had washed the goose poop from his brickwork one last time, and then he had purchased the air rifle.

Bernard stopped staring out the window at the empty houses staring back at him and returned to the kitchen stove to turn the bacon. He broke eggs into another pan and fried them to look like sunny daisies. He had just finished sliding the eggs onto two plates, bracketed by neat rows of crisp, brown, bacon and buttered toast, when Meghan shuffled out of the bedroom. She had disguised her lithe, young, form beneath an oversized sweatshirt and baggy sweatpants. Her bleach blonde hair hung in bedraggled, greasy, strands, a rubber band pulling a handful off-center to one shoulder. Bernard tried to remember her smooth, naked, body as she had glowed in the soft bedside light the night before, instead of this slouching, slacker brat who had just crawled out of his bedroom. He had pulled the blanket away from her as she slept beside him, to drink in the grace of a young woman's form. She could have been Helen of Troy as long as she remained unconscious. This morning, she was Quasi Motto's sister. A memory of his own wrinkly, flabby, arm resting beside her sculpted hip sobered him to the reality of his crimes. But her god was money, and he was a high priest in a small town. An entire congregation of neophytes awaited his blessings at the health club, or a back street bar at 2:00 AM.

When Meghan finally looked up at him this morning, her expression said, "Dirty, old, man." She passed the eggs and bacon by, taking only a slice of the buttered toast. "I've got to hurry into town to catch my mom. My rent is two weeks past due. She would rather pay me up to date than risk my moving back home," she tossed out, pretending she could care less whether Bernard had any interest or not.

Bernard looked at the uneaten breakfast. "How much is your rent?" he asked.

"Five hundred a month," she quoted casually, scuffing on her sneakers without lacing them up.

"If you eat some of this fine breakfast I have cooked for us, I will write you a check for both last month's rent and this month's," he offered.

"Aren't you sweet!" she chirped, "I *am* a little hungry." She pulled up one of the stools to the counter and began to pick at the eggs on one of the plates with a fork. Bernard left the kitchen for his study to write the check. He hoped that he could remember her last name.

When he returned, an empty plate rested on the counter and Meghan stood by the door. "I'll stop by this afternoon for my stuff if you are home, Barney," she said.

"Will you be spending the night?" he asked, holding out the check.

"Maybe, we'll see," she said, taking the money. Then, flashing a phony smile, she cooed "Thanks Barney," and was out of the door.

Bernard sighed to himself and sat down to eat his own breakfast alone. Money could buy a bed-warmer for an old man, but it could not buy class. He had lost all the class in his life in a hospital bed, six months ago. Someone like Marie would be as absent from the remnant of his life as a unicorn. Finishing his toast, he opened a cupboard to toss the garbage into the trash can. His precisely cooked, daisy face, eggs, and the accompanying crispy bacon, lay on top of yesterday's waste, where Meghan had tossed them while Bernard had paid her for her services. He dropped the lid on the trash can and closed the cupboard door in disgust.

Bernard caught sight of humming, green, blur crossing the front window in his periphery vision. Old Carl was out on his greens-keeping duties already this morning. The truth be known, Carl was probably younger than Bernard, but he had lived a lot harder. He bumped along industriously in one of the Elkhorn's John Deere "Gator" utility tractors. Somewhere in the little utility box of that Gator nestled a pint bottle of cheap blackberry brandy. Raking dead grass and leaves in November was certainly chilly work, and Carl certainly had no intention of ever freezing to death.

The pickled greens keeper used to stop at the Dibble house at least once a day to visit Marie when she was ill. Bernard had not minded his invasion of their privacy very much. Carl and Marie's chats on the back patio had given Bernard some time off from catering to Marie's every physical and emotional need. In truth, Bernard had become somewhat callous and condescending to Marie's repetitive conversation. Carl apparently had more patience, or perhaps her stories and opinions had all been fresh to him in his limited existence. Either way, Bernard had not felt jealous unless he had actually witnessed Marie smiling and laughing during her visits from the shabby, old, greens keeper, and he had easily avoided that situation by retiring to his study. In fact, toward the end, Marie had spent more of her conscious time with Carl than she had with Bernard.

Bernard remembered Carl watching from the seat of his Gator, out across the fairways, as the ambulance had come to get her. Carl did not visit the house after Marie had gone to the hospital. Bernard did find a sympathy card on the rear patio table beneath a small polished stone, after she had died. "I am sorry," was all that was written inside, without any signature – along with a single, gray, goose feather. Sometimes Bernard wished he could shoot Carl with the air rifle to make him disappear. If the old derelict had continued to haunt the patio like the geese, Bernard might indeed have shot him too.

* * *

Meghan never returned to the Dibble house that afternoon for her things. Bernard had spent the day in Buffalo, doing errands and shopping for the weekly groceries. He had avoided the health club intentionally so that he would not bump into her. Her unspoken "dirty, old, man" expression still burned in his brain. Tomorrow or the next day, she would come to retrieve her clothing and his memory will have scarred over, replaced by other needs. Next month's rent probably had not been paid yet. "Her appetite will return," he thought to himself with a cunning sneer.

No geese loitered on his back step tonight. He left the lights off and sat by the patio windows, commiserating with the stark cottonwoods stiffening their arteries with the chill waters of the pond against the coming winter. November's setting sunlight lanced through his front windows from the mountain peaks in the west, gilding the oak moldings of his house in bitter, red-gold. He swirled the bourbon in his glass to watch the harsh, platinum, light glance fire from the ice cubes within. Paler sheets of fire spread up the tall, glass, panes of the houses perched on the hill behind his own. Finally, the sun set beyond the mountain peaks. Purple darkness rose up from the earth to extinguish the flames.

But not all of the windows went black. Here and there, some rooms, and even entire floors of houses, remained illuminated. Bernard could make out vague figures moving around inside the rooms - large groups of figures. "Some people must have returned for a few days," Bernard thought to himself. "The Coxes must be back from Arizona. People are doing things in the Dunhams' great room as well." The longer Bernard watched the more certain he was that at least one party was in progress in the houses on the hill. He had not noticed any new traffic on the roads of the Elkhorn since he had returned home, but then he had been gone most of the day. Both the Coxes and the Dunhams had been good friends and golfing partners of Marie's and his. They should have invited him to any party they would be conducting. Perhaps they simply didn't realize that he had remained at the Elkhorn.

Bernard turned the lights on in his kitchen and found the phone book in its drawer near the telephone. The Coxes' number was written on the inside back cover, as well as that of the Dunhams. The Dunham party looked bigger, so he dialed their number first. The phone rang, and rang, and rang. The party raged on with no answer. Disgusted, Bernard tried the Coxes next. Someone picked up, laughed, and immediately hung up. "How rude!" Bernard shouted at the dead receiver. He dialed again with the same result. "I will just crash their blasted parties then. They will be delighted to see me and very sorry for their oversight. I'll find out who the giggling ninny is that hung up on me at the Coxes, and stifle her social agenda for the winter," he growled to the insolent phone as he slammed it into its cradle.

Pulling a cream, leather, jacket from the hall closet and fluffing his thin, silver, hair out with his fingers, he turned the dead bolt on the front door and went into the garage. In five minutes, he stood at the bottom of the Dunhams' long stairway beneath their front door. Bernard had always felt that this castle stairway was a little too pretentious, even by the architectural standards of the Elkhorn. It certainly was a tiresome nuisance to climb at his age, but the lights and laughter beckoned. Bernard placed his feet carefully on the steep, stone, staircase in the darkness as he climbed. Finally reaching the top step, he looked up and reached for the door bell – and the lights extinguished.

Only the relentless Wyoming wind writhed about his ankles in the utter silence. Bernard tried the knob. It remained as unyielding as a sealed crypt. He beat upon the door with his fist, and heard the echo of his efforts progressively fade against other closed doors deeper and deeper within the darkened house. "Very funny!" Bernard snarled to the empty house.

Turning to descend the steps of Castle Dunham again, he saw the welcoming lights of the Coxes' home two lots further up the street. Gossamer images of young women could be seen through the translucent curtains, interposed with darker shades of immaculately suited, young, men. Bernard knew someone would answer the door there. He didn't bother to drive his Escalade on up the two spaces to the front of the Cox house. Striding across the withered grass of the lawns instead of using the concrete path, he decided to walk straight in and apologize later. He might as well have attempted to walk through one of the exterior walls. Neither the knob nor the door yielded a whisker. Bernard bounced off with a thump to land on his skinny keister in the groomed arborvitae next to the front step. All light snuffed out within, as soon as he had touched the latch. Little breezes mimicked laughter among the dormered windows of the second story.

Bernard rubbed his bruised shoulder and struggled to free himself from the clutching arborvitae. Other lights kindled in other empty houses throughout the visible expanse of the Elkhorn. Some homes belonged to familiar owners. Some were unknown territory. Angered by the rebuke of the silent houses, Bernard resolved to solve the mystery of parties he was not invited to attend. He roared his Escalade to the closest glowing structure. This time, he thought he might be wise to observe the festivities from a short distance before attempting to join the party.

Creeping up to a dry-stone, retaining wall, he peeked over at the figures moving within the dwelling. Perhaps it was the bourbon, or perhaps age really was stealing away the sharpness of his vision, but he could not make out any facial details on any of the frolicking participants within. What details he could discern greatly unsettled him. Men wore soldier's uniforms from the post Civil War era and women wore flowing gowns of the same period. Bernard steeled his rapidly frazzling nerves. "Ah, a costume party!" he told himself. "I won't intrude. I'll just get a closer look." As he scrambled over the wall into the illumination radiating from the windows, all inhabitants turned their blank visages to the windows, gaped silent, black, circle, mouths in shock, and vanished like colored smoke scrolled up into the high ceilings - leaving darkened, lifeless, windows of rejection. Bernard actually looked up to the roofline and chimneys involuntarily, expecting the see the specters escaping into the night sky. Only the cold, sickle moon in the east returned his gaze.

Much the same happened at half a dozen other houses. Only the garb and episode of history varied. Where soldiers had waltzed with their elegant sweethearts in the previous house, coal miners jigged and polkaed in their grimy, miner's, clothes with buxom, brawny, women in gingham dresses and bonnets. Cowboys swung their best, pony-tailed, gals around in a dosey-doe as a fiddler called the square, in another house. Spurs struck showers of sparks as they pranced, but neither a nose nor an eyelash could be discerned. A black-tie-and-tails ball swirled around and around in a great, cathedral ceilinged, hall of one of the larger houses, to the exquisite music of a full orchestra. Indians, holding up bloody scalps, war danced around a roaring bonfire in another dwelling, with absolutely no apparent damage to the structure. Bernard did not show himself to the glow of their campfire in that home.

At the last house Bernard dared to approach that night, a group of young people in their teens and twenties drank beer and smoked pot to the strains of Led Zeppelin. That party spread throughout several rooms of the house it occupied. As Bernard looked into rooms, progressively further toward the rear of the building, the views became darker. Young people snorted lines of white powder from tabletops and stabbed needles into their arms. At the rear of the house, only naked legs and arms writhed out of the soupy darkness, caught in a flash of red light from some unknown source. Sometimes only a hand or bare foot splayed against the window pane for an instant. Once or twice, the back of a long-haired head bumped against the glass, but never a face. When Bernard sneaked around to the front of the house and tried to peek over the bottom of a window sill, he saw one of the figures turn toward him and mouth out the words, "It's the cops!" with its ink well mouth and, as before, everything vanished in a vacuum.

Although lights shown in many other windows throughout the abandoned community, Bernard's nerves could not take any more phantom encounters. He returned to his big, safe, SUV fortress, frightened of every cottontail and tumbleweed that crossed his path. As he unlocked his truck door, a narrow pair of headlights crested the hill above him and descended in his direction. The familiar whir of the John Deere Gator identified the silhouetted driver as Carl. Bernard was grateful for some true, flesh-and-blood, company, even if it was only Carl.

"So you have seen them too," Carl said. "I've been watching them for three nights now. Gets to be more and more houses every night."

"Can you get close enough to see their faces?" Bernard asked.

"No, every time I reach a place where I might be seen, they disappear. But I don't think they have true faces that you or I can see anyway."

"What do you mean? They must have faces. All people have faces."

"Living people have faces, at least faces that other living people can see. I am not sure what these creatures are, but you and I are not allowed to join them. And from some of the parties I have peeked in on, I would rather not join them," Carl said with a hunch of his shoulders. Both men stood silent for a moment, recollecting their worst experiences so far. "Are you going to look into any more of these ghost parties, Bernard?" he asked.

Bernard shook his head and climbed into the driver's seat of the Escalade. "I have seen enough. I am going to go home, pull the blinds, turn on the TV quite load, fall asleep in my recliner, and forget that I ever saw any of this."

"The lights will be here again tomorrow night and you will look again. You can't forget them," Carl said solemnly.

"You watch for me, Carl," he replied, closing the truck door and starting the engine.

Carl watched him back into the nearest driveway, turn around, and drive down the hill toward his own home. "What happens when they fill the houses next to you, Bernard?" he thought to himself, "What happens if you come home some night to find them dancing in your own living room?"

* * *

Carl had driven around on the many roads of the Elkhorn, gazing in at the faceless celebrators in the empty houses. He had given up trying to make out who or what these beings really looked like. They all seemed so very happy in whatever form of reverie they chose to practice. Most of all, they were not alone — and he was. What was the point of being real, if one had to be real alone? He felt no superiority simply because he could feel time passing and they apparently could not. When his brandy bottle had run empty, he had run along home to his lonely apartment above the Elkhorn maintenance building.

It was afternoon of the next day now, and Carl watched a pair of Canadian geese on the bank of the big pond in front of the maintenance building. He could distinguish the gander by the shape of its head. The gander stood peering expectantly at his mate resting on the cool sod with her neck bowed and her head nearly touching the ground. "That bird's got something wrong with her," Carl said to himself. "He wants to be on their way south, but she cannot get up." The longer Carl watched the pair, the sadder he felt.

Finally, he could not watch any longer without trying to help the injured goose in some way. Carefully, he walked out toward the injured bird. Her mate hissed and backed away, but the female remained as she had been, head down, indifferent to his approach. Carl knelt down beside the injured goose, while the gander could take no more of his presence and fluttered out onto the safety of the pond's surface. Cradling the goose's neck in one hand, Carl lifted her from the ground a little to examine her. He could see that some kind of injury had misplaced the feathers at one spot on her breast, but he could not tell the extent of the injury. She quivered in his hands, whether from fear of him, or from cold, he could not tell. Either way, Carl was almost certain that she would never make the journey south with her mate again. He knew there was nothing he could do to help her, but he felt he must do something to ease her discomfort until her ending. But how does a man comfort such a foreign creature as a wild Canadian goose? Unable to think of any other gesture, he pulled off his old, Woolrich, coat and formed a warm nest beneath her. Then he retreated to the interior of the maintenance building to watch discreetly from the window.

The gander soon swam to the shore and returned to rest beside his mate. After a half hour or so had passed, Carl could not bear to watch the good-bye of the geese any longer. He remembered some snow fence, far away over on the other side of the Elkhorn development, which needed stretching out and propping up. Slipping out of the side door of the maintenance building, he climbed into the seat of the Gator and drove away as quietly as he could.

The goose lay motionless, with her neck stretched flat on the ground, when Carl returned at dusk. The gander stood off to one side, watching her. Carl knew she was dead. So did the gander. A quarter moon rose in the east, beckoning all travelers of its sky to be on their way, but the gander lingered. "I'll help you make up your mind, poor fellow," Carl spoke to the bird. He walked slowly out to the dead goose resting on his woolen coat. "Nothing you can do for her now, old boy. You best be on your way to whatever life is left for you. I'll do right by her for you," he soothed as he gathered the dead goose up in his coat.

The gander moved away a few paces, but did not hiss this time. Carl backed away, carrying the goose in his coat. The gander watched until Carl reached the gravel near the front of the maintenance building. Then, turning his noble head toward the moon, he launched himself into night air, flapped his wings out over the smooth surface of the pond, and turned south, rising into the darkening sky to fade into the distant blue.

Carl placed the goose in a cardboard box on the garage floor and shook the feathers from his coat. He hung the coat over the back of the seat of the Gator and retired upstairs for a meager supper. Somehow, he had lost most of his appetite.

* * *

Bernard sat at his granite kitchen counter, sipping his morning coffee. He was remembering an afternoon when he had watched his father, Chester, lie down beneath the family's grand piano and proceed to repair the differential of an imaginary truck. In Chester's imaginary world, he had returned to the days when he had worked on the construction of the Alaskan Highway. The piano had actually sounded better when his father had finished, even though he hadn't touched any of the instrument's delicate innards. In Chester's world, spacemen landed in the back yard and threw horseshoes with him. Teddy Roosevelt stopped by to ask his opinion on fiscal budget problems. In the final years of his life, Chester Dibble had gradually slipped away completely from Bernard and his mother Janet, to retreat into a fantasy world of his own imagination.

Grandfather Pete had supposedly exhibited some of the same tendencies before a stroke had finished him at the age of sixty-two. Bernard pondered the possibility that he might also be showing signs of senility, dementia, or some other hereditary instability. His memories from two nights ago of the phantom parties certainly qualified him for a padded room at the nearest Booby Hatch. Having his visions confirmed by a drunken grass custodian was in no way reassuring. Last night, he had sat in the dark in his own dining room and watched the haunted houses through binoculars. If any lights appeared in otherwise vacant houses tonight, he would pull the blinds, jump in his car, and spend the night at the bar in the Occidental Hotel, watching mindless television. Carl wouldn't get as much as a wave from him from now on.

Carl was standing outside now, tapping on the glass doors to the patio. His face was flushed with something more than the morning cold. "Let me in, Bernard," he called through the thermo-pane door, his voice muted and slurred, "I have to tell you what I saw last night – who I saw." The steam cloud he made on the glass looked as if it were stained purple from blackberry brandy.

"Go away, Carl. Marie is dead. Remember?" Bernard shouted callously to the shabby, old, drunk.

"No, I saw her last night, Bernard. She was at the MacPhersen house. She was dancing and happy," Carl bellowed, loud enough to make the door shake.

Bernard leapt to the door like a young puma. Wrenching the door open, he raised his fist as if to strike poor Carl down with a mighty backhand. "Get off of my property you crazy, drunken, old, coot, or I'll drown you in the pond! How dare you mention her name in one of your booze induced nightmares! I'll have you fired and barred from setting foot in the Elkhorn again if you don't shut up and leave this instant," he screamed.

Carl stumbled backward a few paces and fell to his knees. "She smiled at me, Bernard, but she left a message for you. Please let me tell you the message. I can't rest until I have delivered her message to you."

Bernard snatched up one of the patio chairs high over his head. "I'll put you to rest!" he howled, lurching toward the cowering greens keeper.

Carl raised his arms over his head in a futile effort to shield himself from the impending blow. He looked down at the earth, but continued to speak. "She breathed on the window and wrote in the fog. She wrote, 'Tell Bernard to come.' Then she turned back to the party. I lost her in the crowd."

Bernard set the chair back down in front of him and leaned upon it, as if the wind had been kicked out of him. Carl slunk away toward his Gator before Bernard decided to thrash him with the chair again. When he had reached the Gator, he turned and repeated, "The MacPhersen house, Bernard. You know it. The biggest one at the top of the hill. End of the road." He started the Gator and whined out of sight.

So…, Bernard found himself standing in the middle of the turning circle in front of the grand MacPhersen house, on top of the highest hill of the Elkhorn, an hour after sunset, waiting for a party to begin. He expected nothing to happen, or at least, an excruciating delay of events. He dreaded some other horrid gathering, such as the Indian War Dance, or the Hippie Drug Party, but, certain as the moon rising in the east, pale lights began to waver at the bottom of windows and doors like stage lights behind a curtain. The illumination climbed steadily up the glass and strengthened. Figures dressed in attire from the 1950s swam in and out of view in a billowing crowd. Familiar gestures, posture, or styles of walking stirred memories of long, lost, friends and acquaintances from decades ago.

Soon, a particular small, slender, female, figure began to arrest his attention as she milled ever closer in the circulation of the party. Every few steps, she would almost turn to face him, but someone would touch her elbow or call her from across the room, and she would turn away again. Bernard knew that black hair, cut to shoulder length. His hands remembered the curve of those hips. That woman, walking in that room, was Marie, even if he had not gazed into her face yet. She was the exact woman he had married fifty years ago.

He could not wait any longer. Running to the door, he shouted, "Marie! Marie!" The young woman began to turn at the sound of her name beyond the window. Bernard seized the heavy, bronze, door latch. This time; this time, he would join the party. He would join Marie. But the darkness once again swallowed another glimpse of a vanished age. The shadows of a tomb replaced the glitter of the 50s, like Elvis shooting another television set.

So desperate had Bernard's plunge been to hold his Marie once again, that he burst into the foyer of the MacPhersen house like a comet. No lock had resisted his gallant entry into a darker night. Feeble starlight illuminated vague walls and lumps of blackness that must have been furniture. Bernard's knees buckled and he thrust a hand out against an opposite wall. "Marie?" he sobbed futilely and began to weep. His hand brushed a light switch and he immediately found himself facing his own pathetic, weeping, reflection in a full length mirror. The image so shamed him that he fought to gather his emotions – as if anyone inhabited the vacant house to see him in such a pitiful state. Rising to his feet, he noticed another, smaller, mirror positioned across the entry way which reflected an endless, receding, procession of red-cheeked, ghostly-pale, Bernards, trailing off into infinity. No matter how distant and minute his image got, he still looked feeble and old.

Bernard straightened himself and strode into the next room, then fumbled for a light switch along the door frame.

Finding the switches, he turned off the light in the disgusting, mirrored, voyeur and turned on the lighting in the main, great room, chamber. A huge, monolithic, stone, fireplace yawned open its black mouth at him from across the room. Yet another mirror reflected his own withered frame down to him from above the mantle. Artificial candlelight from the chandelier glinted off his bare, boney, cranium through his combed over, fluffed up, hair. His lower eyelids sagged, exposing their blood red, inner, liner.

"What is it with all these mirrors?" Bernard cursed to the empty room. He turned his back to the offensive reflection and found several magazines featuring the same gorgeous, young, woman on their covers. She had different hair and wore different fashions on each magazine, but she was definitely the same girl. Picking up one of the tabloids, he discovered that it had been issued at least ten years ago. In fact, on closer inspection, all of the issues were from ten to twenty-five years old. Now he remembered the gossip, during the construction of this monstrous trophy house, about the aged, super model who would be one of its inhabitants. Perhaps this was the clue to all of these mirrors in this carnival, side show, shack.

Bernard began to explore the other rooms of the empty home, moving slowly, turning the lights on and off as he progressed. Each room held at least one ghastly, looking glass. No mirror held any magic for flattery. Instead, it cast back an image of its victim in cold, hard, brutal, honesty. Not a single aspect of Bernard's appearance was left to the enhancement of his imagination by the time he had reached the rear of the mansion. In defiance, Bernard grinned his best Andy Griffith smile from Mayberry into the last, small, mirror of the house. The mottled, antique, glass hung in what must have been a sun room during daylight hours. His teeth looked blunted and gray, tipped this way and that, like neglected tombstones. Snubbed, he closed his mouth with a frown and shut out the lights in this final chamber as well.

A faint glow, emanating from withered flower bushes in the rear garden, beckoned him out to a brighter, living, moonlit, landscape. When he exited the awful house of flattery, he discovered some small, solar powered, accent, lights still casting their fairy glow beneath the freeze-dried rose bushes of the small, semicircular, garden. One single, elaborate, white, wrought iron, chair occupied the center of the elevated mound. Some small, dark, object, about the size of a big, bed pillow, rested on the white chair. Bernard climbed the brick steps cautiously to find out what had been forgotten on this chair of exaltation. A wicker basket rested upon the cushioned seat of the white chair, and in the basket lay a dead goose. He recoiled in disgust. Obviously it was one of the geese that he had dispatched with his air rifle.

"That drunken, dirty, bastard!" Bernard exclaimed to the empty garden. "He set me up for some kind of sick joke. Use my grief for my lost Marie to lure me up here for his own private, little, sick, justice, will he? I'll have his job for this! He has no right to accuse me! No proof of anything!"

Bernard stormed around the outside of the MacPhersen house to his waiting Escalade. No other lights shone in any of the other houses of the Elkhorn resort community. He did not forget the luring lights that he had seen, or the image of his wife. But just how the deception had been accomplished by Carl, he was not certain. Perhaps the shabby greens keeper possessed some hypnotic talents from a previous career with the circus. He certainly was the same caliber of person as any carnie freak. Well, Bernard would put an end to his pranks tomorrow. First thing in the morning, he would go to the main offices of the Elkhorn and enlighten the powers-that-be about the side show scum whom they had employed. He would tell them about the disturbed sense of humor Carl had chosen to inflict upon one of their most affluent members. There would be no more Carl sneaking into houses at night, turning lights on and off, casting slide shows on chintz curtains to break a poor old man's heart strings - not after tomorrow morning.

* * *

Feeling had completely left Carl's hands and feet. His face barely tingled in the bitter wind, strengthening from the mountains, as it brushed the previous storm out onto the prairie. The chill still made his eyes water, and the stars twinkled merrily in his blurred vision. The Elkhorn director of personnel had fired him that afternoon, on grounds that he drank too much. Well this would prove her correct when he was found frozen to this bench in the morning, surrounded by empty brandy bottles. He was on his third bottle now and feeling no pain. She had told him to gather his personal belongings so that the Elkhorn Agency could haul him and his things away to whatever relative or shelter he chose to go to. No relatives existed that would have him, and a homeless shelter did not appeal to him at all

The Elkhorn had been his home. If he could manage to put his full stash of booze down fast enough, he might manage to die at home. Then, they could send his stuff to whatever relation or shelter they might choose. Pulling another bottle from the bag at his side and cranking the top off with his numb palm, he slugged down another generous swig. A false, friendly, warmth filled him inside. His eyelids drooped and the stars faded.

Bernard wheeled the snappy, little, Alfa-Romeo Spider around the turn onto Bucktail Lane toward his home. The sports car power slid around the turn and snapped to correction. Bernard chuckled to himself and belched bourbon fumes up, warming his nose. He was not drunk, just self satisfied with the accomplishments of the day. "Linda had nice, strong, thighs when she was running on that tread mill this afternoon," he reminisced to himself. He knew she would be delighted, and oh so thankful when she discovered that he had paid her dues at the health club for another two months. Her man had been transferred to work in Grand Junction, Colorado over four months ago. Daddy hadn't sent much money either, for the care and upkeep of their little girl, for quite some time now. Linda's hours had been reduced at the bank where she worked. Her membership in the health club had to go on the chopping block now, but Bernard had fixed that for her. A casual lunch with her was the next step. She would readily agree to such an innocent proposal in gratitude for his paying of her dues. Lunch would lead to a dinner, helped along by something nice for the little girl.

The car shied on the slippery road, and Bernard whipped the wheel in the opposite direction. Perhaps the Spider had not been the best choice for a November ride. Sudden, short, storms were common in Wyoming in November. If he had bothered to check the weather, he might have been warned. He was almost home now though. The morning had been clear and bright, and he hadn't taken the car out for a while. The snazzy, little, convertible was always good for picking up chicks, too. He had needed a pick-me-up after the events of the night before.

Perhaps he *was* slowly going crazy. So what if he was. He was the only person who needed to be satisfied with his mental faculties, or his moral fiber either for that matter. It had pleased him to have Carl fired, whether the old geezer was completely responsible for the nightmares of the previous evenings, or not. The old man had been too much of a reminder of Marie's final months. Now he would be gone. Perhaps they would hire some athletic, young, woman to take his place. Bernard might have some candidates to suggest for the position.

Chasing young skirts thrust no shame into Bernard's soul either. It wasn't his fault that they had chosen the wrong man and the wrong career to survive a little economic adversity. The proper education and the correct choice of mate were always available to a young woman in this day and age. But foolish choices made them desperate fools, and fooling them into fooling with him had become the greatest entertainment this old fool had found in quite a long time. Most other pursuits were far too dangerous.

The car shimmied on the icy road again. Bernard whipped the wheel in annoyance, and promptly slid into the left-hand ditch, Ka-whump! The impact had been minor and he had been wearing his seatbelt, but he knew by its angle that the car was high-centered on the berm. Unbuckling the seatbelt, he climbed out of the Spider to survey his predicament. "Definitely high-centered. Nuts!" he muttered.

The icy wind cascaded down the collar of his thin, leather, jacket. "Another poor choice for a November outing," he thought to himself. Well, home wasn't far away; less than a mile. He locked the car and strode off briskly toward his house. An unfamiliar, disturbing, shape slumped on a wrought iron bench placed along Bucktail Drive by the Elkhorn Agency, near one of the tee-offs. Bernard stomped into the unmarked snow to investigate. It was a man and, by the smell of him, Bernard knew it was Carl.

Grabbing the inert man by his coat lapels, Bernard shook and shook. No evidence of life came from the stiff lump on the bench. Carl's face felt cold to the touch. His hands were stiff as icicles when Bernard pulled off the gloves. No pulse beat in the wrists. In a last ditch effort to find some sign of life, he reached beneath the scratchy, wool, collar of the dirty coat to feel some faint heartbeat in the frigid flesh of Carl's neck. Nothing. Bernard let the body slump back to the bench in defeat. Carl's eyes opened and his jaws parted.

"Marie is waiting, Bernard. Have you seen her?" he wheezed.

Bernard recoiled from the man who had been dead seconds ago. "Shut up, you old fool! I haven't seen anything except phantoms of my own imagination, instigated by your lies. I will not chase any vanishing lights again. Now let me get you into some place warm, and then to a hospital, although I should leave you here to finish dying. Lord knows, you have caused me enough trouble lately," he cursed.

"You cannot save me, Bernard. My heart has already stopped. It only beats for a few more strokes, as a busted watch, if shaken, might move its hands for a few more seconds. Take my coat. Wear it when you go to see your wife. It has covered a dead man tonight and will serve as a talisman. They may take you as one of their own."

"I will not! I will break the door down in the nearest house and get you inside!" Bernard shouted, grabbing Carl's arm. The frozen man's head lolled back on his shoulders. Ice already began to glaze his sightless eyes. Bernard let his arm drop.

Lights flicked on in the house nearest to the two men. "Hey there!" Bernard shouted, "Hey there! I'm so glad you are home. Come help me, quick! I've got a frozen man here. I need to get him to a hospital right away." The house stood less than fifty yards away. Anyone inside certainly would be able to hear his pleas for help in the stillness of the winter night. No doors opened. No outside lights cast a bright welcoming path from the back door or garage. Bernard ran toward the shining house.

Halfway to the house, he could see figures moving beyond the windows. Music from the 1950's wafted out on the still air. A woman with shoulder-length black hair stood a few feet from the other side of the window and peered out into the darkness. Heat from the reverie inside caused the window to steam slightly and her features to blur. But Bernard knew who she was. Without hesitation, he spun around a sprinted back to Carl. He practically tore the buttons loose that held the Woolrich coat around the old man's corpse, stripped the sleeves from the stiffened arms, and shook the coat loose from its occupant. Carl crumpled into a heap, face down in the snow. Bernard stripped off his fine leather coat and tossed it on the bench to retrieve later. Shuffling the smelly, old, wool, coat across his own shoulders, he strode with defiant determination toward the phantom house and Marie. The new snow was slippery and the window sill was low. Clasping his hands behind his back, he waddled up to the shining picture window and stretched out his long neck to peer inside. Beautiful, young, Marie came up to the window to gaze out at him in the snow. She turned to the young, handsome, man in the cream-colored coat beside her. "Look Carl!" she exclaimed, "A single goose out in the snow. He must have lost his mate."

"Yes," Carl agreed, "He will have to travel on alone now. Winter is here and it is time for him to leave."

The beautiful, young couple turned away from the window to rejoin their party. Bernard opened his mouth wide to protest. A load, forlorn "Honk!" was all that came out. In a moment, other mournful honking drifted down from far, far up in the bitter, cold, sky. Bernard could not resist the beckoning. He turned away from the window and its warm company within. Looking over his shoulder wistfully one last time, he flapped his long, gray, wings, and leapt into the sky. Before long, he found himself following one branch of a long 'V' of geese in the midnight air. They called and he called with them. They called for their mates long lost and never to be found again. He could not remember the Elkhorn and he could no longer remember Marie. All he knew was the terrible longing for something he too had lost, and that nowhere, in any part of the vast, endless, sky before him, would it ever return to him again. "Who-wheeeere…?" his fellow ganders honked ahead of him. "Who-wheeeere…?" he honked in reply.

SHE WORE A YELLOW RIBBON

Humid air blasted alkali dust into Jared's face as he climbed the hill toward the cemetery. Sand mixed with the dust to increase the sting. Atmosphere and lighting did not match the definition of afternoon. Black storm clouds boiled across the Mexican sky, shutting out nearly all hope of sunlight. Night would have begun at noon, except for a white-gray light that trickled through fault breaks in the smothering cloud blanket. A hurricane was whirling in from its spawning grounds in the Gulf to tear its way up through the funnel of Mexico.

No moisture had struck the ground in Guanajuato as yet, but the storm had waylaid Jared here just the same. The bridges had already been washed out between Guanajuato and Mexico City. Enricho, the antiquities smuggler waiting for Jared in Mexico City, would have to tuck his newest acquisitions back into whatever rabbit hole he hid them in. His Aztec and Mayan treasures had lain hidden in the ground for centuries. A few more days wouldn't make any difference in their value.

Perhaps Jared would hang around Mexico City a few extra days after the floodwaters subsided. Who could tell what wonders might wash out due to this latest storm? With a little leg-work, and the odd peso slipped into a bony, brown, peasant hand here and there, Jared might be able to eliminate the need for Enricho entirely on some of the best buys. In the mean time, he would sit out the storm here in Guanajuato.

Raymond had been right about the beautiful, manicured, nature of the town. Jared appreciated its colonial charm, even as it braced for the coming storm. He would poke through some of the shops this evening to see what he might turn up. Usually, by the time an artifact made its way from the field to a shop, even in a little town such as Guanajuato, the price had inflated so much that Jared could no longer make the profit that he was accustomed to. But he would look anyway. Sometimes locals noticed strange Gringos wandering in and out of the curiosity shops. Well-informed natives had taken Jared aside in the past, with a tug at a sleeve and a tip of their hat. Some of his most profitable purchases had been made when these local guides had led him to some secluded farmhouse or back street hovel. The starving waifs within were more than willing to sell greatgrad-mama's tapestry for the price of a potato or two. Jared smiled to himself, remembering the codex fragments that he had bought two years ago from a withered, old, beggar-woman on the out-skirts of Zagategas.

She had looked to be a hundred years old, but she had a child with her - a little girl of maybe seven or eight years. The child had tuberculosis bad and would not live to see another Christmas - any fool could see that. Jared certainly was not a fool. He had spotted immediately the Mayan codices hanging on the crumbling adobe walls in the candlelight of the beg-gar-woman's hut. Forgetting momentarily the stench of the filthy dwelling, he could smell the crisp, green, bills that the stinking rich collector from New York City would pay him with. No wonder these people died like rats from TB and a hundred other diseases when they chose to live in such squalor. *Anybody* aught to be able to find a broom, a vessel of water, and some rags to scrub the place out with, no matter how poor they were. That girl could have been swatting a few of those flies buzzing around while she wasn't doing anything else.

The gimpy worm of a man who had guided Jared to the beggar-woman's dwelling had meant for Jared to buy a pottery bowl with a jaguar design in its glaze. Busloads of these ceramic bowls had already crossed the border into the States. Every coffee table from Pasadena to Baton Rouge had one perched on a corner. All had been legitimately imported, nice and clean. No profit in that kind of thing.

"What does she want for the pot?" Jared had asked.

The worm scratched his game leg and eyeballed the sickly girl. He spoke to the woman in Spanish and she replied with a voice like cornhusks in the wind, "Mi hija est'a muy enferma. El docter es costoso."

"She needs medicine for her little girl," informed the worm.

The woman spoke softly to the little girl who immediately wrapped her twiggish arms around her cracker box chest and began to cough. Jared glanced out the hovel door to hide an expression of disgust. If they were going to con him, they should at least try to be a little more subtle about it. He would soon see who would con whom.

"How much is the medicine to cure this poor innocent child?" he asked the worm.

"200 pesos, Senior," answered the worm without consulting the woman.

"I have only seventy pesos with me tonight and I am leaving town first thing tomorrow morning, after the wire services open. I must contact my father in DeMoines to send me money for my train fare to get home," Jared lied like a spider spinning silk.

The worm spoke to the woman again. The sickly girl coughed and wiped her mouth on her shirtfront. The woman went to the girl and put her arm around the child's quacking shoulders.

"Ciento cincuenta pesos," she said without looking away from the little girl.

"175 pesos," the worm said in English.

"No, all I have is 75 pesos," Jared said, playing the stupid tourist, "Not 175."

The worm smiled, "You said 70 pesos, Senior."

The girl began to cough uncontrollably, clutching her knees to her chest in a constant spasm. Her mother rocked the girl in her arms, calling softly, "Martina, Martina." The worm wrung his hat brim in his hands and looked pleadingly at Jared.

Jared rubbed his face and hoped that his cheeks looked red. Mastering his most grievous expression, he stammered, "Okay, okay, I'll skip my dinner tonight. I've got one hundred pesos and that's all! She can have that. But she must throw those old Indian pictures she has got pinned up on her wall into the deal as well. Mom loves that kind of stuff and Dad won't mind me wasting his money so much, if it makes Mom happy."

The worm relayed the offer to the old woman. She rose to her feet without a word, while the girl continued to hack away on the dirt floor. Jared winched secretly when she tugged the priceless codices loose from the wall, rolled them up carelessly, and handed them to the worm. As if she were passing on the Holy Grail, the woman lifted the worthless jaguar bowl tenderly from its place of display on the rickety table and presented it to Jared. Jared took the bowl and dipped his head slightly, saying, "Gracias! Gracias!" The mother returned to the child who now wheezed prostrate on her side upon the floor.

The worm tugged at Jared's elbow, "We should go now, Senior. The child is very ill. Such things can travel to others if they linger too long - even to generous Gringo gentlemen."

Jared had made thousands on the codices. He had separated the images into six different fragments and brokered them to six, different, wealthy, patrons. Each deal had been a secret transaction for clean, untraceable, cash. Jared kept the jaguar bowl on the corner of his desk for an ashtray and as a reminder of the best buy he had ever made – so far.

Guanajuato's famous cemetery with its curiosities beckoned all travelers when they visited the region - whether they had arrived there of their own free will or not. Jared found himself with time on his hands. Violent weather might confine him to his hotel room or the nearest cantina all day tomorrow. He had decided to see the mummy catacombs today. The ornate iron gate of the cemetery sang its own two-note funeral dirge as it swung to and fro in the gusty wind. Close inside the stone wall of the cemetery, a couple of plots to the right, two men pecked away at the sun-baked soil of a raised grave with shovels. Their backs were toward the gate. They cursed in Spanish with low voices as they worked. Placing his steps carefully to avoid being heard, Jared crept up behind the diggers. He leaned forward so that his head came just behind and between the two. He said, "Hey!"

"Aiye! Aiye!" shouted the shorter man on the right and jumped behind the head stone, brandishing his shovel. The taller man on the left went from a stooped digging position to a full sprint in the blink of an eye. Upon hearing Jared's hysterical laughter, he turned from his position halfway across the graveyard to see what ghoul had risen from the grave to snatch him. Jared leaned on the man's abandoned shovel, incapacitated with glee.

The tall man stalked back and snatched his shovel away from Jared's grasp. "Who are you and what is your business here?" he demanded in Spanish.

"Take it easy," Jared said, "I don't speak much Spanish. Can either of you speak any English?"

"Si," the tall man answered, regaining a little of his composure, "a little. What do you want?"

"Get rid of him," the shorter man said in Spanish from behind the headstone. "We must dig this one up before the heavy rains begin and she is buried much too deep. Her people promised to pay forever and then promptly died away themselves. We should have saved their stinking carcasses and shoved them all into this great cavern that we will have to dig to bring *this* one up. Get rid of him quickly."

"What do you want here, Senior?" the tall man asked again.

"I came to see the mummies," Jared explained.

"Ah the mummies! Always the mummies!" snarled the short man, still in Spanish. "Send the damned foreigner down the hole with the dried up ones so we can get back to digging up a new leather doll for the Gringo tourists to gawk at."

"I should not send him down there alone. He might slip upon the stairs or damage one of the bodies," protested the tall man in Spanish.

"He can do no harm to the residents down there and it would serve him justly if he fell on the stairs. We could stick him in this big hole we are making, in revenge for scaring ten years of life from us. Send him down there and get back to work."

Grabbing Jared by the arm, the little man pointed across the cemetery toward an ancient knarled oak tree. Near its roots, a wooden door stood propped open above a circular shaft leading down into the ground. "Go visit your friends and leave us to our work. See if they will jump for you when you sneak up on them!" he shouted angrily into Jared's face in Spanish.

Grasping Jared's other hand, the taller man pulled him away from the graveside and his angry partner. "Come," he said, "I will show you the stairs."

The blustering wind intensified as Jared and the gravedigger made their way across the maze of haphazard burial monuments and raised plots toward the rickety wooden door. The bottom corner of the door was sandwiched between an ornate, iron, cross jabbed into the ground and a loaf sized, broken, block of marble. But the relentless wind had loosened the cross in its socket and pried the block away from the door. Smaller branches of the oak clashed against each other violently in the gathering wind to create a deafening racket above the two men. The tall gravedigger grasped the scrapwood door by its top edge and beckoned for Jared to come closer.

"Please hold this door, Senior, while I make the prop more secure," he shouted.

Jared obliged his request. Picking up the marble block in both hands, the tall Mexican struck the top of the cross three strong blows, driving it more solidly into the earth. With the third blow, the block split in two. The larger piece landed on the Mexican's toe.

"Godammit!" the man cursed and hopped away on his uninjured foot.

"Marcos! Dejede perder el tiempo con que Gringo enganosa y obtenga sobre aqui," the sort man bellowed from his excavation, "La lluvia vendr'a pronto."

"Si, si," Marcos shouted back. Pointing down the dark, circular, shaft that the door was meant to cover, he directed, "The dry ones are down there. Go and see all you want. They are through the glass doors when you reach the bottom of the stairs. Be careful on the old stairs. They are very worn."

"Are there any lights down there?" asked Jared.

"Si, there is a lantern and matches by the door. Some light comes in through high windows. You will see as much as you want if you wait a moment or two. Now I must hurry back to Paulo, or he will get angry." The gravedigger turned to leave.

Jared caught him by the arm. "Please replace the stone at the base of the door," he requested.

"Si, si," Marcos agreed, slamming the bigger fragment down on the inside edge of the door and adding the smaller piece on top of it. He hurried back across the cemetery then, leaving Jared alone on his quest for the dead.

Jared climbed down the spiral, stone, staircase into the darkness. The vault did not smell musty like his grandmother's cellar. It had no smell at all, but rather robbed the nostrils of moisture progressively with each new intake of air. Some daylight trickled down the shaft to penetrate the gloom, enough so that Jared could make out grounds-keeping tools of various shapes leaning against the walls of the catacomb entryway. A rake and hoe protruded from a neat pile of white sticks gleaming faintly in a far corner.

"Bones," Jared realized to himself.

He spotted the outline of the lantern where it rested on top of an overturned wheelbarrow. The barrow had no wheel between its shafts.

"Even the wheelbarrow is dead," Jared mumbled to himself.

His eyes grew accustomed to the dim light rapidly. Multipaned glass doors stood closed at the opposite end of the entryway.

"Nuts! I'll bet Marcos Mudhead forgot that the doors are locked," Jared grumbled.

He wove his way through the tools to the glass doors and pulled at the large brass handles. One door creaked open on its dry, rusty, hinges.

"It's open," Jared sighed with relief, "Miracles will never cease."

Pulling the door open, he stepped inside to the long hallway. He could already make out the shapes hanging at their assigned stations on the walls at either side. The light was stronger here, entering the long hallway from small windows near the ceiling. Jared wondered why the windows were not visible from the ground above. He decided that they must be concealed in some fashion by the surrounding gravestones. Before closing the door, he looked back at the lantern on the dead wheelbarrow. The entryway was much darker than the catacomb hallway in which he now stood. He decided that he would enjoy the gloomy atmosphere of the unlighted hall of the dead first, before finding the matches to light the lantern.

His eyes adjusted to the gloom quickly, the irises dilating to match the wide-open maws of the corpses hanging from the shadowed walls. Jared stepped closer to the nearest mummy for a better view. Once upon a time, some slender, young, woman might have inhabited this husk of a body suspended from wire before him now. Something resembling a discarded party gown hung entangled from the jutting hooks and angles of the human remains. Road-killed animals displayed more evidence of species than this distortion in the pale blue frock. Black hair hung from the small skull like burnt hay. Eyes, nose, and cheeks were all wadded back behind the rigid, brittle, howl of the lips. A full set of sparkling, clean, white, teeth jutted out toward Jared, like a barrier fence around a mineshaft. No evidence of a tongue could be discerned in the black cavern of the throat.

"Ah, at last I've found you," Jared said to the mummy princess, "My dream girl. Young, slim, and pretty - and no tongue."

A shriek, accompanied by a chorus of soft moans, filled the silent catacomb. Wind, gusting violently outside, was forcing its way through cracks around the tiny windows above and giving voice to the dead. Jared realized this; a split second after his reflexes had forced him to leap back from his mockery of the mummy princess.

"Please forgive my insolence, My Lady," he said with a bow. Noticing her shriveled feet were bare, with some evidence of heavy callusing still remaining on the bottoms of the dried flippers, he quickly added, "Not really a princess, but only a pauper wench anyway."

Turning to survey the rest of the hall's inhabitants, Jared spied a great, dark, hulk bound to the wall several stalls down from the princess. He shoved his hands into his pockets and strolled cockily down toward the hulk in the black suit. This mummy's mouth was strangely shut tight. Its eyes still gleamed like two black beans from the bottoms of their sunken sockets. Jared had to stoop to see this detail because the carcass wore a black fedora hat pulled down low on its forehead. The man must have been quite immense in life. Even now in his freeze-dried form, he took up a great deal of space. Other mummies hung suspended from their mounting wires with little stress, but this character slumped against the bottom of the wall, a bamboo cane looped over the crook of one arm. The wind continued to increase its velocity outside, as did the intensity of the moaning choir inside.

"Everyone else is singing in here, My Good Man. Now why are you so close-mouthed?" Jared asked the hapless mummy. Pulling a pencil stub from his pocket, Jared bent in closely, face to face with the dark hulk. Using the eraser end of the pencil stub to push up one corner of the dead man's lip, he asked, "Hiding some gold choppers perhaps, Old Boy?"

Thunder rumbled the windows in answer and lightning glow flickered about the hall to illuminate Jared's orthodontic examination. Nothing but clenched brown gums grimaced back at him from behind the tightly drawn lips.

"No money in this wallet," he observed, returning the pencil to his pocket.

Rain tapped its fingers tentatively against the windowpanes above. Finished with his shake down of the old-man mummy's mouth, Jared moved on down the long rows of dehydrated lives pinioned to the earthen walls. No guard was present to prevent him from groping a pocket on some poor wretch here or uncurling a furled ear over there in search of the overlooked earring. But the relatives and gravediggers had been much too thorough in the past and no valuables could be squeezed from the discarded, brown-paper-bag, people.

Finally, Jared stood before the mummy of what had apparently been a little girl of perhaps nine or ten years old. He guessed this by her height, dress, and long, dark, hair. A yellow, satin, ribbon bound her glossy, deep walnut-colored, hair back from her parchment face neatly. In truth, the face retained much of its recognizable countenance, even after the drying effect of the earth. Perhaps due to the lack of extra flesh in a child's face (especially in the faces of some of these malnourished, Mexican, children) little contortion of the girl's features had occurred. The hide had only shrunken and tightened on the delicate, little, skull. Her eyes remained closed, her lips only slightly parted, her chin tilted down in submission to her fate.

"A perfect shrunken head," Jared thought to himself. He fingered the jackknife in his pocket idly. "She must be fairly fresh. In a couple of years she'll curl up at the edges and be just as ugly as the rest of them," he thought.

Crash! Something slammed to the ground with brutal force beyond the glass doors at the top of the spiral stairway. The noise startled Jared back to reality. He had better be on his way back to the hotel soon while some daylight still strained its way through the edges of the hurricane. A great blast of wind must have already knocked the hatchway door loose from its haphazard bracing. He had seen enough of these Mexican pre-serves - not even a decent souvenir among the lot. It was time to go. He took one last look at the solemn, little, girl suspended in front of him.

"Who am I kidding?" he said to himself. "Your little face would spoil like a Florida Jack-O-Lantern if I tried to sneak you out of here. You will have to remain here with the rest of the uglies." On a whim, he patted her fine, kid-glove, cheek with one hand gently - while slipping the yellow ribbon from her silken locks with the other. Her head seemed to sink lower onto her birch bark chest without the ribbon in her hair. The hair cascaded down freely now to nearly cover her face. In the deepening darkness, Jared observed droplets of water fall-ing from the overhanging ceiling to collect on the scalp of the child mummy. Slowly, a trickle of water formed, coursed down the girl's forehead, and dripped from her long eyelashes. Guilt nearly gripped him for a moment, but the thought of attempt-ing to retie the ribbon around that mess of nasty, wet, hair and flesh hardened Jared's heart immediately. Stuffing the ribbon into his shirt pocket, he walked toward the glass doors.

Dampness began to make its way down through count-less, minute, fissures in the catacomb walls. It seeped in around the long-neglected windows. A mist began to form low on the catacomb floor. It swirled around Jared's feet like the ghosts of long lost pets as he hurried toward the glass doors. He heard the splash of water and felt its chill dampness oozing in over the tops of his loafers when he stepped into an unseen puddle. He reached the doors and gave one a gentle push to exit. The door gave back an unexpected stiff resistance, opening only a few inches. Jared put his shoulder against the wood frame and shoved. The door shuddered open grudgingly and Jared stepped through to find himself standing in four inches of water.

"The damn thing must have swollen shut. Amazing how fast that happened," he muttered. "Oh well, I'm out now," he chuckled as he strode up the stairs.

Without slackening his pace in anticipation of any resistance, he raised his hand to brush the flimsy hatchway door aside on his way out. The scrapwood door did not budge an inch. Jared had a split second to register surprise before the crown of his head struck something extremely hard and immobile. The blow tumbled him backward down the stairs into the fowl darkness of the entryway below.

Senseless from the blow and the fall, he rolled, and then crawled around in the mists and puddles of the catacomb hallway aimlessly. Eventually, he ceased his crawling to sit in a pool of dim light, clutching his skinned knees with one arm, and rubbing the new goose egg on top of his head with the other hand. Mist swirled to eye level, obscuring his view in the fading light. Something slithered along his right foot and hooked around his ankle. With a violent tug, he was on his face before he might clutch at the hook or spring free. Jared twisted around against the slow, dragging, force. In a panic, he grasped the unseen hook and pried it loose from his ankle, just as a brilliant electric-pink blast of lightning brought the interior of the catacomb into full view. Jared held the hooked end of a bamboo cane. The black hulk in the fedora hat held the other, his toothless maw agape in a hideous smile. Thunder plunged the long tomb into darkness again. Jared's pathetic scream knuckled under against the thunder's earth-shaking rumble. He crab-walked away from the darkness where the hulk could last be seen. Another flash of lightning revealed the black hulk still firmly attached to the wall, but writhing slowly against his bonds.

The thunder became relentless, sometimes distant, sometimes practically in the hall with Jared and the dead. Forks of lightning stabbed the interior with an uneven glare every second or two. Jared could not believe his horrified eyes. Forms wiggled and twisted in their wire harnesses on the walls as moisture trickled and dripped onto them from the walls and ceilings above. Some portions of the hideous forms seemed to be rehydrating. Grotesque, swollen, lumps of flesh hung juxtaposed in the same body, next to withered leather stretched tight over black bone. When the thunder boomed more distantly, Jared could make out the sound of ancient joints cracking and, most horrifying of all, the gurgling choking sound of voices trying to speak.

"Fire!" Jared's brain shrieked, for the ancient comfort of man. He crawled franticly down the center of the hallway toward the glass doors of the entryway. If he could find the lantern and matches, he could somehow hold the corpses at bay. Already, the sound of rusty wires snapping free, followed by gurgled cries of victory, intermixed with the din in the catacomb. So far, none of the fiends seemed to have broken completely free from the walls, but Jared spent little time gazing around the tomb space in the intermittent light. He struggled to his feet to cover the last few steps to the entryway. He reached the doorway and placed his hand to the frame. On the far side of the doors, a match flared. Jared slumped to the floor in relief, oblivious of the large pool of water that had gathered there. Marcos or the shorter gravedigger must have returned to make certain that he had left the catacombs.

Match met lantern wick and Jared found himself staring into the grinning skulls of three skeletons. The skeletons guarded the doors like sentinels, each brandishing a hoe, rake, or scythe for a weapon. A great crowd of dissimilated bones and skulls swam through the air behind in a hellish dance. The skeleton guards stomped a rhythmic dance to the sound of the thunder.

Jared slammed his shoulder against the door in desperate terror, figuring he had a better chance against the brittle skeletons than he would have against the rapidly reanimating muscle behind him. The doors did not budge, swollen shut completely now by the puddles of water gathered at their base. Jared kicked his heel through one of the lower panes of glass. A soldier skeleton slashed his ankle with a hoe immediately. Jared screamed in pain and jerked his injured foot back. Crawling a few paces back from the doors, he examined the deep wound while the skeletons looked on and laughed silently. Had the wound been made with the scythe, he would have been crippled. Jared cast a frenzied gaze around the hall with the next flash of lightning. None of the mummies had freed themselves from their wire bonds completely yet. Perhaps the mummies could not reach him if their wire bonds held through the night. The skeletons seemed to be contained by the jammed glass doors.

Jared closed his eyes tight and covered his ears with his hands. This nightmare couldn't be real. It must be a result of the bump on his head, something that hatched from the goose egg. This hallucination would fade soon. At least, he was certain, the horror would end with the morning light.

Something feathery trailed across Jared's left wrist. He pulled away and looked toward the touch with the next lightning flash. To his horror, he could see root-like feelers growing from many of the appendages of the mummies. Much as mold grows on an old bread crust, one of these feelers spread almost imperceptibly next to him. Other webs of the mold feelers seemed to be spreading across the mausoleum floor - directly toward *him*.

Jared crept backward toward the glass doors again. Glass shattered behind him as the skeleton bearing the hoe smashed out several of the panes in one door. Skeleton parts began to swirl through the openings and reassemble in the catacomb hallway, as the skeleton soldiers demolished the doors. In absolute terror, Jared crawled in the only direction he had not tried yet - toward the corner of the tomb where the little girl hung. Perhaps her bonds were stronger because she had been wired fast to the wall most recently. She was also small and not very strong. Perhaps he stood a chance with her.

Several of the soggy mummies had nearly freed themselves from their imprisonments by pulling upon the floor with their mold roots. As they pulled themselves apart in their struggles to get to Jared, a stench of newly rotting flesh filled the air. Two of the skeleton soldiers wriggled through the shattered glass doors and stood at attention with a hoe and a rack. The third soldier handed his scythe through to a tall skeleton that had just reassembled itself inside the hall. This new skeleton joined formation with the first two. The trio advanced toward Jared in a slow, determined, march, their weapons at ready. Jared backed away, screaming, "No! No! This is impossible! This isn't…"

A strong, young, hand snared him by the throat from behind, stifling his final shriek. Rooty fingers twisted him around to face the darkness in the corner. One great blast of lightning provided illumination for his final vision - the little girl peering impassively into his face as she squeezed her fingers tightly closed around his throat.

* * *

Marcos approached the cemetery with great trepidation. It had been four days since he had last been there. The hurricane had raged so strongly for two days that everyone had remained indoors. On the two days that followed, Marcos had worked with the rest of the men of Guanajuato to clear the rubble from the damaged buildings. Five people had been killed in the terrible storm and several others injured. Now he would have to face the devastation that the storm had wrecked upon his place of livelihood.

The storm had sprung the cemetery gates wide open. One gate hung by its lower hinge only. The other lay flat on the ground, completely wrenched free. Stones and markers were tilted and scattered everywhere. Even a thorough search of the parish records would not reveal precisely where all of the grave markers properly belonged. Marcos stopped at the edge of a small, muddy, pond. It filled the excavation that Paulo and he had started on the day of the storm. Paulo would probably decide to push the soil back into the hole as the water subsided, rather than deal with the ghastly remains waiting beneath the muck in the bottom of the grave.

The catacomb and the mummies within would be another matter. Paulo and he would have to sort out which bodies could be salvaged for display again and which bodies must be discarded. Bones would have to be hauled to the surface and dried in the sun. God only knew what damage had been done to the structure itself. At least now there would be room for more bodies to be stored in the future. Paulo and he had dreaded the task of digging an extension to the display hallway to provide room for new inhabitants. Now they had an entirely different problem to dread.

One great limb of the cemetery oak had split away from the trunk in the violence of Hurricane Martina. The limb had fallen across the hatchway to the catacombs. Suddenly, Marcos remembered the Gringo who had entered the crypt before the storm. He hoped the Gringo had possessed enough sense to get the hell out of there - before the limb had fallen. Marcos rushed to the entrance of the crypt. When he reached a point where he could look over the top of the massive limb, Marcos nearly jumped out of his own skin. Something brown moved there on the remains of the hatchway. With another stride and to his great relief, Marcos could see that it was only a little girl playing there on the splintered remains of the door.

"Get home, you silly, little, waif!" he snarled, in a voice he had learned from Paulo. "This is no place for a child to be. Get out of here or I will take you down below to stay."

"The poor little girl looked up at him with primal horror in her eyes. She leaped to her feet and ran as though Hell itself yawned beneath her. Marcos chuckled to himself for the first time since before the storm had struck. "There will be new life in the world again today; as there is on all other days," he reminded himself. It was a saying that he often told himself when his work in the land of the dead became too depressing. He watched the little girl bound off through the sunlit fields - a yellow ribbon in her hair.

RED HORSE

"Who would do such a thing!" Ansdel growled to himself, "Ruined! Four days work and no fix for it." The crude image of a red horse sprawled diagonally across one third of the expensive paper, obliterating most of Andsel's detailed watercolor of old ranch buildings against a western landscape. Someone had entered his studio and deliberately daubed the equine image with their fingers, in fiery, red, paint, across his artwork. His unbiased artist's eye involuntarily acknowledged that, had the horse been alone on a single color field, and oriented in an interesting fashion on the paper, it would have been a beautifully crude and powerful icon. Whoever had created the horse had scuffed the body and head in with one, single, precise, gesture of his hand. Andsel noted with disgust that the orientation wasn't even on a strong diagonal of the composition. As if the vandal couldn't even see the carefully executed watercolor beneath his own creation, the horse's image was skewed on a haphazard bias.

"Well, even an elephant can get lucky, given enough paint and paper," Andsel muttered to himself to refute the scurrilous artist's talent and to soothe his own ego. He peeled the water tape from the edges of the ruined artwork and stripped the painting from the work board. The Alhausers would have to wait another month for the watercolor of their homestead ranch buildings to be finished. "Great art never arrived on time anyway," he consoled himself. "Extended anticipation always made the final product more worthy of the commissioned price."

Who could possibly have been in his studio since he had last worked on the painting? His wife Tiffany certainly had unrestricted access to his studio. She sometimes visited to give insincere appreciation for his artwork, but he knew that she could not recognize his latest artistic effort from some painting that he had done a year or two ago. She wouldn't know what to damage, even if she had reason to.

In fact, his artwork was an ally to her, keeping him in the studio late into the night, and out of her bed. The complex activity of painting soaked up his mental concentration like an emotional vampire, leaving little remaining energy for romantic interests. They were both far too old for such foolishness, she had decided. After a year of trying to convince her otherwise, Andsel had stopped fighting the battle and retreated to his studio and his fantasies of colored paper. Whether newly created or old familiars, the denizens of his studio sanctuary held no interest for her whatsoever. The hand that had created the red horse was far too large to have been hers anyway.

Joan, the cleaning lady, entered the studio once or twice a week sparingly, but, for fear of Andsel's painting props and artifacts, spent so little time in here that she could not have accomplished the graffiti. Though her hands were certainly beefy enough, she used them only to pick up the scrap paper from the floor, to hurriedly run a vacuum cleaner over the paint-stained carpet, and to haul out the trash. She refused to dust his western history souvenirs, even for any additional amount of pay. The lances and tomahawks displayed on the walls made her cringe away behind her feather duster. Andsel's favorite antiquity, a crownless skull, grinned innocently from its quilted coverlet on a shelf and kept her from entering that half of the room entirely.

At arm's length, she would push the Hoover franticly back into the domain of the skull, pawing only the dust bunnies within her mechanical reach, and carefully averting her gaze to the side, lest the skull catch her eye and call her name. Andsel had turned the face of the skull toward the wall behind it, where, years ago, a painting of a New England farmstead had settled from the studio's clutter. But Joan still imagined that it might turn part way around on its own and wink one yellowed cheekbone at her, as if to say, "See you in your dreams, baby." Those shelves remained undusted until Andsel found the time for the task himself.

"Cats or kids," Andsel muttered to himself, knowing full well neither creature existed on the property nor had access to the inner sanctum of his studio. Dismissing the mystery of the ruined painting as too complex to bother with anymore, and certainly too distressing, Andsel reached for a cardboard box, which UPS had delivered yesterday. Whatever the box contained was not very heavy. Whoever had shipped the item had not bothered to package it very securely either. One single layer of packing tape sealed the top flaps shut, and no other tape had been applied to the bottom or sides to reinforce the cardboard. "I may have to write a complaint letter or make a call to the vender if this is damaged," Andsel thought to himself, as he slit the seam of packing tape apart with one blade of his work table scissors. A hand written note in a familiar script lay on top of the contents. Andsel suddenly deduced that this package had never seen the inside of a UPS truck. Lou Palzella, of Carter Drilling, had written the note. Lou must have personally dropped this box off by the Edgar doorstep, and delivered it extremely discreetly as well.

The note read:

"Don't ask me where this turned up. I will not
remember. One of my most dependable hands
will be attending his bachelor party at the Mint

Bar next Wednesday night. I'll expect a large prepaid tab to be waiting at the bar for him and his friends - courtesy of you. It is his second marriage, so no need to be too generous. If you are too stingy though, these young men will not be able to sufficiently forget where this item came from. If the memory cleansing funds are not adequate, I will temporarily refresh the tab and hit you up for the balance later. Enjoy. Burn this note.

L. P.

Andsel pulled the wadded newspaper away from the box's contents. A jagged half-dome of yellow-brown bone gleamed dully up at him. One small hole, about the diameter of his little finger, pierced the intact cranium of a human skull. He plunged his hands into the box to lift the ancient skull out and shake the box free onto his work table. The box struck the table top with a dull thud, sounding much too heavy for cardboard alone. Andsel turned the grisly trophy, retrieved from some unknown gas well platform or remote access road, to peer up at him with surprised, accusing, sockets. It must have been quite a shock for some dozer operator when he had rolled up this relic of the long ago Indian wars to snarl at him from the red sand and clay of the Powder River Basin; or perhaps, some roughneck had kicked it out from beneath the gnarled limbs of an ancient sagebrush. Andsel had received a few odd finds in the past from Lou, an arrowhead or two and a rifle barrel of indeterminate age, but never anything like this. No wonder Lou had hastily boxed the thing up and told his hands to keep their goddamn mouths shut if they wanted to finish that hole and get paid. Between the Indians, archeologists, and the police, that area would have been shut down for a mile in every direction against any further drilling.

Remembering the heavy thump in the box, he groped around inside it with one free hand, while continuing to examine the skull. The V shape of a snaggle-toothed jawbone looped over the heel of his fumbling hand. "A complete skull!" he whistled to himself as he pulled the lower mandible from the box. Some teeth were missing from the front incisors of the jaw, but no evidence of dental work appeared upon first inspection. Andsel fit the jawbone into place beneath its upper mandible on the skull and rested the complete assembly on the edge o his work table. He knelt down to look at this ancient traveler, face to face.

The skull stood long and a bit narrow, with high, prominent, cheek bones. One hundred and fifty years or more of wind and water had softened the edges of the bullet hole and its exit fracture. Sediment had stained the ivory-white bone to nearly the color of suntanned flesh. Perhaps the hide, which once had covered this skull, had been genetically, a beautiful red-brown. The bullet hole was not that large, probably a 36 caliber Colt Navy. Chances were good that this man had been and Indian. But then again, Indians had used pistols on white men too. Plenty of Caucasian soldiers or homesteaders had been long faced, high cheek boned, Swedes or Irishmen. Perhaps this poor man could have been some disillusioned homesteader, putting a bullet into his own head from sheer despair. Perhaps a rusty .38 revolver lay buried only a few inches beneath the soil where this skull had been found. Who could even be certain that this skull had belonged to a man and not to a big, horse faced, woman? Perhaps the man had shot his horse faced wife. The real story was anyone's guess. Only someone skilled in forensics or paleontology could say for certain what race this person had belonged to, and that kind of examination would bring the same hurricane of trouble down upon Andsel that Lou had avoided by hustling this relic off to his doorstep.

Andsel studied and admired the skull for several minutes more, then looked around his studio for a place to display his new acquisition. He decided to place it at the opposite end of the same shelf on which the scalping-victim skull rested. In peevish anticipation of Joan's personal discovery of his chamber of horror's newest inhabitant, he positioned the skull so that it stared directly toward the entry of the studio. Andsel hoped to be sitting quietly in the living room, in complete innocence, when she shoved her Hoover down the hallway and trundled through the door of the studio. He chuckled to himself at the thought of her reaction. Soon, Andsel would be responsible for the cleaning of his studio entirely on his own, if Lou brought any more of his finds for Andsel to display,

Tiffany called, "Dinner, Dear!" from the far end of the house.

Exchanging one last glance with his new boarder, Andsel flicked off the lights of the studio and pulled the door shut behind him.

CHAPTER TWO

Joan sat in one of the Edgars' patio chairs, holding a small boy who looked to be about ten years old. The boy's face was buried in Joan's ample bosom, and Andsel could see that he was either crying or laughing hysterically, as he drove up his driveway in his pick-up truck. When the truck's engine had stilled, and Andsel opened the truck door, he could tell that nothing was funny. Joan glared at him over the crown of the boy's head.

"Is this your son, Joan?" he asked innocently.

"No, he is my grandson, Mr. Edgar," she answered tersely. "I am watching him for my daughter for a few days."

Andsel decided not to ask about all the tears. He did not see any blood dripping from the boy, and all of the child's limbs and digits seemed to be in place and in the proper form. If Andsel was supposed to know what the boy's problem was, he was sure one of the two women currently in the house would inform him very soon. He would rather not verbally walk head first into it, so he walked into the house without a further word to Joan. His wife met him at the door to the kitchen with a glass of milk in her hand. Her expression was not pleasant.

"Your collection of horrors has frightened that poor child completely out of his wits," she stated testily.

"What was he doing in my studio, or, better yet, what is he doing here at all?" Andsel threw out, as a logical and obviously idiotic defense.

Tiffany Edgar brushed past her husband with a scowl. "I'll discuss your newest trophy with you after I give this boy his milk. I have put a little Bailey's in it to soothe his nerves. He has had quite a shock."

Andsel watched through the dining room window as his wife administered her sedative-laced potion. After a tentative sip, the boy took a hearty swig, obviously starting down the road to a fine career of future DUIs. "Tiffany will be proud in years to come," he thought to himself. The two women exchanged knowing glances like generals before the slaughter. Andsel decided to take their onslaught sitting down and retired to his recliner in the living room. He flipped on the news with the remote and pretended to be absorbed in the woes of the world. Pretty soon, his view became obstructed by a small, irate, woman, resembling his wife.

"If you are going to continue collecting gruesome, morbid, objects from the local past, I will have to insist that you lock them up!" Tiffany snapped at him.

"Now listen here, Tiff! All of the house is yours to do with as you see fit – except my studio. That area is my domain. If you choose to allow Joan to baby-sit her grand children at the same time that she is supposed to be cleaning our home, that is your business. If the house stays clean, I do not care. But I will not have unsupervised children rampaging through my things. If she chooses to bring a child here, she had better keep it on a short leash – literally if need be," Andsel huffed until he was short of breath.

Tiffany puffed up nearly all of the available oxygen in the room for her next tirade, leaving precious little remaining for poor, suffocating, Andsel. "That new skull with the bullet hole is obscene!" she began. "The first one was bad enough, but at least you kept it turned toward that tacky, New England, painting, away from anyone's immediate view. Most people took it for a piece of primitive, Indian, pottery. But this new one! Grinning at a person, with the back half of its head blown away so hideously! Enough is enough!

"You've got hatchets and spear points bristling from every wall, some of them with hair still stuck to them. I tell people the hair is only cobwebs and hustle them out of the room before they look too closely. That poor boy poked his head in your studio door and came out screaming as if the devil himself stood in there. Joan refuses to clean the studio at all now. You will have to take care of it yourself."

"I ask you again," Andsel defended, "What is that boy doing here, and why was he allowed anywhere near my studio? He ruined a painting of mine yesterday, you know; smeared red paint all over it."

"Cody wasn't here at all yesterday, Andsel. You probably spilled the paint on your picture yourself, clumsy as you are. Joan's daughter and her husband are going through some tough times right now. They took a long weekend to spend some romantic time together in Deadwood. Joan volunteered to watch Cody, like a good grandparent. You could be a little supportive, and you could apologize for leaving such ghoulish objects out for anyone to stumble across."

"Cody Boy had to stumble all the way down a long hallway, around a corner, and through the laundry room to luck on to my studio door. I am glad the skull was there as a kind of watch dog. No telling what mischief he would have done in there today. And by-the-way, it was *you* who was not here yesterday – remember? You spent the day at the farmer's market and at the various yard sales in town, turning over old clothing. You only know that Joan *says* she did not bring this boy with her yesterday."

"Mr. Edgar, I am ashamed of you! Joan has never been anything but honest and straightforward with us. The poor woman has problems enough right now without your childish accusations."

Andsel could see that he would loose this battle. Tiffany would resort to bringing Joan and the boy in for a tearful confrontation if the argument continued much longer. He decided to exchange one verbal engagement for another waiting outside in the patio chair. Opening a second confrontation might be risky. Such strategies had not worked out so well for Hitler or Harold the Great, but maybe he would have better luck. After all, Joan was no William the Conqueror. Given her limited intellect, he might survive the battle without getting an arrow in the eye.

"I'll go talk to Joan and the boy," he offered, "But she is not to let him out of her sight if she brings him here again. I will close the door to the studio, but I will not install a lock. I refuse to have to fetch up a key to go into my own, personal, area of this house!"

"You had better make some kind of appeasement to Joan for your little prank, or she may decide not to clean for us at all," Tiffany scolded.

"This damned skull is getting terribly expensive," Andsel thought to himself as he rose from his chair and headed for the front door. He would give her two more bucks an hour – three tops, but she would continue to clean the studio; that was for damn sure!"

Cody had ceased his blubbering. He slumped in Joan's lap in a stupor, gazing down at his sneakers. The Bailey Milk was taking effect, no doubt. Joan remained silent and expectant. Most likely, she had already calculated a figure for her raise.

"I understand your grandson, Cody here, found a little surprise while he was exploring my studio this morning," he started.

Joan unstopped her bottle of self righteous indignation, "Such remnants of the body belong in a cemetery, Mr. Edgar, not displayed on a shelf to frighten innocent children. If you choose to deny the dead proper burial and hoard their poor bones in your home, that is your business – even though such a practice is a sin in God's eyes. Could you please have the decency to but your relics out of sight from those of us who still hold some respect for the remains of our dead?"

Andsel was tempted to ask Joan just how well she had known the deceased, but decided to get this confrontation over as quickly as possible. "I am sorry, Joan, I was not aware that you were bringing your relatives to work with you," was the sharpest comment he would allow himself to make. "The collections in my private studio are only inanimate objects of metal, wood, and bone to me. I forget that a misguided child might see them as something else if he is allowed to wander into my private area alone," he continued.

Cody looked up at Andsel with wild eyes. "The Indian motioned for me to follow him. His hand appeared around the corner of the hallway and waved for me to follow him. When I came around the corner and through the doorway of the room, he stood in the far corner. He was huge! His war bonnet curled back and spread like fire across the ceiling. He held a long, curved, stick, with many flaming feathers and bands of color twisting around it. He reached out to touch me with the hooked end of the stick, but I ran!" the boy sobbed out.

"That is a coup stick, Cody. Never let an Indian touch you with his coup stick, or he will steal your soul," Andsel lectured, unable to stop himself from enjoying Halloween urges many months out of season.

The boy buried his face in Joan's pillowy chest again and resumed his whimpering. Andsel noticed the milk glass was empty. Perhaps the boy needed a refill, if Tiffany could spare it.

"Don't encourage Cody's vivid imagination, Mr. Edgar!" Joan reprimanded. "I won't be able to get him to sleep for the next few nights as it is. Some monster is always under his bed already without any help from you. This trouble his mom and dad are having has put his tender, little, nervous system all a' jitter."

"Shall I take him back to my studio and show him that the skulls are only dry, harmless, old, bones, Joan? Would that help?" Andsel volunteered in desperation.

"Mr. Edgar!" Joan shrieked, as the boy seemed to attempt to crawl beneath her very skin, "You apparently know absolutely nothing about raising children! I think that I had better take Cody home and finish cleaning your house another day. Your home is far too upsetting for a child to spend any time in. Perhaps when Cody can return to his parents' care, in a week or so, I may return to clean for Mrs. Edgar."

Now the situation had become critical. Even if Andsel moved to a hotel for a week, the house would never remain clean enough to suit Tiff's demanding standards. His life would be a living hell for months. Time to make an offer. "Go ahead and take the day off with pay, Joan. In fact, I'll raise your pay three dollars an hour because you do such an excellent job maintaining sanitation in this house. But please come back to finish tomorrow. Bring little Cody if you like. I will keep the door to the studio closed and you needn't clean in that end of the house at all while he is staying with you."

A faint smile passed like a second ghost across Joan's face as she rose up from the patio chair and set the boy on his own two feet. "That is very generous of you, Mr. Edgar," she said, "I will return tomorrow, if Cody has calmed down enough by then. Hopefully, by this time next week, all of this Indian business will be put behind us."

Andsel rummaged through his pockets to find the loose bills remaining from paying for his breakfast at the Country Cottage with his Thursday morning coffee group. A five and a couple of ones came out in a wad. "Stop down at the Dairy Queen and have yourselves a sundae on the way home. Maybe some ice cream will take Cody's mind off of spooks," he offered, holding the bills out to Joan. She thanked him and led her grandson out to her late model Ford parked on the street. Andsel retreated to the house. "Well that is settled," he tossed off to Tiffany as he passed through the living room on his way to the studio.

"Is she coming to finish her cleaning tomorrow?" Tiffany demanded to his departing backside.

"Of course," he answered, as if no traumatized child had ever complicated his sunny morning at all.

Nothing appeared out of place in the studio – no scorch marks on the ceiling from flaming feathers, no furniture bashed about by a magic coup stick. The new skull grinned at Andsel from its corner like a toothy puppy dog, ready to play. He walked over to the skull and patted it fondly. "Good doggy. Good boy," he cooed. "You drove out the nosey, naughty, little, sissy boy, didn't you. You're a good watch dog." The skull warmed rapidly to his touch. When Andsel pulled his hand away, the skull's brow ridges no longer seemed bowed in friendly arches. Even though the bone was as permanent as granite, some trick of light gave the brows a much more cliff-like ridge of defiance. Andsel tapped the bullet hole with his finger in a gesture of subjugation, then turned to his tilted work table to begin again the Alhauser ranch painting.

Selecting another sheet of rough-toothed, watercolor paper from a large folder stacked against the wall, he taped the paper down to his work board on the table. He arranged several preliminary sketches of the buildings, which he had drawn on a previous visit to the ranch, around the blank paper, and then began to rough in the shapes with faint, water-base pencil, lines. When the building forms had been established, he poured fresh, clean, water into a plastic bowl and spread several blobs of raw watercolor paint out onto his main pallet.

Andsel first washed some sky tones across the top of the virgin page, followed by other earth-tone washes in the ground areas toward the bottom of the space. Andsel's mind watched his domain through the windows of his eyes from a high tower and drove the hands to obey his will. Like slaves at his command, his fingers mixed the colors and moved the brush across the page. Geometric building planes asserted their forms on the landscape, beneath his hand. Barn boards were sawn, shaped, and weathered, then hammered into place on the paper, with precise, intricate, strokes of his indentured digits. Sharp lines of prairie grass and sagebrush spurted from the ground, rising as much from the earth of the stained linen paper as raining down from the bristles of the flourishing brush. Andsel worked on, within the harmonious world of his own contrivance. Time moved around him at his work as a stream flows around a stone, forming swirling eddies and deep pools of wonder in its shadow. Sunlight kindled in his mind's eye to bleach the whiteness of the paper and shoot yellow through the tawny grass. His breath stirred winds of Payne's Gray that rippled through the sky.

Initially, the fingers responded as directed, but, as the Alhauser painting progressed, the serfs began to rebel. At first, they only wandered a little, creating a different shade here, an unruly line there. Andsel snarled at the five-fingered slave subconsciously, and it toed the line again for a few minutes more. But the hand soon meandered off on a task of its own contrivance once again. Beads of sweat oozed out onto Andsel's forehead as he struggled to contain the rebellion. Errors manifested themselves within the commanded blueprint. Andsel conjured up tricks to repair or conceal the damage. Numb fingers revolted again to set different parameters. The artist chose a different blueprint and redirected the slave.

Something brushed his back and distracted his attention out of the window to the Wolf Mountains in the distance. Five minutes passed.

Andsel suddenly realized that he had been painting without even looking at his artwork. Turning his gaze back to the work table in disbelief at his own carelessness, he could make no sense of what had morphed upon the paper during the absence of the master. Low, rectangular, ranch buildings had become A-frames with open rafters. Instead of four walls connected at right angles, these structures exhibited evidence of many, many, sides – much like the facets of some crazy, wooden, jewel. No conventional surface of log or clapboard gave texture to these corruptions. Instead, skins of mottled brown, tan, and yellow covered the buildings. Here and there, a regular, rectangular, window or door stretched itself out from the slanted membrane of a building, in an effort to show some submission to the master's will. On closer inspection, little patches of horizontal log or weathered planking, like structural psoriasis, did blotch the smooth, skin, surfaces, as further appeasement toward the original design.

While Andsel surveyed the wreckage, his hand continued to fidget on one side of the painting. Realizing the corruption of his grand design continued, he ripped his hand away from the painting and heaved the brush from his grasp. Little, brown, blotches were erupting from a distant hillside, like melanoma, where his rebellious hand had last flailed. "Son-of-a-bitch!" he cursed to the empty studio. "The entire day's efforts were ruined!" What could have possibly gotten into his head? This muck and splatter did not resemble anything. He considered tearing the paper from the board and beginning again, but his head began to ache and fatigue dragged at his limbs. Hurriedly, he flushed out the brushes and shaped the bristles with his unreliable fingers, then set them in the brush jars with the handles down. Wrapping the palette in some cellophane to preserve the paint, he washed his hands at the work sink.

An old couch rested beneath the large sunny windows that Andsel had been looking out of while his painting hand had taken on a mind of its own. He decided to stretch out on the couch for a while, perhaps to relieve his throbbing head. The warm sun felt good upon his face, painting his eyelids with a cheerful orange glow when viewed from the inside. Where in his inner psyche had the corrupted A-frame outhouses come from? Remembering what exactly the Alhauser ranch buildings had truly looked like seemed impossible. He tried to visualize the barns and outbuildings of other properties of which he was familiar. A yellow dirt road led him along through red and orange forests, to pass by hip-roofed barns in green, green, pastures. White, clapboard, houses stood near the barns. Horses and cattle grazed placidly in the barnyards, while children frolicked about the lawns of the houses.

One house had pumpkins ringed all around the bottom of its exterior and on every step of the stairs before the front door. Other pumpkins lined the railing of the front porch. Every pumpkin had been carved into a jack-o-lantern; each with a different expression. Not all pumpkins wore happy faces, but most were cheery. Andsel's job seemed to be to light the candles in all of the jack-o-lanterns. He held a pumpkin in his hand and touched his long, wooden, match to the candle inside. A smiling lantern gazed up at him with a grateful, yellow, glow. Andsel turned to retrieve the stem top for the pumpkin to seal it up, but no top could be found. All of the other pumpkins began to roll and hop in his direction. Even though the topless jack-o-lantern was the first that he had lighted, the rest began to glow with lights of their own, and their colors were not comforting. Purples and greens flashed from the triangular eyeholes and snaggle-toothed mouths in the gathering darkness. Red, snake, tongues of light writhed out from the gash mouths to reach for his ankles. Jack-o-lanterns floated off of the porch railing and joined up with other bigger pumpkins to form hideous, orange, snowmen and totem poles. They leaned over him, blotting out the dark, blue-black, dusk, and he ran. He dropped the topless pumpkin and he ran. He ran back down the darkening, dusty, road, beneath the black-shadowed trees, into the body of a man dozing on a couch, beneath an east-facing window, at sunset.

Andsel had slept the entire afternoon away, yet somehow he did not feel rested. At least his headache had abated. Something growled in the darkened room – something very near. Andsel realized it was his empty stomach. Rubbing the sleepy seeds from his eyes, he rose from the couch and strode out of the studio, closing the studio door behind him, and never casting so much as a glance at the disgusting, disappointing, art work of the day on the table.

CHAPTER THREE

Supper with Tiffany was a subdued affair, consisting of macaroni and cheese from a box with little conversation. "I'll boil you a hot dog if this isn't enough to eat," she offered in a flat tone, as tasteless as the macaroni.

"No need to bother, Tiff. This will sustain me," he replied.

Tiffany's culinary skills were sumptuous, and she exercised them on a daily basis. Her choice of menu tonight was a distinctive statement. Referring to the meal as "mere sustenance" had been a fitting return volley. Customarily, he would carry his plate and silverware to the sink and rinse them up in consummation of yet another wondrous dining experience. Tonight, he left his soiled plate and utensils on the dining room table in silent statement that nothing worth acknowledgement had occurred there. Plumping down into his easy chair in front of the TV, he commandeered the remote, while Tiffany cleared away the aftermath of the macaroni affair from the dining room table.

A rerun of "The Waltons" was playing on the Hallmark Channel, and John Boy's irritating facial mole captured Andsel's attention immediately. In the currently running episode, the fictional young man with the permanent, mud-spot, blemish on his cheek struggled to drag his grandfather away from the clutches of the Baldwin sisters and their Papa's moonshine recipe. A snort of Papa Baldwin's recipe sounded pretty tasty to Andsel after his trying day in the studio, culminated by such a scrumptious meal as he had just experienced. He went to the liquor cabinet, retrieved a bottle of Tobermory scotch from the bottom self, and poured four fingers-worth into a tumbler. Ice would have been a nice addition, but he would have had to brave the chill atmosphere of the kitchen to get cubes from the refrigerator. He took the bottle with him to his chair instead and drank his scotch neat.

The Hallmark Channel announced that it was interrupting its Waltons Marathon temporarily to market cell phones, or something or another, for its sponsors. Tiffany was coming through the living room door with a paperback, romance, novel in her hand as he set the scotch bottle down on the end table next to his easy chair. Since she no longer pressurized the box canyon of the kitchen with her frigid animosity about Joan and the skulls, Andsel carried his tumbler to the friendly refrigerator to collect a couple of ice cubes from its door dispenser. Sipping the chilled single malt, he wondered if John Boy was trucking any pumpkins around rural Virginia in his old Model A. He would love to see an episode where John Boy found himself trapped in the Model A with fifty, evilly grinning, jack-o-lanterns glowering devilish neon light from the back seat. Andsel smiled at the thought of John Boy screeching in terror, - his pre-melanomas mole sticking out like a black nipple - as he ran from a riot of goblin pumpkins chasing him down a Nelson County road.

"Do you think radio and television waves can influence a person's dreams?" he asked Tiffany as he settled down again into the numbing grasp of his easy chair.

She studied him incredulously for a moment. "Not as much as that bucket of booze you are cradling," she responded.

"I fell asleep in my studio today and had some nasty dreams. They were quite a shock. I need to calm my nerves," he paraphrased her words from the morning's incident and consequent medication of Cody Boy. She would either be miffed at his mockery or miss the private joke entirely, but he said it anyway, to please himself.

"So now your grisly skulls are giving you nightmares too. Well it serves you right. Did that flaming Indian chief hook your soul with his cop stick too?" she retorted.

"It's a coup stick, and no, the dreams weren't about skulls or Indians at all. They were about pumpkins and Appalachian countryside. With this Walton Marathon thing going on, I'm wondering if a subconscious brain can absorb television waves and corrupt them into strange dreams," he continued. As if to corroborate his theory, John Boy and Grandpa Zeb began loading huge, orange, pumpkins into the back of John Boy's Model A for deliverance to the Baldwin sisters.

"Even if you could have heard it from your studio, the TV has been turned off all day. I am certain that paint and turpentine fumes, added to *last* night's whisky for your nerves, had more to do with your bad dreams than Walton reruns. Now why don't you leave John Boy in peace and flip the channel to something modern and violent, like you usually watch?" she urged.

"American Idol isn't on tonight," he responded and continued watching Zeb and John Boy.

"Put a coaster under that whiskey glass," she growled in consternation.

Andsel pawed a ceramic coaster with a white wolf depicted on its surface from underneath some magazines on the end table. He set the tumbler of pale, amber, whisky down on the coaster and frowned at the way the tumbler and whisky turned the white wolf yellow and rosette. John Boy was whining to Grandpa Zeb about not having enough money to go to college in Charlottesville. Zeb mumbled something about searching for pearls in pumpkins instead of getting one's feet wet. John Boy ignored him and kept on whining. Andsel took another pull at his scotch, then fished through the magazines on the end table. John Boy and Zeb would reach the Baldwin sisters' house soon and the dialogue would improve. A National Geographic roiled to the surface of the magazine pile. Emperor penguins crowded together on its cover, in a bitter Antarctic twilight. Andsel set his whisky down on the penguins – after taking another generous slug of Papa Mull's recipe – and smiled at the new, golden, glow around the dreary, frigid, fowl.

The Waltons had reached the Baldwin's home by now on the TV. Zeb had a water glass of the recipe in his hand already. John Boy was hacking away at a pumpkin in his lap with a Barlow knife that Zeb had given him. One of the Baldwin sisters produced a picture of Papa as a model for John Boy's jack-o-lantern, and John Boy went to work. Zeb prattled on about what a shame it was that all of the pumpkin innards might go to waste when they might make a perfectly good pumpkin pie, especially with so many hungry people suffering from the Depression; or did he say, "suffering from depression?" Andsel sipped his whisky and wondered if pumpkin pie could help fight depression. After a meal of Kraft macaroni and cheese and cold shoulder, a slice of pumpkin pie would certainly help *his* personal depression. A tin bucket appeared for John Boy's pumpkin leftovers so that Zeb would get his pie. Those Baldwin ladies began to look pretty foxy, creaking away in their porch rockers. Pretty soon, John Boy had produced the Virginia Rembrandt version of a jack-o-lantern, helplessly dripping with talent as he was. Andsel was certain he could make out a huge, black, pumpkin mole festering out of the right cheek of the Papa Baldwin pumpkin. He poured some more Tobermory into his glass and wondered why none of the other Walton brats exhibited any large, facia,l moles. Now Yancy, the local poacher, he had a mole, or was it a wart? Andsel would have to watch a few more episodes in hopes that Yancy might show up. Then the true origins of John Boy's wart might be revealed.

Damnit, Andsel's eyelids felt heavy! He dropped them for just a minute and the next thing he knew, everybody in Schuyler, Virginia was standing out in front of Ike Godsey's store, admiring John Boy's pumpkin - whoopee. Andsel swilled another gulp of scotch and let his eyelids droop again.

Dark shapes moved in the blue-gray murk around him, pushing in close. Damn, it was cold! He knelt on a frozen dirt floor with his numb fingers jammed in the crease between his groin and his thighs. They ached as if splitting down the middle, if he tried to move them. Some rag of a blanket draped around his naked shoulders in pathetic defense against the cold. Undistinguishable others, in their own shapeless coverings, shuffled in tighter to him, and he responded in kind to gather their warmth. Stale body odor, mixed with the smells of leather, fur, and musty wool, permeated the frigid, dim, shelter crowded with people. No one seemed familiar, but that didn't matter, as long as they gave off heat and were willing to share it. They pushed in closer and pushed their own coverings up over his shoulders and head. He snuggled in toward the center of the cluster and found a small fire burning. People ground their teeth, in the feeble fire light, rubbed their bellies, and moaned. Andsel's own stomach twisted into a dried knot trying to digest itself for nourishment. Strange noises came from the innards of the bundled human beings around him, as if they were smothering puppies beneath their shabby coverings.

But Andsel held a treasure between his knees; a secret treasure that he must hide for himself alone. One by one, the figures began to lean over to one side until they each stretched out on the glacial earth and turned to burial effigies like those resting in English cathedrals. Dark shadows began to circle around the translucent wall of the shelter. A single, low, door allowed a pale, winter, light to visit the interior of the rude enclosure. The shadows flitted across the opening intermittently. They seemed to increase in size and their images became more distinct as each inhabitant of the dwelling succumbed to the cold and hunger. But Andsel huddled tight within his garments and fondled his little package between his knees. He remembered what it was he horded now by the touch of it. A crumpled box of unopened

Kraft macaroni and cheese lay safe between his knees, safe and warm, cradled from all others, for him and him alone.

Finally, the last occupant, other than himself, collapsed in slow motion to the ground and turned to stone. In a moment, when he was certain that the last contender for the precious contents of his crumpled box had died, Andsel would gnaw at the uncooked macaroni and lap up the cheese dust with some snow. A huge, sinister, shape swelled up beyond the door of the shelter and, before Andsel could open the box, a mighty wolf leapt upon him through the open space. It crunched his feeble fingers into bloody stubs when he thrust them at it in futile defense. The beast bit his face, completely covering his eyes in a stinking pink flash, as if Andsel stood inside a lightning bolt and could smell his own flesh burning. The gigantic wolf withdrew its maw to grin down at its victim. Throwing back its head, it howled a cry of victory, - long, vicious, and despairing - then plunged its jaws down to close on Andsel's throat. The last vision Andsel remembered was the color of the wolf turning from gray to scarlet as Andsel's own blood gushed from his crushed throat to cover the monster above him.

"Boom!"

"Aaaahhh!" Andsel awoke screaming and clutching at the vanished, gory, red, wolf. He sat in the warm, well-lighted, living room again with John Boy staring at him from the TV screen. Tiffany soon joined John Boy, in her nightgown.

"What the hell is the matter with you?" she bawled. "You woke me out of a sound sleep, in abject terror, you old fool!"

Andsel sat forward in the Lazy Boy chair with his arms clutched about his chest, still trying to drive off the frigid cold from his dream.

"Are you having a heart attack?" Tiff asked as she moved closer with concern.

He unclasped his arms from his chest, "No, I heard a shot. Didn't you hear a shot close by somewhere?"

Tiffany shook her head in disgust. "There was no shot, Andsel. You've been dreaming again. Now shut that TV off and come to bed." She grabbed the remote and turned the television off herself, then stormed off to the bedroom again.

"It was the macaroni and cheese that caused it. Stuff always gives me nightmares," he complained as he rubbed his eyes. A gun shot had definitely rang out somewhere, just as that damned wolf was killing him. He shuddered involuntarily at the memory. A swallow of scotch remained in his glass. Quickly downing the remains, he climbed out of the easy chair, turned off the table light on the end table, and followed Tiffany into the bedroom. She had already fallen back into deep slumber when he disrobed and climbed into bed beside her.

The scotch hammered his subconscious fantasy faculties into black silence for most of the remainder of the night. In the final hours of late, light, slumber, John Boy did make another appearance, but he was a much older man. Andsel's wandering, sleepless, eye saw him across a holiday table laid out and loaded for a feast. The setting was Thanksgiving, or Easter perhaps. A middle-aged John Boy sat across the table from Andsel. He wore a dark green, military uniform, and his face was turned to the left to receive a dish from someone seated to his right. When he turned to face Andsel, a long, white, evil looking, scar streaked his cheek where the mole had been.

"What happened to your mole?" Andsel blurted out.

John Boy grinned a crooked grin. "Grew out of it," he explained and held out a small dessert plate. "Have a slice of pumpkin pie."

Other hands moved a serving dish containing a complete roasted chicken between Andsel and John Boy.

"No turkey?" Andsel asked.

"Fox got in the hen house," John Boy explained over a mouthful of pie. "Got a' hold of one before I shot him. Take my gun if you're goin' out again," he said, motioning toward a Sharps carbine in the corner of the room. Andsel awoke with the taste of pumpkin pie in his mouth and wondering why someone dressed in a World War II uniform would be carrying a weapon from the Civil War. Scotch dry-mouth soon replaced the pumpkin pie flavor, driving Andsel out of bed and into the bathroom. "Perhaps it was Zeb's old gun, or even Zeb's father's," he wondered to himself as he brushed his teeth vigorously. Then he wondered why the hell he cared.

CHAPTER FOUR

Tiffany already had the coffee poured into a big mug for him when he entered the kitchen. He looked over her shoulder to discover what egg-powered delight might be taking shape in the pan. A golden omelet steamed and bubbled in the skillet, with chunks of ham and onions poking out of its sides and an orange filigree of cheddar artfully inscribed from tip to tip. A crispy reef of hash browns waited in a smaller pan to complement the omelet masterpiece. Tiffany wanted something special from him for sure, but he didn't care at the moment. He waited expectantly at the dining room table, nursing his first cup of coffee. Soon, she slid the magnificent, omelet, smile, with its frizzy, hash brown, hairdo, beneath his raised coffee cup and said, "Get to it." She went back into the kitchen, but returned with her own coffee mug and the coffee pot. He stopped wolfing down the omelet just long enough to thank her for refilling his cup. No need to prompt her to reveal her purpose for him in the day to come. She would bring it up any time now. He would try to enjoy every nuance of this scrumptious breakfast which she had prepared as enticement to get him to do her bidding. After all, it might be the high point of the day.

"Are you going to work in your studio today?" she asked in her most innocent, cooperative, voice.

He chased the last of the hash browns down with his fork, flushing them down his throat with a long slug of coffee. An answer had already formed in his brain, but he forced himself to pause for a nonchalant ten seconds before responding. "I should make another try at the Alhausers' homestead painting. Third time is a charm, so they say."

"Having trouble with it?" she asked.

"I have started it twice. That Cody boy ruined it the first time. Something weird happened to it yesterday – colors all ran together, and the shapes twisted out of proportion. It was the damnedest thing. Perhaps I can still save it today. Sometimes my efforts look more hopeful in clear, morning, light," he mused.

Tiff gazed away out of the curtained window. Andsel knew his morning plans did not sound at all like her plans. He also knew that there would be no salvaging of yesterday's painting, but something drew him to survey the bizarre damage. Usually, something useful to be learned would surface from the quagmire of color; some new, unknown, technique would make itself clear to enhance a better effort on another painting.

"Perhaps you need to leave it for a day. Maybe even revisit the subject," she suggested.

"I was thinking," he began, "If Joan shows up with that snoopy boy again, I should be in my studio to keep an eye on things."

"I'll keep track of that child, Andsel. You needn't concern yourself with him," she offered with a little too much snap in her voice.

Andsel did feel lost from the visual direction he had originally planed for the Alhauser homestead painting. A visit to the Alhauser ranch did sound appealing, but any suggestion from Tiffany this morning should be approached with a large dose of rattlesnake repellant. He could not spot the coiled threat, but it was certainly laying about somewhere in his future. He needed time to think.

"Maybe I *will* go for a ride today,' he began, raising her hopes, "But first I think I'll look over the damage from yesterday's painting session for a little while this morning. Thanks for that delicious breakfast, darling," he concluded as he rose from the table.

The Alhauser Ranch painting was as big of a disaster as he had remembered. Rectangular ranch buildings morphed into odd, multi-sided, gothic, torrents. Teepees, stretched over two-by-fours instead of lodge poles, wore patches of clapboard siding pasted over ragged holes. Something brushed his right shoulder from behind, and he turned to survey the shelves behind him. Everything seemed to rest peacefully in its proper place. Each skull peered at him dispassionately from opposite corners of the room. "Well, what are you going to do about this unsatisfactory situation?" they both seemed to ask, but each perceived a different situation, and each had its own solution in mind. Andsel stood silently, wondering how to negotiate a compromise to some unclear dilemma, as if he were a man caught between two unhappy wives. For an instant, the skulls were replaced by the pretty, brown, faces of two, young, Indian, women. With the hallucination of the pretty squaw faces, the silent conflict of the skulls broke off abruptly. The new skull went gray in disgust, and its sockets darkened with black indignation. A rosy glow of amusement momentarily flushed the cheekbones and gums of the older skull in the opposite corner.

Andsel became aware now, that his right hand held a brown, colored pencil, and, while he had stood in hypnotic dialog with the skulls, he had also been aimlessly scribbling at one corner of the surreal ranch painting. Heaving the pencil away, he turned to study the damage done by his prodigal hand. The little, brown, blobs that he had created on a far hillside of the painting yesterday were more defined now, as some form of bovine animal. In fury and fear, Andsel snatched up a rubber eraser and scrubbed brutally at the grotesque cows with his left hand, keeping his right clutched into a punitive fist.

"Rubbed out!" he muttered to himself repetitively as he worked. Eventually, the heavy paper tore through, and he stopped his feverish torment of the picture. For a moment, he considered cutting away the deformed buildings to save them for an amusing curiosity some other day, but another wave of violence gripped him, and he crushed the ruined painting into tight wad. "Burn them!" a voice shouted in his brain, "Burn them out!" Tossing the defiled landscape into a metal tray that he used to contain thumbtacks, Andsel ripped open the drawer beneath the work table's surface and searched frantically for a box of matches. Finding the matches, he soon had the bit of Wyoming countryside ablaze within the metal bowl. He stood watching the fire with a savage grin on his face until the smoke alarm went off and jarred him back into his present surroundings. He grabbed a bowl of water which he used to wet his watercolor brushes in and doused the little inferno out in the metal tray.

Tiffany burst through the studio door shouting, "What the hell is going on in here?"

Andsel turned to pull the circular smoke alarm down from the wall opposite from the couch and windows and rip out the batteries. Recovering his dignity quickly, he answered as innocently as a new-born babe, "It disgusted me, so I destroyed it."

"Are you trying to destroy the whole house with it?" she demanded in shock.

"Burn it! Yes, burn it all!" a voice seemed to whisper from behind him. Confused, Andsel absent-mindedly fumbled with the tools arrayed upon the work table surface until his right hand clutched a razor knife which he often used to crop paper. The blade felt good in his fist – like a good scalping knife.

"What *is the matter* with you?" Tiff asked, completely oblivious to any danger.

Andsel looked down at the pathetic, little, knife in his right hand, tossed it onto the work table, and then stirred the soggy ashes of the Alhauser Ranch in the metal tray with his finger to make certain the flames were extinguished. "I promised Homer Alhauser that this watercolor would be finished by the end of this month, and I haven't even managed a good start," he muttered.

"Open a window! This place reeks of smoke. I won't have my house smelling like an ash tray," she snarled as she pulled the studio door shut. Andsel moved to a smaller window at the side of the big picture window to crank it open. "You can't work in here with all of these fumes, so you might as well take that ride you were talking about at breakfast," she suggested.

"It is just a little smoke from clean paper," Andsel replied obstinately.

She pulled the studio door open again and growled, "Go!"

For an instant, an old woman's face fleshed out the older skull, behind and beneath Tiffany's right elbow, and shouted "Go!" in harmony with Andsel's wife.

"Who is an old woman now?" chuckled the whisper from the opposite corner.

Reality was becoming far too twisted for Andsel to endure.

"I need to go out to Homer's to have a look around; refresh my memory of the layout; maybe get a different point of view on the subject," Andsel declared to all of the different people who seemed to be crowding up his little sanctuary, and stomped out of the studio with great purpose. Presently, his truck door slammed, the engine chugged to life, and tires crunched on the gravel driveway as he backed out. Tiffany crossed the empty studio, picked up the metal container of homestead ash soup, and dumped it out of the open window. The skulls glared at her from their apposing corners when she turned away from the window to return the tack container to the work table.

"I need to do something about you two," she said to herself. "Joan will be here any minute. I need you out of sight and out of mind." Snapping her fingers in solution, she walked out of the studio, closing the door firmly.

A large, narrow, walk-in, closet opened from the hallway, adjacent to a bathroom, on the way back to the main area of the house. Tiffany opened the closet door and turned on the light. Somewhere on the jam-packed shelves around her were some ornately decorated Christmas boxes which she used from year to year to contain presents. She had remembered that a couple of these boxes were about the right size to contain those hideous skulls. Andsel could remove his grisly, little, friends from their new homes whenever he longed for their company. A highly decorated corner of one of the boxes poked out from behind several disheveled rolls of wrapping paper on a top shelf. She really needed a step ladder, or at least a chair, to reach the nested boxes, but she didn't feel like lugging a stepladder in from the garage or a chair from the dining room into the closet. Putting the heel of one foot on the shelf behind her and stepping up onto the second higher shelf in front of her, she raised herself up to a position to reach the Christmas boxes. Andsel would have had a fit if he had caught her practicing these acrobatics in the closet, instead of getting the proper equipment for the job. Concern over her safety would not have brought about his consternation. Concern for a broken shelf would have. His anxiety would have been unfounded. After all, she did not weigh a fraction of what his fat butt weighed. If he were to try such a stunt, the shelf probably would come crashing down.

Tiffany lifted the boxes free with one hand from the other items stuffed on the shelves around them while she kept her balance with the other hand. Tossing them to the carpeted floor, she climbed down from her precarious perch. A dull click sounded in the silent storage closet as she took her weight from the lower shelf behind her. "Nuts!" she thought to herself, "I probably did crack something or pry it loose from the wall or its braces." Wiggling and pushing on the shelf yielded no evidence of damage, so she turned her attention to the boxes on the floor with their intricate, abstract, decorations.

The two outer boxes of the nested assortment seemed to be about the right size to contain the skulls. Tiff put the two boxes aside and tossed the smaller, remaining, boxes back up on the top shelf from which she had retrieved them. Her throw had not been the best lay-up, for the little boxes bounded off of the edge of the target shelf and ricocheted against the bare light bulb in its socket. The bulb burned out with a tiny "tink." Total darkness did not engulf the closet. Some faint illumination penetrated around the door jam and bottom of the door, leaving the space in deep shadow. "Double damn!' she muttered, stooping over to pick up the larger boxes and taking a stride toward the exit door, while snatching at the knob in the same motion. The door refused to open and the cold, brass, knob slipped from her hand, as she slammed into the unyielding panel. "Son-of-a...." she began to swear as she bounced back away from the door and tumbled to the narrow floor. The bottom shelf clipped her head just behind her right ear, bringing stars to her eyes. The little room swam for a few seconds, but she did not loose conscientiousness. Stars faded from her vision, to be replaced with sharp pain behind her ear where the shelf had caught her.

Tiffany decided a good plan might be to lie still there on the floor for a minute or two. She rubbed the injured area gently. The flesh and bone felt tender to the touch, but no serious damage seemed evident. When the ringing pain had subsided to less than car accident level, she pulled herself up gingerly on the shelves. "The damn door must have swollen shut," she thought to herself. "Probably, if she put a little muscle into it, the thing would wrench free, " but repeated twisting and yanking on the obstinate portal yielded no better results. Tiffany folded her arms across her chest in disgust. Perhaps if she riffled through some of this junk in the closet, she might find something stiff and flat to use as a crowbar to pry the door open.

As she stood in the gloomy shadows, the sound of humming filtered from the bathroom, next door to the closet. "Joan," she called, "Joan, the closet door is stuck shut. Can you push on the outside of the door while I pull on the inside? Perhaps we can free it so I can get the hell out of here."

Childish giggling rippled through the wall from the bathroom.

"This is not funny, Joan. The light bulb has burned out and I have clipped my head on a shelf here in the dark."

The laughter answered again for a moment, then Joan called out, "I'm sorry about your head, Mrs. Edgar. I'll come push on the door right away."

Tiffany grabbed the door knob with both hands and leaned back with her full weight. Muffled footsteps sounded from the adjacent bathroom, and a shadow crossed the thin slivers of light emanating around the door. Some solid weight thumped against the other side of the obnoxious door, but nothing moved. The door knob somehow seemed to grow chill in Tiffany's hand. "Push harder, Joan!" she called. The panel seemed to creak as if it might splinter, but still, nothing gave free.

"I think the lock is jammed," Joan speculated from the freedom of the hallway.

Suddenly, the door knob in Tiffany's hand felt as if it had been dipped in liquid nitrogen. "Son-of-a-bitch!" she managed to utter completely this time, releasing the door knob and shaking the circulation back into her hand. The chill seemed to be radiating from the door now, filling the little, narrow, space with a creeping, subterranean, cold. "Has the weather gone cold outside, Joan?" she called. "Could you turn the heat on for me? It's freezing in here. If I'm going to be stuck in here all day, I need the heat on."

"It is a beautiful day outside, Mrs. Edgar. Are you feeling all right after you bumped your head?"

"My head is fine. Turn up the thermostat. It's cold as hell in here!" Shadows moved across the slivers of light around the door again. Tiffany assumed that Joan had moved down the hallway to the thermostat. Five minutes passed. "Joan," she called, "Joan, where are you?" Five more silent minutes passed. Light seemed to fade around the door frame. Perhaps clouds had begun to overcast the sky outside. "Joan? Joan? Turn on the light in the hall, dear, when you come back," she called. Shuffling noises returned to the hallway, but the hallway remained dark. In fact, the person on the opposite side of the door seemed to block out any remaining light from penetrating the darkness of the closet. No verbal response sounded beyond the bitter door. Tiffany pleaded again, "Joan, turn on the light in the hall, dear. Turn up the heat for me."

A faint, but distinct, earthy, odor oozed through the cracks around the door. Still, no comforting voice sounded beyond the barrier. "What is that smell?" Tiff questioned meekly.

"I remember when I was a little girl, my grandmother died," Joan began from the safety of the hallway.

"What the hell does that have to do with getting me out of this god damned closet?" Tiffany bellowed to her domestic beyond the door.

"I loved my grandmother dearly," continued Joan, as if Tiffany had never spoken. "Her home was always warm and cozy, full of good smells and soothing sounds. But she died."

"I am sorry about your grandmother, Joan. Please turn up the heat. It is positively cold as death in here," Tiffany begged.

"Several days after the funeral, my mother took me to Grandma's house to began the removal of her things and prepare the house for sale."

"Yes Joan, something very similar happened to me as a little girl. It was very upsetting. Now turn on the hall light. Turn up the heat. Go to the neighbors and ask them to help you free the closet door."

"The heat had been off in the house ever since Grandma had been dead. It was in winter. The house was very cold. Mama left me in the car with some coloring books and toys while she went inside to begin the cleaning. But I got bored. I went out into the yard to take one last walk around Grandma's house. Someone had left the cellar doors open, perhaps when they had turned off the heat and drained the water from the pipes."

Tiffany was struck speechless. Her mother had also left her in the car to ready her grandmother's house for sale after she had died. That was a very old and unpleasant memory, long forgotten.

"I heard a voice coming up faintly from down in the cellar," Joan continued. "I thought my mother had descended into the cellar from the stairway within the house, so I went down the cement steps from the outside."

"Stop it, Joan! That's *my* memory!" Tiffany screamed. "I don't know where you got that information, but you are evil to mock me with it now! Why would you be so cruel?"

"No one was in the darkened basement. Probably Mother's voice had only drifted down from above as she talked to herself about old memories of days with her mother. The cellar was dank, dark, and cold. I began to think about Grandma lying in her cold, dank, dark, coffin, sealed in that massive, concrete, vault, beneath several feet of musty dirt and sod."

"Shut up, Joan!" Tiffany screamed, pounding her hand against the unyielding door. Something cold and stringy curled around her finger through the crack in the door jam. She clutched at the mysterious fiber, hoping it was a strand of Joan's hair. In the darkness, the familiar form of plant roots caressed her hand and she recoiled from the door.

"It was windy that day and the cellar door blew shut. I was just little girl. The wooden door was much too heavy for me to push open by myself. Darkness smothered me in the bitter, cold, cellar, like it smothered Grandma not so far away in her lonely grave. 'Momma!' I screamed, but she couldn't hear me way down in that freezing hole in the ground. I could hear her though. She was singing in a room high above me. She was singing a song that Grandma and she used to sing together when they had worked in the kitchen or garden together."

"I remember that horrible song," Tiffany cried, "And I don't ever want to here that cursed song ever again!"

"Marezy dots and dozzy dots, and little lambzy jivey, a kiddly divey too, wouldn't you," Joan sang softly. "Is it getting colder and darker in there, Tiffany? Come on, sing along with me. I think you know the words."

"Shut up! Shut up, you wicked bitch!" Tiffany screamed. More roots squeezed their way through the cracks around the door, bringing the damp musk of the grave in with them. Frost began to crust on all surfaces in the closet. Boxes began to shift and tumble off of the shelves with the grating sound of stone on stone, and Joan continued to sing the exasperating tune in the warmth and light beyond the door.

"How do you like it in there in your cold, dark, box, Tiffany? Is it discreet? Is it sanitary? Hide the dead away and sing a silly, little, song to forget. Sing with me, Tiffany. Marezy dots and dozy dots..."Joan purred.

"Please Joan, please Grandma, let me out. I am so sorry for anything that I might have done to offend you. Yes, it is dark and bitter in here. Set me free," she cried.

"Sing with me, Tiffany," her grandmother's voice came through the door.

"Oh Grandma, I am so cold! Help me please!"

"Sing with me, Tiffany," the old lady cooed.

"Marezy dots, and dozy dots," Tiffany began in a quivering, little, voice. A warm whisper of air brushed her check for a split second. "A kiddly divey too, wouldn't you?" and the room warmed decidedly. "If the words sound queer and funny to your ear, a little bit jumble and jivy." The door cracked open to let in the light and warmth of the day. All clinging roots had vanished. No one knelt outside of the door. Tiffany bolted out into the hallway. "Joan," she called tentatively, but no one answered. She looked into the adjacent bathroom. No evidence of the cleaning woman's presence in that room existed either. Expecting a soggy, tumbled, mess in the closet, she found no dripping frost or tumbled boxes. Everything rested tidily on its appointed shelf. Two, mashed, Christmas boxes lay crumpled on the floor. Joan must be escaping from her evil prank. Perhaps Tiffany might catch a glimpse of her car leaving the neighborhood. She fled from the oppressive house and burst through the front door. Joan's car approached her home from down the street. She knelt in the yard and began to weep.

CHAPTER FIVE

Andsel began to feel better as he drove out of town on Soldier Creek Road. A man was always in control behind the wheel of his own truck. His mind cleared from the morning's distortions in the studio. He would pick another view of Homer's homestead; attack the problem from a different angle. Perhaps taking the back way over gravel roads to the Alhauser Ranch would help him capture the ambience of the countryside for the painting.

Green hills rolled away on either side of Soldier Creek Road, gradually rising to meet the Big Horn Mountains a few miles to the west. Spring snowstorms had been generous to the northern Big Horns, and thus generous to the high plains below them throughout the summer as the deep white blankets melted. Some winters had been too skimpy for moisture in the past, leaving the foot hills parched and brown by mid-summer, but not this year. The road had been graded to remove the washboard ruts in the recent past. Andsel's truck whizzed along smoothly without rattling on the gravel surface.

Homer Alhauser reefed on a large end wrench impaled into the working depths of a hay swather when Andsel rolled through the imposing, timber, entry arch of the ranch building compound. Homer tossed the wrench into a battered tool box at his feet and picked up a grease gun from the top of the hay machinery. Andsel rolled down the truck window as his pickup came to a stop, to meet the rancher's steady, silent, gaze. No comment or greeting parted Homer's lips in acknowledgement of Andsel, as he fitted the grease gun's hose to one of the multiple zerk fittings of the swather.

"How is the hay crop this summer?" Andsel asked to break the silence.

Homer pumped the handle of the grease gun a few times, then moved its nozzle to another fitting. "First cutting was fine; nice and heavy. This second cutting's not as tall, but tolerable for August," came his taciturn reply.

"I am having some trouble getting the atmosphere correct for the watercolor of your ranch here; the one I am painting for you. Do you mind if I wander around the ranch buildings, Homer?" Andsel asked.

"Most days, it's sunny. Some days, it rains. Take your pick," Homer muttered, pumping another dollop of grease into the multiple, moving parts of the machinery. "It's the *wife's* painting. She saw one on the wall of the Draper's place over in Gillette and had to have one for herself. *I* know what the place looks like."

"Do you mind if I look around?" Andsel persisted.

"Suit yourself. Close the gates. Watch out for snakes."

"Thank you, Mr. Alhauser. I will be careful," Andsel replied courteously. "Say 'hello' to your lovely wife for me."

Homer barely nodded as Andsel started the truck and drove further on into the ranch grounds. Parking the truck near the main barn, Andsel opened the glove box and fished out a digital camera. A few, new photos might help inspire new beginnings in his efforts to depict the homestead. He studied the features of the immense, main barn and machinery shed, complex. Dun-colored, plank, siding covered the exterior of the livestock barn in a common, horizontal, pattern. A gray, galvanized, sheet metal, extension had been grafted to the barn on its west side, to serve as a machinery shop, several years ago. No collection of deer or elk antlers adorned the planking of the barn. No faded lettering, or even o blotch of rust, marred the vertical, metal, siding of the machinery shed. The usual collection of ancient junk, too good to throw away, had not gathered by the shop entrance to give evidence of the passage of many years. Dull and expressionless as their main occupant, these buildings were not at all suitable for the image now slowly focusing in Andsel's subconscious.

One, lonely, log building tilted on a gentle, manure-covered, slope, perhaps a hundred yards from the east wing of the main barn. There, discarded in the muck, stood one, single, remnant of the original habitations of the homestead. Much as a fly might be drawn to the strong odor of the muck that the structure succumbed in, Andsel was drawn toward the little log relic. Abandoning the modern, sterile, world of the barn, he strode out into the fertile pasture and stepped gingerly through the shallower fringes of its fetid wallow, around to the east side of the log building. Perhaps a view of the weathered cabin as the center of interest, with the newer ranch house and buildings in the background, would present an interesting composition. A grimace of disappointment and disgust wrinkled across Andsel's visage. "Son of a bitch1" he snarled. Some past ranch hand had sawn, chopped, and torn the east wall completely from the building to make use of it as a livestock shelter. More recently, someone had rolled the remains of an old freight wagon into the cavity of the old log structure, to protect the antique from the weather. This ancient carriage had at least blocked the cattle from crowding into the structure over the many years and wedging the walls completely apart, causing the cabin's complete destruction.

Slime did not lie too deeply between Andsel and the gapping opening where the wagon had been pushed in. He walked to the weathered structure as if crossing thin ice. Before reaching the opening of the log cabin, he framed a few pictures in the digital camera for reference for his third attempt at a homestead portrait, then he moved up to the building entrance to examine the interior and its contents. The old wagon itself seemed to be mostly intact, although the wood of it was weathered, dry, and brittle. Andsel decided to take several photos of it from different angles. These pictures would come in handy for future paintings. Unfortunately, the interior was far too dark for effective pictures, even with the aide of the built-in flash of the digital camera. He surveyed the space for some solution. Perhaps a scrap of old sheet metal, - shiny on one side - or a shard of window pane, could be found and positioned to reflect some sunlight into the log cavern. He discovered a better remedy in the form of a light switch of the old, antiquated, porcelain-mounted, variety. By running back through the previous images on his camera, he did discover a line of rough poles, standing all a' kilter, and supporting an electrical wire from the barn to the log shed. Upon further examination of the interior, a lone, filthy, cobweb-entangled, light bulb hung from some electrical wire in the center of the building. Andsel would have liked to have wiped away some of the debris from the bulb before trying it, but the fragile wagon and its contents blocked his access to it. Using a stick of scrap lumber which he found in a corner, Andsel tentatively pushed the old light switch into the "on" position. Miraculously, the bulb lighted. Andsel quickly snapped the reference pictures of the wagon, keeping an eye on the hazardous bulb for any signs of ignition.

A familiar shape caught his eye from the ground at the rear of the wagon, deep inside the little building. "Well now," Andsel said to himself as he tucked the camera away in his shirt pocket, "A McClellan saddle." Such a fine example of the government-issue saddle from the 1860s would be an excellent addition to his artifact collection. He did not have any intention of stealing it, but he might be able to buy it from the Alhausers at a reasonable price. Who knew, perhaps Bonnie Alhauser would give him the saddle as partial payment for the homestead portrait, or, better yet, in additional gratitude. At least the old saddle should be picked up out of the cow manure and placed up on top of the wagon until someone found better storage for it. He began to inch his way toward the saddle, but was stopped cold in his tracks by a sound that reached to his most basic, primordial, animal fears – the sound of a rattlesnake's buzzing tail. He watched in horror as the hideous reptile slithered through the opening in the center of the wooden McClellan saddle. Slowly, he backed out of the viper's den, toward the safety of the sunlight. The snake did not follow, but remained inside, within the rectangular frame of the McClellan.

"Well, at least I'll get an interesting picture," Andsel thought to himself. He quickly pulled the camera from his pocket again and snapped a few pictures of the cabin's guardian. Then, using the same, scavenged, stick of lumber that he had utilized before, he flipped the light switch down to the "off" position. No flames had erupted in the dry cobwebs and dust around the bulb during its brief illumination. No snake bites, no fire, and some excellent photographs; all in all, he was quite pleased with the results of this little adventure. Homer would probably come out to the cabin and shoot the rattlesnake if Andsel mentioned its existence to him. Perhaps he would bring up the snake as an opening remark when he inquired about purchasing the old cavalry saddle.

Homer only looked up and nodded slightly when Andsel drove up to the man and his machine on the way out.

"You've got a rattlesnake using the old homestead cabin for a den. Did you know that?" Andsel probed for a response.

"What were you poking around that old derelict for?" Homer asked as he continued working on the swather.

"I thought your ranch portrait might look good with the original cabin in the foreground. Is that where it was first constructed?"

"Hell I wouldn't know!" he growled in annoyance. "Bonnie's granddad bought this place from the bank, back in the thirties – the old carpet bagger. The original cattleman who settled it in the 1880s went belly-up broke. Either of those two men may have skidded it away from its original foundation, for all I know about it. Paint it where ever you damned well want it. You won't offend any of *my* family memories, and Bonnie's only go back to the thirties."

"I'll ask Bonnie about it then," Andsel suggested and began to roll up his window as he rolled out of the ranch driveway. The taciturn rancher apparently couldn't care less about the painting of his ranch buildings. Bonnie's esthetic tastes were the only ones that really mattered concerning the results of Andsel's artistic efforts. He drove the additional five or six miles north to Highway 14 and turned east to get on Interstate 90.

Multiple headlights quivered through a pavement-induced mirage, far down the road ahead. A squad of bikers approached from the opposite direction, on their way to Yellowstone Park. After touring the park, they would swing south through Teton National Park and Jackson Hole, and then return east to the hedonistic extravaganza of the Sturgis Rally. When a man reached fifty, buying a Harley and then wrestling it around a region of the country of which he was totally unfamiliar had always seemed extremely foolish to Andsel. A wiser strategy might be to buy a little Maita or MG sports car. Most of these executives-on-a-spree would be much more familiar with such a vehicle, and they certainly would be safer driving it down the highway. Throw a six pack of beer into the equation, and the sports car made a hell of a lot more sense than the two-wheeled Harley. Riding a custom Harley trike, instead of driving a sports car, was just flogging a dead horse, in Andsel's opinion.

Waves of mirage rippled across the road from the midday heat, expanding across Andsel's view of the bikers as he approached, instead of dissipating in their usual manner. "Why were these goofy, old, wanna-be, bikers all dressed as Civil War

Cavalry?" Andsel wondered as he roared closer. Involuntarily, his foot pressed down harder on the accelerator pedal. Harleys morphed upward into charging horses. Soldiers pulled rifles and sabers from scabbards; pistols from holsters. Andsel let out a blood-curdling scream and pointed the pickup directly down the center line of the highway. Franticly, cavalrymen split right and left around his pickup juggernaut. Two soldiers struggled to control their mounts and prevent them from rolling into the dusty barrow ditches on either side. Cutting loose with another war whoop, Andsel checked his rearview mirror, only to discover a maelstrom of motorcycles and dust, instead of mounted cavalry, attempting to sort itself out after his attack. The image shocked him back to reality. What the hell had he just done? He could have killed one of the riders, or himself, or both!

"Were any of them authentic bikers?'" he asked himself in panic. "Were they turning around to chase him down and stomp him to a pulp? Would he have to fend them off with his truck?"

"Let them come!" a voice shouted in his head.

Andsel checked the mirror again. None of the bikes appeared to be lying on its side with crowds of riders scurrying around it. None seemed to be giving chase. Somehow, no one had apparently been injured, or pissed off enough to seek revenge. Seeing no point in returning to the scene of the engagement to offer apologies, or to count coup, Andsel kept his foot jammed down on the gas pedal until he reached the on ramp to Interstate 90.

CHAPTER SIX

Traveling down the southbound lane of Interstate 90, Andsel struggled to regain his composure. Bizarre incidents happened on the road all of the time. The bikers would probably assume he had dropped a cigarette in his lap or simply dozed off. If no major harm had occurred, they would probably rather ride on to the next bar and calm their nerves with a beer or two, instead of spending the afternoon with a Wyoming Highway Patrolman, discussing Andsel's description and his motives for running them off of the road. Andsel planned on having a shot of something strong himself as soon as he arrived home.

Most Wyoming residents constantly kept an eye peeled for wildlife as they traveled the empty highways of the state, and Andsel was no exception. Even now, with his thoughts still centered on his frightening loss of self control only moments ago, he subconsciously searched the terrain for an eagle, elk, or deer. An antelope buck stood down by the rim of a dry gulley. Andsel's eye instinctively compared the length of the animal's horns to the length of its nose. When the horns exceeded the length of the antelope's face, as this one's did, the comparison indicated a respectable buck. Andsel remembered sighting another fine antelope buck standing atop the banks of Upper Prairie Dog Creek in much the same manner, several years ago.

On that afternoon long ago, the buck had worn a much larger pair of heavy, black, horns. The antelope's horns jutted up so high that Andsel had pulled off of the highway and dug out his binoculars from behind the truck seat. As he studied that fine buck standing on the rim of Upper Prairie Dog Creek, Andsel noticed something shiny, white, and bowl-shaped, poking out of the red, clay, soil, at the feet of the buck. Forgetting the antelope's marvelous head gear, Andsel concentrated on the gleaming, white, object in the dirt. Beyond any doubt, it was a human skull.

Putting the binoculars down, Andsel surveyed the fence line along the highway. A posted, no trespassing, sign adorned a nearby fence post. "Damn It!" he cursed to himself, realizing he could not plead ignorance if he were caught on a stranger's private property without permission. He scanned the distant highway in either direction. No other vehicles appeared within the confines of the vast valley. Without further hesitation, he climbed out of his truck, hopped over the four-wire fence, and sprinted down toward the astonished antelope. The buck vaulted the stream and loped up the steep slope on the opposite side of the valley, its white rump a taunt to any pursuers foolish enough to attempt to match its superior speed. Andsel, his attention locked on the skull protruding from the earth, never looked up from the edge of the stream bed. Gasping for breath, as much from excitement as from the two hundred yard run from the roadside, Andsel reached the creek side and grasped the rim of the skull. He quickly twisted it loose from the ground entrapping it and began to examine the gruesome bowl of the empty cranium.

Obviously this poor victim had been scalped, but, worse than a typical removal of the head skin, the entire top of head had been chopped away with a tomahawk. As Andsel had ran down to the stream, the thought had crossed his mind that the skull might have belonged to some recent victim of a crime, but the weathered condition of the crude, brutal, hack marks belayed any risk of disturbing a fresh crime scene. In fact, upon further study of the ground near the skull, a faint outline of a gentle mound could be discerned. Survivors of some long ago Indian confrontation must have buried their unfortunate companion along this creek side nearly one hundred and fifty years ago. The poor pilgrim had lain there undisturbed for all of those years until the stream, swollen with the spring run off, had shifted its course enough to wash out the head of the lonesome grave.

"Perhaps there were more artifacts buried in the packed, red clay of the mound," Andsel thought to himself. "If the victim had been a soldier, anything, from buttons, buckles, to pistols, might remain with his bones."

The distant roar of a tractor trailer bellowed from the north as the truck downshifted to slow its decent into the valley. Andsel had totally forgotten about the risk of being caught trespassing. He quickly scanned the highway again to the north and south. The trailer truck approached from the north, but it did not concern Andsel. He calculated that most semi drivers seldom took time to stop and arrange the prosecution of petty criminals such as trespassers. Whoever approached in the brown pickup from the south though, might take a troublesome interest in what he was doing out at the streamside. Andsel dropped down over the rim of the bank into the stream bed and lay down. Peeking through the long grass and sage along the top of the bank, he watched the brown truck meet the semi at the bottom of the valley where his own truck was parked. The pickup continued on up the north incline of the highway to disappear over the horizon. When both the truck and the semi vacated the valley, he waited to hear the sound of any further intruders to the scene of his grave robbing activity.

While he listened for other vehicles, Andsel studied the contours of the mound from his eye level vantage in the creek bed. Browner bone knobs protruded from the soil where the skull was buried. "Aahhh!" he hissed to himself, "The jaw bone must still be buried there just beneath the surface. Grasping the boney knobs, he attempted to wiggle the mandible free from the earth, but it remained firmly interred. He was forced to dig it out. Fishing his jack knife out from his pants pocket, he unfolded the blade and began to gingerly gouge the gumbo away from the knobs of bone. The clay pried away tougher than gum from a church pew. He had to dig the jaw bone nearly completely free from the compacted clay with his pocket knife before he was able to wiggle it loose from the clinging earth, while keeping a close watch on the interstate for any approaching vehicles. Scraping some of the remaining red clay free from the jaw bone, he wondered how he might ever dig through the rest of the grave to recover more artifacts, with only a pocket knife. Someone would surely spot him at his work before he could ever manage to turn over all of the resilient clay.

Another car crested the south hill and whizzed down into the valley, slowing a little as it passed his silent pickup. He scooched down into the stream bed again to avoid detection. Cool water lapped at the heel of his loafer. "Perhaps he should grab his trophy and get the hell out of there before he got caught," he thought to himself. "Perhaps he should let the stream and nature take their course to wash away the clay from the grave. Each, new, heavy, rain would carry away more of the soil, bit by bit, eventually exposing the scalping victim's bones like new teeth in the red gums of the clay. After every future downpour, he could sneak past the grave site to pick over any remains that might rise into the present."

Another automotive engine hummed in the distance, this time from the north. Without further debate, Andsel leaped up over the creek bank with his booty in hand and raced back to his truck. He barely managed to reach his truck and thrust the skull into the passenger seat before a red Jeep Cherokee approached close enough to identify his purposes. Andsel smiled innocently and waved as the Cherokee passed across from him.

Little rain fell during the remainder of that summer, and Andsel found little reason to travel south of Sheridan toward Upper Prairie Dog. Heavy run off from the melting snows the following spring completely tore the grave away from the clay bank of Upper Prairie Dog Creek. A half-acre, u-shaped, bite was ripped from the land where a body had rested peacefully for more than a century. Andsel surveyed the dismal void with his binoculars from the interstate one year later, not even bothering to dash down in the hopes of finding a brass button or a silver ring.

Now, the skull rested tranquilly on the shelf in his studio. Yes, the shocked stare from its empty sockets had disturbed him a little at first when he would enter his studio without remembering the presence of his new guest. On a whim one day, to restore a harmonious atmosphere in his work space, he had simply twisted the skull's countenance away from the door, toward the old, New England, landscape painting resting behind it.

The reminission of the recovery of the scalped skull had carried Andsel all of the way from the open countryside into Sheridan and into his own neighborhood. His shocking escapade with the cavalry bikers suddenly resurfaced, fresh and raw, into his memory. Perhaps none of the bikers had read his license plates, and white Dodge pickups were as common as sage brush in Wyoming. Andsel hit the automatic door opener on his visor as he approached his house from the street and briskly piloted his truck into the concealment of the garage. Hurrying from the truck, he slapped the switch for the power garage door opener as he entered the house from the garage and watched the overhead door rumble down into place, with relief. The bikers would be long gone in a few days, and no one would be the wiser. Sturgis would be over in a week or two, exterminating most of the Hell's Stock Brokers and Thundering Accountants from the western states for another year.

Tiffany slumped at the kitchen counter with a tall glass of clear, effervescent, fluid in front of her when he entered the room from the back hallway. "What's the occasion?" he asked, undoing the laces on his hiking shoes.

"Grandma visited today," Tiffany slurred, "And she wasn't very pleased with my house keeping."

Tiff had obviously started a relaxing weekend several hours ago, even though today was only Friday. Andsel didn't have a clue why she had stirred up a gin and tonic so early in the day, but he decided the best strategy would be to humor her. "Your grandmother has been dead half a century at least, dear. Beside that little fact, she should take up her complaints about the cleanliness of our home with Joan," he offered.

"Oh, Joan was there too," Tiffany acknowledged.

Andsel found himself at a complete loss of a direction to continue in, in the conversation with his inebriated wife. He glanced out of the kitchen window and spotted Joan's vehicle parked down the street. "Did Joan, by any chance, happen to speak to your grandmother?" he asked.

"Well, they were together, but they didn't discuss anything amongst themselves. Neither one of them like your new guest in your studio though."

Joan came into the kitchen from the dining room at that moment, carrying a hand broom and a dust pan. "Hello Mr. Edgar," she greeted Andsel in a reserved tone.

"Hello Joan," Andsel responded cheerfully, "Tiffany tells me that you met her grandmother today."

"As I told Mrs. Edgar this morning, no one was in the house except us two women. She apparently got locked in the hall closet somehow this morning. She slipped and bumped her head in the dark. I am not sure what she imagined while she was disoriented from the blow, but it frightened her very much. I found her sobbing in the front yard when I arrived.

We searched the house for any intruders, but no one had been here of course."

"So she has been calming her nerves with gin and tonic ever since?"

"Tiffany was extremely frightened. I offered to take her to the doctor or emergency room, but she wouldn't go."

"Yes, she has become quite a practitioner of homeopathic medicine in the past few years, preferring to self-medicate," Andsel observed.

"You should be concerned about your wife, Mr. Edgar. She has had a bad bump and a bad shock this morning."

"I will keep an eye on her to make sure that she doesn't do herself any more damage. Thank you, Joan. What was she babbling about my unwelcome guest in the house?" he inquired to redirect the subject.

"Get rid of that damned Indian skull with the bullet hole!" Tiffany squalled, "Or I will throw it out myself!"

"You should let the dead rest in peace, Mr. Edgar. On display on your bookshelf is no place for a soul to find God," Joan chimed in with Tiffany's sodden sentiments.

"I imagine that Indian, if Indian he was at all, was more of a heathen then a Christian, Joan," he defended.

"I'll send them both to the dump, and they can find whatever, particular, god they like best from the garbage heaps," Tiffany slurred. "I'll be goddamned if they are going to force me to sing hymns, nursery rhymes, or Kumbuya with them in *my* house!"

"Those are *my* things in that studio, Tiffany. If you don't like them, then stay out of there," Andsel declared sternly. He immediately regretted antagonizing his drunken wife with defiance. She glared at him demonically and raised herself up from her stool.

"Damn you, Andsel! I'll go pitch the damned things out right now!" she raged. The gin had too much control of her feet by this hour of the afternoon, and she nearly collapsed to the floor. Joan caught her by one elbow while she propped herself up on the counter with the other rubbery arm. "Come on Joan. Gimme a hand," she directed.

Andsel pointed his thumb toward the bedroom for Joan and added, "I'll put my new friend in my truck cab for the night, Tiffany. You get some rest, dear."

"Get them both out of this house!" she bellowed. "Nothing separates the garage from our bedroom but a two-by-four wall."

"I'll lock the truck, dear. The topless skull has been in this house for years without causing any problem."

Tiffany slumped again on Joan's arm, nearly taking the stalwart cleaning lady down with her. "Come along to bed, Mrs. Edgar. You seem very tired," Joan soothed and led the intoxicated woman down the short hallway to the master bedroom.

So far, Andsel's day had been plenty disorienting, without the help of gin and tonic. He decided to keep the biker-cavalry episode to himself for the time being. A late lunch might help calm his nerves. Even some of last night's macaroni and cheese might quell the gnawing pains in his stomach, especially with some catsup on it. A disgusting surprise greeted him when he browsed the refrigerator for the macaroni and cheese. Gray-green mold had begun to form on top of the orangey leftover. "Son of a bitch1" he muttered to himself. There would be no warmed-up mac and cheese for lunch today. Looking into the cold cut tray for sandwich makings, he noticed a thicker layer of the same repulsive mold growing on the container of shredded cheese. "No wonder we are seeing things today1" he exclaimed. Tiffany must have used the grated cheese, without noticing the mold growing on it, when she had prepared the macaroni and cheese the previous night. Probably the mold was only slightly formed at the time and not blatantly noticeable. Andsel pitched both the macaroni and cheese and the spoiled shredded cheese into the kitchen garbage can. He pulled out some sliced roast beef, with a jar of horse radish, and made a sandwich, washing it down with a cold glass of milk.

Tiffany would be sleeping off her nerve medicine for the rest of the day. He would be on his own for supper. The project of the Alhauser Ranch painting still occupied his thoughts. Perhaps a fresh start with some real progress could be accomplished in the remainder of the afternoon. Sitting on the couch in his studio, he reviewed the pictures of the forlorn log cabin and its contents. No definite image of the commissioned painting's composition had, as yet, formed in his imagination. He picked up a sketch pad and a soft-lead pencil. Sometimes, idle doodling helped his subconscious resolve random images into a formal plan. The McClellan saddle still tugged at his desire. He sketched out the saddle's outlines as he had seen it, tilted on its side, lying in the gloom of the cabin, and then added shading to give it form. One, single, gray, hair dropped from his own head to land upon the drawing and curl about the saddle, much as the rattler had done earlier that day. On a whim, he traced the form of the hair across and through the saddle, then filled in the image of the serpent.

Andsel's pencil came to a halt. He could not expand the image of the snake and saddle into a more complete composition to fill the page. He moved his hand to another corner of the paper. The strange vision of the biker-cavalry charge from earlier that afternoon floated to the surface of his memory. Soon, a riderless horse appeared from listless pencil scratchings beneath his fingers. The bridled horse stood facing away from the viewer with its hind quarters oriented toward the saddle and snake. Andsel quickly drew in a horizon line designating a knoll, behind the horse. Then he added some diagonal lines in front of the snake and saddle to give the appearance that they rested in a tuft of long, prairie grass in the foreground. Putting the pencil down, he studied his evolving picture and smiled softly to himself. He quickly resumed work with the pencil, adding some wisps of cloud to give the sky some definition, and to project an overall depth of field in the picture.

Stopping to rest his hand on the paper, Andsel gazed into the hollow sockets of the new skull with the bullet hole in its forehead. His creative thoughts were diverted away from his artwork to daydreams of what those eyes might have seen so long ago. Time pulled him along like wind, over trackless, sunlit, prairies. His soul wandered among the golden grass without direction, drifted beneath the blue sky without a care. Days coiled into seconds; minutes unfurled into years.

Faintly, from the far end of the house, the telephone rang, and the skull released its spell over Andsel, with a sinister smile. An ugly, gray, smudge marred the new drawing along its horizon when Andsel lifted his hand from the paper. Lead, which had accumulated along the edge of his hand as he had worked on the drawing, had melted off with perspiration to stain the picture. "Damn it!" he growled, cursing himself for his negligence. Every artist learned from early experience never to leave his hand resting on the page for any length of time, or the paper would be stained. That was an elemental lesson, never to be forgotten. Andsel had carelessly allowed his mind to wonder so far away in an instant that he had spoiled yet another piece of artwork. Attempting to erase the smudge would only make it worse. "You've been nothing but a bad influence as far as my art work is concerned," he accused the leering skull with its bullet hole. The skull returned his gaze dispassionately.

The telephone rang again in the distant kitchen. Andsel tossed the sketch pad and pencil onto the couch and hurried to the kitchen where the phone hung. Catching the phone up on its last ring, before the answering machine would take command of the call, he gasped into the receiver, "Hello, this is the Edgar household."

"You tryin' to burn my place down for some particular reason, Edgar?" Homer Alhauser snarled from the telephone.

"Burn it!" Andsel exclaimed, then caught himself, "What do you mean burn it, Homer? I only took some pictures out by that old cabin. I didn't go anywhere else on your place."

"The cabin is what caught fire! Didn't anyone ever tell you not to just toss your cigarette butts any place you please around a ranch?" Homer continued to growl.

"I don't smoke, Homer. All I did was turn on the light to take some pictures, but I am certain that I turned it off when I had finished."

"You damned fool! That light hasn't been turned on in probably ten or fifteen years! No telling what the wiring was like anymore, nor what filth it was running through?" Burnt the roof off of the place entirely, and most everything inside is coals and cinders now."

"I swear Homer, I turned that light out and remained there long enough to have seen any smoke or flames lighting up. Did the fire spoil that beautiful, old, wagon in there?"

"Hell yes! Bonnie is *not* happy. She wanted me to haul that thing out into the front yard for display some day. Personally, I don't care if it never made it to the yard. I won't ever have to mow around it now. But I *could* have sold it for a pretty penny. Now, it's not even good for firewood."

"Geez Homer, I *am* sorry. How about that old saddle that laid on the ground in the back of the cabin? Did it burn up too?"

"There aint no damn saddle in that shed. We sold off all that old horse tack years ago, and no one ever kept saddles or bridles or harness of any kind in there. That kind of gear belongs in a barn with a good roof and walls, not out where the weather can get at it."

"I swear that I saw a McClellan saddle tucked in behind that old wagon. I tried to wiggle back in there to pull it out of the dirt and toss it up onto the wagon, but that big rattlesnake I told you about crawled across it. I have even got pictures of it."

"I couldn't care less about your damned pictures, Edgar, and it will be a long time before Bonnie forgets about her wagon. Don't be in any hurry to come back out here to peddle your artwork."

"I'm sorry to hear that, Homer, but I did not burn your shed down. It was just a coincidence that I had even been there today, I guess."

"Well you and your coincidences can just stay to hell away," Homer stated flatly and hung up.

Andsel hung the receiver back in its cradle and shook his head in disbelief. He knew that he had turned off that light. He had been looking at the pictures of the snake and saddle only minutes before. When he returned to the studio, he would look at them again. Damned, careless, old, ranchers anyway; Homer should have disconnected that shed light from the barn wiring years ago if he had felt that it was untrustworthy,

Upon returning to his studio, Andsel immediately picked up the digital camera to scroll through the pictures of the afternoon. Images of the cabin, with the barn and other ranch buildings behind it, were present. Evidence of the now destroyed wagon remained in the modern, magical, little, metal, box. When he reached the point in the camera's memory where the snake and saddle should have been recorded, a blazing, red, smear greeted his imploring eyes. He ran the menu of the camera up and down through its files several times, even turning the camera completely off and back on, but nothing remained of the saddle. Only the fiery, red, blot mocked him from the little viewing screen.

"Burn it!" a voice hissed from the shadows of his memory.

Andsel turned the camera off in disgust and retrieved his sketch pad from the couch. Something odd about his drawing caught his attention immediately. Silhouetted against the sky, beyond the horse, an Indian brave raised a dripping scalp to his pagan gods where the graphite blot had disfigured the drawing before. The body of a cavalry man, also in silhouette, lay at the Indian's feet on the crest of the knoll. Andsel heaved the sketchpad to the top of his work table in shock. What the hell was happening to him? How could he create these bizarre images on paper and not recall executing them at all?

The atmosphere in the studio seemed heavy, as if the space contained a multitude of people, standing silently, waiting. Ranks of soldiers stood at attention with Andsel among them. They waited, eyes front, ready for a command or an attack. The odds were not good. Andsel must steel himself, muscle up his self control. He could not run from this assault, could not let his comrades down. Far away, a horse whinnied. He looked down at the drawing on the table. It was a good drawing – simple - but everything worked in the composition – a brutal beauty. Might could make right, and life was right when your enemy lay bloody before you. Wrong was defeat and death. The horse whinnied again, and a drum began to beat. Warriors at his sides began to raise their feet in a muffled, stomping, dance, and Andsel raised his feet in syncopation. He found himself humming a primitive chant. His horse ran swift, his lance flew true, he too would take scalps in the morning. Raising his fist into the air, he screamed his blood-curdling war cry in challenge. A cavalry bugle trumpeted "Charge!" from the enemy, so loud that books shifted on the shelves and the windows rattled nearly to the point of breaking. Doubt filled Andsel's heart with the peeling of the bugle. A roar of distant hoof beats shook the floor.

"Whose horse you gonna' ride, Andsel?" a voice demanded at his ear. Then the room went silent.

Andsel's heart pounded like a war drum. "Damn that bad cheese!" he gasped as he caught himself against the work table. His knees buckled as if he had danced all night. The clock on the wall read six o'clock. Had he really stood there for three hours? Impossible! He simply wouldn't accept it! A phrase from Dickens's *A Christmas Carol* flashed across his mind. After Marley's ghost had left him, Scrooge had uttered "A crumb of cheese, a fragment of underdone potato," as cause for the apparition. "Humbug!" Andsel puffed, and stormed out of the room.

CHAPTER SEVEN

"I am sick of playing cowboys and Indians," Andsel growled to anyone interested as he slumped into his easy chair and picked up the remote. Whole new worlds blinked to life in front of him at the thump of his thumb. After surfing the sitcom sea, he halted at one of the news channels where glittering pieces of jewel-encrusted, Saxon, gold sprawled across the screen. Apparently, some amateur, metal detector, enthusiast had stumbled onto a huge number of gold, sword-and-armor, fragments in a field in Staffordshire, England. Mass media had dubbed the find the Staffordshire Hoard. Nothing like these ancient, Anglo-Saxon, artifacts had been uncovered since the excavations at Sutton Hoo. Images from the famous, long ship, burial at Sutton Hoo were used as reference and enhancement for the news story. A brief documentary clip explored a virtual mock-up of the extravagant burial chamber inside the Sutton Hoo long ship, via computer graphics. Unbelievably intricate golden armor, weapons, and jewelry, - embellished with garnets and glass cloisonné - had accompanied the mighty warrior into his long ship grave

"An entire ship, filled with priceless loot; now *that* is some kind of special coffin," Andsel thought to himself. "Those Saxons really knew how to treat a corpse."

The documentary continued with a discussion of the life style of Saxon warriors in the seventh and eighth centuries. Andsel began to get the impression that - other than possessing iron and steel technology - the people of jolly, old, England during the Middle Ages did not differ very much from the horse culture tribes of the Great Plains before the arrival of Caucasians in the 1800s. Tribes in both England and North America had fought against each other continuously to gain control of new territory and to retain it. If time was like a slide show, and one projector's cast image could be thrown across the landscape of another's; if Cheyenne and Comanche had met Angles and Saxons on the battlefield, a bookie would probably have been obligated to give even odds on all bets.

Saxons had possessed bronze, iron, and steel, while the Indians had used only flint, but both technologies made a lethal hole. Through superior technology, the Europeans might have won the early battles of the campaign, but when the Indians had collected enough iron points for their arrows and had swapped their stone lances for steel, they would have stolen many an Angle maid and taken plenty of Saxon scalps. Saxons had worn metal armor, but the Indian cavalry, mounted on faster, nimbler, ponies, might have cut them to pieces, once weak points in the Saxons' formations had been discovered. Had history reshuffled the war-like races of the world, combining the horsemanship of the Plains Indians with the steel of the Saxons, the Normans might have been driven back across the English Channel in defeat, but time had been treacherous to Harold and his Saxon army.

Time had been a treacherous god to the Native Americans as well. So many coincidences of circumstance and technology had converged against the red man, in such a small window of decades, that his culture had never stood a chance. If the Great

Plains had been wider, and trans-continental railroads had not been completed so rapidly, relations might have developed more slowly and fairly between the red man and the white. Andsel held no illusions about the aggressive, militant, nature of the tribes of the plains. Had European civilization brushed up passively, in stead of aggressively, against the Indians' domain, the Indians often would have attacked it as raiders and as conquerors just the same. Such behavior was a warrior's nature, his culture, and his religion.

Across the border in Canada, the two races seem to have been exposed to each other more gradually. The white population had been smaller. Vast areas of marsh and stunted, coniferous forest had slowed the progress of white men. Colder, harsher, climate had forced both races to concentrate more time on providing food and shelter, with very little time for war. Cold climate had given rise to cooperation instead of combat.

Winter had also interrupted the trains of covered wagons across the American plains, but it did not halt the trains of the railroad. The locomotives hauled a river of people across the land. The railroad carried food and materials for shelter. It carried progress; it carried change; it carried time, and time was a new god of the white man's whom the Indians had never met.

Even so, the distances of the plains were immense. California and the Oregon Territory on the Pacific Coast were much more suitable regions for white settlement. Whites might have bled more gradually out onto the forbidding, arid, grasslands in the middle of the country, allowing ample time to reach a parody between the two races.

Before the Civil War, the United States Army maintained a minimal force on its western frontier. Most soldiers carried only single-shot, muzzle-loading, rifles, and the bows of the Indians were relentless in attack. Properly treated, the Indians' iron-hard, rawhide, shields often turned the primitive military ammunition of the period. Had the Native Americans been allowed more time to procure repeating weapons of their own, and had they learned to use them better; the match might have been more equal. But fate did not have that equity in mind for the Indian in the United States.

The Civil War ulcered forth thousands of professionally trained soldiers, competent in the use of the most modern weaponry of the era. When the war ended, many of these men spilled onto the plains to find a new market for their deadly skills. The trains sped the new military across the ancient world of the Kiowa, Sioux, Comanche, and Cheyenne. The tribes fought valiantly, but their old gods could not turn away every bullet. Disease and starvation had already decimated their numbers far beneath a population large enough to sustain a war against the U. S. Army. Time was a god they had never acknowledged, so time rose suddenly in the East before them, and snuffed out the sun of their prairie kingdoms.

One constant undertone had always intrigued Andsel throughout all of the books that he had read about the white men's interactions with the Indians during the settling of the West. Although Indian culture had been completely different – pagan, barbaric, and savage – an obvious natural intelligence lay behind every aspect of it. Even in rank hatred, white people had held some admiration for the Native American. Grudging respect for the adversary had developed on both sides of the conflict. Unfortunately, after the Indians' defeat, other white people, with little or no respect for the abilities of the Indians, were given control of the Indians' well being. Time tried to leave the Native Americans by the wayside, hoping that they would fade away. Yet the bright colors of their culture have endured.

Montana, to the north, contained several Indian reservations. Two tribes, the Crow and the Northern Cheyenne, held reservation lands just across the state line. Crow and Cheyenne from across the border intermixed commonly and equally in northern Wyoming society. Andsel had been to several of their festivals on the reservations, that were open to the public. From what he could observe, even though they had their full share of social problems on the reservations, the Indians looked forward to the future with their culture decidedly intact. They would work through their problems to their own unique solutions, and they would determine their own future with little or no outside help.

On the television, Staffordshire and Sutton Hoo had been replaced by the current debate on healthcare reform. Andsel could listen to that issue at any hour of the day if he wished, and now was not one of those hours. He had not checked on Tiffany since he had gone to his studio hours before. . He flipped off the talking heads on the TV and walked to the bedroom to see that his wife rested safe and sound.

Tiffany lay on her right side on the bed, breathing deep and evenly. Joan had removed her shoes for her before leaving. Andsel pulled a spare blanket from the closet and spread it over her. He stood at the side of the bed for a moment and gazed at her in the soft light of the reading lamp on her night stand. She still was a beautiful woman to him after all of their years together. Sure, she drove him crazy on a regular basis with her continual standards for his behavior, but he knew that she still cared for him because of this constant assessment. Other men's wives waned into apathy towards their husbands, regarding them with little more interest than a house plant. He hoped the day would never come when she showed him no more attention in a week's time than a potted cactus. Yes, on a moment-by-moment basis, she chafed him like sandpaper underwear, but all moments of his life orbited around her existence within it. Even during the time he spent painting, the time of his utmost personal concentration, part of his subconscious knew where she was. This, he knew, was love. It was not a flaming, uncontrollable, love of youth. It was the unbreakable, bedrock, love of two people who had grown into one.

The day had been a long one for both of them, not so much in hours as in experiences. Hunger did not nag at him, even though supper time had come and gone. His place beside his slumbering wife beckoned to him. Perhaps he would stretch out beside her and read for a little while.

A Scientific American magazine lay on his nightstand. Leafing through the periodical, he stopped at an article about strand theory and the shape of universes. He could grasp the concept of what the experts quoted in the article and proposed as fact, but his practical mind kept stumbling over the sheer vastness of the distances which these people pulled their evidence through. "My god," he thought to himself, "When I was a child, people had only recently comprehended what a galaxy was. Now, we supposedly know what the limits of a universe might be. Last that I knew, a handful of men had barely walked upon the Moon. That surface was the only heavenly body that could be attested to with certainty from first hand accounts."

Viable pictures of other planets had been transmitted back to Earth from spacecraft which had recently left the hand of man. Andsel had faith in the technology behind these spacecraft and the ministry of scientists who created them, but the priestly theories of the physicists held little more substance for him than Greek mythology. He would rather read Beowulf than the pages of math equations predicting the existence of Dark Matter in the Scientific American before him. Grendel's Mother, now there was some dark matter to be afraid of. Barring the odd comet or meteor, modern man probably wasted his time worrying about the stars for any more moments than the ancient Saxons did. As long as the starlight kept shining and didn't begin to wink out a few stars at a time, man could happily gaze at them over a campfire or through a telescope, making up stories about them for his amusement. If that ocean of diamonds ever did began to thin, then the human race would perceive the true edge of the universe approaching – like a tidal wave of time - coming to claim its final due of deity.

A wave of fatigue sloshed over Andsel as he thumbed through the rest of the magazine's articles; one on DNA, and another on the substances composing the Earth's mantle and core. He rolled over on to his left side and shinnied his back up against the warm posterior of his wife. In a last ditch effort to remain conscious, he strove to concentrate on the text of an article about how earthworms were slowly destroying the American deciduous forest, but his efforts were to no avail.

Mature John Boy had returned. He bent over a shovel behind a New England barn, turning over cow patties. Turning to look at Andsel, so that the battle scar became apparent across his cheek, he pointed to the freshly turned earth. "Here is the best place to find worms for fishing, youngster," he explained. Andsel knelt down beside the shallow hole to help John Boy sift through the dark, pungent, soil and pull the wriggling, red, worms free, depositing them into a waiting tin can. The question of how he had suddenly become a ten-year-old boy, instead of a middle-aged man, never crossed Andsel's mind. Uncle John was taking him fishing! He always caught fish when he went with Uncle John! Soon the can seethed with glistening, red, worms. "Time to go catch some fish," John said, picking up the can.

In an instant, they stood at the stream's edge in the deep woods. Crystalline water tumbled over a slate shelf to form a wide, still, pool. The little waterfall made beautiful, tinkling, music as it dropped from the shelf, but the ripples that it created soon dissipated into a surface clearer than glass further down the pool. "We have to sneak up to the pool, Andsel, so the fish don't see us. Keep low now," Uncle John instructed. Dozens of trout spiraled around in schools within the cool, green, depths of the forest pool as Uncle John and Andsel crouched at the edge. "Now bait your hook, boy, and drop it about an arm's length from one of those schools," Uncle John said, holding out a fat, red, earthworm for Andsel.

Andsel took the worm and began to stab it onto his fish-hook. The hook shone like silver in his hand as the tortured worm squirmed.

"Wrap him on there tight, boy. Don't let it bother you none. Everything dies sooner or later, and today that worm's time has come. Now plunk him down in the water gentle, so as not to scare the fish. Just kind of lower him in real slow."

Andsel followed Uncle John's directions, and the school or rainbow-painted fish immediately swarmed around his bait. A flash of white underbelly and a violent tug on the line signified a strike.

"Set the hook!" Uncle John shouted.

Andsel reared back on the pole, and the sparkling trout leapt from the water in defiance. Diving back beneath the troubled surface of the once tranquil pool, it tore yards of line from Andsel's reel as it dashed from one side of the water to the other. Andsel hung on for dear life. Eventually the fish tired, and Andsel brought it to shallow water near the shore.

"That's the way to bring him to justice, my boy!" Uncle John shouted and slapped him on the back. "Now get a hold of him by the jaw, and I'll get something to put him in."

Andsel knelt down at the water's edge. He carefully pulled his line in with one hand, then slid his other hand up behind the exhausted trout. Grasping the fish around its middle, he grabbed its jaw near his silver hook with his other hand, and lifted it from the water. Uncle John held out a large, open, glass, jar, filled with the clear creek water,

"Drop him in there now. That'll keep him out of trouble," he said with a wink.

"Where did you get the jar?" Andsel asked, and found himself instantly awake in the bed beside his wife. "These bizarre dreams are getting worse," he thought to himself as he reached across her to switch off her bedside lamp, "I hope the effect of that damn moldy cheese has worn off in the morning," he mumbled to himself and turned off his own reading lamp.

John Boy did not take him fishing anymore that night. His slumber was uninterrupted for several hours by any hallucinations. But, as his chunk of the Earth's crust began to swing back toward the rays of the sun, Andsel found himself transported to Merry Old England. Instead of a fishing rod, a mighty, two-handed, battle axe rested in his gloved hands, and battle seethed all around. Heavy chain mail weighed him down. A steel battle helmet muffled his ears and obscured his vision. Andsel looked up from his battle axe just in time to dodge the lance of a mounted knight bearing down upon him. Instinctively, he swung his battle axe as the horseman passed. His vicious weapon struck home across the leather clad knee of his opponent. The horseman screamed and dropped his lance. Another warrior, on foot and on the opposite side of the passing horse, stabbed at the horseman's helmet with a lance of his own, driving the man from his saddle. Andsel lunged forward and chopped the enemy's head from his shoulders as he struggled on the ground.

"Grab your shield, man!" They are soon to send another volley!" shouted the foot soldier with the lance.

Looking around him on the body-strewn ground, Andsel spied an almond-shaped shield with many arrows imbedded in its outer surface. He quickly raised the shield, shouting "Come to me, my King. My shield will serve us both." A black cloud of deadly slivers hissed into the sky from down the slope.

"Send me my horse!" the man called from behind Andsel.

Arrows thudded into Andsel's raised shield and into the ground around him. "Come Harold, before they shoot again!" he beckoned, but no answer came. Another charge of Norman cavalry massed at the bottom of the slope, awaiting the results of a third volley. Again, the evil swarm of iron-tipped arrows hissed into the sky.

"I am pierced in both leg and side and cannot ride," moaned the King. "Take my horse and escape."

Another rain of arrows thudded into Andsel's shield. The evening air shivered with screams of the stricken men around him. He turned to help his savior with the lance, only to find the fallen man prone upon the ground with an arrow buried in his head through his left eye. Despair welled up in Andsel's heart at the sight of his fallen sovereign. A boy ran toward him, leading a heavy war stallion bedecked in fine armor and harness. Andsel laid his shield over the body of his king. A rearing, red, stallion emblazoned the shield, beneath half a dozen Norman arrows. Handing Andsel the reins, the boy turned and ran into the forest at the rear of the battleground.

"Hurry!" whinnied the horse.

With an agility completely shocking to himself, Andsel leapt into the saddle. Other Saxon soldiers, both mounted and on foot, were turning from the advancing charge of William's forces to flee down the wooded slope to the rear. Andsel yanked at the reins of the king's charger to turn in retreat as well. To his horror, the leather snapped free from the horse's bit, leaving the useless reins dangling in his hand. Only then did Andsel notice that the stallion he rode was red – as red as the hair of a Northumbrian lass. The horse turned his head to peer at Andsel with one evil eye and to grin a devilish, equine, grin. In an instant, the red demon leapt forward toward the oncoming, mounted, knights of William.

"Whoa you cursed fool!" Andsel bellowed, grabbing the pommel of the saddle with one hand, and snatching at the animal's laid back ears with the other, but his command went unheeded. A sword hung in its scabbard at his side. If he must meet his death in a single charge against the Normans, he would do so valiantly as a Saxon warrior; not curled up and cowering like a dung beetle on the saddle of his horse. Releasing the ears of the renegade horse, he drew the sword and raised it in both fists while gripping the horse with his thighs. On came the Norman assault. The red stallion deftly cut between a knight's lowered lance and the shoulder of his steed, slamming head-on into the Norman and his mount. Andsel swung his shining steel with all the force he could muster, compounded by the force of his momentum. The blade chopped down at the juncture of his opponent's neck and shoulder, cleaving completely through the man's chain mail jerkin nearly to the opposite armpit.

The red horse reared and kicked itself free of the slain knight's flailing horse, and Andsel kicked out as well, into the torso of his butchered victim to pull his blade free. Another knight veered toward him, with a sword held in both hands like a short lance to impale him. At the last moment, the red horse spun with the flow of the Norman charge. The thrust of the Norman's sword passed behind the red horse's head and in front of Andsel's chest. Andsel snatched a firm grip on the knight's tassets and heaved the man from his horse to land on the ground beside him. Quick as a flash, the red stallion spun upon the dismounted knight and stomped him into the earth. The red horse neighed in triumph. Andsel roared his battle cry in unison. Two invaders had fallen to his blade and he still stood upon the battlefield. Blood lust roared through his veins as a burning fire. How many more could he slay before they cut him down to join his king?

Most of the Norman cavalry had already passed Andsel and the red stallion in their pursuit of the remainder of Harold's army. One knight turned his mount from the pell-mell charge up the slope to face this singular Saxon. Three men had died easily by Andsel's hand thus far. He had simply reacted on the instinct of a soldier, with little time to think about the combat. This knight looked him right in the eye with fatal intent, and he had time to consider the consequences. Even if he wanted to turn tail and run, he knew the insane beast beneath him would not obey such a command, but he had no intention of running. Blood of two men covered him, who had lived only a moment ago. Dead and dying men littered the battlefield around them. On a far hill, the last rays of the evening sun lighted the brilliant colors of an autumn forest against a deep blue sky. Many would not see that beautiful hill, nor the sunrise tomorrow, and their deaths would be for nothing. Certainly, this was the fault of men. War had always been so. Suffering of all kinds had always existed. Certainly, this was *not* all the fault of men. Andsel had seen enough suffering. His king was lost; his land was lost; his home was lost. He would meet this knight, and one of them would soon meet the gods who made men suffer and die. Better for a man to meet the gods with a good horse beneath him and a strong blade in his hand, than to let the immortals steal his legs with old age and force him to crawl for mercy. Were it Andsel's day to die, he would stand before the cruel gods himself to exact an answer for the suffering. If the Norman soldier fell, Andsel would steal the strength of the gods, to live another day.

Odds were in the Norman's favor, for he held a long war lance and his shield. Andsel still held his broad sword, but this knight was likely skilled enough to skewer him easily from his mount in a formal joust of single combat. He would be pierced upon the ground long before he might ever swing a fatal blow. The lance of his first victim protruded from the sod between his new advisory and himself. Unfortunately, the lance would be on the wrong side of his mount as he passed it in the charge. With a roar in his throat, Andsel spurred the red battle steed to thunder toward his enemy. The Norman gave steel to his mount in answer. Halfway to the clash of battle, Andsel passed the grounded lance on his left. Dropping his sword, he seized the tail of the spear in both hands. In an instant, the point of the Norman's lance was at his chest. Twisting away from the thrust, he swung his own spear above his horse's head and drove it down over the top of the Norman's shield. Shocked surprise flashed across the face of William's man in the space of his last heartbeat, before the lance struck home between his neck and collar bone. The lance sprung skyward from his chest as if it were a flag pole without a banner, then it slowly tilted downward, as its dying bearer slumped back in his saddle and tumbled to the ground.

Lightning strikes of pain shot through Andsel's right side. The Norman's lance had not entirely missed its mark. Blood splattered from a gash bigger than he might plug with his fist, between splintered ends of his ribs where the glancing blow of the lance had torn the mail away. Each broken breath beckoned mortality with crimson streamers from his lips. He smiled to himself in spite of the pain, and leaned forward onto the pommels of his saddle to gaze one last time at the glorious light on the distant hill. Two warriors would stand before their gods to demand justice for their cruelty before night had closed the day.

The red horse twisted its head far back, in a contorted, completely unnatural, position to peer into its rider's face. Andsel looked into the visage of a red man, transposed onto the craned neck of his battle charger. "Well done, Andsel," Red Horse commended him. "You are brave enough for any warrior to be proud to fight beside. I will carry you from this field of battle as any fallen warrior should be carried away on the shoulders of his comrades." Red Horse turned his face away to become all steed again and leapt into flight down the slope toward the coming darkness. Raising his head one last time to see where his final resting place might be, Andsel saw the white cliffs of England drop away to the sea beneath the plunging hooves of Red Horse. Shrill winds of the fall whistled in his ears. He struck the sheets of his own bed and he was awake.

CHAPTER EIGHT

'Five-thirty' gleamed from the digital alarm clock on Tiffany's night stand. She still slumbered in her cloths beneath the blanket. The night sky was still dark, but a barely perceptible brightening in the east foretold of dawn to arrive within the hour. Andsel's memories of his recent, nocturnal, adventures in medieval England had him completely awake now. He rose from the bed and striped off his shirt from the day before. Leaving the light off in the bed room, he tip toed to the bathroom to wash his face, closing the door behind him. The hot water felt good on his skin. He raised his arm and looked down at his ribs. No hideous gash punctured his side.

Andsel studied his face in the mirror. Something needed improving. His complexion seemed so pale and wrinkled, not at all the steel-helmeted, hawkish, visage he had worn in England a few short minutes ago. Tiffany's rouge, eye shadow, and lipsticks stood in battle array across the back of the vanity. A little red lipstick across his cheek bones seemed to erase some of the feebleness of age. Rouge smeared on the chin and beneath the nostrils added a certain carnal aspect. Green eye shadow covered his pale cheeks nicely. White moisturizer, caked on his forehead and the bridge of his nose, nearly completed his war face; some color was still missing though. Yellow - yellow was required for the ultimate, menacing, intensity. No yellow compounds seemed to be available from Tiffany's repertoire. That problem was simple enough to solve. Andsel had every color in the rainbow waiting in his studio. One minute later, he stood in his studio daubing yellow oil paint beneath the red lipstick on his cheek bones.

A noise of movement, back in the main part of the house, caught Andsel's attention. He grabbed a tomahawk from the collection of artifacts which he had mounted on pegs on his walls and retraced his steps to the bedroom. Tiffany would appreciate his latest artistic endeavors; he was sure of it. He should share it with her. Switching on the overhead light, he crept to her side of the bed and leaned over her. As the light flushed across her closed lids, she rolled onto her back and opened her eyes. Her corresponding scream at the sight of an old, white, Indian man in full war paint, leaning over her with a raised tomahawk, was not the reaction Andsel had expected — but he was *delighted* with the response. Memories of his sword as it had cleaved through the second victim of his charge against the Norman cavalry, came to his mind with her shriek, and he grinned a vicious grin.

At that critical moment of art appreciation, the alarm clock rang. Andsel chopped the obnoxious device nearly in half with his tomahawk, every bit as neatly as he had cleaved the Norman soldier. His war whoop shattered the stillness of bedroom. Tiffany screamed again and rolled off of the bed. In the blink of an eye, she threw open the closet door and lurched inside. Andsel launched into a Sioux war song at the top of his lungs and shook the sparking remains of the alarm clock from his tomahawk, then swung the weapon at his fleeing wife. She slammed the closet door behind her, just in time to avoid the lethal steel. Andsel buried the blade deep into the doorjamb, shearing off the door knob in the process. Tiffany began ripping the clothing from the racks on either side of the walk-in closet to bury herself beneath for concealment and protection. Andsel had taken care of his lippy squaw for the time being. He would decide her ultimate fate later.

Brilliant morning sunlight burst through the bedroom window to paint the closet door red. The sun was rising. A warrior must ask blessing of the sun god before a battle. Andsel left his tomahawk buried in the closet door molding and hurried to the east-facing picture window of the living room. Blazing sunlight streamed across his bare chest as he ripped the curtains apart. He spread his arms in worship and sang the sun song. Morning breezes stirred the foliage of the trees across the street in the neighbors' yard. This house was antiseptic. Tiffany had not allowed a window open in this part of the house in decades. A brave needed to smell the dawn to decide what action to take in the day ahead.

A smaller pane of glass could be opened at the bottom of the big picture window. The latch and handle were hidden behind a big, glass, fish bowl resting on a wooden stand in front of the window. The bowl contained a small terrarium. Nothing actually grew among the polished stones and colored marbles at the bottom of the bowl. All of the little plants and cactus protruding from this concocted gravel were made of plastic or fabric. Supposedly, the terrarium's purpose was to catch the light in interesting effects throughout the day, but the curtains behind it were so seldom opened that Andsel really couldn't see much reason for it to be there at all. It was just something else for Joan to dust.

The window latch operated like a pair of opened scissors. By pulling the handle away from the sill, the scissors blades, positioned between the outside of the sill and the bottom of the window sash, closed together and extended, pushing the window open. Andsel first tried to pull the lever of the window latch by reaching around and over the offensive terrarium. A slight gap opened at the bottom of the window at first, but movement stopped as the seldom-used, latching device seized up. Putting his foot against the wall, Andsel shouldered the terrarium out of the way to crash across the floor, grabbed the latch lever with both hands, and yanked it away from the sash. The window sprang free with a bang. Fresh, morning air streamed into the living room, along with the warmth of the sun. Andsel breathed in deep the scents of the new day.

Some, particularly familiar, odor tickled his olfactory senses on the breeze; something familiar from the night before. "Horses! That's what it is!" he thought to himself. Andsel rushed out the front door in his bare feet to follow the scent. The wind flowed out of the west from behind the house. As he turned the corner of the house, a horse's faint whinny came to Andsel from a couple of blocks away. Town folk who possessed horses kept them boarded at a local stable and pasture grounds only a couple of blocks away on the edge of town. Andsel smiled to himself, "A horse stealing raid, that was the work of the day."

Rushing through his back yard gate, he sprinted across the grass and leaped over his neighbor's low fence, with one hand on the top rail. An astonished woman peered out of her kitchen window, with her morning cup of coffee suspended in mid air between its saucer and her gapped mouth. Andsel flashed by her without acknowledgement and cut through a side alley to cross the remaining block to the boarding stables.

A twenty acre pasture provided space for the horses to roam or be ridden for exercise. Several of the stock loitered across the field, grazing. Andsel did not even break his stride to climb over the high plank fence to be among the horses. He strode out toward the center of the pasture, making subtle clicking sounds, and holding out his hands to call the horses to him. The fact that he hadn't ridden anything in his entire life other than a pony at a carnival when he was a six-year-old boy did not deter him from approaching the creatures. Surprisingly, they responded immediately. All animals turned their heads toward the bare-chested, war-painted, elderly, man clucking among them in his bare feet. Each horse moved at a walk, trot, or gallop, depending upon its distance away, to come and stand within an arms length of Andsel as if he were made of oats. When perhaps twenty or more horses had closed in around their new master, they turned in unison and began to circle him in a clockwise direction, en mass, as if they were trained Lipizans at the circus. Faster and faster, they whirled around him. Closer and closer, they spiraled inward. Andsel watched them intently, trying to measure the timing of their strides. A big, red, roan seemed to be leading the herd's inward spiral. One more turn and the roan would be close enough. Andsel coiled to leap upon the roan's back when it passed again. He felt his calves and thighs tighten for the spring. He raised his arms slowly to snatch the horse's mane.

A bugle trumpeted from the east, back toward Andsel's home. Something *did* leap from the place where Andsel stood. The red roan's mane curled tightly around phantom fingers. Some ghostly weight settled perceptibly onto the horse's back, and the animal stretched and lengthened its stride. But Andsel, the mortal man, remained rooted as a post in the center of the whirling horses at the sounding of the distant bugle.

The equine whirlwind began to widen slowly with the change in the red roan's gait. Andsel should have felt relief as the distance increased between him and the flying steeds. Unfortunately, he was no longer the center of their arc. Horses continued to move in closer behind him, nearly brushing his back as they passed, while the space in front of him increased. "Stand stock still," a voice whispered in his head, "None of them will touch you." Terror made Andsel comply without question. Horses cut in front of him on the next turn, as well as behind, enclosing him in a mass of thousand-pound juggernauts oblivious to his existence. Andsel closed his eyes. For an instant, he was Red Horse the warrior again, astride the red roan. The great prairie spread out before him in the golden morning sunlight. His stolen horse herd streamed out behind him like an extension of his flying black hair. Pungent sage filled his nostrils. The mighty roan thundered between his knees. He was free.

"Now run!" a different voice thundered in Andsel's ears. He opened his eyes to discover that the herd had ceased its spiral and turned to gallop out across the pasture, leaving him alone. He too was free – but he must hurry. His climb over the plank fence was not nearly as graceful as his entrance had been. After cutting through the alley as before, he decided to circle around his own block in normal fashion using the street, instead of crossing the neighbor's yard and back fence. His heart pounded as he stumbled through his own front door. Time would be short. Red Horse could only ride the roan, as a spirit free, for so long, then he must return to the body of his host.

Since the revelry call of the bugle had sounded, some new entity seemed to be influencing Andsel's terrified thoughts. Andsel found himself searching frantically for a container of some kind. The emptied terrarium globe caught his eye where the sun glinted from its surface on the floor. He snatched it up and hurried to the kitchen sink to fill it with water. Yanking open the drawer where Tiffany kept the larger silverware and utensils, he selected two large, silver, salad forks. He closed the drawer over the handles of the salad forks and slammed his hip against it to lock the handles in a primitive vice. Pushing downward on the fork tines, he forced them toward the floor. Opening the drawer, he freed the utensils, reformed as two crude hooks of silver with wide paddle handles.

Red Horse had turned the horse herd at the far side of the pasture when he had come up against the fence boundary. He followed the fence line at a desperate gallop, searching for a breach of some kind. Round and round the pasture, the herd sped behind their phantom leader, but the thief could not escape with his booty.

Andsel left the water-filled globe on the dining room table and hurried to his studio with his silver hooks. Red Horse's skull did not gaze at him as he burst through the door. It stared away out of the sunlight window, lost in desire to be free. "Strike now and set the hook!" shouted the voice of Uncle John from an old cavalry bugle that hung by the door of the studio. Andsel sprang forward with his salad fork hooks and snatched up the bullet-holed skull by the eye sockets.

Out in the pasture, Red Horse pulled the roan up short in a cloud of dust. The horse herd streamed past the roan and scattered across the pasture in all directions. In a panic, he dropped from the back of the horse and fled toward the plank fence and the last vestige of his mortal remains beyond. "Damn that treacherous white man! He would take his scalp for this deceit, or at least the hair of his squaw!"

Andsel ran to the open window in the living room, with the Indian skull suspended at arms length. He righted the little wooden table in front of the window, and set the skull down upon it. "You must face your enemy," King Harold spoke behind him. Andsel twisted the skull around with a salad fork so that the empty, dead, sockets faced him. "Retrieve your shield!" warned Harold. Andsel raced to the studio again to snatch the bugle from the wall. He chanced to look down at the remaining, scalped, skull in the studio where it rested beneath the bugle. A paint brush protruded from the left eye socket where its handle had been jammed, as if shot from a Norman bow. Andsel turned with a shudder, slung the bugle on its leather strap over his shoulder, and ran back to the living room to await the return of Red Horse.

He heard the savage's spirit rattle the fence as it leapt across into the front yard. The sun seemed to blaze brighter upon the grass as Red Horse passed across the lawn. As if time itself regressed one hundred and fifty years within the spirit's presence, a sliver of the neighborhood vanished where he passed, to reveal a panorama of distant prairies filled with buffalo. The sliver of the past broadened and shimmered with radiance as Red Horse charged the house. A mighty blast of wind struck the front of the house. A massive gust burst through the open window to set the skull dancing upon the little table. The dead eye sockets glowed with the sunlight: the boney eyebrows above, arched in anger. In an instant, Andsel snatched up the silver, salad-fork, hooks again. Swinging them like a Saxon battle axe, he snatched up the evil skull by its cheek bones and carried the hissing cranium at arm's length into the dining room, like the head of Goliath.

"Drop him in there," Uncle John directed. Andsel dropped the skull into the water-filled globe on the table and twisted the hooks free. "That'll keep him out of trouble," Andsel said to himself. The water began to churn and bubble. "Got to get a lid on this pot," he decided. He scanned the dining room and the adjacent living room for a solution.

Several framed pictures of family gatherings from the distant past were displayed on a shelf in the living room. One picture was from a reunion of Andsel's own family at least forty years ago. Andsel had been a teenager at the time. He stood in the front row next to his pretty cousin Linda. For a moment, he remembered standing beside her in the hot sunlight. "Let your hair down, Linda," the photographer had called out. "You look like a boy." Andsel had reached behind her neck and tugged the blue scarf from her ponytail, letting her dark hair fall forward to frame her soft, pretty, face.

"That will do," he muttered, returning to the present, and snatching the picture from the shelf. He pried the cardboard from the back of the picture, then shook the picture and its protective pane of glass loose upon the soft carpet of the living room. Linda stared up from the floor, wide-eyed, her lips parted in surprise. She had been a beautiful, young, woman on that day forty years ago. She was a heavy woman now, with her white hair dyed a garish blonde. Andsel was glad that he *had* snatched away the ribbon on that sunny summer day to catch the woman as she was. Having other spirits to catch, he grabbed the glass carelessly from the floor. "Damn it!" he growled, as the sharp glass cut a neat slice in the tip of his right, index, finger. Blood trickled across the surface of the pane.

"Ah no! A bad turn," Harold gasped in his ear.

"Oh shut up," murmured Andsel, and stuck the injured finger in his mouth. He carried the pane in his left hand to the simmering bowl, and slid it across the rim. The bubbling stopped immediately. His own blood dispersed into the water of the bowl, tinting it rosy pink. He pulled his injured finger from his mouth to examine it. The bleeding had stopped. Suddenly he felt very tired and alone. Slumping into a chair, he wondered to himself how he was going to keep that pane of glass secured to the rim of the bowl.

Tiffany would think he was insane, and he probably was – at least he *had* been. Nobody else seemed to be sitting there on the living room floor inside his skin with him now. *She* would probably leave him too, as soon as he let her out of the closet. Should he release her now, so that she could scream and holler, pack and leave, or should he wait until after he had finished with Red Horse? Somehow, he already did have a definite plan in mind for his genie in a bottle. Tiffany might call the cops on him before he ever got away with the skull in the jug, if she were set free. Well, she deserved that chance, he guessed. After all, if he left her locked in there all day, she certainly would call in the law. She might not act immediately if he turned her loose this morning. She might mull it over for an hour or so before taking any action, especially if he left on his mission right away. Perhaps he should back the truck out and prepare his escape first, then pull the hatchet from the door.

Rising to his feet, he went to the garage, hit the automatic door opener, and climbed into his truck cab. A caulking gun with a half-used tube of clear silicone hung from a nail on the back wall of the garage, among the many other tools. "The silicone would work perfectly to seal Red Horse in his tomb," he thought to himself as he backed the pickup out into the driveway. After shutting the truck off, he retrieved the caulk gun and cleared the dried silicone from the tip. Returning to the dining room, he ran a bead of silicone around the outline of the bowl rim on the glass pane. He took a deep breath, then grabbed the glass pane and flipped it over, deftly sticking the bead of silicone down onto the rim of the bowl. Even so, the surface of the rosy water puckered in an effort to boil. The cavalry bugle still hung from Andsel's shoulder. He unslung the instrument and set it down on its bell end on the glass pane to hold it in place while the silicone hardened. Now, to release Tiffany.

When he had removed the bugle from his shoulder, he had realized his disturbing appearance. He wore nothing but yesterday's slacks, rumbled from having slept in them and filthy from the exploits of the morning. His face felt stiff with paint and make-up. Maybe he shouldn't greet Tiffany at the closet door in his war paint with a tomahawk in his hand. After all, he vaguely remembered being in that state when she had dived in there. He stopped at the kitchen sink where he scrubbed away as much of the paint as possible with some dish washing soap and a dish towel. Surveying the mess on the towel when he had finished, he decided to use it to wrap the fish bowl in, and then dispose of it afterward. A rumpled shirt from the cloths hamper in laundry room covered his pale, old, hide. Sneakers without socks would do fine for the day's work.

Bracing himself for the female storm to come, he walked to the closet door. "Tiffany Dear, are you in there?" he cooed, feeling magnanimously stupid instantly. Of course she was in there. The tomahawk still jutted from the door jamb. He grabbed its handle and wrenched it free with an upward tug. Tossing it out of sight under the bed, he called again, "Tiffany. It's all right now. I am feeling completely myself now. I don't know what came over me. Some kind of bad dream, I guess. Kind of a walking nightmare. It won't happen ever again, I promise."

No answer came from within the closet.

"Please dear, speak to me. Scream at me. Call me filthy names. Anything at all, please, just speak to me."

Tiffany's soft voice crept through the door in gentle song, as if she were in her grade school chorus. "Marezy dots and Dozey dots and Little Lambzy divvy," she sang, "A Kidley Divey too, wouldn't you?"

"Tiffany?" Andsel questioned, "Are you all right?"

"No Grandma, I really don't want a cookie. When Grandpa ate one of that kind of cookie, he had to go to the hospital and he never came back."

"What the hell are you talking about?" Andsel shouted.

No answer came from the closet.

"Tiffany?" he called again after a few minutes.

The gentle sound of Tiffany's soft, contented, snoring emanated from the closet.

"Okay Tiffany. You rest a while longer. I've got some errands to run. We can talk about this when I get back. I have made a little mess in the living room. I will try to call Joan to clean it up, because I really must be on my way. If she can't stop by, I will pick things up when I return,"

The sounds of tranquil rest continued behind the door.

Andsel decided to get, while the getting was good. After exiting the bedroom, he did try to place phone call to Joan, but made contact with her answering machine only. "Hello Joan, this is Andsel Edgar. We have had a bit of a messy accident this morning in the living room. I was wondering if you might have time to stop by and tidy it up for me," he recited into the impersonal, skeptical, device. "I have several errands and appointments that I must get to on time, or I would clean the mess up myself. Mrs. Edgar is still feeling under the weather and has remained in bed. If she is still there when you arrive, it would be best not to disturb her rest." He added, "Thank you, Joan," and hung up the receiver.

Returning to the living room, he reslung his bugle as a talisman, scooped up the heavy bowl briskly, and headed for the garage. He found a shallow, cardboard, box of about the correct dimensions to cradle the bowl, in the garage. Placing the bowl in the box and then in the front seat, he returned to the kitchen for the paint smeared, dish, towel. Just in case the bowl spilled or he needed to handle the skull for any reason on his journey, he retrieved his salad forks and stuffed them in his front pockets. Their wide forks protruded from the tops of his pockets to poke him uncomfortably in the belly when he slid into the pick-up seat. The towel cushioned the bowl nicely when he packed it in place. He pulled the passenger seatbelt around the box and snapped it in place for extra security, then backed out of the driveway.

Even though he wished to be done with the task ahead of him as soon as possible, he drove well under all speed limits, pointing the truck northward out of town toward the mountains. A skull with a bullet hole in it, submerged in blood-soaked water, might be rather difficult to explain to a highway patrolman who might pull him over for speeding. More glittering, motorcycle, headlights on the horizon jolted Andsel's memory back to his assault on the Iron CPA, Harley, gang yesterday. He glanced in his rear view mirror involuntarily, anticipating the lights of a cop car pulling him over in response to a report of his escapade the day before. The highway stretched clear and empty behind him. He pulled down his sun visor and twisted it to the side to obscure the view of his profile as the phalanx of bikers passed him in the opposite lane. None slowed or cut across the median to follow him.

He turned onto Highway 16 toward the Big Horns. Five miles further west, he began to climb on switch backs into the mountains. Grass-covered foot hills gave way to lodge pole pine forests. Andsel turned off the air conditioning and rolled down his window. Forty miles per hour was about as fast as anyone could comfortably drive on the twisting road, so the breeze entering the cab was pleasant, but not overpowering. Sweet pine scent inundated the interior of the truck. Red Horse's skull seemed to smile as dappled sunlight flickered across the surface of his globe. Forty minutes from the bottom of the

Big Horn Range, Andsel had reached Burgess Junction and the end of travel on a hard top road. He took a gravel road to the north, slowing to twenty-five or thirty miles per hour. Washboard ripples had formed in the dirt road's surface over the summer. They caused a constant vibration in the truck and set Red Horse's teeth a'rattlin. The skull looked as if it were speaking, chattering away rapidly in some foreign language. It gave Andsel the creeps. He kept his eyes on the road. Another forty minutes of bumpy traveling, and several turn-offs later, he reached his destination.

Dry Fork Point was about as far as a passenger car could drive, or a truck could pull a camping trailer in the Big Horns, and then only during the dry summer months. Two camping trailers were parked at the base of the massive granite boulders of Dry Fork Point. Lawn chairs were folded up and stuffed beneath both trailers. Blinds had been drawn inside. The heavy, opaque, plastic, rock shields, which doubled as awnings, had been dropped over the front windows above the hitches. Whoever used these campers had simply locked them up and left them for the week at Dry Fork while they had returned to Sheridan, Casper, or Gillette to work at their jobs. It was a common practice. A camper could remain at a camp site for sixteen days before it must be moved to a different location. Other people seldom tampered with the unattended trailers.

No other vehicles were parked in the turn around. If another car or truck were to approach, it could be heard for miles before arriving. He had the place to himself. Pulling the keys out of the ignition, he walked around to the passenger side, opened the door, and pulled out the bowl in its box. The trail up over the house-sized boulders was steep. Cradling the box carefully against his chest, he picked his footing with care. A stiff wind from the east blew at this exposed altitude this morning. Winds seldom came from the east in the Big Horns. They often brought unsettled weather. Several small islands of cumulus clouds were cruising rapidly toward the mountain peaks, sending their shadows slithering up the slopes far ahead of them. Andsel puffed hard for breath by the time he had completed the hundred yard climb to the top of the point. Setting his box down gently on the bare granite of the look out, he took a moment to appreciate the magnificent view. From Dry Fork Point, a person could see fifty miles or more to the north and east across the high plains of Wyoming and Montana. Cloud shadows marbled the Wolf Mountains in the distance, across the Tongue River drainage. "This was as fine place as anyone could ask for to take his final view of the mortal world," Andsel thought to himself. "Perhaps he too might have his ashes tossed to the high winds here some day when he shook off his own mortal coil. Five hundred feet below, a harrier hawk rode the gusts of wind low above the grasses in his search for rodents. Thunder rumbled faintly over the Wolf Mountains far away. Andsel caught the shimmer of distant lightning beneath purple clouds. A larger clump of clouds scudded closer to the point, threatening to envelop it in mist within a few minutes. Red Horse should leave in the sunlight, as any warrior would wish. Andsel should get on with the task at hand.

He lifted the heavy, glass, globe from the box and raised it high over his head.

"Do not send a warrior to his end sealed in a prison," a voice spoke inside his head.

Andsel had indeed intended to send the skull, globe and all, hurtling down to the rocks below, but somehow, even though he had suffered torment at the hand of Red Horse, even though Red Horse had caused him to nearly kill his wife that morning, it did not seem proper to confine his spirit at its ending. Andsel lowered the bowl to rest beneath his sneakered feet. He pulled the silver forks from his pockets and reversed his grip so that the broad fork ends pointed away in normal fashion. Pushing the tines against the silicone seam, between the glass pane and the bowl rim, he levered downward. The pane popped off neatly without breaking. He slid the plate glass carefully to the granite, then reversed the forks, and hooked the skull gently by the eye sockets. The water did not seethe when the glass had been removed. Even so, Andsel braced himself mentally for Red Horse's possible onslaught when his skull was removed from the water. At the first hint of any inner turmoil or mental disruption, Andsel would fling the damned skull as far out over the chasm as his strength would allow. Carefully, he lifted the skull out of the bowl and lowered it to the rock. Nothing but peace flowed through his mind.

"There is no need for those weapons between us now," Red Horse spoke in his mind again, as clear as if the Sioux brave stood beside him.

Andsel tossed the silver hooks into the water-filled bowl with a little splash. Picking up the skull without hesitation, he stepped to the shear edge of the precipice. The little cloud had drifted between the sun and Dry Fork Point, casting gloom across it and the chasm below. He lifted the skull high above his head and picked out the largest boulder he could see below for a target.

"Wait a moment for the Sun," Red Horse requested.

The cloud drifted slowly toward the west and, as it passed, shafts of sunlight filtered through its misty edges and shimmered across the rock face. Just as the cloud passed completely from between Andsel and the Sun, one mighty tentacle of lightning reached its sinewy path across the blue sky from the Wolf Mountains to strike the little cloud, exploding it into a golden mist.

"Now! Send me now!" shouted Red Horse, and Andsel sent the skull hurtling down, down, to the rocks below.

The skull shattered into a million pieces when it finally struck the boulder Andsel had selected so far below, accompanied by a mighty clap of thunder. When the shards had settled and sifted to their multitudinous, permanent, resting places among the cracks and crevices of the boulder field beneath the cliff, the harrier turned in its lazy search for food to drift over the site of the impact, perhaps to discover what all the ruckus had been about.

"A truly fitting end for a warrior," Andsel said to himself as he watched the harrier ride the wind currents westerly. More lightning flickered over the Wolfs and the corresponding thunder grumbled. "Guess I had better get the hell off of this mountain top before the next bolt catches me," he muttered as he poured the water from his bowl. Stuffing the salad forks back into his pockets and retrieving the glass pane, he turned away from the precipice to shuffle his way carefully back down the narrow path to his truck. Tossing the bowl and cover into the cardboard box, he fired up his faithful steed, backed into the gravel road, and started his long journey back to the hard top, and eventually, to Tiffany.

CHAPTER NINE

By now, she would have packed, but who would she have packed for? Would she have neatly folded her things and arranged them carefully in her various suitcases and bags; or would she have gathered up heaps of his clothing to toss out into the yard? No, she wouldn't air his dirty laundry in the front yard for all of the neighbors to see. She would hurl it into the garage where he parked his truck. Most likely, she had phoned their lawyer and then the police. The restraining order was being drafted as he was driving along this beautiful, scenic, gravel, road. His future scudded away as fast as the silver clouds drifted across the perfect, blue, sky. A fork in the road appeared ahead. As best he could recall, the right fork would take him away from the hard top road, to pass through stunning alpine valleys with sparkling trout streams flowing parallel to the road. He hadn't been that way in years. He was in no hurry to get home to face Tiffany, an attorney, and possible arrest.

Before he had even given the choice much thought, he found himself on the right-bound fork. Spruce, fir, and lodge pole forests flanked the old road most of the time. Now and then, the trees ended to reveal vistas of vast, open, meadows studded with huge gray and pink boulders and cliffs. The stone monoliths mimicked grotesque figures or fantastic creatures. Andsel wondered if they moved in the moonlight, perhaps danced one miniscule step a night, over eons of time. "What an insane, silly, idea," he thought to himself. So many of these twisted, warped, fantasies had flamed into his mind unbidden over the last few days. Perhaps he was suffering from some mental ailment which was causing these bizarre dreams and hallucinations. He wasn't getting any younger. Maybe he could plead to Tiffany that he was suffering from some undiagnosed mental or emotional condition. He could beg for her understanding, tell her that he hadn't been feeling well, promise to see a doctor immediately. She would probably call their family physician, herself, in the morning. He would gladly submit to any tests or evaluation to keep her from leaving. Perhaps there truly was something wrong with him. Painting oneself with make-up and chasing the local horse herd, while wearing nothing but yesterdays Dockers, in the wee hours of the morning, was certainly grounds for a trip to the booby hatch. Andsel began to contemplate his potential brain surgery. An image crossed his mind of his family doctor, Wayne Burkholtz, holding the bowl of his cranium in one hand and peering into the empty interior of his skull as he lay upon a gurney. Dr. Burkholtz would be saying, "Now here is your problem, Tiffany. His brains have been completely removed by someone."

Tiffany would answer, "I can't imagine why anyone would bother. I'll bet a squaw couldn't even tan a weasel hide with them. Andsel certainly never found a reasonable use for them."

Andsel burst into laughter at the image. He wanted to hear Tiffany laugh with him again. God, he did not want her to leave him! Sure, their life had become rather hum drum over the years. They had gotten into the habit of picking at each other for entertainment. Beneath the constant, low-key, antagonism, he still loved her deeply. No one else truly mattered even remotely as much to him as she did. He had known all aspects of himself, the good and the disgusting, for a long time now, but Tiffany was the unknown world beyond. Yes, he had known her for all of the years of their long marriage, yet something new revealed itself about her every day. His constant efforts to annoy her now seemed like a pathetic strategy to evoke some new facet of her character – each facet always understandably negative. If she might see her way to forgive this recent, temporary, insanity of his, he resolved to find new ways to surprise her in only a pleasant manner in the future, instead of swinging a tomahawk at her head.

Who was he kidding? At best, he would be required to spend endless, expensive, hours talking to a shrink. He wondered if he should find a cheap hotel to hole up in for a week or two, or if he would be banished from his home long enough to justify renting some shabby, cold, lonely, apartment. None of his prospects sounded the least bit enjoyable. Begging for forgiveness had never been one of his stronger talents. He had better rehearse his plea many times before he reached his doorstep tonight, and pray she did not turn a deaf ear before he even had a chance to speak.

Many miles of empty mountainside had slipped by the truck window while Andsel pondered his fate. He now found himself at an intersection with the asphalt road again, several miles further to the west. Time to return to face the music. A small, white, dome on top of the mountain peak to his right caught his eye. Wyoming had erected an astronomical and meteorological observatory there on the top of Medicine Mountain several years ago.

It was not the first use of the 10,000 foot peak by humans. Ancient Native American tribes had constructed a place of worship on the peak several centuries before. The Medicine Wheel, as it was called, consisted of a large assemblage of loose, rough, stones in the shape of a spoked wheel approximately one hundred feet in diameter. Several cairns also had been erected within the wheel. Tourists could visit this Indian holy place by driving a short distance on a gravel road, then parking their vehicles, and walking the remaining three quarters of a mile on a groomed path to the Medicine Wheel. Even though the Sioux, or any other modern-day tribe, did not claim creation or ownership of the Medicine Wheel, they did hold it sacred. Members of many different tribes frequently visited the Wheel to honor memories of deceased loved ones, or to pray for strength and guidance through life's travails. It was considered as sacred as any church, and a visitor was required to treat it as such.

Andsel had not visited the Wheel in many years. Still in no particular hurry to go home, he turned toward the west. Soon, he found himself parking his truck in the wide gravel area provided at the end of the Medicine Wheel access road. No other vehicles occupied the parking lot. Finding the historic monument vacant at this time of year pleased Andsel a great deal. A moment at the Wheel alone, without camera-bearing tourists in shorts, from New Jersey or Florida, was rare in August. Vacation travelers did tend to thin out as summer faded closer toward the first day of school. Ripples of glowering clouds, like the washboards of the gravel road he had been driving on earlier, marched toward the Big Horn Basin to the west and the Absoroka Mountains beyond. Andsel remembered the random blast of lightning that he had witnessed on Dry Fork Point a couple of hours ago. He locked his truck doors and hurried up the walking path. Perhaps the tourists from New Jersey were a lot smarter than the locals when it came to standing on a mountain peak with impending thunder heads hurrying in from the east.

Forest Service Rangers monitored the Medicine Wheel site during the summer months from a small utility shack at the edge of the parking lot. No lights illuminated the interior of the shack to signify an occupant busy inside. The door remained closed. Either the ranger inside was taking a nap or he just did not care to brave the increasingly chilly wind to check out one, single, old, man foolish enough to climb the path to the Medicine Wheel, with an impending storm brewing up. By now, the temperature down on the prairies below would be approaching ninety degrees. Andsel had forgotten how truly chilly several thousand feet of altitude could make a summer day. Add the intermittent shade created by the bands of clouds, and the stiff breeze that pushed them along, and anyone would wish they had brought along a heavy jacket. Andsel strode along briskly up the path to overcome the coolness. Soon, he stood by the rope fence which protected the archeological wonder against people wandering among the stones to pick up souvenirs. If not for the fence, the structure would have been carted off to the four corners of the world long ago. One of the two rangers stationed at the site, was supposed to stand on casual guard near the Wheel. The ranger was also there to answer any questions, when the site was open for visitors. Andsel surveyed the area for the ranger on duty. No one seemed to be around. Another of the harrier hawks hovered over the short grasses and talus rocks of the mountain top, searching for picas or marmots. Andsel had always admired the way these hawks could fly so slowly and so close to the ground as they searched for their daily meal. A small white patch, located in the area where their tail feathers flared out from their bodies, made them conspicuous as they floated among the mountain flora. To Andsel, they seemed to be in constant contemplation of the beauty that surrounded them - peaceful sojourners across a timeless landscape.

Various, colorful, little, bundles ornamented the ropes of the barrier fence. These were prayer offerings from the many Indian worshipers who visited each summer. Sometimes the offering consisted of a colorful scarf or a single feather. Other small tokens of hope or respect had been laid among the rocks of the monument itself. Andsel circled clockwise to the left, as was indicated by a sign. Common Indian belief held this to be the appropriate direction. Bits of antler or bone sometimes poked out from between the weathered stones. Someone had draped a ball cap and a dog collar over one of the boulders.

"That hat and collar is one of the more poignant mementos I have seen up here," a soft voice spoke from behind Andsel.

"Great!!" Andsel thought to himself, "Now I am hearing a totally new voice in my head, and this one is female." He turned around to find the missing ranger standing close behind him. She was a tall, dark-haired, young, woman, looking very attractive in her green uniform and hat. A pale blue scarf tied her long, straight, hair back in a pony tail, giving a youthful accent to her formal attire. For an instant, he thought his Cousin Linda had materialized from the old photograph to haunt him in Red Horse's place. "You gave me a start just now," he commented. "I thought I was alone up here."

She smiled softly and said, "You are never alone up here."

He turned back to the Wheel to look at the cap and collar offering again. "Who do you suppose died first, the dog or his master?" he asked.

"Perhaps they died together," the girl commented.

"I suppose, with an Indian, the dog might have been offered as a meal," Andsel said with a laugh.

"You're one of those people who are always quick with the smart answer, aren't you/" the girl retorted.

She lifted her chin a little defiantly when she spoke, and the sun lighted her face from the shadow beneath her hat brim. Her skin shown with a hint of mellowed copper.

"I am sorry," he blathered hurriedly, "I didn't realize you were Native American. I didn't mean to be disrespectful."

"It doesn't matter what I am. This is a holy place for everyone, regardless of what deity they believe in. You would not have made such a disparaging remark in a cemetery, would you?"

"Yes, I am sorry to say, I probably would have. Sometimes I say things for my own amusement, and for no one else. It is a poor habit of mine that most people certainly do not appreciate."

"If you are frightened by sacred things that you do not understand, don't try to belittle them with snide humor. Sentiment and spirit sometimes cling to them. Careless jokes might be conceived as a dangerous challenge. Dangerous for you."

"Again, I am sorry for my thoughtless comment, Miss," Andsel stammered. "What do you think might be the story about the collar and the cap?" he asked her, in an attempt to diffuse the conflict.

She stepped to the rope beside him. "The only thing for certain is that the dog loved the owner of the cap and probably the love was returned. They are represented together here. Any sorrow of loss between them is ended in this hallowed place. That knowledge is enough for me."

"That is a beautiful thought," Andsel said, to himself, as much as to the young woman.

"What did you come here looking for?" she asked, without turning away from the Wheel.

An image of Tiffany looking out at him through the widow of their closed and locked front door came into his mind. "Courage," he answered with a smile.

"Another smart-ass answer, I think," the girl responded, with out looking away from the sacred circle, as if it were a crystal ball for reading minds.

"Not really," he responded.

"Then you must leave an offering here for the Great Spirit. If he is not too greatly offended by your wise crack about the dog, he will send a spirit helper to bring your courage to you," she directed, turning toward him with a secretive smile.

"Well I guess I am out of luck as usual. I came up here with nothing except the clothes I am standing in," he said.

"What are those things sticking out of your pockets?" she asked, pointing to the forgotten salad forks.

Andsel pulled his abused kitchen utensils from his pockets and stood there with a sheepish look on his face. "Uh… something I found discarded on one of the campground picnic tables?" he mumbled, for lack of a believable, honest, answer.

"Lying is never a good way to present an offering, but, lucky for you, they are made of silver, and that metal is always respected. You must have meant to hang them on the fence as an offering against whatever vial offense you are seeking forgiveness for, or you would not have bent the handles into hooks. Silver or not, I suspect the gods will make the task that you request their help with, a little harder than it might be, because of your jests and your deceit," she observed. "Make your prayer and hang them on the fence, like everyone else has done."

"She doesn't exactly talk like your average, teenage, junior, ranger, sent up here for summer wages to pay her college tuition," Andsel thought to himself as he hung the shiny forks on the barrier fence. "She must read a lot of cheap paperbacks to pass the time up here. It has affected her language." He prudently kept these thoughts to himself. Perhaps she was wearing a gun. He stepped back from his offering to stand beside the girl and they contemplated the out-of-place objects, together. The forks clattered together in combat in the strong wind.

"They sound like swords coming together," the girl commented.

"She has definitely been reading too many Gothic novels," Andsel confirmed to himself.

"They won't last long in this wind," the girl said as she pulled the scarf from her hair. She twisted the scarf into a complex knot around the rope and the hooks of the salad forks. "That should hold them," she said with satisfaction.

Andsel moved to untie the scarf, saying, "You needn't waste your beautiful scarf for such a silly offering, on my behalf, Miss," but the knot proved far too intricate for him to undo.

She put her palm against his chest with surprising force to push him away from the offering. "Leave the scarf where I put it. You are going to need all of the help you can get, I think," she demanded.

"Okay, if you say so," he acquiesced to this mighty strange young lady of authority. No firearm appeared to hang from her hip, but considering the remoteness of the location, he began to get the feeling that now would be a good time to leave. "I just remembered an old stained towel that I have down in my pick up truck. I will leave it down at your ranger hut and you can use it to replace your beautiful scarf on your next trip up," he said. All he received in response was an ice-cold stare from the ranger girl. "Okay then. Good-bye," he said and waved as he turned to complete his circuit of the Medicine Wheel and then hurry back to the safety of his truck. Without answering, the girl turned to walk away toward the cliffs behind the Wheel. "Why is it that every woman I meet scares the hell out of me anymore?" Andsel wondered as he hurried down the path to the parking lot. Thunder grumbled close overhead in reply.

Big, heavy, raindrops began to splat into the coarse sand and gravel of the path. Tongues of lightning flashed across the nearby peaks to the east. Andsel roared into the parking lot on a dead sprint. A short, stout, man shouted, "Anyone else up there?" to him from the little porch of the ranger hut as he passed.

"No one except your partner," Andsel shouted, as the rain increased to a steady downpour.

"Partner? I don't have any partner up here today. He stayed home, sick, at the main station this morning," the stout man shouted back over the rumbling thunder.

Andsel came to a dead standstill in the battering rain and shouted back, "The girl, your partner. She wore a uniform exactly like yours. She must be your partner."

"There isn't any ranger here but me today, Mister, and certainly not a woman. If there is a woman up on that mountain, she better get the hell off of there or she will be lit up like a Roman Candle," he shouted back indignantly.

Suddenly, Andsel remembered checking the embroidered name on her uniform because she had resembled his cousin so much, when he had first seen her. "Harriett! Her name was Harriett!" he shouted back to the man on the porch. Lightning ripped the sky in two directly above their heads, striking the peak near the astronomical observatory. Both Andsel and the ranger cowered beneath the blast and its accompanying crush of thunder.

"I don't know any goddamned Harriett!" the ranger shouted and ducked inside the safety of his ranger hut, slamming the door behind him.

Andsel turned away to sprint to his truck. He spotted the painted dish cloth in the box on the truck seat. Grabbing the rag from box, he ran to one of the posts at the entrance of the walking path. A chain, used to block off the path when the site was closed, hung from the post. He knotted the rag to the eye screw that held the chain to the post and streaked back to his truck, beneath another incredible electric discharge from the heavens. Whoever the young, uniformed, woman was, she had better find a crack in the rocks to climb into, or she was going to be a fricasseed, forest ranger, for sure. As far as Andsel was concerned, he had seen about enough mysterious happenings for one lifetime in the last couple of days. It was time for him to go home to face the concrete reality of Tiffany's wrath.

CHAPTER TEN

Rain had settled into the Bighorns to stay for the remainder of the day. Mighty winds shoved curtains of water across the crooked road from every angle. Andsel drove slowly down the long descent of Route 14, gripping the wheel with both hands. Fatigue settled into his bones with the dampness of the afternoon. The mysterious Harriett still haunted his thoughts, perhaps because she had resembled his Cousin Linda. Andsel had quickly decided that the young female ranger had only resembled the teen-age Cousin Linda in a superficial, general, sense of coloring and stature. Linda had been of a very pale complexion, while the girl at the Medicine Wheel had been darker. The ranger girl's eyes were deeper set within her face, more secretive. Only coincidence had caused Andsel to choose the old picture containing the likeness of a young Linda to rob his glass plate from hours before meeting another tall, dark-haired, girl. Stranger or not, Andsel hoped that she had found shelter from the storm. He had finished his dealings with spirits with the shattering of the skull on the rocks below Dry Fork Point. Cousin Linda was still as lively as a firecracker. Her ghost did not roam the forlorn peaks of the Big Horn Mountains. He was certain of that. After concluding his unwilling involvement with Red Horse, Andsel decided that he was finished with any further contemplation of the supernatural. Ranger Harriett had been composed of flesh and blood as far as he was concerned, and that was that.

Bikers in down parkas hurriedly packed their precious Harleys into covered trailers in the parking lot of the Mountain Inn Bar when Andsel had reached the bottom of the mountains. When the bikes were adequately secured, the riders and their support drivers would pack themselves into the bar for black coffee or a stiffer toddy against the chill. After a drink or two, they would wad themselves into the crew cabs of the pick-ups hitched to the covered trailers and drive back to Executiveland inconspicuously.

Andsel considered delaying the pending confrontation with Tiffany by ducking into the bar and buying a round for these waterlogged road warriors, in secret compensation for running their compadres off of the road the day before. The sudden thought that one of them might recognize him or his truck gave him cause to reconsider. He turned his eyes away from the warm, glowing, bar, back to the rain-blackened highway, and steadied his foot down on the accelerator again.

Twenty minutes later, his home street and the ruination of his marriage loomed beyond the hood of his Dodge. To his surprise, the overhead door on his side of the garage scrolled upward in anticipation, before he had ever reached for the remote opener clipped to the visor. A brief sense of driving into the maw of hell washed across him, as he crossed the threshold of the garage. The door clumbered to a solid close behind him, as he switched off the ignition and extracted his keys. He sat in the truck seat, trying to gather his nerve and clear his mind to deal with the drama to come. A new battle would begin as soon as he stepped into that kitchen beyond the side entry. His cavalry bugle talisman gleamed dully from the truck seat beside him. Perhaps he should wear that in to the house for protection. The overhead light on the electric door opener clicked off after its timed interval had expired, erasing the gleam from the bugle and leaving Andsel alone in semi-darkness. Cold dampness began to creep into the truck cab like the sealed atmosphere of a grave. Soft, warm, yellow, light beckoned from the little panes of glass in the entry way door. "At least it would be warm in the house," he thought to himself, "Plenty warm." He fully expected to spend tonight in a hotel room. If he could at least get inside of the house for one last time, Tiffany might allow him to gather up some clothing to stuff into a travel bag before she demanded that he leave. With final resolution, he heaved the truck door open, climbed out, and strode up the steps as if he still owned the place.

No scowling Tiffany grimaced at him from behind the glass, nor did her stern silhouette bar entrance to the short hall-way that led to the kitchen. She probably waited in the kitchen with the meat cleaver, or the cops. He wasn't sure which would be worse. She might only wound him once or twice with the cleaver before he could disarm her, but the cops would ruin him forever. Then again, one deft chop with the cleaver and all of his troubles would be over. Opening the door quietly, he stepped softly into the hallway and wiped his feet on the rug. He started to shuffle out of sneakers. then considered the possibility that he might need to make a quick exit out into the damp night, and these might be the only shoes that he was allowed to leave with. "Better to die with my boots on," he thought, and stepped to the doorway of the kitchen. Taking a deep breath, he swung around into the full glare of the kitchen and Tiffany.

Steam roiled up to encircle her face softly in a silver hal-low, from the pie she held in her oven-mittened hands. "I had to pull this out of the oven before it burned, or I would have met you at the door, dear. Joan brought me some fresh rhubarb today when she came to help clean up the mess I had made. I don't know what came over me yesterday, really!" She looked down at the muddy sneakers on Andsel's feet. "Don't forget to take your shoes off before you come to supper. This strawberry-rhubarb pie is for later." Andsel stood with his mouth agape as she turned to set the pie down on a cooling rack on the island counter. "Hurry along now, dear, The roast will get cold. I'll put a salad together while you wash your hands and face."

Andsel turned back into the entry way to remove his muddy shoes. Tiffany broke up a head of lettuce to add to the bowl of chopped onions, tomatoes, carrots, radishes, and other various greens, as Andsel passed her in the kitchen on his way to the bedroom. His face was a ruddy mess of paint and mud. A quick shower might have been a good idea, but supper waited on the table. He risked a quick glance at the closet door as he passed through the bedroom on his way to the bath. An ugly scar still marred the door jamb. All residue from the shattered alarm clock had been removed. Andsel wondered if the tomahawk still lay hidden beneath the bed. After scrubbing the muck from his face, he took stock of his filthy attire. He ripped off the grubby shirt and slacks and stuffed them in a cloths hamper in the corner of the bedroom. Stepping to the closed closet he pulled the door open hesitantly.

"Your supper will get cold, Andsel," Tiffany called from the dining room.

"I'm changing into clean clothes," he answered as he pulled a pair of slacks and a shirt from hangers in the immaculate closet. Tugging on a dry pair of socks, he peeked beneath the bed. The shadowy outline of the tomahawk appeared, undisturbed, beneath the center of the box springs. He hurried to the dinning room, buttoning his shirt.

Roast beef steamed on a large platter in the center of the table. Real mashed potatoes flanked the roast, in a dish on one side. Buttered corn provided a golden, yellow, contrast from the other side.. Tiffany had already served herself beef, potatoes, and corn. Remains of lettuce and ranch dressing on a small plate beyond her glass indicated that she had already eaten her salad.

"I'm sorry that I didn't wait for you to join me. I know that it was impolite, but I hadn't eaten anything all day, and

I was famished. Obviously, I had entirely too much to drink yesterday. My appetite struck me like a lightning bolt when you came home," she apologized. "Would you like some salad?" she asked, offering him the bowl.

He used the big, stainless steel, spoon and plastic spatula in the salad bowl to serve himself a portion of green salad, without so much as a raised eyebrow at the unusual serving utensils.

"I seemed to have misplaced the set of salad forks temporarily," she apologized. "Things seemed to have gotten displaced quite a bit yesterday. In fact, I seem to have confused the floor of the closet with my own bed at some time during the night," she added meekly.

Seizing the initiative, Andsel ran with her confusion. "The alarm clock must have startled you," he conjectured. "You woke me up when you smashed it on the night stand and, before I could find out what the trouble was, you had crawled into the closet and pulled the clothing down on top of you." He poured some dressing on his salad and began to crunch down the crisp, fresh, greenery. Some unfamiliar, tangy, flavor enhanced the tossed salad this evening. The strange seasoning caused a strong, tingling, sensation in his nasal passages. "You seemed to settle down comfortably in there, so I left you alone. Were you having a bad dream? You babbled something about your grandmother and a cookie," he added.

Tiffany frowned and changed the subject. "I must have needed some fresh air at one point in the day yesterday. The front window in the living room was wide open and I had spilled the terrarium across the floor. Joan helped me clean that mess up when she had first arrived today. Lord only knows what happened to the glass bowl!"

"It was shattered into a dozen pieces across the carpet, dear. I picked up the pieces and threw them away, so that you wouldn't step on them, before I left the house this morning," he ad-libbed.

"Where *did* you go in such a hurry this morning, Andsel?" she asked.

His re-direction of recent history had been going so well that Andsel had forgotten to consider that *he* might have to account for any of *his own* bizarre actions of the day. He stuffed more salad into his big mouth in a hurry, to buy some time to concoct an answer. "I had left my camera out at the Alhausers's ranch, the day before yesterday. I was afraid that the rain might ruin it so I drove out there and retrieved it. Then I took a ride up the mountain to do some sketches of the Medicine Wheel and a couple of other regular tourist sites. I thought perhaps I might be able to sell one or two drawings at the lodges up there next year. I won't have them finished in time for the remainder of this year's tourist season," he composed eloquently. "My, this salad has a particular zest to it tonight!" he added to redirect the conversation.

"Do you really think so? It is made with the same, old, vegetables as usual. You really must try some of the beef before it gets cold."

Andsel pushed his salad plate aside and forked two slabs of the roast onto his main plate aggressively. A dollop of potatoes and a hefty scoop of the corn joined the beef immediately.

Tiffany rested her silverware on her plate, to address Andsel. "I truly am sorry for letting my drinking get out of control yesterday, Andsel. I am terribly embarrassed by my actions," she apologized sincerely.

Resting his own fork and knife on the table, Andsel studied her earnest face. "According to Joan, you had experienced some sort of unusual fright in the morning, after I had left – something about being locked in the hall closet. She said that you were terribly shaken. I can understand that you might need a little sip of something to calm your nerves."

"I hallucinated that my dead grandmother had locked me in the closet and then buried me alive," Tiffany explained solemnly.

"Why on earth would you have such a horrible illusion concerning your grandmother?" he asked.

"I have never told you this before, Andsel. It seemed best to let old rumors disappear with the dead, and you never knew the woman, but my mother's mother was suspected of poisoning her husband. I was never actually left alone with the woman for any length of time. As an infant, this did not seem unusual to me, but in later childhood, I knew that something might be a little threatening about her. Now why that ancient, implied, danger might manifest itself to me yesterday morning, while I searched for something in the hall closet, I will never understand."

Contemplating his own outrageous visions and actions of the past few days, Andsel knew full well what entities might have influenced his wife's buried subconscious. He prayed to God above that such supernatural forces had been dashed completely from both of their lives, with the shards of the skull, upon the rocks at the bottom of Dry Fork Point. Continuing with his fictional rearrangement of the past two day's events, he offered her a salve for her concerns over her mental state. "You know, I found mold growing on the left-over macaroni and cheese yesterday. I found mold on some other cheese in the refrigerator as well. Won't some funguses and molds cause illness and hallucinations, Tiffany? I haven't been really feeling myself over the last couple of days either. Perhaps it was a bit of bad cheese that has set us both out of sorts lately, and not the booze at all. I threw the spoiled food out last night, after you had gone to bed."

Andsel's appetite began to slack away immediately. His stomach fluttered and wrinkled beneath the fresh roast beef deposited there.

"Speak for yourself, Andsel. I, for one, know that I had drunk way too much gin by the time you had arrived home yesterday," Tiffany confessed. "If you can forgive me, I would like to forget about the entire, frightful, shameful, past, forty-eight hours."

Something definitely crawled around inside Andsel's stomach. He salted the potatoes heavily, forked down a couple of mouthfuls, and washed them down with iced tea. When the piping hot potatoes, alternated with the ice cold tea, splashed down Andsel's gut, the unruly gob inside of him dug in its claws. Andsel covered his mouth with his napkin and wrestled the gastric demon down before it could climb out. His flesh began to feel clammy with a cold sweat.

"You don't look so well, my dear," Tiffany observed. "Is there something wrong with your dinner tonight?"

"No, no, Tiffany! It is all delicious," he said, gathering another fork-full of the tender beef. Concentrating deeply on its rich aroma, he stuffed the succulent meat into his maw and chewed with determination. After thorough mastication, he swallowed resolutely. The beef might as well have been burning, liquid, India rubber by the manner in which it bounced back up his esophagus, upon striking the churning mess in his stomach. Andsel clutched the napkin to his mouth and hurtled toward the toilet in the master bathroom. Tiffany serenely finished her meal, undisturbed by the sound of his retching from the bathroom.

After a few minutes, his coughing and gagging subsided. She carried her dirty dishes to the sink and then deposited his unfinished dinner into the trash. "Can I bring you some more iced tea or juice to clean that awful taste out of your mouth?" she called sympathetically. More coughing and gagging resumed in the bathroom, followed by the sound of flushing. Tiffany took a clean glass from a cupboard, added some ice from the refrigerator, and then filled the glass with cold tap water. She carried the water into the bathroom, where Andsel lay slumped between the wall and the toilet bowl. Holding out the glass to him, she instructed, "Sip it slowly."

He took the extended glass of water and sipped a small portion. His stomach visibly contorted immediately, and he covered his mouth with his hand, but he kept the trickle of water down. Panting heavily, he handed back the water. His hand shook violently. In fact, he now shivered violently from head to foot as if naked in the Arctic.

"I'm so sorry that my cooking has made you ill, my dear," she apologized.

"Supper was delicious, Tiffany. Your cooking is always pure magic. I think maybe I have spent a little too much time out in the damp and cold today. That's all."

"You certainly didn't leave the house dressed for wet weather, from what I saw you come into the house wearing this evening. Are you chilled?"

"I'm freezing! Except my lips and tongue are on fire! My throat feels like I swallowed broken glass."

"My poor dear," she cooed. "No rhubarb pie for you tonight then, I am afraid. Come on. I'll help you into bed." She put an arm beneath his elbow and lifted him onto his wobbly legs. He clung to her for support as she braced him on his way to the bed. He leaned against the closet door, holding on to the stub of the knob, as she turned the blankets back. "Can I help you with your shirt and pants?" she offered.

"No," he said, slumping into the bed, "I'll crawl in just as I am. I'm freezing."

"Poor dear," she soothed, "What have you done to your nose? Did you bump it in the bathroom?"

Andsel put his hand to his nostrils. Warm moisture covered his upper lip. He pulled his fingers away to examine them in the light. "My God, I'm bleeding!" he exclaimed.

Tiff pulled a couple of Kleenex from the box on the night table and held them to her husband's nose. "Tip your head back," she instructed. "I'll get a cold cloth with some ice." In a moment, she returned with the ice and cloth. "The bleeding doesn't seem to be too bad. I'll go clean up the kitchen and check on you in a few minutes," she said.

"Okay," he mumbled through the tissues and wet cloth.

Returning to the dining room, she picked up the half empty salad bowl from the table and carried it into the kitchen.

She tossed the stainless steel spoon into the sink, then tossed the salad - bowl and all - into the trash bin. Andsel's salad plate also landed in the trash receptacle. Tiffany placed his main dining plate into the sink and then, as a second thought, she pulled the stainless spoon from the sink and threw it into the trash as well. A pie server rested at ready beside the strawberry- rhubarb pie. Cutting a generous slab from the warm, pristine, pie, she placed it on a dessert plate. She brought a new tub of French vanilla ice cream from the refrigerator freezer, pried out a large scoop to plunk down beside her pie, and then returned to the dining room table with her solitary dessert. Tiffany scooped up a bit of the pie with her fork, but stopped, with the morsel suspended in mid air. Retuning the bite to her plate, she got up from her seat and went to the liquor cabinet. In a moment, she returned to the table, accompanied by a large gin and tonic to wash down her just desserts.

Tiffany enjoyed her pie and tonic in leisurely fashion. Then she covered the leftovers and arranged them in the refrigerator for another day. The few dishes could wait until morning. Andsel might need her attention. He huddled in a fetal position on his side of the bed, bundled tightly in the bed covers. No conscious acknowledgement occurred when she touched the back of her hand to his forehead. He simmered with low fever. Crusted blood rimmed his nostrils raggedly. "That's disgusting," she thought to herself. The soggy cloth lay beside his head on the sheets. Picking it up, she went to the bathroom sink and wrung the blood stains out with hot water. Returning to her patient, she wiped the crusted blood from his nose hairs briskly.

"Ow!" he shrieked to consciousness, "What the hell are you doing?"

"You'll get blood on the sheets, dear," she said softly, "Feeling any better?"

"I'm freezing and my head is splitting," he groaned.

"I'll bring you some aspirin," she offered and returned to the bathroom. In a few minutes, she shook him awake gently.

"Here are a couple of aspirin and some cold water to wash them down with."

He raised himself long enough to swallow the pills with a sip of water.

"Better take a couple more to last you through the night," she suggested, holding out two more tablets. He took the tablets dutifully. "And drink as much of the water as you can get down to avoid dehydration," she recommended, pushing the water glass to his lips. He guzzled down the last of the water to appease her.

"Now please leave me alone," he growled.

"Yes dear," she answered, "I will bring you another blanket."

Tiffany found another blanket on a shelf in the closet and returned to spread it over her ailing husband. She noted a slight trickle of blood had begun again from his nose. A smile crossed her lips as she spread the damp cloth out beneath his proboscis to catch the thin, red, stream. The heavy dose of aspirin should help to keep his blood flowing. On one final thought of preparation, she retrieved the garbage can from bathroom and placed it close to his head at the edge of the bed. "He just might have need for a bucket before this night is over," she said to herself, then shut off the light and exited the bedroom, softly humming a familiar nursery tune.

After mixing another gin and tonic, she settled into her easy chair in front of the TV, propped her feet up on the otto-man, and punched the remote. Shelly Winters and Debbie Reynolds shared the screen in a movie from the early Seventies. Before long, Shelly had pushed her husband off of the back of his tractor to roll under his disc harrow. When he came out the back end of the machinery, he looked like a sliced, polish, sausage ready for a shish kabob skewer. "Hysterical!" Tiff gur-gled over a good slug of gin, "Better than the Roadrunner and Wyle Coyote! Cartoons for old, married, people! Hah! Hah! Hah!" Pretty soon, Shelly was ventilating Debbie Reynolds with a kitchen knife. Tiffany cackled along with the screaming. Commercial breaks finally concluded the carnage, so that Tiffany could catch her breath. A commercial about E. D. Eddy and his romantic problems provided a pensive moment for her to finish her drink and nod off.

Meanwhile, Andsel wandered through a foggy dusk up a crooked gravel path toward an abandoned house. Broken stairs with upturned steps caught at his toes to send him sprawling. Icy rain on a rising wind began to sting his face. Knarled trees slapped and banged their limbs together in the gale, like hockey players fighting for the puck. In terror of becoming their slap shot, Andsel struggled to his feet and scrambled up the miserable path. Another loose step flipped up to smack a vicious blow on his ankle that left him limping. One, thorny, old, limb snapped free from its ancient trunk to slash him across the backside as he stumbled up the rotted steps of the old house and collapsed on its sagging porch. He lay gasping on the safety of the porch.

Strong, horny-knuckled, hands slapped against his ribs, high beneath his armpits, and hoisted him to his feet. "Come on boy! You're missing your party!" a fierce, cold, voice bellowed. Andsel's toes barely tapped on the floor boards as the troll behind him slung him through the open front door and slammed him down into a ladder-backed chair. Two withered crones grinned at him across a splintered kitchen table. He could make out nothing of the features of one of the crones beneath her huge, starched, black, hood, except the tip of a hatchet nose and her ghoulish grin.

"No woman that old should have so many, huge, pointed, teeth," Andsel thought to himself, "Not a gap in her head. Even crocodiles had more spaces in their smiles to hold a cigar than she did."

The other old skag's face was all too evident. If any skull bone still resided with in her blob of filthy, tallow-colored, flesh, it had shrunken to the size of a peach pit. Contorted miles of wrinkles wrapped around the blob, interrupted by two, languid, runny, green, pools of eyes. Lurid, red, lipstick denoted parallel, cracked, dry, flaps as lips. No teeth gleamed behind the fiery lipstick. Only a fathomless, black, void howled within, while brown drool, perhaps tobacco juice, drizzled out of the corners of her maw, to course beneath the double chins.

"Give us a kiss!" she rasped and grabbed him by the back of the head with a disproportionably long arm. In an instant, his lips were plastered up against the vile, red, maw. The stench blasted into his own mouth was decidedly *not* from chewing tobacco. Her long, powerful, arm slammed him back down into his chair, so hard that the brittle relic nearly crumbled beneath him. Blubberhead Betty cut loose with three, deep, turkey gobbles, as a substitute for laughter. The Hooded Hatchet joined in the revelry with her own, file-on-bone, sounds. Lumpy remnants of Betty's drool wriggled on his lips, squirming to re-enter. Frantically, he wiped his lips on his own ragged sleeve, then gagged and wretched in a violent dry heave toward the filthy plank floor to his left.

When the convulsion had abated, he rolled back to vertical in his chair, just in time to find an orange goblet slammed down in front of him, in the mahogany fist of the troll creature. Configured more like a brandy snifter, the curious vessel looked all the world like a small jack-o-lantern with the top removed. Andsel starred at his giant, mummified, waiter, his own dry mouth agape. Definitely a living man once, the creature looked to be a re-animated bog man, dredged up from the depths of some Celtic, peat, bog. Only one eye peered back at Andsel from the peat-pickled skull in its saddle leather skin. If an iris existed in the orb, it was as black as the pupil itself, and as lightless as the maw of the crone who had recently kissed him. A charred wooden stub protruded from the other puckered socket, its other imbedded end tipped with a rusted, iron, arrow head. Bog man held a great, stone, pitcher in his tarantula hands. Green vapors steamed from a molten, yellow, liquid within the pitcher. The bog man stepped to the table and filled pumpkin goblets in front of each of the hags, then leaned forward to fill Andsel's goblet with the yellow liquid. A smell of rancid butter and musty burial vaults rose to his nostrils with the green vapors. Andsel noticed a ragged ridge of scar across the left cheekbone of the bog man.

"What's the matter, Andsel? Don't you recognize your old Uncle John?" thundered the bog man.

"You are Zeb Walton, not his son John!" screeched the Hatchet, "Or are you John Boy tonight?"

"I thought you called yourself Harold," Blubberhead gurgled.

"I am whomever Andsel sees tonight, with a little help from the colonel's recipe. Now drink up, boy!" he roared, "The Baldwin Sisters' recipe is not to be wasted!" He snatched Andsel's nose between two tannic knuckles, pushed his head back, and poured the viscous, yellow, fluid into Andsel's open mouth.

Andsel sputtered and gagged, but swallowed the vile potion. It burned his throat and stomach like turpentine. The Baldwin Sisters slugged down their portions of the elixir and held out their jack-o-lanterns for more. Uncle John downed a pumpkinfull of the liquor himself, before refilling all of the goblets.

"Pretty good moonshine, huh?" he hissed and slapped Andsel on the shoulder.

"The moon had nothing to do with this batch," Hatchet said. "This stuff was brewed in the darkness of a *new* moon. It is an especially powerful distillation."

Blubberhead's visage began to flow like hot mud upon her shoulders, before Andsel's eyes. She slowly began to morph into someone Andsel had known many, many, years ago. He struggled to bring the new female face to recognition in his floundering mind. He turned to ask Uncle John, who this woman really was. Uncle John's clothing flickered through several different modes as he watched. First the tall, umber, mummy wore gleaming chain mail. In an instant, the mail faded to cavalry blue of the mid 1800s. Khaki, green, military fatigues, familiar to World War II, replaced the deep blue and gold brocade, only to rotate back to the cold, cruel, glitter of the chain mail again. Andsel's head began to swim with the changing colors of Uncle John's attire. He turned back to ponder the new profile of Blubberhead Baldwin. His memory rolled back through old, faded, slides and photographs of acquaintances long dead to snap to a stop upon his mother-in-law Viola's upturned face as she lay in her coffin on the day of her funeral. Viola closed her eyes placidly to confirm his identification.

Opening her eyes, she cackled, "You know me now, don't you, boy."

"We are not exactly sisters either," spoke the other female seated at the table. The Hooded Hatchet now turned her head and raised her chin to look Andsel directly in the eye. His own wife Tiffany, her skin a vibrant, frog, green, her features honed sharp with cruelty, gazed back at him from beneath the black death's hood.

Andsel reeled back from the table and backed toward the door.

"Leaving so soon?" inquired Uncle John. "You will miss your rhubarb pie."

"R-Rhubarb is p-poisonous," Andsel stammered.

"It doesn't matter. You're dead already!" John thundered with deep, maniacal, laughter.

Sharp, boney, knuckles pinched his nose again and he dropped his jaw open involuntarily a second time. A different, but equally disgusting, liquid poured down his throat. Whoever had clutched his nose released it, so that he could roll to the edge of the bed and heave his quacking guts empty into a waiting trash can. He hurled up the last remnants of his supper, dark green bits of salad he guessed by the texture and taste. The salad was followed by a couple of bouts of dry heaves.

Tiffany's gentle voice soothed his shattered nerves, "That's it now. Clear it all out."

Andsel finally quit coughing up and rolled back into the bed. He slowly opened his eyes, wondering what color his wife would appear in. Tiffany gazed back at him with her normal, healthy, complexion and soft, rounded, features. "What was that awful liquid you just poured down my throat?" he asked.

"Syrup of ipecac. I found a box of my mother's things in the closet this morning. A bottle of ipecac was in there. It actually might have been my grandmother's. It is old and powerful medicine. Mom used to give it to me to clear a sour stomach."

"Please don't give me anymore," he begged.

"You won't need any more," she replied. Andsel lay silent for a moment and then let out a long sigh. His breath smelled like rancid butter as it wafted by Tiffany's face. A faint smile crossed her lips. "You missed your pie," she said.

"Please don't talk to me about food," he replied.

"Your stomach should be empty now, dear. The ipecac will have taken care of that. People don't use it much nowadays. I am not certain that a person can even purchase it anymore. It may be considered poison now. A little hard on your heart, I guess, but I like it. It is one of those good old potions that you know will get the job done. I have moved it and a few other old remedies from Mother and Grandmother's reserves into our medicine cabinet. Now you settle down and get some rest, Andsel. I'll sleep in the spare room tonight so that I won't disturb you."

She picked up the smelly trash can and took it to the bathroom, along with the blood-stained wash cloth. Andsel heard her humming a jaunty, little, tune to herself as she emptied the can and rinsed it out in the bath tub. He had fallen sound asleep by the time she returned to place it beside the bed again. Tiffany pulled her robe from the hook on the bathroom door, turned out the light in the bedroom, and left Andsel to rest in peace. "Pleasant dreams," she whispered as she closed the door tight.

CHAPTER ELEVEN

Andsel found himself back at his own dining room table. A normal colored and regularly featured Tiffany stepped up beside him and slid a generous wedge of strawberry-rhubarb pie in front of him. "Would you like some coffee with your pie?" she asked.

"Yes please," he answered.

She placed a steaming mug of black coffee beside the pie. Thank God, the cup was not carved from a pumpkin, but it did have a slightly orangish hue to the glaze. He decided to ignore the cup's color as coincidence, and began to examine the pie. It looked delicious with a beautiful flakey crust and juicy red filling. A light coating of brown sugar glistened on the upper crust. Still, his stomach shrank from receiving any sustenance within, no matter how delectable the pie appeared.

Tiffany came back to the table, with a piece of pie and a cup of coffee for her own enjoyment. She began to cut off little bites of the pie with a long steak knife, pushing them into her mouth with gusto. Pools of red juice began to puddle in the dessert plate. She gulped a generous slug of the steaming hot coffee down and continued to attack her pie. Andsel watched in awe.

"You're not eating any of your pie," she observed.

"No, my stomach is still a little quezzy," he explained. "You go ahead. Enjoy your pie."

Tiffany shoveled the rest of her pie into her mouth ravenously. Trickles of the deep red juice coursed from the corners of her mouth, which she promptly wiped away with the heel of her hand and then licked it clean. Raising the empty plate to her lips, she tilted it back to drain the juice. "I think I'll have another slice," she said, and immediately left the table to cut another wedge in the kitchen. Andsel watched his famished wife pursue the second piece of pie.

"If you are not going to eat that, then I'll take care of it," a familiar deep voice grumbled at Andsel's other elbow.

He looked down at his pie, only to find the peat bog claw of Uncle John snatching it away from him. Uncle John pulled up a chair to Andsel's right and began to eat the pie. His table manners were much more refined than those that Andsel's wife had exhibited. Andsel hooked a finger through the handle of his coffee cup defensively. Mother Viola appeared behind Uncle John, then moved further around the table to seat herself directly opposite Andsel. She placed familiar jack-o-lantern mugs of coffee down in front of John and herself on her way to her place.

"What are you people doing at my dinner table?" Andsel shouted.

"You will be with us always now, Andsel," a third, shadowy, figure spoke from a chair to the right of Viola, a little further back away from the table and out of the light.

"And who the hell are you?" Andsel shouted at the shadow.

"I am your wife's namesake. I am her Grandmother Tiffany."

Tiff returned to the table with an immense chunk of pie. "Hi Grandma," she called casually to the bulky shadow. She immediately began to attack the pie as she had done before. Her teeth seemed longer and more pointed, but other than this, she still appeared normal in every other characteristic. Again, her plate filled with thick, red, strawberry-rhubarb juice. The liquid eventually lapped over the edge of the plate and dripped onto the table top, with an incessant "Tap, tap, tap," to form large puddles.

"You evil, ugly, people can not be here in this house," Andsel declared. "Tiffany and I live here. You are all dead."

"You had better get used to our company, young man. You are as lost as we are," Uncle John declared as he finished his pie. He stood up from the table without ceremony, and went to the kitchen in pursuit of another helping.

"What do you mean, I am lost? I haven't done anything." Andsel cried.

Mother Viola reached her flabby, cold, hand across the table to grasp his own. Her fingers wreathed about his clenched fist like frigid earth worms. "Do we frighten you, Andsel?" she asked. "Would you like us to go away forever? I am sorry, but we can never go away. Even though your mortal eyes cannot see us, we are always around you. The Indian's spirit should have taught you this lesson."

"I got rid of the skull of Red Horse today. You ghouls need to keep abreast of current events in this household. You are wasting my time and my rest."

"You can't get rid of the dead, my poor boy, because you are always one yourself. What you call living is only a temporary interruption. Your mortality is only a bright, shining, lie. This cold, dark, world in which we are seated now is the permanence you must get accustomed to," she explained.

"Nonsense!" Andsel snorted, "This little tea party is simply a bad dream, brought to me courtesy of some bad stew. You will all be a faded memory by tomorrow night."

"We had roast beef tonight, dear," Tiffany corrected him.

"I'll make a stew for you that you won't ever forget," hissed the black shadow from the corner of the room.

"I am informed, Grandmother Tiffany, that you probably poisoned your husband. I believe that I will pass on any dinner invitations from you. In fact, I am not certain who baked this pie, so I will allow Uncle John to have my portions. He doesn't look like much more harm can come to him."

"I baked the pie, you sarcastic little snot!" Viola snarled.

"My apologies Viola, I do remember eating several excellent meals at your table, long ago. Tiffany has become a marvelous cook under your tutelage. I do know that you goaded and nagged your poor husband Bill into an early grave, but I have never heard any rumor of your poisoning him."

"What you don't know about me won't hurt you!" Viola snapped, "Unless Tiffany has need of it."

"Hmm, mm, mm," Tiffany hummed in agreement, over her mouthful of pie.

Andsel looked at his lovely wife, enraptured in her mastication like a gator in a goldfish pond, and looked away in revolution. "I have never done anything to harm her." he declared.

"There is an ugly scar in the wood work of your bedroom closet that indicates otherwise," Grandmother Tiffany pointed out with emphasis from a mummified, green, finger.

"Red Horse made me swing the tomahawk. I lost my head for a moment. His spirit influenced me to do bad things."

"The Indian served only as a reflection of yourself. He reminded you of your lust for killing. It was your own face cast back at you from the mirror when you put on your war paint, not his," Grandmother Tiffany retorted. "Tomahawks, poison, axes, or swords, the mystery of murder is as alluring to you as it is to any one of us seated here at this table."

"I never harmed a soul, before the skull of Red Horse showed up on my door step. He made me nearly kill my wife, so I got rid of him. *I* am not at all like any of you," Andsel shot back.

Mother Viola threw her blubberous head back and shook with gurgles of horrid laughter. "You!" she shouted, "On your own, you couldn't part with a strand of hair from the point of someone else's lance. You covet the remains of the dead; treat our bones as your playthings; hold them as trophies of your victory over death.. No one can defeat death, Andsel. To deny it is to deny yourself."

"The skull is gone and Red Horse is gone," Andsel declared. "I do not have any little bits of any of you hanging around this house; so, when this family reunion is over, none of you have any right to show up here again."

"There is a piece of one of us still in your possession! He gets no peace! He gets no rest!" Grandmother Tiffany shouted. In her enthusiasm, she leaned forward into the light surround-ing the table. She was the spitting image of his wife Tiffany, hatchet-faced and green, as she had appeared in the derelict house of the earlier visit. Andsel looked from one generation to another, and back again. His wife began to take on a greenish tint and her features grew harsher as she ground the remains of her dessert. Grandma Hatchet leaned back into the shadows and slowly faded into nothingness.

Something slammed down on the table in front of Andsel. He looked down to find another piece of the disgusting red pie in front of him again. It had not been served on a plate this time. It rested in a curious shallow bowl. Andsel tilted the bowl up to examine it and found that he was staring into the hollow sockets of grimacing skull. Uncle John plumped down in the chair at his right to start on his second helping of pie.

"What the hell kind of dish is this?" Andsel shouted, look-ing up at the bog man.

Uncle John shoveled bites of pie down a gaping black hole between his boney, brown, shoulders. He had no head to answer Andsel from.

"Take your damned head and got to hell!" Andsel screamed and hurled the skull and pie at the headless bog man.

In an instant, all of the unwelcome guests had disappeared from the dinner table. Only Tiffany and Andsel remained. The smears of red juice were gone from Tiffany's placid face and the puddles of fluid on the table had vanished. A young waitress with long, dark, hair appeared at Andsel's elbow. She placed a new, white porcelain, coffee cup in front of both Tiffany and Andsel, along with new silverware, and blue, cloth, napkins.

Filling the cups with fresh, black, coffee, she said, "Now why don't you two have a nice cup of java together and bury the hatchet?"

"I'm not sure where he left it," Tiffany answered. "The last place that I knew where it had been, was buried in the door jamb of our closet."

Andsel awoke with a start. The bedroom was pitch dark. The curtains and blinds had been drawn tight. He rolled to the floor, then slowly rose to his feet. His stomach still twisted into knots, keeping him hunched over, with one hand against the wall for balance. After pushing the curtains aside and tugging on the Venetian blind cord, he peeked out of the bottom of the window to see if the dawn had begun yet. A sword slash of yellow light swung from a slit of sky between the distant horizon and a heavy, black, cloud bank above. Bloody gills of crimson wavered along the bottoms of the thunder heads. Andsel half expected immense purple eyelids to open, uncovering languid green eyes in the threatening behemoths, but they only crept across the land blindly, searching for the scent of his soul. Andsel slapped the blinds closed. His mouth puckered down upon his throat like a frost-withered rose. He hobbled to the bathroom for a long drink, but even pure water set his innards to wringing up another knot. The water had at least relieved his parched mouth and throat. Before returning to the bed, he pawed around on the floor beneath it until his fingers found the tomahawk handle. Tucking the comforting weapon beneath his pillow, he dropped off into near-death sleep almost instantly. The ghoulish family reunion did not reoccur in his dreams. No dreams at all disturbed his coma.

He awoke several hours later, during mid morning, with a mighty desire for coffee – strong, black, coffee. His legs supported him much better now, but his knees still did not lock securely beneath his weight. Andsel gimped out to the kitchen where Tiffany stirred a hearty, brown, stew in a large pot on the stove. She still hummed the same childish tune to herself as she worked.

"Is there any coffee?" he croaked.

"Why good morning, Sunshine! How are you feeling?" she cooed.

"Puny," he replied. "Is there any coffee?"

"Yes, but the coffee maker has been off for hours. I am afraid that you will have to heat up a cup-full in the microwave."

Andsel retrieved a cup from the cupboard. He involuntarily checked for any of orange hue, but thankfully found none. Pouring a cup of the black medicine from the half-empty glass pot, he placed it in the microwave and set the timer for sixty seconds. He hovered near the microwave like a junkie on a street corner. With a "ping', the machine released his salvation.

"I need you out of the kitchen, dear. I am making a stew for an early supper tonight, and you are in the way of the cooking. If you will go sit at the table, I will start some breakfast for you, if you think that you can keep it down. Does an omelet sound appetizing to you?"

Andsel took a second cup from the cupboard and filled it with black coffee. He placed it into the microwave and set the timer as before. His stomach did not convulse at the thought of an omelet, nor did it reel at the possibility of hash browns.

"I've had all of the coffee that I want, long ago, this morning, Andsel," Tiffany said, as she added chunks of celery to the stew.

"The second cup is for me because I won't be long finishing this one," he replied.

"You are creating an extra dirty cup for me to wash, but no matter. Do you want that omelet?"

"I'll rinse out both cups for you and put them in the dish washer. Yes, I do want the omelet. Can I have some hash browns with it also?"

"Certainly dear," she replied and shook a bright red herb into the stew. The hearty, brown, mixture frothed up to yellowish foam for a second or two until Tiffany subdued it with a wooden spoon. "There, there," she soothed, "Can't we all just get along?"

Andsel downed his first cup in hefty gulps. Tiffany handed him the second cup across the kitchen island. He savored this cup more slowly, swirling the marvelous liquid around in his mouth to replace the vile vestiges of the previous night of illness. Tiffany had placed a medium frying pan on a second burner of the stove and had poured some pre-mixed omelet batter into the pan. She rustled through the refrigerator to find some sliced ham, which she deftly chopped into little cubes to add to the omelet. Her staccato enthusiasm with the big kitchen knife made Andsel involuntarily clench his fingers beneath his palms into protective fists. Hash browns soon warmed and browned in a third, smaller, pan on the stove.

"Sorry that I am using premixes for your brunch, dear, but the day is getting away from us, and I have to finish trimming the flowers and potted plants around this place this afternoon. Fall will arrive soon enough, and the perennials have to be prepared for their long sleep. I must clear out the weeds from the beds so that I will have room to mulch in the plants for the winter."

"Won't the flower boxes beneath the front windows freeze?" Andsel asked from idle curiosity and in an effort to make conversation.

"Those are full of red petunias. They die for keeps," she dictated with firm finality.

"Why plant flowers that will not survive? It seems like a huge waste of effort," he asked.

"Some of the most beautiful flowers are only meant to last one season. I cannot change their fate. The enjoyment I receive from them is worth the effort."

"Some people dry them for the winter or press them in books."

"Wouldn't that stain the pages, make the story hard to read?" she asked looking up from her cooking.

"You could place them between sheets of wax paper," he offered.

"Too much trouble for old dead things, I'd say. Chop them up for fertilizer for next year's growth. If you want to preserve them, then paint me a picture, instead of all of those old cowboy-and-Indian pictures you are always painting." She attacked some more hapless vegetables on her cutting board with the menacing kitchen knife. "I have some peppers and onion left over from the stew. Would you like me to add them to your omelet?"

"Yes please," he replied. "That sounds delicious."

She cleared a portion of the small pan containing the hash browns and scraped the butchered veggies into the pan to sauté them, sliding the omelet to an iron trivet for a moment, while the ham and vegetables caught up.

"I could paint a floral still life for you, Tiffany. Homer Alhauser isn't in any hurry for the ranch picture anymore. Painting a simple vase of flowers could be a nice change."

"Don't make it a still life. Paint them in the window box with the breeze moving them, and perhaps a hummingbird hovering nearby to take their spirit."

"Their spirit? Plants don't have a spirit," he laughed.

Tiffany frowned and placed the omelet back onto a burner. She slid the ham and veggies into its center, then rested the little skillet of has browns on the trivet. With a deft flip of the spatula, she turned the edge of the omelet over into a pleas-ant, happy, half-moon, shape. "When the hummingbirds drink the nectar, the flowers curl up as if they have been drained of life. But, for a moment, both the beauty of the petunia and the beauty of the hummingbird are in the picture together."

"What catches a hummingbird, do you suppose?'

"Only time," Tiffany answered. "All things surrender to time."

No one spoke for a few minutes. Tiffany stirred the stew and finished the omelet. When both sides were a lovely golden hue speckled with patches of brown, she flipped the omelet onto a plate, added the waiting hash browns, and carried the breakfast to Andsel at the table. "I'll bring you a fork," she said.

"What do you think the hummingbird does with the petunia spirits that it collects?" Andsel asked with a smile.

"He takes them to South America and deposits them into orchids to start a new life. Now stop teasing me about my silly notions and eat your breakfast," she snapped.

"It is a lovely notion, Tiffany – not silly at all. Very Buddhist. But I wonder if the orchids don't curl up as well."

"Very logical, Mr. Spoke. Thanks for being such a kill-joy with my dreams. Who the hell knows where a spirit goes? How is your omelet? Is it settling on your stomach okay?"

"The omelet is delicious. Sorry that I stepped on your fantasy, although I wish someone would put a damper on some of my night time adventures," he apologized. With a second thought, he added, "Maybe the flower souls become little hummingbird chicks. That might be an improvement over an orchid. Some orchids are parasitic plants, I think."

"Are you having bad dreams?" she asked.

"Well let's just say they don't involve hummingbirds and flowers," he replied, not wanting to involve uncomplimentary images of her deceased family in the breakfast conversation.

"Perhaps you should spend more time with pretty, living, things, instead of a room full of old, dead, artifacts from tragedies of the past. I could use some of your help with a shovel and a wheel barrow by-the-way."

"Bring me some flowers and I'll consider it," he said and then dug into his plate of food in earnest.

"Rinse your dishes when you are finished and put them in the dish washer, please. I have to get back to my gardening outside. The days are getting shorter. I already did the inside plants while you slept."

Andsel finished his brunch alone, then took care of his plates and silverware as requested. Reconstructing the events of yesterday, he remembered the cavalry bugle and glass bowl in his pickup cab. The bugle could be returned to his studio at this time, but the bowl would need to be disposed of. Slipping into the garage, he retrieved the bowl from the truck cab. "I told her that she had broken it, so it had better become broken shards in the trash," he thought to himself. He held the bowl deep within the confines of the large trash bin of the garage and smashed it with a rusty monkey wrench that had lain upon a window sill for several years. "Monkey wrenches – a fix for anything," he muttered to himself. A tiny shard of glass splintered upward to strike him on the chin. Andsel winched at the tiny pain, but did not cry out. A drop of blood splattered on the concrete floor as he closed the lid of the garbage bin. An oddly recognizable, red, effigy formed where the blood struck the floor. Andsel pressed a finger to the miniscule cut on his chin and smudged the blood spot away with the ball of his foot. He tossed the cardboard box and paint-smeared towel into the bin, on top of the shattered bowl. Retrieving the bugle, he closed the truck cab door and exited the garage for his studio at the other end of the house. Tiffany was visible through the front windows, picking weeds from a flower box of petunias, as he passed through the house. She did not look up from her work as he slipped through the living room, but he shuffled the bugle to the far side of his torso anyway to avoid any unnecessary suspicions. He hung the talisman on its customary peg as he entered the studio.

The paint brush still protruded from the eye socket of his single, remaining, skull. Pulling the brush free, he slipped it back into the jar of brushes, bristles up, as it should be stored. Tiffany came around the outside corner of the studio, lugging a small, white, plastic, table. Placing the table a few feet out from his studio window, she disappeared around the corner of the house again. Andsel decided to wait stoically to discover what kind of gardening madness she was up to. He gazed down idly at his work table. The sketch of the McClellan and the snake lay haphazardly at the top of the table.

"A good sketch, none-the-less, for all the trouble that it cost me," he thought to himself as he picked the sketch pad up and scrutinized it. Pulling a razor knife from the drawer beneath the table top, he carefully sliced the sketch free from the pad. On a whim, he turned and propped the drawing up in the corner of the shelf where the bullet-holed skull had once reposed. His remaining skull seemed to thump softly, and the bugle above it hummed a nearly imperceptible sigh, stirred by some miniscule eddy of air current in their corner of the room. A shiver passed through Andsel's scalp, and then he laughed at his own sensitivity. "I probably didn't get the thing settled down firmly when I pulled out that brush from the eye socket. A slight vibration must have caused it to rock down to a solider position when I placed the drawing on the opposite end of the shelf. Probably something in the same vein happened with the bugle," he rationalized.

Tiffany appeared around the corner of the house again. She was lugging an entire window flower box, full of red petunias. Andsel stomped to the window and swung it open. "I would have gladly helped you with that if you had only asked," he shouted out to her.

She waved him off with a gloved hand. "Paint me something living," she replied, pointing to the petunias.

A gentle breeze shouldered its way into the studio through the opened window. The bugle hummed a little louder behind Andsel and shifted on its nail. "I knew it," he affirmed to himself, "Just an errant breeze."

The lidless skull gazed back, as if to say "Wait and see what the wind brings in."

Andsel glanced away from the lifeless bone, in disgust at his own rampantly out-of-control imagination. An Indian basket from Arizona, on the top shelf, above the topless skull, caught his eye. Putting a knee on the shelf that held the skull, he stretched his arm upward and retrieved the basket. Plopping it over, upside down, on top of the skull, he muttered, "Nigthty night now. Rest in peace. And shut the hell up."

A biblical phrase popped into his mind as he tipped the basket over the skull's eye sockets, "Thou shalt not hide thy light under a basket."

The breeze curled beneath the McClellan drawing, tossing it to the floor. Andsel scooped it up and returned it to its rightful place on the shelf. Then he adjusted the window closed a bit more, so that lighter items would not be rustled out of place in the room. He hadn't worked with pastels for quite some time and the media lent itself well to flowers. Selecting a pad of rough toothed paper, especially milled for pastels, from a storage cabinet, he placed it upon his work table so that he could look directly out of the window at the flower box in the yard. He pulled the drawer beneath the work table open again to retrieve his large box of pastels and to replace the razor knife where it belonged.

The Wyoming wind swayed the brilliant red petunias in a hypnotic rhythm, setting his fingers to dancing with the chalky colors upon the paper. Andsel hummed to himself as he worked and the breeze ran adoring fingers through his hair. Pastels were a very loose, fluid, media to work in, lending themselves to long, sweeping, strokes with lyrical curls and flourishes. Soon, vibrant, crimson, blossoms waved across his paper like green limbed maidens tossing their lusty skirts to the wind. Petals burned red, as sunlight through a delicate earlobe, the blood pulsing in passionate streams within. Andsel's mind drifted back to a hot summer's afternoon many years before, when he had gazed up in wonder into the face of his maiden Tiffany. Passion had pulsed in blue rivers beneath the gossamer skin of her throat. Her eyes were wide blue windows, carrying the azure wonder of the wide open sky above her through to share with him, beneath the royal golden curtains of her hair. She swayed in rhythm with the breeze, just as the petunias swayed in their window box beyond the studio window. Andsel's hand stitched blue and gold into the wind and sky of the picture to enhance his gift for his wife.

An emerald fairy, and then another, hummed its way on the currents of the wind to the window box. Hummingbirds! Tiffany wanted hummingbirds in her picture and here they were! The jeweled creatures flitted from blossom to blossom, sampling the nectar, and Andsel's pastels flitted in tiny, frantic, strokes to capture their souls on the paper. Eventually, the miniscule birds' thirst for petunia wine was assuaged. With a flick of their tail, they buzzed off to sample some other brand of elixir from a different colored goblet trembling in the wind.

Andsel leaned back from his table to study his creation. Stained-glass petals fluttered in airy currents of blue sky and golden sunlight upon the page. A winged, iridescent, sprite thrust its saber beak at the nearest glowing cup from one corner of the composition. Another creature tugged at a flower's ear from the opposite side of the picture, but this was a bird of a different color. A bat-winged goblin, in bog brown, stood on the edge of the flower box. Andsel stared out of his window to see if he had somehow captured a toad in his picture of the petunias. The flowers had withered and closed up like busted umbrellas, from the onslaught of the hummingbirds. He dropped his eyes back to the permanence of his artwork. The bog troll had buried his head in the cup of the flower and drank its life in great gulps, collapsing the blossom like flesh around a tick. The green bird, more mantis-like now, stabbed at the shackled flowers, one by one, shriveling them into leathery husks, while the troll drained the blood from each victim in turn from his end of the picture.

"No!" Andsel screamed, slamming his hands to his eyes. The chalk dust stung his eyes instantly, bringing tears coursing down his cheeks. He tore his fingers away from his eyes and slammed them to the table top again, as his tears dotted the paper. His tears slowly cleared the dust from his eyes, leaving trails of bog brown down the lines of his face. Gradually, the original picture of exuberant, ruby, petunias, fluttering in a radiant, blue and gold, August breeze, resolved itself again upon the paper.

Leaving his restored artwork on the table, he stumbled to the work sink of his studio and bathed the pastel dust from his eyes and face. After drying his eyes with a towel, he took a can of art fixative from a shelf to spray upon the drawing before it might change again. His intended image remained as he had left it, minus the brown and green hobgoblins. He sprayed the pastel drawing liberally with the fixative. "That'll hold you," he commanded to the hummingbirds. A sudden inspiration crossed his mind.

His eyes still stung from the pastel dust, so he returned to the sink to rinse his eyes and face one more time. Glancing into the small mirror over the sink, he noticed what a poor job he had done at his initial emergency cleansing. Streaks of blue, gold, red, and brown combined to form the ashen grays and purple browns of old bruises. Uncle John's face peered back at him from the glass for an instant; not the concocted Uncle John of moldy cheese and rhubarb green delirium, but the real Uncle John, who he had known from his earliest childhood. A kindly, tall, old, gentleman, named John, had actually existed in the days between his infancy and grammar school. Uncle John *had* taught him to dig worms and spit them onto cold, steel, hooks, without squirming. That beloved, old, man had indeed taken him fishing beneath shadowed cathedrals of dark pine, where speckled trout patrolled the tannic pools. Andsel had nearly forgotten those few idyllic hours spent with his grand uncle, as if they were only nursery rhymes, no longer fit for adult consideration. But a true Uncle John had existed; one whom he had loved with the innocence of a child.

Andsel wiped a steak of gray from his own cheek and remembered wiping gray from the cheek of his beloved uncle, except something was reversed in the memory. He had not wiped away gray to reveal pink flesh upon the cheek of Uncle John. He had wiped away false pink of flesh to reveal the gray pallor of death. Now the memory blasted back, clear as the moment it had happened some sixty years ago. Andsel had been taken to say "good-bye" to his Uncle John one last time. A reunion of the extended Edger family sat quietly in chairs, wearing their Sunday best, while Uncle John slept soundly in a beautiful, dark wooden, box in the center of the room. The box shone like the wood of Grandma Edger's prized china cabinet - the cabinet no child was allowed to play within miles of. It was no wonder that Uncle John slept so peacefully while so many of his family watched and murmured reservedly among themselves. His special box had been lined with the softest of white satin comforters from one of Grandma Edger's feather beds. Andsel broke away from his father's grasp and ran to the gleaming special box. He jabbed his foot into one of the shining brass handles on the side of the box, just as Uncle John had taught him to step into the stirrup of the saddle on the neighbor's Shetland pony, and hoisted himself up to look into the placid face of his beloved uncle. "Uncle John!" he called, "Uncle John, wake up! Everyone is here waiting. It must be Thanksgiving." He reached out to caress the old man's cheek and wag his chin to awaken him. The flesh was cold and soggy as a pumpkin in November. Greasy, pink, paint came away on his little fingers, revealing skin the color of wet newspapers where a living man had been. Uncle John did not wake up that day and his memory had slept with Andsel's innocence.

CHAPTER TWELVE

Andsel turned on the hot water and splashed the steaming jet to his face vigorously, rubbing away the last remnants of the pastel dust as though it were dried varnish. No malicious spirit would steal the identity of such a cherished soul as his real Uncle John to corrupt his dreams and sanity! He would find a way to halt this intrusion of the decency of his world. He had turned back the assault on his image of the flowers. Perhaps he could entrap the images that had been forced upon his mind involuntarily, within the created reality of his own contrivances. Perhaps the ghouls that came to dinner could be sealed there forever, and burned like so much Monday morning rubbish.

He turned on his heel with a military snap and strode to his work table with determined purpose. Pulling a fresh piece of the heavily toothed pastel paper from the pad, he picked out blacks and heavy browns from the pastel pile on the table. Closing his eyes, he forced the ghouls' visages from the previous night's dreams to reappear in his memory. Opening his eyelids a slit, like the yellow gash he had seen on the horizon early that morning, he sketched in an umber outline of peat bog Uncle John. Dropping the umber and snatching up pure black, he squiggled in a rat's nest of snarled black evil to form the shadow of Grandmother Hatchet, on the opposite side of the composition from Uncle John. Fiery red ensnared the globular form of Mother Viola, seated between the first two hideous caricatures. Andsel swept an arch of sienna, using the pastel laid on its side, to form the table top in front of the ghouls. He smudged in sinuous muscle volume to the wiry form of Uncle John and topped it with the trollish visage worn by the hobgoblin who had so recently tried to drain the life from the pastel petunias. A black stub of a broken arrow protruded from bog goblin's eye socket, nailing him to the page. Greens, blues, and purples stitched Grandmother Tiffany's volume into the fabric of the page, entrapping her forever like a spider's victim within the initial, black, silken, threads drawn by Andsel - bonds stronger than iron. Fetid sacks of yellow, ochre, and orange took form within the red, netted, lines that cinched up the decomposing Viola. Andsel sealed her mouth shut eternally with sutures of crimson. As a final detail, he sketched in shards of broken pumpkin goblets across the table top. Snatching up the art fixative, he sprayed down the pastel liberally. "That should hold you bastards!" he sneered. "I'll take particular pleasure in burning you at the stake in the backyard tomorrow."

The room reeked of aerosol fumes from the heavy applications of fixative. Andsel's head swam from his artistic and magical conjuring efforts. He tottered over to the open window and wedged his face into the space to inhale the fresh air. Soon, his mind began to clear. Tiffany's petunias still waved in the breeze beyond the studio window. The pastel of the flowers should be matted and framed before he presented it to his wife. Returning to the work table, he cleared the pastels from the surface, into their proper storage. He placed the picture of the ghouls' coffee break in the corner to dry, on top of the overturned basket, then opened the studio door to increase the ventilation. The flower composition was placed beneath the fresh air of the open window, while he sponged away any remaining chalk dust from the work table top.

Andsel placed a large scrap of cardboard, scored with many slashes, upon the surface of the table and dug his razor knife out from the drawer beneath. He sorted through a stack of matte board sheets on one of the studio shelves. Selecting a pale green sheet, he placed it on the cardboard and began to measure out the matte frame for the petunia pastel. Laying a steel yard stick across the measured pencil marks, he slashed out the center of the matte frame with the razor knife. Tinny voices seemed to murmur angrily behind him from the lidless skull's corner. Andsel turned to see what the disturbance might be, but nothing appeared amiss in the corner. For an instant, some trick of reflected light seemed to create hanging shimmers of color between the ghoul picture and the bell of the bugle above it. He gripped the razor knife tighter in his fist combatively, but the illusion vanished with a blink of his eye. He turned back to the task at hand. Retrieving the petunia picture from the window sill, he slid it beneath the matte and centered it. Holding the assemblage in place with one hand, he raised one corner of the matte with the other hand, and slipped a small piece of masking tape beneath, to tack the picture into place. He delicately flipped the matte and picture upside down, then taped all edges of the artwork in place securely. When the artwork was again right side up, he checked it one more time for proper centering. Satisfied with the job thus far, he stepped to another shelf which held a pile of picture frames and glass.

Tiffany had returned to the interior of the house momentarily from her gardening. She also had heard the murmuring of vaguely familiar voices drifting down the hallway from her husband's studio. Odors of fragrant blossoms wafted on a lost spring breeze from the direction of the studio. A familiar shadow from long, long, ago seemed to cast its silhouette along the inside of the open studio door. She could not resist investigating the wisps of memory tantalizing her from the far end of the hall and crept silently to the portal.

No one but Andsel occupied the studio. He stood at the far corner of his work room, examining an old picture frame. The room was as still as a tomb. A stiff, ragged, edge scrapped her elbow. She looked down to discover what had caused the irritation. The anguished faces of her mother and grandmother stared back at her from Andsel's latest artistic efforts. The two women and another man were bound in brown, red, and black wrappings, like mummies, with only their heads, from the nose up, exposed. The captives seemed to squirm within their vicious bonds on the fixed paper. She should have cried out in shock and disgust at this outrage against her family. She should have torn the thing to bits and flung it into her husband's face. Instead, a coldness, like the chill of the closet two days before, began to settle in her heart. An odor of musty earth and rotted roots began to replace the scent of flowers. Revenge was the only appropriate response to such an assault on her loved ones. Turning away from the hideous drawing on its shelf, she left the studio in silent fury.

Andsel felt a chill breeze brush the back of his neck, reached to the open window, and pulled it closed. He took the selected picture frame to his work table and began to mount the petunia composition in the frame, completely unaware that his wife had so recently been in the room. When the job was finished, he viewed it momentarily with satisfaction. Leaving it on the work table, he turned to leave the studio. As he reached to doorway, he glanced at the other art work of the day. Mocking laughter seemed to emanate from the mouth of the bugle on the wall. Andsel snatched up the ghouls' portrait and wadded it into a tight ball. He stuffed the paper wad deeply into the throat of the bugle with a vengeance. "Choke on that, you son-of-a-bitch," he muttered to the inanimate instrument, then strode out the door and slammed it behind him. The skull chattered on the shelf in silent laughter.

Tiffany had returned to her grounds keeping tasks. A wheelbarrow-sized pile of weeds rested at corner of the house, not far from the spot at the curb where the Edgers customarily placed their garbage. Pulling on her leather gardening gloves, she went to the pile and began sorting through the various uprooted plants. She soon found the particular herb that she was searching for. It was a small plant with small, white, star-shaped, flowers and a few, grasslike, leaves at its base. Each of the six petals of each blossom began from a yellow-green node. Most distinctive of all were the onion-shaped bulbs from which the plants had sprung. Vile, black, scales covered the bulbs. Tiffany lifted the bulbs to her nostrils and inhaled gently. A smile, worthy of her namesake grandmother, crossed her face. No onion odor came from the evil looking bulbs – only the odor of moldering flesh. Carefully snipping three of the bulbs from the plants with her garden scissors, she replaced the plants back into the weed pile and returned to the house. Placing the bulbs on a heavy paper plate in the kitchen, she selected her sharpest paring knife from the rack and began to peel away the black scales from the bulbs. When they shone as white as the marble beneath the full moon, she minced them repeatedly until only a fine powder remained.

Death Camas was a potent toxin, but he still must ingest a proper dosage. She could add it to the stew, but its potency would be severely diluted. If he did not consume enough of the stew, he might only become ill again, and that was not the result she had in mind. She selected the salt shaker from the spice and condiment caddy at the center of the dining room table. The shaker was less than half full when she unscrewed the top. Folding the paper plate into a taco shape, she poured the fine, white, camas powder into the salt shaker and screwed the top back on. She shook the shaker gently, from side to side, to mix a little of the existing salt with the new mystery powder and then replaced it in the caddy on the table. She wadded up the paper plate and stuffed it deeply into the trash can of the kitchen. Bumping the faucet on at the kitchen sink with the back of her glove, she soaped up her gloved hands with dish soap and washed them in the steaming hot water. She washed the garden scissors and paring knife as well. After taking the scissors and gloves to the garage to dry on a window ledge, she returned to the kitchen and washed her hands, like a surgeon before an operation. As a final precaution, she mixed a solution of bleach and water, then used it to scrub down the counter where she had prepared her seasoning.

How was she to insure that he salted his dinner heavily? The stew had been seasoned somewhat already, but he would probably add some salt to his serving. Would it be enough? His sour stomach from the night before would probably also make him crave salt at the supper table. Perhaps she could flatten the flavor of the stew with the proper spices. She opened the cupboard where she kept her large assortment of spices and stared into the dark recesses. Far, far, in the rear, were one or two seldom used powders of ancient names. Removing eight or ten common spices from the front rows and pushing the other bottles aside, she reached into the shadows and drew out two vials, both nearly full. "Here we are. My old friends from biblical times, hyssop and fenugreek. Both dry as the dust on a mummy's knuckles, bitter as King Richard the Last," she said to herself. "I'll have to set my portion aside first before I add your desert breath to the dinner stew." Pulling the big, stainless, pot from the back of the stove, she removed the lid and dipped out a generous serving for herself into a large porcelain bowl. She placed her portion into the microwave, but did not turn the machine on. The untreated serving would be warmed, just a few minutes before she called Andsel to the table.

"Now you get to join the party," she said to the little vials. "You hyssop, bearer of vinegar to Christ on the Cross, add your dry, parched, thoughts to the meal of sacrifice," she mumbled as she shook in liberal quantities of the spice and stirred vigorously with the large, wooden, spoon. Trading the hyssop for fenugreek and turning the burner on low beneath her modern cauldron, she chanted fervently, "Swell the breasts of vengeance, Oh fenugreek! Let flow the bitter milk of retribution for my ancestors!" She stirred the stew to a brown whirlpool and imagined poor Andsel clutching at the bits of carrot, potato, and beef as the maelstrom sucked him down. Lifting the spoon to her sneering lips, she tasted the broth. Her mouth puckered involuntarily. "No more flavor than grave dirt," she remarked to no one else in the room but her.

"But would he salt it enough even so?" she thought to herself. "What else might she serve with the stew, to gather his medicine for him?" Tiffany pulled open the pantry closet door and peered at the canned goods within. "Lima beans," she snapped, "He always likes lima beans, and I know he will add salt to them." She plucked the can from the shelf and opened it with the electric can opener. Dumping the contents into a small sauce pan, she lighted the burner beneath the pan and stirred more gently with a big, stainless, spoon. "Perhaps a little help for you from the ancients as well," she muttered. "Just a couple of shakes from each, or he will notice," she said as she added a pinch or two of the hyssop and the fenugreek. "Blood in your throat, blood on my door. Curse of your blood, trouble *my blood* no more!"

Tiffany continued to stir the pots on the stove as if she were conducting a symphony, a symphony which only she could hear. Eventually, she began to hum the same children's ditty that she had been singing to herself for over two days. As the stew began to simmer and the beans began to steam, she reached over to the microwave, set the timer, and punched the start button. When the timer dinged, she opened the door and stirred the contents with her finger. "A little longer," she judged, and set the timer again. When the timer dinged again, she turned the fires off beneath her cooking and set the spoons on the edge of the sink. Then she retrieved her own bowl from the microwave and placed it in front of her chair.

"Andsel! Andsel dear!" she called down the hallway to his studio, "Come to the table. Supper is ready." Turning to pick up the lima beans from the stove, and placing them in a serving dish, she bumped her elbow into the hot, stainless, cauldron of stew. "Damn it!" she cursed and grabbed her scorched elbow with her free hand. She could have sworn the stew pot had been on the other burner only a moment ago and not nearly so close to her. Her unburned arm had struck something on the counter when she had instinctively grasped her injured elbow. Rubbing the singed flesh, she surveyed the counter to her right. "Ah, the fenugreek and hyssop had gotten in the way." She had knocked them over, scattering a fine mixed powder across the counter's surface. Andsel would enter the kitchen at any second. He mustn't see the rare ingredients she had added to his dinner, even if he wouldn't understand the dulling effect they might have upon the flavor. She scooped up her little helpers and quickly placed them back in the spice cupboard. With one mighty puff, she blew the spilled remainder into the ether of lost evidence. Andsel's steps sounded at the living room threshold. She looked up to see him smiling and standing at the entry from the living room. Before he could speak, she directed, "Set the table, will you?"

"Certainly, dear," he replied as he pulled open the drawer that contained the silverware. Tiffany selected a second serving bowl from the cupboard and ladled a portion of the stew from the pot on the stove into it, then placed the bowl in front of Andsel's place at the table. Andsel selected knives, spoons, and forks from the drawer and placed the utensils on either side of the bowls of stew. He pulled open the drawer which held the table linen and selected two sky blue napkins. Tiffany turned to place the lima beans upon the table.

"Where did *those* napkins come from?" she exclaimed.

Andsel looked at her with mild surprise and amusement. "They came from that drawer just now. Before that, I can't answer you, because you buy the linen. Don't you remember buying them?"

Tiffany could raise absolutely no recollection of buying any blue napkins. It bothered her a little more than such a simple lose of memory should have, but she had bigger fish to fry at this meal than worrying about some unaccounted for, strange, napkins. "Never mind," she replied, "I hope that you are hungry. I know that dinner is a bit early, but I have more work to do outside before dark."

"I'm famished," he answered. As he spoke, a faint, strange, odor passed his nostrils, bringing a chill to his spine. For a moment, he smelled the odor of a crypt - or at least a root cellar - a root cellar in which all of the contents had gone bad long, long, ago.

"Well… have a seat, Andsel. You can't eat standing up," his wife directed.

Andsel complied with her wishes. The stew wafted its aroma to his nostrils as he pulled his chair closer to the table. He unfolded the blue napkin and laid it at the side of his bowl, then picked up his spoon and scooped up a mouthful of the aromatic stew. Strange, his wife's stews were usually much more flavorful than the serving he tasted tonight. He took a second taste. Yes, definitely flat as cardboard. Tiffany waded into her bowl with gusto. That stale, mortuary, odor, which he had first scented upon entering the kitchen, interceded between his nostrils and the stew. Wherever it emanated from, the stinky-foot smell was curdling his enthusiasm for his supper. Andsel reached for the salt to enliven his dinner. His stomach knotted up instantly when he touched the salt shaker, and he grimaced involuntarily with the pain.

"How is your stew, Andsel?" Tiffany inquired.

"Fine, dear, just fine," he replied, "I'm afraid my stomach is still a little queasy from last night, though." He took another spoonful of the stew and his stomach puckered like winter dried fruit. "Could I have something to drink, please?" he asked.

"Oh how forgetful of me!" she snapped and rose from the table. "Will iced tea be all right?"

"Yes, that will be perfect," he replied.

She went to the refrigerator and pulled out a pitcher of tea from within. Filling two, tall, glasses, she returned to the table to place one in front of Andsel and one on the table for herself. Andsel guzzled a big swallow of the tea. Tiffany began devouring her bowl of stew with famished enthusiasm again. Andsel tried another mouthful of the bland, brown, broth and meat. He mulled a bit of beef around in his mouth half-heartedly.

"Something wrong with the stew, dear?" she asked.

Andsel looked up from his bowl. Some trick of the light in the dining room seemed to give his wife's complexion a greenish hue for an instant. A moldy-wood smell wafted from beneath the table, like an unearthed coffin.

"Perhaps you need to add a bit of salt. Mine seems to taste delicious, but you often prefer a little more seasoning to yours, and your illness may have unsettled your appetite," she suggested.

Her recommendation seemed like a good idea, but when he considered reaching for the salt shaker, his innards wrung so violently that he nearly doubled over in his chair. "No dear, I have just salted it heavily while you were pouring our drinks. The stew tastes outstanding. I'll just need to eat it a little slowly tonight, to give my stomach time to absorb it."

An image came to his mind from some long ago dream of bitter cold and gnawing hunger. People shuffled about him in the frigid dark, moaning from hunger. He could hear their bellies growling for the stew available to him. "Remember the winter days of starvation, and eat!" they thundered in his ears. He picked up his spoon and found that he could muster an appetite for the tasteless stew. Soon, he had eaten half of the bowl. Tiffany watched him eat with a faint smile, as she consumed her own serving. Andsel pushed his bowl back from in front of him.

"Is that all you are having?" she asked.

"I think that I will have to wait a little, before I can eat any more. Your stew is as delicious as ever, darling, really. My stomach is a little fragile tonight. That is all."

Tiffany scowled for an instant, appearing a little more intensely green, then her face brightened with sudden recollection. "For goodness sake! I have forgotten the lima beans!" She jumped to her feet and stepped to the stove top. "I have prepared some lima beans to go with your stew tonight, and had forgotten them entirely. Would you like some of them now? Perhaps they will settle in your stomach more easily," she offered.

His face brightened at the thought of something else to fill out his supper. "Yes, please!" he answered enthusiastically. She selected a smaller bowl from the cupboard and spooned lima beans into it, then placed the bowl in front of Andsel on the table. He readily tasted the green vegetables, noticing that they had much the same hue as his wife's skin was taking on. The beans tasted like wet wallboard. He gulped down the last of his iced tea.

Cold shadows crowded around him again. "Eat for us, Andsel," they pleaded. Other, different, shadows gathered around the dining room table as well – unpleasantly familiar guests to Andsel. He took two more bites of the lima beans. "Aren't you having any of the beans?" he asked his wife.

"No, dear, the beans are for you. I'm not as fond of them as you are. The stew is enough for me," she replied. "Finish your bowl."

"I drew a pastel for you this afternoon," he said, in desperation for a distraction.

She looked up from her own dinner, with arched eyebrows, her mouth a tight, grim, line. "Did you now? I cannot wait to see the results," she said earnestly.

"I'll go and get it for you," he offered, half rising from his chair.

"I am sure it can wait," she said. Rising up from her seat, she picked up the salt shaker, reached across the table, and began to apply the seasoning liberally to Andsel's lima beans. "This may improve the palatability of them for you," she offered.

For an instant, the bowl of beans appeared to be the hollowed out hull of a small pumpkin. The familiar, shadowy, guests loomed in closer to him at the table, bringing the stench of decay. "Could I have some more tea?" he pleaded.

Tiffany snatched up his glass and turned toward the refrigerator again. He deftly lifted his bean bowl and scooped half of it into the remains of his stew, stirring the beans beneath the surface quickly. Returning his bowl to its place in front of him, he wiped the spoon on the blue napkin, and stuck it into his mouth. Tiffany returned from the kitchen, looked at the spoon, looked at the bowl, and smiled.

"How are your lima beans?" she purred.

"Excellent! They were the perfect complement to the stew," he replied. His small intestine folded itself into a foot and kicked his stomach up against his spleen. One hand clutched his midriff while his other pulled the blue napkin to cover his mouth. Neon blue vapors wavered before his eyes. Something, brooding and dark, hovered over his head; waiting, waiting, for him to buckle. The neon vapors slithered up his nose and misted his vision, while muffled wings battered his hearing. He slumped sideways in his chair.

"Andsel dear, are you all right?" Tiffany called from many miles away.

He felt her hand under his arm, on his ribs, over his heart. Much like his stomach before, his heart began to constrict and slow, as if he were drowning in frigid water. Terror crept into his fading consciousness.

"It is okay to let go, Andsel," a soft female voice spoke. "You can come back from falling through the ice. I will allow it."

He slumped to the floor. Blue vapors closed over him like the softest woolen blanket. Tiffany should have been calling him. She should have been shaking him, pulling him back. All he could hear was laughter, or was it the crackling of breaking ice.

CHAPTER THIRTEEN

The blue blanket stretched above him now, as a cool, blue, winter, sky. A hawk flew across the sky to pass behind him. A woman's soft voice called his name, "Andsel, I brought your horse," she said.

When he turned toward the voice, a slender, young, woman with long, dark, hair stood beside a tall, red, horse. No saddle or tack of any kind adorned the animal, and its eyes burned fiercely. Andsel took a step back.

"You know this horse, Andsel. You set him free to run on to a new day. Now he returns to pay the dept. He will carry you into battle."

"But, I don't want to fight. This seems like a nice, quiet, place. I would just as soon stay here," he answered.

"You do not have a choice, Andsel. Like it or not, your visitors have arrived, you have turned on the lights, and set the locks behind them. While you polished the keys of bone, the guests in your house have been at each other's throats. Sukawaka Luta was set free when you threw his skull from the cliff top, but your blood has mingled, and now your spirits are kin. Red Horse will fight beside his brother to evict the unwelcome guest."

"But I *am* dead, aren't I? Please, let me be dead. I don't want to start all over again. Living is just too damn hard, and the dying wasn't really all that difficult – a little unpleasantness for a brief moment, and then I was through. I shouldn't have to endure it again now that I have arrived here where it is quiet and peaceful."

"You are here because I allow it, or, at least, I am allowed to allow it. I hold you here." The dark-haired girl held out her closed fist. "You are neither dead nor alive. There is no death or life; only existence."

"Then I choose to exist here," he declared, and sat down on a convenient pile of rocks. A young man and a dog played fetch with a stick in a nearby meadow. The dog caught the stick, rolled over, and walked away as a little girl, without looking back. A tree grew where the man had stood a moment before. Andsel thought that he might like to change into a stone, like the ones he was sitting upon. As a simple stone, he could dance slowly in the moonlight, free of thought and trouble, for a hundred thousand years.

"You are not prepared to be a stone yet, Andsel. You could not endure the memory of a million years. The sadness of forgetting would drive you down dark paths, like the soldier whom you must fight has been driven. Without the road of time, all existence would become gray, melancholy, monotony to you. Those that you love would gall you with their absence. Eventually, you would hate them for *their* escape from your loneliness. You would slash out at everything to find a path of your own – forward, backward - and further down into the black well of nothingness."

"It isn't dark here," Andsel retorted defiantly. "This place is bright and clean and warm. You and the horse are here. I have noticed other people existing here as well. Your threats or intentions don't matter the least little bit to me. I think I will stay."

The dark haired girl turned away from him and began to walk away, leading the red horse. "The light that is here is not yours," she replied over her shoulder. Blue sky began to fade into grayness as the strange pair receded from him. His new world slipped into dusk beneath heavy cloud until it became a complete darkness, as the woman dwindled out of sight in the distance. Andsel was plunged into an utter blackness as if he had no eyes - nor had ever possessed any.

"Light your candle for us, Andsel. Show the world the brilliance of your soul!" shrieked some horrid banshee from the blackness.

No earth touched his feet. No sound murmured in a skull without ears. A minute passed, an hour, a day, who could say? Only the name "Andsel" remained, but no one was there for him to shout it to. He *so* wished that Tiffany was there, even if she shunned him for his past cruelties. If she were there, he would possess something to know, something beyond his own imagined contrivances. He tried to imagine her, as if she were real to his touch, but he always found himself looking back from a mirror, covered in ridiculous make-up. Soon, he knew, he *would* despise her for her absence. After the hatred had passed, would he forget her face? Would he forget his own? Time had abandoned him here in this blackness, left him to tumble into that pit of oblivion. Existence alone would be a prison without doors. Terror gripped him, but then he realized nothing existed to threaten his destruction. At least destruction might be an escape from oblivion, perhaps even a chance to start again. What would he become if he were allowed to start again? Would that thing be better than what he already was, or would it be worse? What was the point of starting over at all?

"I am Andsel!" he began to shout in his mind. "I am Andsel! I am Andsel!" he raged, over and over, until the declaration became only the chant, "I am! I am." But his voice became quieter and quieter until it was only a whisper, which no one else could hear.

Somewhere, a horse neighed. Dawn's glimmer brought faint gray where there had been no sight at all. The woman and the horse approached with the daylight. "Stardust in the farthest corners of the universe puts out more light than you can muster, Andsel. And you would be a stone?" she questioned.

Andsel dropped his gaze to the earth and did not speak for a long time. Finally, in complete despair, he responded, "Then I am lost."

"You *do* have light of your own, Andsel, even though you could not perceive it yourself. How else could I have found you in that darkness in which you stood an instant ago? The soldier stands in a much deeper darkness. Other creatures, not as benevolent as I am, have found him and would possess him forever - as you would hold Tiffany. *He* would hold Tiffany. *He* would *possess* you!"

"How can I save her from them? I cannot even save myself," he cried.

"You must open another door for her, set her free, as you set Sukawaka Luta free. The shadows will run in terror from your light."

"I haven't any flame; none that I can see. How can I combat the soldier and his companions? How can *I* destroy *them* when they are like the Sun to her, and I am not even a match stick?'

"Would you destroy another spirit? Can you be destroyed? In the darkness, you thought that time had abandoned you, but time is not a river that you ride upon. Time is only your own, ever growing, understanding of the world. It circles around you, spiraling ever inward, but it does not support you. When its wind ceases to blow around you, you do not cease to exist: even when you long for your own destruction. If that mighty emptiness can not destroy you, then how can you hope to destroy the shadows?"

She paused in her speech for a moment, waiting for a response from her pupil, but Andsel remained silent with his head bowed in desolation.

"You still fear these dark creatures, but do these evil spirits walk in your world like open fire? Even to the soldier, they are only misshapen shadows, smudges of flickering light; but to him that is everything. Are you a mere shadow in your own world? Have you not loved others in your life? Some of them are gone from your eyes, but not from your heart. Nor are you forgotten from their hearts. Time stretches paper walls between those who love, but when time ceases its illusion, love's light illuminates the world for those who are bonded in love."

"I did not see any light reaching out for me in the darkness," Andsel replied in despair. "If the light is there, I do not have the eyes to see it."

"From your mind, Andsel, you make your paintings real. You sign them into being with your name. From your heart, Andsel, you must *remember* all of those creatures you have ever loved and continue to love them as if they still walked beside you every moment. Even though you cannot touch them, you must have faith; you must *know* that they still hold out their love for you. If the darkness did not destroy you, then it has not obliterated them either. Have *faith* that their light and yours can make the world of your heart more real than any painting. Hold fast your world's existence with your *soul*."

"I am afraid that I have never loved enough in my life to muster the bountiful light which I see here," Andsel sighed.

"I have lived a long time and have gathered many loves. Yes, my love lights this place for you now, but you have not lived in hatred. Some people grow love like great plots of exotic flowers and give them out freely in magnificent bouquets. Orchids are beautiful and certainly have their place in the world, but bitter winds often wither them. Life has seasons of fall and winter, as well as summer and spring. Where are the orchids when the weather turns gray?

Others may only grow small, green, moss and lichens on barren stone, yet just such a vivid green patch of hardy moss is a welcome sight to any traveler through the harshness of the mortal world. Those souls whose love is subdued yet sturdy like the moss have just as much value in the world as the hot house gardener. Barren time does not kill the love firmly rooted in their endurance. The love continues to grow and provide what simple beauty it can at every opportunity.

Common decency is truly not so common. A helpful hand given without condition does not go unnoticed. Many little kindnesses mean a lot. Your gardens are subdued, Andsel, but they have always continued to thrive for anyone who has had need of them. Though you do not count every traveler who passes through your life and moves on a little less road weary because of a warm smile, a bit of humor, or a trivial, kind, gesture from you; there have been many. You would be surprised at the amount of love held out to you. Those of us who understand love as I am trying to make clear to you, hold it out as casually as a dandelion plucked from endless meadows to those in need - and *we* are *many*. If you remember, and believe that love is still there, you have nothing to fear from the shadows."

"Even if I can save myself from the soldier and his companions, how can I ever tear Tiffany away from her own darkness?" Andsel wailed in despair.

"Whose touch has Tiffany loved in the darkness? Hold out your hand to her and she will remember. Then, hold her from them with your love. Love is your light."

"How can I return to save her if I am dead?" he asked. "Am I really dead?"

"The dark ones would have her kill you. Then she would be bound to them forever. There was poison in the meal."

"Then she hates me enough to kill me now. I cannot save her," he sighed.

"The shadows have tricked her into fury against you. They chose the faces of loved ones from her past and wore them as disguises. They tell her that life and death are only two sides of a game, a game which can be played over and over again. Tiffany believes them because the faces that she sees were dead and have been returned to her. To appease her anger, she would beat you once at this innocent game to teach you a lesson. In her mind, she believes that you would rise again and all would be forgiven."

"I have eaten the supper, then I am certainly dead," Andsel exclaimed.

"You are not dead. I have helped you to avoid that change," the dark haired woman replied. She held out a folded, blue, cloth and opened the fold. A small, brown, plant bulb rested within the crease. "I hold you with me for a time, but the time is nearly spent."

The red horse shook his noble head and neighed impatiently. He lurched forward to brush against Andsel, pushing him off balance. Andsel felt himself falling, much as he had felt himself sliding from the dining room chair only a few moments ago. Instead of striking the ground, or a floor, he found himself seated astride the red horse with the woman-in-blue standing at his side.

"Remember who is the light and who is the shadow in your world, Andsel. Trust your own powers of illumination," she called out to him. "Now hold out your hand in love to your wife, and all evil will be forgotten." Plucking the bulb from the blue cloth with her free hand, she tossed it up to his outstretched hand. He caught the bulb reflexively, and the Red Horse took off at a gallop. In an instant, they approached the brink of a familiar precipice. With a few strides more, the Red Horse plunged off of the Dry Fork Look Out into the mists of a storm. A mighty river of lightning tore the sky apart, blinding Andsel completely, as the horse and he plunged toward their deaths. Thunder struck him harder than the fall.

He found himself awake and alone on the dining room floor where he had fallen an unknown age ago. He felt as if he had just crawled out from a deep freeze. Dried spittle caked the corner of his mouth. His eyelids hitched and grabbed as he struggled to drag them across dry eyeballs. Moving a limb required deep concentration, but after several attempts, his mind resumed control of its outer provinces again. Hysterical laughter erupted in random bursts from the distant living room in response to some unintelligible prattle from the television. Were he in pain, he might have cried out for help. Instead, he felt dread at being discovered not dead. Rising on shaky hands and knees as silently as possible, he began to crawl toward the hallway leading to the back door and the garage. Tiffany continued to cackle sporadically from her chair in front of the TV.

Directions of up and down did not seem to matter much to Andsel in the first moments of his consciousness. Indeed, objects only seemed to be patches of color and shade, representing nothing cohesive in his mind.

His crawling seemed more like swimming to his fuzzy comprehension of the real world. When he reached the rear door, he could not seem to decide what to do next. The round, shiny, thing protruding from the door had some significance for further progress, but how it could be useful totally escaped Andsel at the moment.

For a moment, he was no longer in his own home. He crawled in high grass on a rolling expanse of prairie, aware of soldiers far behind searching for him. A narrow gulley opened before him, providing a hidden path away from his pursuers, but he must move swiftly. Any moment, they would crest the high ground behind him and spot him before he could drop into the concealment of the ravine. He stood up and plunged over the side of the embankment. "Escape," he finally realized, "That was the objective. Escape from the house before he was discovered alive again."

Returning to his familiar world, Andsel found himself standing in his garage with one hand on the mysterious door knob. It was dark in the garage; not too dark to find his way around, but a comforting dark, void of the confusion of dazzling color and bewildering shape that he had first arisen within. Even in the dark garage, his life was still at risk. If he remained there, Tiffany and her shadow handlers could still find him and trap him within the confines of the premises.

"Quickly! Follow the ravine to safety," a vaguely familiar voice whispered in his ear.

Stealthy as a cat, he slipped to the exit door of the garage and let himself out into the cool night air. His spirit began to wear his body more comfortably now, instead of it fitting like a sopping wet sleeping bag. The terrain became recognizable to him again. Something, something of interest, lay back beyond the rear of the house; something familiar, something of power. He moved to the corner of the garage to catch the wind blowing in from the surrounding prairie beyond the town. Horses! He smelled horses on the breeze!

Common darkness held no fear for Andsel after the empty blackness in which the dark-haired woman had left him. In fact, the outside world appeared quite clear to him now. Although illuminated in subdued shades of violets, blues, greens, and grays, all objects stood out distinctly as if lighted from the earth itself. Moon and stars played second fiddle to the light pulsing from the landscape. Andsel strolled calmly toward the horse pastures, enjoying the late summer evening. The neighbor lady halted scrubbing a plate from her family's supper dishes to watch him from her kitchen window as he wandered across her yard like an unsupervised infant who had snuck out into the night for the first time. She wondered if Tiffany would remain in the home alone after Andsel was committed to the continuous care facility in the near future, or perhaps move into something smaller with less maintenance.

A drumming of hoof beats rumbled from the pasture as Andsel approached. The vibrations throbbed up through his stockinged feet as he stood beside the plank fence. He began to stomp his feet rhythmically and chant an unfamiliar song in a strange language. The horse herd marched closer as he watched through a crack in the fence. The red roan led the herd to swirl past the fence close to Andsel. An equine scented wind strained through the plank fence with their passing. Following the roan, the horses turned in a tight spiral to pass the fence a second time. The roan's tail slapped the inside of the fence, brushing Andsel's fingers roughly, as he passed a hair's breadth from the planking. Something rattled against the top of the barrier as the horses passed. Even with his enhanced ability to see into the darkness, Andsel could not discern what had struck the top of the fence. He did notice the silhouette of a large bird circling high above against the stars. Perhaps whatever entity which had struck the fence had fallen down inside the pasture, but Andsel could see nothing resting beyond the planks. A shrill cry, perhaps from the circling bird, echoed down from the heavens. The horse herd continued to turn in an ever tightening spiral. Small clouds of dust rose from the center of the spiral to catch the moonlight, like ghosts from the earth. They drifted outward to dissipate beyond the fence. As the horses circled, they created their own small hurricane of warm, dust laden, air, which pulsed outward with the hoof beats to set the fence a swaying. Another shrill call rang out from the skies. Instantly, the horses ceased their circling and spread out across the paddock in all directions. Silence replaced the storm of the horses as if their dance had never occurred. Andsel's own feet came to rest in the stillness. "Thump!" went the earth next to his own feet, as two moccasin tracks appeared with the puff of a tiny dust devil at his side. Unafraid, Andsel acknowledged the unseen presence with a nod, and both seen and unseen men sprang from the corral to trot away toward the Edgar home.

Andsel and his shadow slid silently beneath the neighbor lady's window as she finished drying the last supper dish. Sensing something otherworldly creeping past her window in the night, she dropped the plate into the sink with a clatter. With eyes as big as the saucers drying in the dish strainer beside her, she searched the darkness for the intruders to her world. Within the small hallow of light cast by her kitchen window, she could see a patterned stirring of the grass. Many pairs of invisible feet seemed to move across her lawn toward the Edgars. "A gathering wind must be causing it, or a hatch of crickets perhaps," she thought to herself, ignoring the goose bumps crawling across her skin.

Andsel slipped silently back into the house through the garage access door. He crept down the short hallway, through the kitchen, and into the bedroom. Raising the Venetian blinds on the bedroom window, he undid the latches and slide the sash open to the night. Groping beneath the bed, he found the handle of the tomahawk. He placed the brutal weapon on top of the chest of drawers near the open window and left the darkened room.

CHAPTER FOURTEEN

Returning to his accustomed place at the dining room table, Andsel resumed his seat. The screams of teenagers emanated loudly from the television set in the living room while Tiffany cackled in hysteria and cheered on the slasher in the cheesy horror movie that she was watching.

"Oh yes! Use that one!" she encouraged, as Jason or Freddie selected a different garden implement from the shed on the TV to butcher yet another, teenage, nubile, slut.

Andsel sat quietly, as mesmerized as Tiffany with her television, as he watched the shapes of the dining room and kitchen décor warp, waver, and ripple as something unseen but not unnoticed circled the table and passed by him to enter the living room. Soon, the screaming of the latest slasher victim was interrupted abruptly by the sound of a cavalry bugle, gunshots, and the battle cries of Indians.

"What the hell?" Tiffany cursed, "The damned TV changed the channel by itself!" She set the gin and tonic that she had been nursing down on the coffee table and reached for the remote. A movement from her peripheral vision caught her attention and she turned to glance at Andsel's Lazy Boy chair. An immense Sioux warrior sat in Andsel's chair, with his elbows resting on his buckskinned knees, regarding her without expression. He held a tomahawk in one hand and clutched the shaft of a magnificently decorated coup stick in the other. The TV remote clattered from her hand to the table top. Red Horse slowly rose to his moccasined feet before her. The myriad colored feathers of his war bonnet and coup stick spread out through his corner of the room and across the ceiling as withering flames. A sinister smile crossed his black painted face as he raised the shining tomahawk above his head and reached out for her with the flaming coup stick. Tiffany shrieked in terror and crab-walked backwards over the top of the recliner which she had been seated in. The chair tumbled backward to the floor, spilling her in the direction of the dining room. Red Horse followed after slowly, snatching at her ankle with the coup stick. She flailed wildly with her arms as she crawled into the dining room, searching for something firm to pull herself to her feet and run from the tomahawk-wielding Indian. Her hand caught hold of a familiar, cotton clad, shin bone and she twisted upward to gaze into the pale face of her deceased husband.

"Hello Dear," Andsel greeted her, "Just finishing my supper. How are you enjoying your old horror show?"

Tiffany recoiled from her crouched position on the floor to cower against the counter which separated the dining area from the kitchen. "It can't be! You are dead! I poisoned you!" she screamed.

"Nonsense Tiff, the stew is delicious. A little bland perhaps, but nothing a dash of salt won't cure. I would hardly call it poison," he answered with a kindly smile. He dipped his spoon into the cold serving in front of him and raised it on an elbow propped casually upon the table. "Why don't you join me for another helping?"

Remembering her feathered pursuer from the living room, Tiffany looked away from her resurrected husband to the doorway she had recently crawled through, but no mighty warrior followed her. When she returned her gaze to Andsel, he no longer wore the pale complexion of death. Vivid hues of war paint lighted his smiling visage. A tomahawk had replaced the spoon. Her savage husband now threatened her from his chair at the dining table. Another burning savage waited unseen in the living room.

Red Andsel rose from his chair to reach out his hand to her. "Please Tiffany, come back into the living room with me and sit down. Are you feeling all right; you look a little green to me?" he asked.

Both the dining room and the living room accessed the front door of the Edgar home through a common foyer. The foyer extended as a hallway, beyond the picture window of the living room, on past the bathroom and hall closet, to end as access a laundry room and Andsel's studio. Tiffany could see into the empty foyer from her position against the counter. Perhaps the Indian lurked in the hallway beyond her view. Perhaps he remained in the living room. Something caught her eye as it crossed the upper edge of the living room doorway. The top curl of the burning coop stick hung there in the door-way where he waited for her to escape from Andsel. She lurched from the counter and sprinted to the front door, ripping it open, and dashed out into the darkness with a scream.

Andsel followed his wife's path calmly around the table and stepped to the doorway of the foyer. He looked out into the darkness but could no longer find any trace of her. A rustle like the sound of feathers brushing the wall drew his attention down the long, dim, hallway toward his studio. A copper-hued hand beckoned for him to follow, from the corner beside his studio door. Andsel obliged obediently.

Red Horse stood in full blazing glory in the same corner of the studio where his skull had once rested, when Andsel entered the room. Multi-colored flames roared out from his war bon-net to spread across the ceiling of the room. Feathers blazed from the coop stick to writhe throughout the room, filling every space with undulating waves of color. For an instant, Andsel felt the same terror which poor young Cody had experienced only a few days ago, but Andsel had too much time in the shadow of Red Horse to sustain such fear for long. They had fought and died together more than once. This spirit held out help to him now, instead of harm.

Red Horse reached out with the blade of his tomahawk to touch the bugle suspended from its nail by the door. Andsel removed the bugle from the nail and turned it upside down with its bell pointed toward the floor. The wadded up pastel of the ghoulish dinner party slipped out of the instrument, fell to the floor, and spread out smoothly without blemish. Red Horse beckoned toward the artwork with his coop stick and Andsel retrieved the picture from the floor. With one more wave of the flaming coop stick, the spirit gestured to the scalped skull on the shelf at Andsel's right elbow. Andsel turned to pick up the skull and tuck it into the crook of his elbow. When he looked up from the shelf, the fiery light had ceased and Red Horse had vanished.

Leaving the empty studio with his burdens, Andsel returned to the dining room. He first placed the skull in the center of the dining table, facing his own accustomed place. Pushing his unfinished bowl of stew around the table to rest in front of the empty chair to his right, Andsel spread the pastel out in front of his own chair. Placing the bugle to his lips, he blew the mess call out shrill and clear as if he had played it every day of his life.

Slowly, a withered, black-shrouded, figure with a familiar, green, face materialized from the empty space behind the chair to Andsel's right. Tiffany's grandmother had answered the summons to dinner. The green-skinned ghoul twisted to escape unseen bonds, attempting to flee to the front door and the darkness as her grand daughter had previously done. A disembodied, copper-hued, hand, holding a tomahawk, appeared above the struggling woman's head. "Crack!" struck the tomahawk down onto the struggling spirit's head. Grandmother Tiffany crumpled to the floor, then regained her feet and slunk reluctantly into the chair in front of her. The hand and tomahawk vanished with the blow, but Red Horse appeared complete, head to toe, standing behind the chair across from Grandmother Tiffany.

"It is appropriate that you should eat Andsel's share of this meal which you have prepared for him," Red Horse declared, as distinctly as the bugle call. He turned his gaze from the woman toward Andsel and nodded.

Andsel placed the bugle to his lips a second time and repeated the cavalry meal call. Viola, Tiffany's mother, appeared in the chair immediately in front of Red Horse, held firmly in place with one of his huge, bronze, hands on each of her shoulders, pressing her into the seat. She squirmed and grimaced in her place beneath his grasp. He released one shoulder to run his long fingers through her poisonously orange-colored hair, as if admiring her scalp, and cradled her many double chins in the brown palm of his other hand, with a sinister smile on his face. He nodded to Andsel a second time.

Again, Andsel blew the notes of meal call from the old bugle. Nothing appeared in the last vacant chair across from Andsel. After a moment, Red Horse scowled, reached across the table with a long arm, and snatched up the grinning, lidless, skull. He swung the skull toward the empty chair and hurled it through the glass of the window directly above chair with a violent crash. Turning toward Andsel again, he nodded a third time.

Andsel pulled in a deep breath of air and blasted a different, more urgent, call from the bugle, the Adjutant's call to Assembly. All faces turned to stare out at the black space beyond the shattered window. All heads turned slowly to watch some unseen entity as it crossed the yard toward the front door. Presently, Tiffany appeared in the front door, standing stiffly, as if possessed in a trance. She carried the skull projectile meekly at her waist. Red Horse beckoned to the empty chair. Tiffany walked to the seat without resistance. She placed the skull in the center of the table again and then took her place in the empty chair.

Red Horse turned his attention to Andsel, gesturing with a down-turned palm for him to take his seat at the table with the others. Andsel obliged the spirit with easy complacency. Something brushed his right elbow and Andsel looked up to see the dark-haired woman walk past his chair and pass behind Grandmother Tiffany. She wore a simple blue dress of medium length with a white apron tied at the shoulders and waist. Grandmother Tiffany cowered visibly as the woman moved behind her. The lady in blue came to a stop beside his wife's chair. He suddenly remembered her as the waitress from the last brief dream which he had experienced the night before, as well as his guide from the other side of the blue ice. Tiffany would be safe now with this powerful spirit at her side.

The dark-haired woman produced a napkin from her apron of the same blue hue as her dress. She pulled it graciously across Tiffany's throat and tied the corners together behind his wife's head with a rather intricate knot for the task. Pulling the knot up snuggly with a severe tug, like a hangman setting a noose, she pulled the half-finished bowl of stew from in front of Mother Viola and brought it to rest in front of Tiffany.

"You must clean your plate, young lady, before you are allowed to leave the table," She chastised Tiffany in a calm, firm, voice.

At the appearance of the young woman, Red Horse had slipped silently to the kitchen. He returned to the dining table now, with the cauldron of stew held by its handle in one hand and the smaller sauce pan of lima beans in the other. Plumping the stew pot down next to the skull in the center of the table, he sloshed the remainder of the lima beans in with the remainder of the stew. Stirring the beans down into the stew with the ladle, he snatched up the salt shaker from the seasoning tray and poured the entire contents into the stew. It immediately began to bubble and hiss in the stainless steel cooking pot. Yellow foam frothed up over the edge of the vessel, threatening to spill down its side and cause untold damage to the polished, wooden, surface of the table. Red Horse stirred the concoction gently with the ladle, cooing softly, "There, there now, can't we all just get along?" The evil looking foam retreated from the rim of the pot and the Indian stopped stirring. He ladled a generous portion of the stew into the bowl of Grandmother Tiffany. The dark haired waitress provided a new bowl and spoon at Mother Viola's setting, while Red Horse dipped up a meal for the green and black wraith across the table. Tipping the stainless pot up, he poured the remainder of the stew into the fresh bowl in front of Viola.

Red Horse finished his culinary tasks and moved to stand beside Tiffany, on the opposite side from the lady in blue. The lady produced a shining, silver, spoon from her apron and began to stir the bowl of stew in front of Tiffany. Steam began to rise from the bowl as its contents apparently began to heat up from the stirring.

"Sacrifice, vengeance, and retribution," she whispered into the ear of the entranced woman, "Such dry, bitter, spices for a lover of pumpkin and rhubarb pies to use."

Tiffany's face seemed to sadden at the whispered words. Her eyes turned away from the table set before her, and her lids dropped as though she were lost in some far off memory.

Dipping the silver spoon into the hot bowl of stew, the dark haired woman held it out for Tiffany to grasp. "You must finish the meal you have started before you can enjoy your just desserts," she declared softly.

""Must I?" Tiffany asked in a strange, deep, voice.

The dark haired woman nodded in admonition.

Grasping the spoon in acquiesce, Tiffany swallowed the steaming potion down and began to eat the serving in her bowl with famished relish as if she had not eaten for years. At the sight of his beloved wife consuming the poisoned meal, Andsel tried to cry out for her to stop; to spit out the vile potion; to choke and vomit out the death of her own creation free from her body, but no sound escaped from his mouth. He tried to rise up and rip the spoon from her hand and hurl the bowl from in front of her, but he found himself bound in his chair. As Tiffany continued to devour the last moments of her life, Red Horse reached over to touch her cheek, unnoticed, with the curved end of his coop stick. Upon contact with the wand, Tiffany dropped her spoon into the porridge and slumped lifeless from her chair to the floor. At the sight of his wife's death, Andsel found himself free of his bonds, but not from his chair. He slumped forward with his face in his hands, sopping in desolation. He remained lost in grief, oblivious to the further proceedings around his dining room table.

All others occupying the dining room paid no attention to Andsel's grief. They had matters of their own to settle. The dark haired woman moved to stand behind Grandmother Tiffany's chair so that she could hold a commanding stare upon Mother Viola. Red Horse had already locked his gaze on Grandmother Tiffany.

"Now share this meal which you have prepared for others," he commanded.

The dark haired woman nodded her head to Viola in kind. Both seated spirits picked up their spoons in resignation to their fate and began to consume their portions the cursed meal. As the level of stew dropped in the bowls, the ghouls and their guardians both began to fade from the world of the living. Fainter and fainter, their substance held the light of the room. Finally, with the clatter of silver spoons dropping into empty china, all vestiges of the spirit world not of flesh and blood had vanished.

Outside, a soft evening breeze shifted from the east to bring the scent of flowers through the broken window. As the perfumed air wafted across his face, Andsel glanced up from his misery to gaze at the slumped body of his wife beneath the window. The breeze swirled about the room like a subtle memory of the wind in the corral. Perhaps the illusion was caused by the tears in Andsel's eyes, but faint lights, like small bursts of fireworks or blossoming flowers, seemed to be carried upon the breeze. More and more of the faceted, colored, lamps flowed into the room through the shattered window until the room seemed saturated with their slow whirling energy. The illuminated wind stirred a curl of Tiffany's hair across her forehead. In her sleep, she tweaked her nose at the delicate scent. She was alive!

"Tiffany!" Andsel shouted with joy and ran to his wife. He knelt beside her and shook her shoulder gently. Tiffany did not awaken or respond to his touch, but he could feel her steady, even, breathing in her sleep. "Tiffany!" he cried again, "I'll get you out of this mess."

Scooping her up into his arms, he carried her into the living room and settled her onto the seldom-used couch that filled the vast distance between their separate reclining chairs. He gazed into her placid face and brushed her hair gently back from her brow. She still wore the blue napkin around her throat which the dark haired woman had placed there. He pulled the cloth around carefully to examine the intricate knot which held it, but the knot slipped free and the cloth came easily away from her throat. Overcome with joy that his wife still lived, he knelt and kissed her on the lips. Tiffany stirred, her lashes fluttered, and her eyes opened a little to look into his worried face.

"Andsel?" she questioned, "What are you doing?"

"I was just settling you out on the couch, dear, where you'll be more comfortable. You fell asleep while you were watching television," he answered.

"I'm sorry. I should have gone to bed. I don't remember a blessed thing after supper," she apologized. "Did you just kiss me?"

"Yeah, I guess so. You looked so beautiful resting there. I remembered that I love you."

"It was nice. You can remember that again anytime that you want to."

He leaned in and kissed her again. She smiled sweetly. "I don't think that I will ever forget again," he said.

"That's good to know, dear. Can I just snooze here a little longer? I can't seem to wake up enough to move much."

"Sure Tiffany, you close your eyes and sleep. I'll clean things up in the kitchen."

He could tell by her breathing that she had drifted back into slumber before he had even finished his sentence. "Perhaps he should call an ambulance to take her to the hospital and have her treated for some kind of poisoning," he wondered to himself, but, miraculously, she seemed to be all right. He would clear the dishes and broken glass from the dining room first and then check on her.

When he entered the dining room again, only two bowls rested on the table. The surface was completely void of any evidence of the meal where Tiffany had dined ravenously only moments ago. The skull did remain in the center of the table, but it was as lifeless as stone, completely devoid of any threat. Andsel reached for the skull to return it to his studio. His foot scuffed on some scrap of paper on the floor near his chair. Ignoring the skull for a moment, he bent over to pull the paper from under his foot. It was the pastel drawing of the ghouls' get-together. Between the thorough drenching of his tears, and the heavy tread of his foot, none of the horrible visages could be recognized. All were just dull brown and gray smudges in a blurry, black background. Andsel folded the picture in half and rubbed the inner surfaces together vigorously. He unfolded the paper, refolded it in half again, but this time ninety degrees in the other direction, and rubbed it viciously a second time. When the paper was unfolded again, absolutely nothing remained of the image that he had created earlier that afternoon.

"It is perfect now," he said to himself as he waded up the drawing. Picking up the docile skull with his empty hand, he carried both relics of the past down the hall to the confines of his studio. Returning the skull to its customary place and tossing the picture on to the work table, he spotted his earlier creation of the breeze-tussled petunias. This was the image he had hoped to end her day with, not the nightmare diner party which they both had suffered through. On a whim, he carried the gift back to the living room and tucked it into Tiffany's relaxed arms. She did not stir at the disturbance, but continued to sleep peacefully. He returned to the dining room and gathered the remaining bowls and silverware. Dropping the whole collection into the cold stew pot on the stove, he carried the entire mess into the garage and dumped it into the rubbish bin. A cool draft still entered through the shattered window, but the strong scent of flowers had faded. Only the normal sweet odors of a late august evening in Wyoming rode upon the breeze. He would find a piece of cardboard or plastic to duct tape over the empty sash tomorrow until he had time to take it to the hardware store for a new pane of glass. Weariness began to catch up with him after all of the outlandish events of the evening. He should have gone to the bedroom and crawled beneath the covers, but he did not want to rest there alone anymore, and he did not wish to leave Tiffany unprotected in the living room either, although he was certain all threats had left the house with the last swallow of the evil stew. Returning to the living room, he pulled a pillow from the end of the couch at Tiffany's feet. Resting his head on the pillow beside his wife's knee, he leaned back against the bottom of the couch and stretched his legs out across the floor. In two slow breaths, he was sound asleep.

CHAPTER FIFTEEN

When the first dim rays of the dawn began to turn the deep purple of 5:00 AM to blue-gray, Andsel found himself awake in the living room. He did not rise from his reclining position against the couch immediately. Tiffany's easy, rhythmic, breathing assured him she still slept peacefully. The house felt refreshingly cool, almost chilly. He should go to his studio and find a scrap of cardboard to cover that busted window in the dining room, but the cool air felt good to him. His old couch felt good against his shoulders, with his beautiful wife gently snoring behind his head. The carpeted floor was soft but solid beneath his hands. He would take a moment to himself, enjoying the peaceful silence in his own home. The trials of the day ahead would have to wait a bit until he was ready.

Tiffany stirred behind him and he turned to see what might have disturbed her. Releasing the picture of the petunias from her grasp, she pulled her arms up around her shoulders as if she felt the chill in the room. Andsel rose quietly to his feet and removed the picture from the couch. He propped it up on the arm of her easy chair so that she might see it when she woke up. Returning to his wife, he pulled an afghan from the back of the couch to spread out across the sleeping woman. Without opening her eyes, she clasped his hand momentarily and pulled it to her cheek with a smile. He cupped her cheek in his palm with love and reassurance and then tucked the afghan beneath her chin, substituting a fold of the woven cloth for his own hand in her grasp. She snuggled over onto her stomach with the afghan pulled about her.

Andsel went into the kitchen and mechanically set up the coffee maker for the morning brew. Pressing the start button, he surveyed the dining room for damage from the previous night's events. Most of the glass from the broken window had gone outside with the force of the skull. He would get a rake and shovel from the garage to scrap up those remains from the yard later that morning. A few tiny shards glinted from the floor beneath the window. Retrieving a hand broom and dust pan from the short hallway between the kitchen and garage, he carefully swept up the slivers of glass from the floor.

Something else gleamed a dull gold color from between the chair legs at the far end of the table. Finishing his sweeping, Andsel studied the familiar silhouette in the gloom beneath the table. Rising from the floor, he first carried the glass fragments to the kitchen trash bin and returned the hand broom and dust pan to their peg in the hall. Then he returned to the dining room, stooped over beside his accustomed chair, and picked up his trusty bugle. With a final survey of the dining room, he turned down the hallway to his studio to return the bugle to its proper peg.

Upon entering his studio, he spotted the crumpled ghoul pastel on his work table. A strong urge to remove it completely from the sanctity of his home gripped him. In the far corner of the studio rested the discarded box in which the skull of Red Horse had arrived so many ages ago. Andsel strode to the box and picked it up, snatching up the crushed drawing as he passed. He tossed the ruined artwork into the box and turned to look for a scrap of cardboard for the broken window. The scalped skull stared back at him from its assigned position next to the door. Without a thought, he stepped back to the door, picked up the skull, and dropped it into the box as well. Sifting through the over-stuffed garbage can next to his work table, he found the first attempt at the Alhauser Ranch painting with the effigy of the red horse smeared across it. Andsel added the red-stained drawing to the contents of his box, along with some other paper scraps for stuffing. For a moment, he considered adding the drawing of the snake and saddle to his trash collection, but decided to keep it as a memento of his adventure at the ranch. The picture of the New England farmstead held no such sentimentality for him and it was plunked unceremoniously into the box as he left the studio.

Andsel carried the box directly through the house, into the garage, and onto the passenger seat of his pickup. He had forgotten to return the bugle to its allotted peg in the studio. It still hung from its leather strap at his shoulder. In disgust at his own forgetfulness, he tossed it onto the truck seat beside the cardboard box and closed the door. Selecting a rack and shovel from the various tools stacked in a corner of the garage, he exited the garage to the yard and quickly racked up the remains of the broken window pane. Returning to the garage, he dumped the contents of the scoop shovel into the big trash bin and wheeled the bin out to the curb to await the city garbage trucks arrival.

Returning to the house, he stepped into the living room to check on his wife. She still slept soundly. Andsel realized that he still wore yesterday's clothing. In fact, he suddenly felt quite seedy and in need of a shower. With a final glance at Tiffany, he went to the bedroom, stripped, and went into the bathroom for a shower. Dressing in a good cotton shirt and slacks decent enough for going out into the general public, he entered the kitchen for the first cup of coffee for the morning.

Tiffany sat at her accustomed place at the dining table when he entered the room. The petunia picture lay before her on the table. Andsel bent over and kissed her on the neck. She reached up to cup his cheek for an instant without removing her gaze from the artwork.

"It's gorgeous," she said, "Better than I had hoped for."

Andsel had stepped back into the kitchen to fill a cup with the steaming java. "Your wish is my command. Would you like a cup of coffee, dear?"

"Oh yes, please!" she requested, still admiring the picture.

Andsel slid the coffee beside her elbow on the table and stepped to the other side of the table to face her. A slight breeze entered the room from the broken window, stirring her hair in the morning light. He waited for her to start any further conversation. Discussing the events of yesterday promised to be extremely difficult. For once, he felt that answering her lead might be a wiser strategy then concocting a reconstruction of his version of the terrible supper and its aftermath. In truth, he wouldn't know where to begin. A lie to Tiffany would have a bad taste in his mouth this morning, he was certain.

Tiffany looked up from her picture and slowly took a sip of coffee. "I'm sorry Andsel, but I seem to be in a bit of a fog this morning. Did I hurt you in some way yesterday? I have the strangest guilty feeling, but I don't remember doing anything specific. In fact, I can't seem to remember much of anything after I finished weeding the flower beds in the afternoon."

Andsel studied his wife for any indication of deception in her face. Her expression belied only bewilderment, without deceit. "Perhaps a little rearrangement of the facts might actually be the best course of action concerning yesterday," he thought to himself. "You were awfully tired when you came in from the yard, Tiffany. Do you remember coming into the house and sitting down in your chair in the living room?"

Tiffany seemed to struggle with her recollection of the previous afternoon. She looked out the paneless window into the morning sunlight for a few seconds. Turning to her husband, she concentrated upon his features for a clue. "I'm sorry but I honestly cannot bring a thing to mind after I entered the house from my yard work. What did we have for supper?"

Andsel took a deep breath. Here was his perfect opportunity to patch over the horrible, dark, ravine their lives had stumbled into over the past few days with one of the verbal rainbows he was so skilled at. If he read her vulnerability of memory incorrectly and she suddenly recalled even a little of yesterday's terrors while he spun his beautiful illusion, the damage to their marriage could be irreparable.

"I'm sorry to say dear, but you did not have any of the delicious stew which you had prepared in the morning. I tried to wake you up for a bite, but you wouldn't be roused. Eventually, I gave up and warmed the pot up myself. It was an excellent stew. I would have saved the remains, but, I must admit to terrible mistake on my part. After my meal, I came back into the living room to check on you. After all, it is not like you to get so exhausted that you collapse in your easy chair in the living room in the middle of the day. You still did not wake up when I touched you, but you did not seem over heated or distressed, so I decided to leave you alone for a well-deserved snooze. I dozed off myself for about forty-five minutes to an hour – just long enough to burn the remains of the stew into the bottom of your big stainless pot. The stench woke me up. I was so ashamed of my foolishness that I tossed the whole mess into the trash this morning before you woke up. I'll buy you a new one this morning when I go into town to do some errands."

He stopped his magnificent yarn and waited to see if it floated well upon the mists in her mind. She seemed to struggle with the recounting of events as he had recited them. Finally with a little shake of her head, she sipped her coffee and looked out of the window again.

"It was just a pot," She said, "They make new ones everyday."

Andsel let out a slow sigh of relief. Perhaps her memory would return another day and he would be in big trouble all over again, but for now he was safe.

"I should probably go to Wal-Mart for some groceries this morning anyway, Andsel. There is hardly a scrap of food left in the fridge. I could pick up a new pot then. You needn't bother. Accidents happen."

Andsel couldn't believe his good fortune. He responded with a simple "Thank you for understanding, Tiffany."

She took another sip of coffee and continued, "I am not very hungry Andsel, even though I apparently have not eaten much since yesterday morning. There is a fresh honeydew melon in the refrigerator. I could cut that up for your breakfast if you like."

Andsel sprang up from his chair. "Oh no dear, you sit there and enjoy your coffee. I can chop up a melon." He opened the refrigerator door and retrieved the melon. Pouring himself a fresh cup of coffee and topping off Tiffany's cup, he returned to dissecting the honeydew. For a moment, the big kitchen knife felt like a tomahawk in his hand and he nearly chopped off a scalp-sized disk from one end of the melon. But he caught himself in the act of babary and proceeded to quarter up the melon properly. Placing wedges of the fruit on two plates, he gathered spoons from the silverware drawer and returned to the table, setting a plate in front of Tiffany before he settled into his own chair and began to eat the delicious melon. Tiffany watched him for a moment and then began to spoon off hunks of the melon and eat them slowly.

"Mmm! It's good," she said over a bite of melon. "I guess I have more of an appetite than I thought."

"A lighter breakfast is good for a change," Andsel observed. "We have had a lot of heavy meals lately."

"Yes, we have," Tiffany agreed. "This is a welcome change. Fresh fruit for a fresh start."

Andsel finished his melon and sat peacefully watching his wife delicately spooning off bites of her own portion. "How are you feeling this morning?" he asked, after a moment or two of silence.

"Better now. My head seems clearer with a little caffeine and sugar from this melon. Whatever had me down yesterday has gone away Andsel. I'll be all right. You needn't worry about me. If you've got things to do, go ahead. You could hand me that notepad from the kitchen counter, and a pencil, so that I can make a list of things to pick up in town."

"Well, I do need to return an item that belongs to an old acquaintance near Fort Phil Kearney," Andsel explained as he rose to his feet and went to the kitchen counter.

"Then, by all means, go deliver your package. I'll be fine," she repeated.

""Thank you, dear," he replied, bending forward to kiss her on the cheek as he placed the pad and pencil in front of her.

She gave him a sidelong look as she picked up the pencil. "You're awfully lovey-dovey this morning, Andsel. What have you been up to that I don't know about?" she inquired.

"What you don't know won't hurt you," he chirped. "If my affection bothers you, I'll back off. I didn't have any intention of irritating you."

She gave a deep sigh and smiled at him. "All of the mischief that I ever caught you at has been harmless enough I guess; so no, I would rather not know what you have been up to unsupervised. You can keep up the mushy, romantic, efforts, just the same, in case I do discover some troublesome misbehavior on your part. Little things might mean a lot on your behalf," she conceded and resumed writing entries down on her list.

A diesel engine rumbled in the street through the open window. Andsel looked up to see the city garbage truck pull up to his curb beside his large, green, plastic, trash bin. With a purposeful hum, the hydraulic arms slid their hooks into corresponding sockets of the bin and lifted it above the side of the truck to dump its contents into the hopper of the truck. Andsel caught a gleam of sunlight shining from the side of the stainless pot as it tumbled into the confines of the truck. When the truck returned his bin to the sidewalk and pulled away, nearly all evidence of the previous night's occurrences had been disposed of. He still needed to repair the broken window. Perhaps if he were to loiter in his studio for an hour or so, Tiffany would leave to do her errands and he could measure the frame for the replacement glass.

Instead of traveling directly through the foyer and down the hallway, he detoured through the living room in hopes of picking up an unfinished magazine to pass the time. The sky blue napkin which had been tied around Tiffany's neck poked out from beneath the couch. Andsel stooped quickly, snatched it up, and stuffed it in his pocket. Gazing around the room nonchalantly in case Tiffany noticed his sudden movement, his eyes came to rest upon the shelves which held the various framed family pictures. One picture rested edgeways to his gaze, with its frame haphazardly tossed on top of it. Andsel knew in an instant exactly which picture it was. He stepped to the shelves and plucked the picture down from its perch. Joan must have placed the family reunion photo back on the shelf, along with the frame, when she had cleaned up the mess from his capture of Red Horse. Here was a small task to keep him busy while Tiffany completed her list and prepared for the journey into the business section of town. He would fit a new piece of glass into the picture's frame and remount it properly. For a moment, he admired the pretty, dark haired, girl in the picture again and reminisced about the long ago reunion. The sound of a shower being turned on in the master bathroom brought his thoughts back into the present and the tasks at hand. He turned from the shelves and strode to his studio to find a scrap of glass.

The reunion picture was a standard eight by ten inch format. He had several panes of glass in that size in his assorted frame collection. Selecting one from the pile on the shelf, he cleaned it with a paper towel and some Windex, then fitted it into the empty frame from the living room. Placing the photo on the back of the glass, he inspected it for dust spots. The dark haired girl peered back at him from the picture. Suddenly, he remembered the blue napkin stuffed in his pocket. Tugging the cloth from his pocket, he smoothed it against the surface of his work table. On a whim, he folded the blue cloth neatly into an eight by ten rectangle and placed it behind the reunion photograph. Placing the cardboard backing in its proper place behind the napkin, he pressed the wire clips around the back of the frame into place to hold the completed assembly together.

"Perhaps that will be good luck for my family and good luck for Linda," he mussed to himself.

The sound of the garage door creaking open broke his contemplation of the picture. Tiffany was leaving on her errands. Picking up a small tape measure form the clutter of tools on the top of the work table, he returned to the living room and replaced the mended picture in its place on the shelf. Moving on to the dining room, he stretched the tape measure against the bottom of the window sash. On closer inspection, Andsel realized that, with the removal of a couple of screws, he could withdraw the entire sash from the window frame and take it to the hardware store to be fitted with the appropriate sized pane. He returned to the studio, selected a screw driver from a tool drawer, and came back to the dining room to remove the sash. With the removal of the retaining screws, the aluminum sash slipped free easily from the frame. Andsel left the screw driver and the screws on the window frame. Looping the sash over his arm, he exited the house into the garage. Tossing the sash into the passenger side of his truck, he climbed in behind the wheel, punched the garage door opener on the visor, and backed out of the garage. He would leave the sash off at the hardware store on his way to the Fetterman Monument. Perhaps the handyman at the store would have a new piece of glass fitted in place by the time he had returned from his mission at the monument.

Perhaps he would get back home before Tiffany returned and he could fit the sash back in place before she noticed the glass was gone. Perhaps her memories would return of the previous night's events and the police would be waiting to haul him away when he returned from his task. Perhaps he should have saved the cook pot and diner dishes as evidence for his defense. Andsel shrugged his shoulders for his own benefit as he drove down the street toward the center of town. No matter what she remembered or chose to do to him in the future, he knew that he would always love her. He had done all he could manage to repair any injuries he had caused to their life. Time would tell if he had staved off all of the damage which was possible. He reached over to the dash and turned on the radio.

CHAPTER SIXTEEN

Kendrick's Hardware promised to fit a piece of single pane glass into the sash for Andsel before he returned from Fort Phil Kearney and the Fetterman Monument. They pointed out that the window had been double thermo pane and should be replaced wit the same for energy conservation purposes. Not carrying such material in stock, they would order a factory glass to fit. Andsel agreed to bring the window back to them in a couple of weeks to have the proper type of pane fitted.

Leaving Sheridan, he drove south along the old highway toward Story, Wyoming. In the bitter winter of 1866, the years before George Armstrong Custer's great debacle with the Sioux and Cheyenne at the Little Bighorn, Captain William J. Fetterman and eighty men met a similar fate a mile or so east of the future site of this picturesque, little, village. Fetterman and soldiers under his command charged over a ridge in hot pursuit of a handful of Indians, only to be snuffed out completely by the fist of Red Cloud's warriors, many thousands strong. A tall, dark, stone, monument stood on the location of the massacre. Andsel intended to end the saga of his ghost soldier with the story of those others on that lonely, barren, ridge today. He passed through Story, drove the couple additional miles to the monument turn-off, and climbed the slope in his pickup. No other cars occupied the small parking lot near the monument.

Slipping the leather sash of the bugle over his shoulder, Andsel gathered up the cardboard box of debris from his studio in one arm and rummaged through the glove box of the truck until he found a pack of matches. Stuffing the matches in his pants pocket, he closed the truck door and walked to the base of the monument. He paused for a moment at the base of the rough stone monument to read the inscription on the bronze, shield-shaped, plaque. He had visited this marker several times in the past and had read this plaque before, but he read it one more time, perhaps as a ritual prayer of respect for those who had fallen in battle. When he had finished reading the plaque, he continued out the foot path which meandered along the top of the ridge where the battle had taken place. Here and there, other small interpretive signs perched on short metal posts at particular points of interest. These signs described the details of the battle which had occurred at that unique location. Andsel did not read any of these signs as he passed. He strode out to the furthest end of the path on a high, grassy, knob at the end of the ridge.

Andsel placed his box on the ground at his feet and looked out across the valley of Upper Prairie Dog Creek spread out beneath him. The stream had been called Peno Creek in the time of Fetterman and Fort Phil Kearny. How or why the stream had been renamed, Andsel had never learned. Its waters had bubbled happily along for eons without the slightest care for what one mortal man in some brief flicker of time might choose to call it. A thousand years from this morning, the waters would tumble down through the prairie grass on their long journey to the sea with the same disregard for the name squeaked briefly through the air by whatever two-legged, self important, monkey who might be passing at that future moment.

Andsel glanced over his shoulder back up the path toward the distant monument. Nothing moved on the path or at the monument. He stooped to his knees and began to clear the long grass away from a circular area about four feet across. When the circle was clear, he placed the box containing the skull and paper scraps in the center. Pulling one edge of the red horse smeared watercolor loose from the top of the box, he struck a match from his packet and lighted the paper. The paper leapt into flame vigorously, surprising Andsel with its hunger to consume. Soon, the cardboard box and its other paper contents burned enthusiastically. Andsel expected the inert bone of the skull to smolder and char once the paper inferno had spent its fury. He bundled up the dry grass which he had removed from the circle and dropped it on top of the fire. To his astonishment, the skull roared into flame beneath the dry grass, as if it were made of balsa wood. The grass gave off a sweet odor as it burned and the white smoke curled about Andsel's face. Pulling the bugle from his shoulder, he stood straight at attention and placed the instrument to his lips. As if he had played the tune every evening for twenty years, he blew the haunting, peace-giving, notes of "Taps" through the old bugle. With the last note echoing across the Peno valley, he dropped the bugle to his side, stepped a pace back from the dying fire, and stood in silence.

When a large, gruff, hand clamped down upon his shoulder, bringing him back to the time at hand, he could not recall how long he had stood there. The fire had mostly died to ashes. "What the hell do you think this is; a place to burn the trash from the inside of your car?" growled the park attendant furiously. He had spun Andsel around to face him with his mighty paw. From the force of the grasp and thrust, Andsel had expected a giant of a man. Instead, a short, fat, plug grimaced up at him from beneath a Smokey Bear hat. "Well, what do you think you are doing; roasting marshmallows?" hissed the red-faced munchkin. Smokey the Munchkin stomped around Andsel and hopped into the middle of the little circle of scorched earth. He kicked and ground the gray ashes into the earth until not even a wisp of smoke escaped. Andsel slouched where he stood, watching the little dynamo eradicate all evidence that Uncle John had ever been. "And what's with the trumpet music?' snarled the human fire plug as he continued his rutting in the dirt and ashes. Finally, the little smoke jumper stopped his manic dance to stand still facing Andsel. "Well!" he demanded.

"I ah… I ah, was disposing of some mementos of a friend," Andsel stammered. "Yeah, yeah, a friend who was in the military. He has been gone a long time now, but I just couldn't seem to part with some things he had left behind – until now anyway. I didn't want to send them out with the trash like common garbage, so I brought them up here. This seemed like a fitting place to say good-bye."

Smokey studied the bewildered trumpet player before him grimly. After a moment, he stepped out of the little circle and began to rummage through a fanny pack he wore backwards so it stretched across his ample tummy. Extracting a small jug of bottled water, he held it out to Andsel. "Here, pour this on your funeral pyre and stir it in. Then get the hell out of here before I write you a citation for defacing a national monument. Do a good job or I'll turn you in to the State Police. I've got your license plate number," he ordered.

Andsel took the bottle, opened it, and began to pour the contents onto the burned patch of earth. He rubbed it in thoroughly with his feet. The attendant had turned and begun to walk back up the pathway. After a few, short, determined, strides, he turned and barked, "I'll come back and check for smoke in a half an hour. You had better be gone. If I find any smoke, I'll make that phone call I just promised, so do a good job with that water, and don't come back here ever again. You hear?"

Andsel nodded his head submissively. He watched the tiny figure of the big voice of authority dissipate into the sage and long grass of the ridge. The whole affair had been very unnerving. The morning's two cups of coffee had worked their way through his metabolism to expand his bladder uncomfortably. He turned away from the receding attendant and relieved himself where the pseudo-officer had stood. Zipping his fly and buckling his belt, he made his own way back to his waiting pickup.

CHAPTER SEVENTEEN

Tiffany was placing a new set of stainless steel salad utensils into the silverware drawer when Andsel walked through the short hallway into the kitchen. A new stainless pot rested next to its packaging on the kitchen counter.

"Shall I put this pot away for you?" he asked.

"I need to wash it first. You could take the box out to the trash for me though, dear," she replied. He picked up the box and took it into the garage where he flattened it out for the recycling pile.

A few months later, he found a new set of antique, silver, salad utensils, along with a matching bowl, in an antique shop up in Billings. He purchased the complete set and brought them home for Tiffany. Picking up the occasional little something for his bride had become somewhat of a habit for him. He liked to slip little presents into her arms when she dozed off on the couch beside him as they read or watched television together. When Andsel dozed off now, his dreams consisted of mostly pleasant adventures. He practiced keeping the world happy, the sun bright, and the sky blue for as long as he could while he slept and dreamt peacefully. For her part, Tiffany tried to refrain from sniping at his occasional foolish remarks.

Sometimes, when he lapsed into a sustained episode of insensitivity, she found herself whistling a particular children's melody from long ago. The tune seemed to bring Andsel to his senses and restore harmony to their lives.

Some nights though, when the moon was full and the Wyoming wind rattled the tree limbs against the roof, Andsel would stir restlessly in his sleep. Far up on the top of Medicine Mountain, the same wind would rattle the offerings tied to the ropes surrounding the Medicine Wheel. Andsel would hear the sound of tempered steel on armor and dream of battles past. He would rise from his bed and wander out into the night to the stand beside the horse corral on the edge of town. Some of the horses, especially the red roan, would meander over to the fence to nicker soft, serious, horse sense through the planks to him. With a brush of a soft, velvet, muzzle, they reminded Andsel he belonged. Then he would return to his own home and his waiting wife. Most times, she welcomed him gently back to rest peacefully beside her. But once in a while, just for a little wicked excitement, she asked him to paint his face with war paint and chase her around the bedroom. She always retreated into the closet, but never remained alone.

THE GOLD OF DEADWOOD

Maureen covered her eyes with her hands as she left the tunnel. Slowly, she parted her fingers, a little at a time, allowing the blazing sunlight to set her flesh aglow like cherries in a line. The blood pink of her own substance infused with light allowed her irises to constrict from their awesome searching of the tunnel's darkness. She always loved this moment, this instant of overpowering escape. As her eyes adjusted, she parted her fingers wider to behold the lush, green, valley below the mine. What would she be today; perhaps a Meadowlark perched upon a sagebrush limb, singing its challenge to the bees; perhaps an Indian Paintbrush, holding outspread fingers to flush red in the sun, much as she had just done? Perhaps something grander? Could she be a buffalo today, running across the landscape unstoppable?

"Wake up, Grandma Rena. Wake up," the voice drifted down from the far reaches of the blue sky like a bull elk's bugle from the mountain side. An autumn leaf brushed Maureen's cheek and her vision swam backward beneath the sighing pines flanking the entrance to the mine. "Wake up, Grandma Rena.

You have fallen asleep at the slots again," Shelly called softly as she shook the white-haired old lady's shoulder gently.

Grandma Rena roused herself from the one-armed bandit that she slumped upon, while the young woman steadied her on her stool. Rena groped for her glasses where she had set them down near the view screen of the slot machine only moments ago when she had lain her head upon her folded arms to rest. The familiar world of Lame Johnny's Hidden Treasure gaming parlor came into focus when she finally managed to prop the spectacles back on the bridge of he sharp nose. The golden prairie was gone.

"Sorry, dear," she said to the petite, young, lady, "I seem to be dozing off much too often these days. I suppose Ricky will put a stop to my coming in here if my napping continues."

Ricky the manager, who stood nearby, overheard the old woman's comment. "If you keep winning those big pay-offs like you did last Tuesday, Rena, I *will* ban you from the premises," he said with a smile. "If you nod off for a couple of extra 'Z's, you won't be bankrupting Lame Johnny's and I won't have to find another job. I know Shelly is close by to keep you from sliding off of your stool, and when she is not, I'll come by to rattle your coin cup."

"You might get away with it now, Richard, but a couple of years ago, you would have probably lost a hand," Rena said, rubbing the sleep from her eyes.

Ricky shuffled away two steps from the old lady and the girl, "You're not still carrying that switchblade are you, Rena? You know how it scares the younger customers!"

"I gave it to Shelly so that she could keep you troublesome, young, men away."

"I'm a married man, Rena, but the blade is not frightening away all of her admirers, or perhaps Shelly isn't waving it at that Greg character who is always hanging around her lately."

Rena eyed her granddaughter for a moment. "So you've been stealing away to flirt with that handsome, young, tour guide again? I guess I haven't been keeping my responsibilities up toward protecting you from the wolves, as I had promised your parents."

"I threw that gaudy, nasty, thing away, Rena. I don't need any old knife to keep me safe in this little town, and Greg is a nice young man who works hard for a living. He is not a gambling loafer like most of the other young men around here."

"You had better not have thrown that blade away, young lady! If you did, you had better find it damn quick. That was magic steel from the ancient sword of Kublai Kahn. A Chinaman brought it all of the way from his homeland to protect against the dark spirits that had been stirred up beneath the Back Hills in the search for gold.

All right, All right, I don't think that I truly threw it away. It might be in a drawer somewhere, or stuffed in a box with a bunch of other meaningless junk. I'll hunt it up tomorrow and give it back to you, Rena."

"Do find it and give it back to me then, to hold for you, but don't dismiss what you know nothing about," snapped the old woman.

"Yes Grandma, I'll look for it. Maybe it is time to get you home for the night," The young woman acquiesced.

"I've got a little change left," Rena retorted, rattling her plastic cup. "When I empty this cup, I'll find my way home. By the way, here is a quarter I owe you from a pot that I won earlier tonight." She held out a coin to her granddaughter.

"You won another pot, Rena? How much?" Shelly exclaimed.

"Never you mind my financial gains and losses. Just put that away for your good luck money on a rainy day." Rena watched intently as Shelly diligently took the quarter and placed it in a small, blue-velvet, Crown Royal bag in her purse. The bag seemed to be perhaps one third full.

"Shelly, could I please have another rum and coke?" an elderly gentleman called from further down the long, narrow, room filled with slot machines.

"Coming right away, Gaylord," Shelly replied automatically. "I've got to get back to work, Rena. Let me know when you are finished with your cup and I'll walk you home."

"I can find someone to see her home, Shelly," Ricky offered. "I'll go mix Gaylord's drink for him and you can deliver it." As the two casino employees stepped away from Grandma Rena, he asked in a lowered voice, "Did she really give that old, two bit, pig sticker to you? She has been clutching it away under her skirt for years."

"Yes, she passed it off to me one night when I had turned sixteen. I'm not really sure if I can truly put my hands on it anymore. I may indeed have thrown it away. By tomorrow, she will have forgotten all about it."

"I am glad it is gone. Rena is pretty sharp for her age, certainly more lucid than *most* of our patrons, but I have been uncomfortable with the possibility that her nasty, little, blade might be floating about the room. If someone awoke her from one of her frequent naps and she was confused, she might have accidentally caused them some harm."

"I've not been sixteen for quite some time," Shelly laughed, "Your gambling parlor has been safe for a few years now, Ricky.

"Thank you, Shelly, for that peace of mind. If you do come across the tawdry thing, throw it away. It would more than likely fold back and injure its wielder than the person it was directed against," Ricky advised.

"You seem to know a lot about Rena's old keepsake," Shelly observed.

"No, I've just seen a lot of cheap novelty knives like the one that she coveted. They were dangerous junk, better thrown away - as I hope that you have already done with it."

"Is Gaylord's drink ready?" Shelly asked to change the subject.

"Oh yes. Sorry that I held you both up. The knife is a trivial matter, more of a conversation maker than anything else. It has probably rusted away long ago in the bottom of the landfill."

Ricky handed the rum and coke to Shelly and she whisked down the curving aisle to a bald, withered, old man cranking away at the handle of one of the slot machines. He laid out a dollar's worth of quarters as a tip without raising his gaze from the one-armed bandit. Lame Johnny's catered to the elderly crowd for the most part. Its owners were content to drain the disposable incomes from busloads of geriatrics, one quarter at a time. Wagers at the slots were meager, but the bandits sucked the silver in slow and steady. Life in Johnny's was peaceful and dependable. Ricky mixed the libations and Shelly delivered the lubrications. Other patrons called for other concoctions as they fed the jabbering, jingling, machines. A fractured calliope of battling, carnival, melodies inundated the gambling hall with a maelstrom of noise. The uninitiated might bolt from this discordant din after dropping a few coins, but the true gambler would never be diverted from his lust to pour the coin of his life into parlor's machinery by the noisome racket within.

"This is my last quarter, Shelly," Rena stated as her granddaughter passed on her rounds.

"Okay, I'll tell Ricky I am leaving and we can get you home,"

"Thank you, dear," Rena answered. She dropped the coin into the slot and yanked the handle down. The machine's rollers whirled, then jerked to a halt, one at a time – apple, peach, pear. "Beat me again! You soulless thief!" Rena cursed the machine. The bandit's music went silent, passively awaiting its next manipulator. "I might better watch a clock all day. It would be cheaper and just about as entertaining. Perhaps a nice Cuckoo clock with a little, yellow, bird to spring out at me and chirp a little song," Rena told herself.

"It won't talk to you unless you pay it," a heavy-set, old lady with orange hair declared to Rena from the station beside her.

Rena got up without answering. The orange-haired woman did not acknowledge Rena's lack of reply. Her attention had already been reabsorbed into the whirling wheels of card suit emblems cascading in front of her. Shelly caught Ricky's attention at the bar and signaled toward her grandmother and the door. Rick curled his finger in gesture for her to come over for a word of conversation.

"Management would like you to make some other arrangements to escort Rena home at night, Shelly. They are saying that they pay you for regular hours and that your time should not be interrupted at random intervals."

"I'm only gone for fifteen minutes. You know she lives just up on Williams Street. I *am* entitled to a fifteen minute break."

"This is not my complaint, Shelly," Ricky defended, "Don't shoot the messenger. I don't mind covering for you at all. Yes, you are allowed fifteen minutes every two hours, but at designated times. If your grandmother can comply with your schedule, there will not be any problem. Otherwise, you will need to find her another escort."

"Rena can keep track of all kinds of things, but time isn't one of them," Shelly sighed. "I'll sort it out with her, Ricky. Can I have a couple of days to come up with better arrangements?"

"You have until Monday of next week," Ricky answered.

"Okay," Shelly tossed over her shoulder as she hurried along to tuck her grandmother's arm under her own and move toward the exit.

Ricky watched the couple disappear into the darkness beyond the glass doors of the casino. A cunning smile crossed his thin lips. Stepping out from behind the bar, he strolled down the aisle among the gray-haired, arm cranking, fanatics. His hand caressed the top of Rena's vacated machine for a moment in absent-minded gesture as he passed. The machine's lights flickered, it bleeped out a few notes of its signature tune, and its rollers scrolled a partial turn. Gaylord looked up from his own bandit, his attention captured by the random, unsolicited, reaction of the inanimate machine. Ricky's eyes met the inquisitive, accusing, gaze of Gaylord. He smiled, fumbled for a roll of coins in his pocket, then laid the coins in the tray at Gaylord's elbow. "Another rum and coke on the house, Gaylord?" he asked innocently, patting the old man on the shoulder.

Gaylord broke the roll of quarters into his money tray and resumed stuffing them into the maw of his bandit. "Sure, one more won't hurt me," he answered and turned back to the siren song of his machine.

Ricky strolled along the aisle, looking at the levels in drinks as he passed and taking an order or two. He returned to his position behind the formica bar and began preparing the drinks. A short, round, man with wispy, sandy, hair entered the main gambling salon of the casino from the rooms behind the bar. "Business steady tonight, Rick?" the man asked as he surveyed the room.

"Yeah, smooth as clockwork, Boss," replied Ricky.

"Shelly taking her grandmother home?"

"Yes, she left about five minutes ago."

"Fine, fine, a fine young woman. Dependable to her grandmother and dependable to Lame Johnny's. We are lucky to have her. I suppose some young scoundrel will steal her away from us to marry her some day soon. You can be on your way now, Richard. I'll man the place for my stretch," the owner directed.

"Thank you, Charles. I'll just deliver these two drinks and leave you to it. See you tomorrow night," Ricky answered, taking the drinks and heading down the aisle. He dropped off the drinks, collected the payments, and left the money with Charles as he exited the casino.

Ricky lived down gulch on Dudley Street in the Ingleside district, but this was not the direction in which he traveled. Instead, he turned eastward to climb the steep, dark, streets toward Mount Moriah Cemetery. The dark little man in his black suit barely stirred the shadows as he made his way to the gates of the famous cemetery. Upon reaching the gates, he turned aside and followed a seldom used footpath which skirted the iron fencing of cemetery. The ground was broken and treacherous, but Ricky strode along with familiar confidence, whistling a jaunty tune. When he had circled around to the back side of the cemetery, Ricky paused and knelt beside one of several leveled patches of earth in the jumbled terrain of the craggy hill.

"Hello Lotus, my dusty bride," He spoke to the unmarked patch of hard packed earth, "I've come to stir you one more time from your slumber. Ah my Pretty, I am sorry to say, tonight will be my last visit to the land of the dead heathens. You see, I've found a new bride-to-be, Sweet Lotus, and our union must be dissolved. I've come to return what belongs to you." Reaching into the breast pocket of his jacket, he pulled out a small, slender, package wrapped in green silk and tied with a white ribbon. Untying the knot, he unrolled the silk and ribbon with a deft, practiced, jerk and caught the contents in the palm of his left hand. A woman's, gold, wedding band gleamed in his grasp; pierced by a tiny, fragile, finger bone - white as ivory

"I remember when the jingling money music awoke me in the depths of the mine shaft where those filthy miners had hurled me. I was *so* lonely when I had crawled from beneath the boulders they had tumbled in upon me. I missed you, Lotus. Remember when I came to this spot by the dark of the new moon and plucked up your hand to place this ring upon your finger? I had purchased it with the very first money I had earned in the casinos - gambling halls in the vernacular of your time." Ricky slipped the ring from the finger bone with the folds of the green silk napkin and stuffed it purposefully back into his breast pocket. "This makes you a free woman again," he said with a chuckle, "But then you never gave it away for free in your profession, did you? I would have paid Old Sally twice or thrice your price, but she wouldn't let me touch you. So I took what I wanted and now I'll give it back." Taking the finger bone in his right hand, he shoved it into the earth of the grave like a needle into a pillow. Down, down, he pushed the little bone, his arm elongating and thinning as it pierced the hardened earth. "Where are you, dear? Now don't be shy. Coyness served you no purpose the last time we met, if you remember, My Love," he spoke to the grave. Twisting his distended arm around deep in the soil and stone, he searched for the remains below. "Ah, there you are," he said with a smile. "Here is your finger back to you, Lotus. We shall see no more of each other ever again. May you rest in all of your tiny, little, pieces now."

Ricky stood up and slowly withdrew his appendage from the earth. He had to back away a few steps from the grave to pull the snakish limb from the ground completely. Holding it aloft, he slowly contorted and shrank the limb back into its original form as a man's arm. When his hand had left the earth, the soil of the grave seemed to shudder and subside a few inches.

"Shrink away if you wish, Lotus. It matters not at all to me now. Soon, I'll have young Shelly as a fresh new bride of living flesh, instead a skinny old bit of pale bone. She makes me wonder what I ever saw of interest in you. But I must remove that nuisance of a tour guide first – that little man Gregory. If you feel my passing tonight, dear Lotus, take no notice. Our time together is finished. You may sleep in peace.

Ricky rose to his feet and confidently picked his way further up the east ridge of the Deadwood Gulch in the pitch blackness of the night. A shadow moved before him, even darker than the lightless world. That shadow crept from the emptiness of his soul, seeking out of the shape of the earth before him. Its fingers crawled like spiders far ahead, until at last they scrambled over a projection of the solid rock of the mountain. Digging, poking, prying, they searched the surface of the outcrop for some tiny crack or fissure allowing entrance to the world below. At last, a crevice appeared and the shadow rushed down, down into the stone, drawing Ricky behind it like molten silk to follow the paths of bedrock into the lightless heart of the Black Hills.

Many veins of gold, fine as angel hair, still remain beneath the gulches of Deadwood - entwined in endless webs throughout the stone. Streaking through the blackness lurking behind the gold, Ricky followed these molecular trails. An electricity of evil, he flowed the twisted corridors, as familiar to him as timber to a termite. Tonight he sought out the tunnels of the Golden Tooth Mine where men had ground away their lives, like the points of their pick-axes, on the stone flesh of the mountain. The miners had gone, but now tourists paid to walk the abandoned paths of the mine. Their green money had supplanted the bright gold that once had flowed from its entrance. Gregg Newtson and other young men led the groups of goggling sun lovers along the paths of solemn darkness where they cringed in delight beneath the threatened crush of the stone above. Strings of incandescent light bulbs violated the sanctity of this lifeless womb so that these transient mortals could view this world of the eternal. Artifacts of the miners' profession had been littered about as props, here and there in the serpentine tunnels, to illustrate how labor had passed in the dayless hours of the mine.

Ricky flowed just beyond the surface of the walls of the Gold Tooth tunnels until he sensed the gooey warmth of the evening's final batch of tourists as they were being escorted from the mine by the nuisance Gregg Newtson. When the tourists had exited the lobby and souvenir bazaar, which now occupied the old head frame structure of the Golden Tooth, Gregg turned back into the mine to perform his final patrol of the passages. It was his duty to make certain all was in its proper place, refuse was collected, and no subterranean adventurers had lingered behind. Gregg strode with confidence down to the familiar depths of the museum mine. As he moved down the shafts and tunnels, Ricky flowed secretively behind. Gregg stooped to pick up a candy wrapper here and an empty water bottle there, stuffing the garbage into a plastic bag he carried for that purpose. "Old pick-axes in that corner as they should be," he noted. "Rusty lantern on its peg in the wall. Almost to the end of the mine and the end of another shift, I'll soon be holding Shelly's hand on the way home from Lame Johnny's," he envisioned and smiled to himself.

Ricky held back several yards short of the final chamber of the mine with its blunt face of impenetrable stone. The structure of the rock was familiar to him here. He had searched it out and marked it in his memory on many a previous swim through the stone of the mountain. Weakness existed; waiting to be encouraged

Gregg began to whistle as he picked up the concentrated clutter on the floor of the last chamber. His cheerful whistling rippled through the stone where Ricky crouched and Ricky began to swell with malice. Greater and greater his hatred grew, pushing out against the rock. The blackness of his hatred heaved out against the walls of the tunnel like hydraulic fluid. As Gregg turned with his sack to begin his ascent from the mine, muffled moans and shrieks began to emanate from the tunnel ahead of him. Fine spurts of gray dust burst from cracks in the trusty walls up the tunnel. A shower of gravel began to cascade from the vaulted roof. Gregg thought to run, but he dreaded the impending crush of the rock. In an instant, his escape was sealed. The roof ahead caved in with a thunder heard by no one - except its victim.

Ricky had chosen his trap location carefully, for Gregg was not crushed by the collapsing tunnel; he was only sealed within like a fly in a bottle. The electric cable and its string of bulbs had snapped in the cave-in, leaving Gregg in terrifying darkness. Silently, Ricky oozed from fissures of the newly broken rock to coalesce into his familiar form within the prison. He watched Gregg in the blackness through his shadow eyes and gloated at the puny mortal's terror. A mocking snicker rose in his throat and blossomed into horrid laughter.

"Who's there?" Gregg shrieked. "I'm here! I'm here! I'm still alive! Get me out!"

Ricky roared in peals of hideous cackling at the pleas for help.

"You think this is funny, do you? You must have got in by the tunnel. Some of it must still be clear. I'll find the way past and then I'll find you too, my funny friend, and then I'll fix you! I'll choke the giggles right out of you!" Gregg bellowed at the darkness. He began to crawl about the chamber frantically, feeling his way along the floor and walls. His hands found familiar posts and railings that had been fastened into place to keep the tourists from handling the props or scratching their initials into the walls of the chamber. Beyond the posts, he found the wooden buckets and rusty picks. His mind's eye recreated the familiar interior of the chamber and he located his position within the room. Tentatively, he crawled toward the exit of the chamber. Ricky watched his progress with delight, stepping silently out of the way as the desperate man moved across his prison cell. Gregg reached the rubble of the cave-in and gingerly groped his way up the tumbled debris. Over and over, his fingers searched the jagged boulders for some sign of a fault or weakness in the barrier, but none appeared. Finally, he shrank back to his knees and began to weep. Ricky burst into new tumults of laughter, mightier and more cruel than before. Gregg spun and pounced through the darkness at the sound of his tormenter, but Ricky sidestepped in the nick of time to watch Gregg sprawl face first in a cloud of dust. The condemned man spat out the bitter dust and sobbed in his misery upon the floor.

"My, my, wouldn't Shelly be impressed with you now," Ricky mocked from behind his captive.

Gregg stopped his sobbing. "I know that voice. I know who you are, Ricky! I may die here of suffocation or starvation, but you will die sooner! Eventually, I'll find you. You can't get out any more than I can and, sooner or later, I'll find you and throttle that laughter right out of you, you crazy bastard! You won't find our situation so funny in the end." He stood up and began to flail wildly about the chamber in search of his cell mate. Ricky easily stepped out of his sightless reach. After many moments of franticly hurling himself around the cavern, Gregg collapsed to the floor again in exhaustion. "If I had a light I'd find you, and then we would see who was laughing. I'll find you yet. You will collapse from lack of oxygen just as fast as me, and then I'll find you. By the rasping of your breathing, I'll find you and choke the life out of you just before I die."

Ricky looked around the chamber and found what he sought. A stub of candle in an old bottle rested in a nook in the chamber wall, along with an old, tin, match safe. He lifted the bottle and match safe from the wall and silently placed them on the floor barely and inch from Gregg's right hand. Nudging the match safe against Gregg's finger tips with his toe, Ricky stepped away and began to dissolve back into the cracks and fissures of the rock. Gregg prodded the little, tin, box tentatively, then clutched it to his chest. He pried it open with shaking fingers. A dozen, brittle, wooden, matches fell into his palm. Holding the tip of one to his nostrils, he smelled the sulfur. Twelve chances at light, like twelve apostles before final judgment. He poured the remaining matches into the little tin and stuffed it into his pocket. Finding a rough stone by brail, he struck the single match against its surface. The match sparked, flared a tiny bit, and then glowered in frail ember. Gregg blew gently on the ember and fragile flame returned. He held the match head downward and watched the flame climb the dry, wooden, shaft. In the match's glow, he spotted the faint glint of light on the dusty bottle, then perceived the candle stub protruding from its neck. The match began to sear his fingers, but he gritted his teeth and held it to the candle's wick. He could hold the burning ember no longer and dropped the spent match into the dirt. "What if the others are no good?" he wondered to himself. Perhaps but one chance at light and hope and he may have wasted it. Should he try them all immediately, or one at a time spread out over the few remaining hours that he might have? Pulling the match safe from his pocket again, he popped it open and the matches scattered across the dirt floor. "God Dammit!' he cried and immediately regretted the curse in fear of offending any deity who might choose to help him. Fingering the inside of the safe in desperation, he apologized to God and begged for one match to remain. No warm wood responded to his touch.

Gregg slipped the safe back into his pocket and placed his hands, palms flat, oh so gently on the ground in front of him. He wiggled his fingers like little, lethargic, worms through the dust of the floor in front of him. One, two, three passes he made, radiating out in front of him without success, but on the fourth he found a single match. The rough stone lay at his right ankle. He picked it up and struck the match to the surface. The shaft cracked, but the flame burst forth. Quickly, he found the bottle and brought the candle to the teetering flame. The candle finally begrudged him a permanent light. Still, he let the match burn down until it stung his fingers again.

Gregg scanned the floor around him and retrieved another seven matches from the dust. He nearly cried for the other three lost matches. Standing upright, he moved to the upper end of the chamber where the tunnel had collapsed. The boulders were huge and hopeless. Perhaps some looseness of gravel, some smaller boulder would present itself upon closer inspection later. Any small gain toward the surface might be cheering in his final hours, even if the mine had collapsed all of the way up to the head frame. He turned away to survey the chamber of his entombment, unable to bear the despair of the cave-in.

Two more candles and a lantern materialized in the faint illumination of the burning candle. Gregg tried the lantern first, but it contained no wick or lamp oil. After all, it and the candles had only been meant to serve as props. At least the candles would light though. Gregg decided to use them one at a time. He returned to the cave-in and studied the heap of boulders from all angles. Selecting the smallest rock from one side, he set the candle down out of harm's way and wrenched at the boulder with all his might. The stone teetered almost imperceptibly. Gregg dropped to his knees and scooped at the dirt and gravel around the bottom of the boulder. Very little debris separated the boulder from the solid rock of the tunnel floor, but Gregg scratched it all away. He tried the rock again and, after great effort, the boulder inched across the floor free from the rubble pile. Gregg collapsed, panting, against the freed stone. He looked to the void vacated by the boulder. A smaller stone could be seen at the back of the cavity. It looked to be wedged quite firmly by the rubble around it. When he had caught his breath, he retrieved a pick-axe head from the wall beyond the railings and attempted to pry the smaller stone loose. After many minutes of wrenching and prodding with the pick-axe, he succeeded in loosening the smaller rock, but it still would not wriggle free. Perhaps it was only his imagination, but for a moment he thought he felt the sensation of cool air around his hand. Desperately, he tugged and yanked at the head-sized stone, ripping his knuckles to bloody shreds. Suddenly the rock sprang free, only to be followed by a further collapse of the surrounding boulders into the cavity.

Gregg slumped to the ground in despair. He held the back of his hand, damp with blood, to the buried site of his hopes. No fresh air cooled his flesh. Gregg leaned back against the first big boulder that he had dislodged. His lungs heaved in and out. Suddenly he realized his efforts, combined with the candle, were exhausting the oxygen in the sealed chamber. His mind raced. Perhaps there *had* been a little cool air before the last collapse of the rubble. He had to manufacture faith that there was fresh air just a little beyond the cave-in. Yes, he was sure there had been. People would dig him out; find him. They must find him alive. Reaching to the candle, he snuffed it out with his numbed fingers. Closing his eyes to shut out the darkness, he quickly drifted off to sleep.

Ricky had listened silently to the efforts of Gregg from the solid rock beyond the chamber. He stifled many a laugh many a time. Newtson would die soon enough, but Ricky wished to prolong the decline as long as possible. He intended to relish every second. The accidental trickle of fresh air had created the possibility of death by thirst, but now that Gregg had inadvertently sealed off his own salvation, asphyxiation would have to suffice; not as lengthy, but Ricky would find ways to make the torment pleasurable.

That same momentary whisper of fresh air which had brought hope to Ricky's condemned man, had also brushed Ricky's sinister thoughts with feathery doubt. People might come indeed, to dig their handsome tour guide out. If the cave-in was not extensive enough, they might even reach him in time. Ricky had better set someone to the task of improving the blockage. He seeped and flowed to the upper end of the collapsed tunnel and oozed out into the open space. Picking up a rail post from the rubble, he began to hammer it rhythmically against a boulder. This was the sound that had first drawn the spirits of the Black Hills from the bedrock into the living air. It was the sound of steel on stone in search of gold. It was the sound of men burning up their lives for the glittering ore, and *that* life could make those spirits aware. Some of these spirits heard that age-old beat again and answered the call. They sped through the pores and voids of the stone, often even molecule to molecule, to find the source. Instead of a warm blooded man with a hammer and chisel, they found Ricky, the worst of their own kind.

They were odd creatures when they manifested themselves in the tunnel. Their faces resembled clocks and only one arm jutted from their short, stocky, torsos. Ricky set two of them immediately to piling more stone upon the collapsed wall. He arranged them shoulder to shoulder so that they could handle the boulders between their two individual appendages. Up and down the tunnel they tottered, prying at a crevice here and wiggling at a boulder there, clumsy in their efforts, but by and by, they added layer after layer against the cave-in wall.

"If you feel footsteps coming, then cease what you are doing and return to Lame Johnny. I have to visit my guest on the other side," Ricky instructed his laborers.

High above in the alleys of Lame Johnny's, Gaylord stopped waiting for the slot machine he had been ratcheting all night to come back to life. He had been patient for ten minutes but the machine showed no signs of resurrection. The curses of the orange-haired, heavyset, lady could be heard above the musical mayhem as she battered the top her defunct machine with her fist. Gaylord picked up his cup of coins and moved on to another vacant machine reluctantly. Soon, the orange-haired lady slumped down at the machine beside him. "I been workin' that damn machine all night. It was due for a big payoff any minute and the damn thing up and dies. I've never seen nothin' like it. Some new trick of the casino's, I suppose. I'll have to start warming this one up," she grumbled and stuffed a quarter into her new addiction partner's maw.

Gregg should have dreamed of pleasant times, big blue skies, and open spaces for his last dreams on earth. He did not. Something came to sit upon his chest and labor his breathing. The something rested lightly at first, no heavier than a goose down comforter. It said, "This is how the earth rests on the chest of my first bride Lotus, peaceful and comforting I suppose. I must confess I was perhaps not as gentle as I should have been with her. Old Sally Sugarloaf would not let me have her, even though she was a whore and available to anyone who could pay her fee. Sugarloaf said I was sick in the head, liked to hurt things, so I wasn't to have her at any price. Well I took her anyway, I did. But she found the knife I had won off of old Drewer in the card game, and she stuffed it into my lung. Well, I throttled her for that. It was a husband's right. Now here comes Sugarloaf Sally, always showing up at the wrong time and sticking her nose into affairs that don't concern her. Well

I told her with my dying breath, 'Your lover Drewer stuck me with this knife. You've seen it before. You know it is his. He was going to pull me off of your little China doll, but I promised to tell all about you and him if he didn't leave me to my pleasure, so he stuck me. Stuck me good and now I'm dead and so is your darling Lotus. He'll hang for a murderer.' That old bitch took the switch blade and hid it from the law so they wouldn't blame old Drewer. Lotus' people tucked her down gentle into soft sand on the ridge of Mount Moriah. Me, they pitched down a mine shaft and tossed boulders in upon me. This is how the boulders felt when they dropped down that long, long, shaft and smashed in upon me," and the creature bounced down hard on Gregg's chest. "One, two, three," he screamed, but he did not stop bouncing at three. As he bounced, he continued his narration. "Drewer was the manager of the old Glittering Curtain Mine. Got himself killed that very night in a cave-in. Now why the manager of the Glit should take it upon him-self to go into the tunnels to inspect the crumbling face of one of the diggings, instead of sending a worthless foreman in his place, escapes me, but he went down there - just like Sally, his secret mistress, sticking his big nose in where it didn't belong, I suppose - and the walls fell in. Squashed him like a bug. I've *seen* him down there."

Laughing hysterically, the creature kicked his heels into the air and pushed on the roof of the chamber with all his might. "This is what the rock feels like on the top of old Drewer's chest way down at the bottom of the Glit Mine," he roared. "The weight on your chest will be every bit as heavy throughout eternity!"

"What happened to the knife?" Greg wheezed.

"Shut up and die," the creature hissed.

Gregg could barely breathe at all. A growing, golden, light slowly filled his closed eyes. 'Perhaps this is how death finally is," he thought, "A golden light, the last gold of Deadwood." Surrendering, he opened his eyes to embrace the light, only to find himself still alive in the same, solitary, stone chamber. All three candles burned brightly to illuminate his tomb. No evidence of his phantom tormentor remained in the cell. "I must be hallucinating from lack of oxygen," Gregg speculated. "Perhaps some fragment of stone struck me in the collapse. I will have to snuff out these candles if I am to live as long as possible." Struggling to his feet, he moved to each candle and rubbed out the flame. He lingered for a moment at the last stub, wondering if it might be the last bit of light to ever enter his eye again. Would he die in the dark, gasping for air and shrieking in silence? Would he go mad and claw at the walls until his hands were shredded and bloody? Better to leave a good-looking, dignified, corpse if he could manage it, but then again, no one might ever see it. In truth, no one except himself remained in his world for certain now to judge his last actions. *He* must choose how he would end. Gregg set his jaw and stood up straight. He was a tour guide at the Golden Tooth Mine in the city of Deadwood, and Deadwood had always been a mining city. Whether it mined the placers of the streambeds or the pockets of the gamblers, Deadwood took care of its own. The people of Deadwood would discover the accident. They would dig him out, live or dead. He still had a chance for the former. Bolstering his hope, he pinched out the final flame and settled to the floor.

* * *

Shelly opened the front door of the quaint, old, house on Deadwood's Williams Street which she shared with her grandmother. The Drewers had lived there since the first decade of the town's existence. Rena Drewer shuffled into the familiar home and hung her purse from its accustomed iron hook on the hall tree. "Before I go to bed, Shelly, I want you to see if you can locate that knife I gave you for protection," Rena dictated to her grand daughter firmly.

"Oh Grandma, I know exactly where it is, I think. I'll find it for you in the morning," Shelly said with a sigh.

"If you know right where it is, then it won't take you long to find it," Rena replied, dropping resolutely into one of the ancient, stuffed, chairs of the parlor and picking up a magazine from the end table at her elbow.

Shelly studied her grandmother for a moment, assessing the old lady's resolve. She glanced at the clock over the mantle and, remembering Ricky's warning about the interruptions Rena was making in her work schedule, she surrendered, "All right, all right! I think I stuffed it in the tool drawer of the pantry, but I'm not really sure. If I can't find it there, Rena, It truly *will* need to wait until tomorrow. Ricky told me management has started to complain about the time I spend walking you home. I can't be late back from my break because I was searching for some silly, old, keepsake of yours."

"That knife was given to me by a grand old lady to protect me when I walked home one dark night long ago," Rena answered. "Her name was Sugarloaf Sally. I was sixteen and not much younger than the girls who worked for her. I haven't a clue why she should care if my life was any safer than that of her employees. I guess she figured my naivety was no excuse for unnecessary injury that evening. 'Take this blade and keep it close to you for protection,' she told me. She pushed the little button and the blade shot out, so that I would know how to use it. Then she folded it up and placed it in my hand. 'It was your father's once and he would be glad to know you have it,' she said. You know I was an orphan, Shelly, taken in by Martha Drewer as an infant after her husband died in the collapse of the Glittering Curtain Mine. Sally must have known my father, whoever he was. Women of her profession knew most of the men of Deadwood from the earliest days, in one capacity or another, I imagine. Mining was a brutal, lonely, profession, and ladies were scarcer than the gold. At any rate, the little knife is all that I have of my true family and all that I can pass on to you."

Shelly had moved on to the pantry while Rena relayed the story, but the houses of Old Deadwood had been built on restricted floor plans in the narrow, steep-sided, gulch, relying on a second story to provide extra living spaces. She could easily hear her grandmother's, strong, clear, voice from any room of the dwelling. Presently, she reappeared in the adjoining doorway of the parlor with a silver-fitted, ivory, cylinder in her hand. "Here it is, Grandma. I have no idea if it still opens. It has been in that drawer for at least four years. You never told me the story of how you came by it. I guess I can understand how this little knife might be important to you."

Rena took the knife from her granddaughter's hand and pressed the little button in the butt of the handle. The shining blade shot out purposefully into the dim light of the old parlor, as if it had been made the day before. "Oh it still works fine," she said, waving the blade beneath the lamp at her side to see the light glitter from the steel. Carefully, she folded up the blade and held it out to the young woman again.

"No Rena, you keep it for now. I don't have any need for that on the streets of Deadwood anymore. We have police officers on regular patrol. If I really need protection, I'll buy a little pistol, but Gregg or Ricky will usually walk me home when I am not with you. You carry it for *your* protection and old memories. I've really got to get back to Johnny's now. Please tell me more about Sugarloaf Sally and the story of the knife in the morning. We can put the knife in a better place for safe keeping now that I know it is a family heirloom of some sort." With the last comment, she whisked out the front door, hurrying on her way back to Lame Johnny's, afraid of being late.

Rena rose from her chair in the wake of her granddaughter's passing. She took the ornate, little, knife to her purse on the hall tree and stuffed it inside. "Then if I am near you, the knife will be near you also," she said to herself. Shuffling back to her chair, she kicked off her shoes and settled her feet up on the nearby ottoman. She picked up the magazine again, under the delusions of reading, yet knowing full well she would be asleep before she had scanned more than a few paragraphs.

Once or twice before in her long life in Deadwood, Rena had felt the tremble in the earth which jostled her now from her sleep in the armchair. She knew exactly what the shudder meant even before she had gained enough consciousness to know her own name or what year it was. A cave-in had occurred in one of the mines. Rena stood bolt upright in an instant as if she were sixteen again. Her hand reached for the phone as she struggled to recollect what mines could still be operating in the Deadwood Gulch. Only the casinos brought gold into Deadwood any-more. All of the mines had been shut down for years. Even the mighty Homestake Mine had finally closed in 2001. Never the less, she dialed the fire department automatically.

"Deadwood Emergency Services, how can I help you?" a woman's voice answered from the receiver.

"There has been a mine collapse," Rena blurted out to the voice.

"Where are you located, miss? What is your full name and address please?'

"My name is Rena Drewer and I live at Thirty-Three, Williams Street. I am in my home now, but I don't know where the mine is. I just know that there has been a cave-in some-where," Rena answered more firmly.

"Well Mrs. Drewer, you are the third person to call in about this in the last five minutes, but no one seems to know where any accident has occurred. Did you feel something in your sleep?"

"Yes, I felt the earth shake. A mine has collapsed some-where. Any fool who has lived in Deadwood for long knows what that sensation means. What mines are still operating?" Rena asked.

"Are you perhaps an elderly person, Mrs. Drewer? You do know that none of the mines have been operating in Deadwood for years now, don't you? Is there someone there with you?"

"Yes, I know the mines have all closed down, but I am telling you some terrible accident has happened. Someone is trapped underground," Rena spoke more impatiently.

"I have heard stories of how in the olden days people could sense when an accident had occurred at one of the mines, Mrs. Drewer, and to be honest, the other two callers have been of a certain mature age like yourself. Perhaps some portion of some mine, abandoned and sealed long ago, has given way. Perhaps that is what you felt, but I am sure it is nothing to worry about," the woman at the Emergency Service soothed.

"No, when we *elder* people feel that tremble, real lives are involved!" Rena snarled into the phone. "What is your name, miss? Mine is *Mrs.* Maureen Drewer-Cummins. I want to know whose name to give your superior when this tragedy is discovered and I am questioned about why my call was ignored!"

A silent hesitation transmitted grave contemplation down the line to Rena. "I suppose the Golden Tooth could be considered an operating mine of sorts," the dispatcher acquiesced to herself, as much as to Rena, to break the silence. "I'll send an officer up that direction to have a look. Perhaps he should have a closer look at the closed up mine complexes as well, just in case."

"Don't waste time, young lady. Alert the rescue people," Rena demanded.

"Is there someone who can look in on you tonight, Rena, a relative or younger friend perhaps, a care-giver?" the dispatcher asked.

"Never you mind about me, just get those people moving! I'll be on my way up the Gulch myself, as soon as I get my shoes on. I'm sure you will find the rest of us *elderly* natives who are able, making our way to help at whatever disaster has happened," Rena retorted and slammed the receiver back into its cradle. She went into the kitchen and splashed some cold water on her face, then wiped away the moisture with the handy dish towel. Seconds later, she had her shoes on, her purse over her arm, and she was headed up the street toward the location of the old mines.

Rena had barely covered one block before a fire siren's wail split the night and the flashing lights of emergency response vehicles began advancing up gulch from the lower end of Deadwood. Rena stopped at the corner to survey the activity in the town below her. She could see black silhouettes of other people flitting through the amber circles of distant streetlights across the steep valley from her vantage point, all moving in the direction of the mines. As she stood observing the rising activity, a police cruiser slowed to a stop at the corner. An officer rolled down the window of his car and shown a powerful flashlight on her face. Lowering the light so as not to blind her, he inquired, "May I help you in any way this evening? It seems kind of late for a lady of your age to be out strolling about on a dark street without an escort."

"You can tell me what is going on up the hill there where all of the lights are going. What mine has had a cave-in? Is it the Golden Tooth?" she snapped.

The officer sighed. "Would you be Rena Drewer? I was sent up here to check on you by our dispatcher. She said you might be on your way up town to see what was going on."

"Yes, I am Rena Drewer and I do not need someone to look out for me, but thank you anyway. Now what is going on up there?"

"Yes, there has been a cave-in at the Gold Tooth. One of the tour guides may be trapped inside. Now please don't continue on up there to try to help out. Those men are trained to do what they can and they do not need other bodies up there wandering around in the way," the officer insisted.

"What was the tour guide's name, do you know?" Rena broke in.

"We never release names until we know the complete situation and we have located and notified next-of-kin," the officer recited routinely.

"Was it Gregg Newtson?" Rena demanded more earnestly.

The hesitation to respond was answer enough, but the policeman finally repeated, "I cannot give out the man's name until we know the complete situation and next-of-kin have been notified."

Rena stepped down to the street to lean into the open window of the police cruiser. "Thank you officer, you have been very helpful," she said.

"Are you going home then, Mrs. Drewer?" he asked hopefully.

"I am going to find my granddaughter. She works at Lame Johnny's Casino. Gregg Newtson is her boyfriend. And no, I do not need a lift. I have walked that way many times. It is only a short stroll and you have more important things to do than worry about an old lady with one foot in the grave already."

"All right then Mrs. Drewer, be careful. Keep your grand-daughter away from the Gold Tooth. She can't be of any help there either," the policeman answered and rolled up the car window. He waited for Rena to step back onto the curb before he pulled away and drove on up the street. Rena turned on her heel and hurried on her way to Lame Johnny's to inform Shelly of the danger to Gregg Newtson.

"What is it Rena? What's wrong?" Shelly asked immediately when she saw her grandmother enter Johnny's for the second time that night.

"Is there somewhere you might sit down for a moment, Shelly?" Rena asked, "There has been an accident."

"Is it Mom and Dad? What has happened?" the young woman asked with fear growing in her voice.

"No, Bill and Janine are fine. Things are fine in Norman. It's Gregg, Shelly. There has been some kind of cave-in at the Golden Tooth and Gregg may be involved."

The girl slumped onto a stool in front of an empty slot machine. Oh God! I've got to know if anything has happened to him. I know he was closing up tonight. I've got to go up there to see if he is all right!"

Rena put her arm around her granddaughter, to restrain her as much as to comfort her. "No dear, you can't go up there. If emergency help is required of any kind, you and I would only get in the way. We have to wait here until news comes down from the mine."

Charles, the owner, had noticed the distress in Shelly's voice and had looked up from the bar to see what the commotion was. He hurried from behind the bar to discover what the trouble was. "What is the matter, Rena? What has got our Shelly so upset?" he asked.

"There has been a cave-in up at the Golden Tooth Mine. Shelly's young man, Gregg Newtson, may be injured or trapped. She wants to go up there to find out the details, but I am telling her that we need to stay here, out of the way of the emergency personnel so that they can do their jobs," Rena explained.

"Can I get you anything, Shelly – a drink of some kind?" Charles asked. "You just sit tight and don't worry about the customers. I can run this little shop by myself with no trouble."

"No, no, I'll be okay Charles. Rena is right. There is nothing I *can* do except wait for news," Shelly answered.

"You take a break to settle your nerve a bit anyway, Shelly. I am ordering you to do so. You may go home if you want to. I know a phone number or two that I will call to see if I can find anything out for you. I am going to bring you that drink, whether you want it or not," Charles replied and returned to the bar. He quickly poured some Coca Cola into a glass and added something clear from another bottle to the soda.

Gaylord stepped away from his machine toward the bar, "I'll take that to her," he offered.

"Thank you Gaylord," Charles replied. "Shelly, this has got a little stiffener in it, so take the first sip a little easy. It will do you good," he called to his waitress. As an after thought, he reached into a bin beneath the counter and pulled out a slot machine token. "Gaylord here is your tip for serving a customer," he said with a laugh and tossed the coin to the old man. Gaylord caught the chip one-handed, without batting an eye, as he handed the drink to Shelly.

"Let's see if we can change you luck," he said, stuffing the coin into the slot machine that Shelly sat in front of. He yanked down the handle with a determined flourish, the machine's rollers spun wildly, and the symbols settled to aces – one, two, three. Money began to pour out of the machine. "Ha, Ha!" Gaylord shouted with glee and began to scoop up the coins from the pay-out tray and the floor around. "Your luck has changed for the better! Your young man Gregg will be fine." He held out the money to Shelly.

"Oh thank you Gaylord, but I don't want it," she said with her hand to her mouth. "Give it to the other patrons to play for luck at their machines if you want to, or keep it for yourself."

"Give it to the others, Gaylord," Rena suggested, "Let them play it for good luck and best wishes for the Golden Tooth Mine."

Charles could be heard talking to someone on the phone. The casino quieted down so that people might catch what he was saying. "I see," he said, "And how many feet is that? Uh huh, how long will it take to clear that? Yes, yes, I understand. Yes, thank you, Good-bye."

The place waited in hushed silence for any new information Charles could give. Only the constant, ridiculous, cacophony of the various slot machine anthems disturbed the tense air of anticipation.

"That was one of the owners of the Gold Tooth. He is a close friend of mine and I have his cell number. He is up there now monitoring the situation. A section of the mine has caved in down near the deepest part. They do believe that Gregg Newtson is trapped in the cave-in. They do not know if the entire tunnel collapsed to the end, or if only a short portion of it has given way. Earl, the man I talked to, said the last chamber of the tunnel was reinforced more heavily because it was the deepest and consisted of the largest open area, so the rescue people have hope that the last chamber is intact and that Gregg may be there. They cannot tell how far the collapsed section is for sure. They do not know how long the removal of the collapsed material will take. If Gregg is still alive in the last chamber and he has enough oxygen, he may be saved," Charles recited grimly.

Shelly covered her face with her hands and began to weep. "Come on now. There is still hope," Rena told her and hugged the girl. The others in the gambling hall murmured among themselves about the news from the Golden Tooth. In the relative quiet, the sound of a coin rattling down into the gullet of a slot machine brought the muttering to an end. The orange-haired lady wrenched the arm of her bandit floorward. The cylinders spun and stopped. "Yes!' she screamed and coins tumbled into the collection tray at her knees. She reached over to the machine in front of Shelly and stuffed one coin of her new found loot into the slot. "For your man up at the Gold Tooth," she said.

Other coins clattered into slots and handles crashed down. "For the Gold Tooth!" became the battle cry. Soon, another patron shouted "Yeehaw!" and began divvying up his winnings to the other players in the casino. Rena pulled the handle on Shelly's machine, but she was not a winner.

"Where is that bag of lucky coins I have been giving you all this time, dear?" she asked her granddaughter. "Now is the time to try out the magic."

Shelly slowly got down from her stool and stepped behind the bar. In a moment, she produced the blue, velvet, Crown Royal bag of coins. She returned to her stool and sat down dully, as if in a trance. Pulling one of the coins from the bag, she slid it into the machine's slot and pulled the handle down. The bandit's drums whirled and stopped. Shelly slumped and collapsed from her stool.

"Help!" Rena cried, as she caught the girl in her arms and broke her fall to the floor.

Charles rushed from behind the bar to aid the stricken young woman. "Has she fainted?" he asked.

Rena gently shook the girl and called her name, but the unconscious girl gave no response. Rena looked into Shelly's face as Charles clutched her wrist.

"Her pulse is steady," he said. Rena did not hear him. Her attention had been captured by a fine strand of silver hair which had suddenly appeared against the rich, dark, youthful, locks of Shelly's head.

"Call an ambulance," Rena said sternly.

Charles turned back to the bar and was soon on the phone again. "Everyone is up at the Tooth, but they will send EMTs down right away," he said when he had finished on the phone.

Rena made her granddaughter comfortable stretched out on the floor with a commandeered jacket folded up for a pillow. She pulled the bag of coins free from the girl's grasp. "This is not your luck, Shelly. This luck is mine," she said. Shaking some of the coins into an empty cup, she stuffed one into the waiting machine and pulled the handle.

* * *

Ricky had sensed the approach of the rescuers down the mine tunnel. He knew his clock-faced workers would break off from their burying and disappear from the cave-in face. None of these developments bothered him. Too much stone blocked the rescuers from his prisoner. Gregg would surely die before they reached him. Ricky moved through the matrix of the stone to watch his victim's slow decline. All was still in the sealed chamber, except for the labored, shallow, breathing of the unconscious man on the floor. Ricky watched and grinned to himself in the blackness.

Suddenly, a faint round glow appeared at the cave-in face inside the chamber, and then another beside it. Stone began to creak and grumble. Rocks began to tumble out of place and be piled in orderly rows along the sides of the chamber. More clock faces appeared and lighted the chamber with an eerie, phosphorescent, glow. In a panic, Ricky stepped to the side of the nearest pair of clock-faced people and attempted to disrupt their work or pry them apart. They brushed him aside with complete indifference. He tried to stop the work a second time, but was again shoved away from the wall, more forcefully this time by more than one pair of workers. "Dammit!" he growled and dove into the substance of the rock with a splirt that dissolved into a stain on the chamber wall and then faded like the trailing slime of a worm.

Moments later, he strode into the casino from the rooms behind the bar. Quickly, he took in the sight of Shelly prone upon the floor and the hall full of patrons madly jamming coins into the machines. A call of "Wahoo! Another for the Golden Tooth!" rang out from deep in the crowd. Rena sat on a stool next to Shelly, watching her unconscious granddaughter, while she mindlessly crammed coins from the plastic cup into the machine in front of her. Rena's eyes were open, but the expression in them was glazed and far away.

"It's a mess," Charles said at Ricky's side where he had quietly stepped up to. "An ambulance is on it way soon for poor Shelly. By the looks of things, they may have more than one passenger."

Turning to face his employer, Ricky held out his closed fist beneath Charles' nose briskly and recited, "Look what I found, way down in the ground, Charles. What do you think it is worth?" With the last phrase, he opened his hand, palm up, to reveal two blackened silver dollars. As Charles gazed at the silver dollars reflexively, Ricky lifted his own jacket collar with the other hand and blew forcefully down the sleeve. A cloud of grit and dust from the tunnel floor burst from the cuff of the sleeve into Charles' eyes, where it burned like acid.

"Aiyee!" Charles screamed in agony, "You son-of-a-bitch!"

"Shhh! you've never met my mother. No one has," Ricky replied, stuffing his hand over the other man's mouth and forcing him into the rooms behind the bar. "Now go into the men's room and rinse out your eyes. You'll be fine in the morning." He slammed the restroom door shut behind Charles and held firm to the knob. Charles' muffled cursing and screaming could be heard through the door, accompanied by gurgling and splashing water. "I am the Sandman, Charles. Now go to sleep," Ricky whispered at the doorjamb and presently the sounds of anger and agony subsided in the bathroom.

Returning to the gaming hall, Ricky understood who had shanghaied his subterranean workers. Their ringleader sat directly in front of him, pawing those damned enchanted quarters into her own obedient slot machine. He crossed his arms over his chest and studied the old lady. She appeared to be in some kind of stupor with her eyes cast down to the face of her granddaughter while her hands autonomously stuffed money into the bandit and cranked its handle. "I can see both Drewer's ugly mug and that old hag Sally in your face Rena, no mistake. I am so glad most of those traits have been washed away from the likeness of Shelly by a couple of generations. What little of that treacherous pair that I have noticed now and then in her face has been softened enough so that I won't mind when we are wedded. In fact, I'll rather enjoy having the last laugh on those two by taking their great granddaughter as my bride," he sneered at the oblivious old lady. "But now I've got to put a stop to your meddling in all of my efforts of the evening. I knew I'd have to get rid of you sooner or later anyway. Tonight is as good a time as any." Ricky stepped forward to the old lady quickly and clasped his powerful, boney, fingers around her neck to throttle the life out of her. Squeezing with all of his might, he starred into the reddening face, with a sinister grin. The other gamblers' hands stopped still throughout the room at whatever task they were doing. The whirring slot machines spun to a halt. Rena's hand tipped over the empty coin cup, searching for one more coin. Her eyes never left the face of her beloved Shelly even as Ricky struggled to crush the last smidgeon of life from her. She reached for the blue, velvet, sac resting on an adjacent stool that she had pulled close to her own. Instead of more coins for the slot machine, her hand found her purse. Ricky heard the familiar click of the little, silver, button just before the blade flamed inside him on its way to his heart. Rena looked into his eyes and twisted the blade in deep.

"I heard every word you said, Ricky. Thank you for that. At last some little good did come out of your existence. I never would have believed it possible," she told the man slithering from her shoulders to the floor as his eyes slowly went dim onto death. Rena kicked the man away from her and dropped the shriveled handle of the switchblade onto the floor. The tiny sliver of bone was all that remained of the weapon, the blade having disappeared inside of its victim. She reached over to stroke the face of her granddaughter. "I *can* see Sugarloaf Sally there," she exclaimed. Remembering old photographs of Nancy Drewer's deceased husband – the gracious woman who had adopted her long ago - Rena thought she could make out a bit of that resemblance as well. "Yes, yes it is there," she told herself, but mostly she saw traces of her own, long deceased, husband George, lost in Korea. "Perhaps I'll see you soon, George," She thought to herself. "You'll be all right now, Shelly. *Everything* will be all right," she told the unconscious girl.

Turning back to her slot machine, she dumped the remaining coins out onto the stool top next to her purse and began stuffing more quarters into the slot. The other gamblers resumed their play as if nothing had ever happened. Her mind drifted back to the place she had been before Ricky had attacked her. She could see Gregg lying peacefully on the dusty floor of the chamber as if she viewed the scene through a window cut into its wall.

She could see Shelly lying beside him. Their eyes were closed and their hands were clasped to each other's. Gregg breathed shallow, but steady. Rena could see the clock-faced people methodically removing the stones from the cave-in on Gregg's side, while the rescuers made rapid progress from their direction. The barrier between had grown very thin now. Soon, the clock-faced people would fade back into the rock of the mountain, released from the servitude of the gamblers in Lame Johnny's. The rescuers would break through in time to find Gregg alone, but alive.

Rena turned away from the window view. She started down the familiar tunnel which she had traveled many times. Veins of gold, fine as angel hair, ran upon the walls of the mine in fine filigree. Rena did not know the name of the mine. It may as well have been called Rena's Mine for all she cared, for she did not believe she would stroll its passageways again. The Gold of Deadwood held many magics within its webs - some good, some uncertain, depending on who unearthed them - but in Rena's Mine, time spun backward. Now Rena was moving down the familiar tunnel for the last time.

Rena covered her eyes with her hands as she left the tunnel. Slowly, she parted her fingers a little at a time, allowing the blazing sunlight to set her flesh aglow like cherries in a line. The blood pink of her own substance infused with light allowed her irises to constrict from their awesome searching of the darkness she had been traveling in. She always loved this moment, this instant of overpowering escape. Slowly, she parted her fingers completely to behold the lush green valley below the mine. What would she be today? Perhaps a Meadowlark perched upon a sagebrush limb singing its challenge to the bees. Perhaps an Indian Paintbrush, holding outspread petals to the sun, much as she had just done. Could she be a buffalo today, running cross the landscape unstoppable? On a distant sunlit ridge, a herd of wild horses burst into view, a wave of many colored freedom. Today, she would be a mustang and run as a little streak of the wind, to roam the endless prairies unbound.

* * *

The paramedics hurried through the doors of Lame Johnny's with their medical valises in hand. They had expected to find an unconscious, young, woman to deal with. The young woman was there, but also a thin, dark, man slumped on the floor next to her, and an elderly woman sprawled across the face of a slot machine, her eyes staring into space. "The girl is breathing steady at least, but the man and the old lady look done for to me," the first paramedic said to his female partner. "You check the woman on the slot machine quick and I'll feel for a pulse on the guy on the floor."

"She's a goner," the female EMT confirmed, "Probably a massive stroke. We can try CPR, but I don't think there is any hurry. What about him?" she indicated with a nod of her head.

The first EMT continued to hold his hand to Ricky's carotid artery, but shook his head. "Nothing here," he said, "In fact, he is as cold as a stone. It's like he has been dead for days."

"How about the girl? She is what we were called for," the lady EMT asked.

The first paramedic turned to check out the condition of Shelly and, as he turned, she stirred, opened her eyes, and rose up on one elbow. The man stooped to steady her as she struggled to gain control. "Easy now," he said, "You have been out for a while and we do not know what the cause was yet."

"What has happened at the Golden Tooth Mine? Have they found Gregg yet? Is he all right?" she asked. The woman paramedic had graciously closed Rena's eyes before Shelly had awakened. Shelly caught sight of her grandmother slumped lifelessly against the machine. "Grandma Rena!" she screamed, "No, I can't loose you now!" She attempted to struggle to her feet to embrace her grandmother.

"I am sorry, miss. Your grandmother is gone. It was probably a stroke or a heart attack," the man attending her explained.

Shelly began to sob hysterically, crying, "Rena? Gregg?" She must have seen Ricky's body sprawled on the floor a few feet away, but she did not acknowledge much loss at his demise. Perhaps the apparent loss of two loved ones was all that her mind would allow her to bear.

At that moment, Charles came gagging and staggering out of the back rooms, still rubbing his eyes. "Where is that son-of-a bitch Ricky?" he bellowed. "I'm going to kill him and then fire him! He'll think blowing sand in my eyes was some funny joke then, he will," he roared.

"The lady paramedic stepped in front of him to halt his charge. "Whoa there mister, let me have a look at your eyes. Stop rubbing them," she commanded, pulling his hands away from his face. She studied his eyes for a moment. "They look plenty red and irritated. You should probably come in with us to the ER to have the doctor take a look at you. We can put some saline solution in to sooth your pain a little for the trip."

Charles caught sight of Ricky lying on the floor. "What's the matter with him?" he snarled.

"I'm afraid he is dead. What happened between you two?" the male EMT asked.

"I didn't do a damn thing to him. He waltzed in here and threw a handful of sand in my face. Then he shoved me in the men's room and slammed the door. I must have bumped my head on the sink or something because I just came to in there. What's wrong with Rena?" he continued.

"Tough night at Johnny's it would seem. She has passed on. Her granddaughter is conscious, but hysterical. We are not going to have room for all of you," the male EMT explained.

"Ah! That is too bad! She was a grand old lady. Her loss, on top of her boyfriend trapped in the Golden Tooth, will be a terrible load for Shelly," Charles said. "I'll be all right. You needn't take me into the emergency room. If I feel the need to go in tonight, I'll get someone else to drive me in. I will certainly get checked out tomorrow."

Her boyfriend huh," The EMT looked up at his partner. "You better call into dispatch and see how things are going up at the mine. Maybe the other ambulance can slip down for the deceased gentleman here, if the mine rescue people have not reached that tour guide yet. We can take Shelly and her grandmother in first."

The woman quickly placed a call into the central dispatch and was connected to the scene of rescue at the mine. "Hi, this is Julie with Ambulance Two. How are things going up there?" she asked. Listening to the radio phone, she nodded her head and a smile slowly crossed her face. "Well that is good news. There is a young lady here who will be very happy to hear that. Can you hold for a minute? Okay," she replied into the phone. "The rescue team has broken through the cave-in and recovered Mr. Newtson. He has suffered some shock and dust inhalation, but he is going to be fine. Ambulance One will take him to the hospital for the rest of the night for treatment and observation," she relayed to the people in the room. "After you deliver Newtson to the ER, can you come down to Lame Johnny's to pick up another? No, no real hurry. The victim is deceased," she spoke into the phone again. After a brief pause, she continued. "Yeah a *real* busy night. Massive heart attack, I'd guess, but I'm not the coroner. We'll stick around here until you show up then. See you in a bit," she replied into the phone and clipped it back to her belt.

The EMTs straightened out the body of Ricky and placed Rena on a gurney. Shelly was able to stand on her own and accompanied Rena to the waiting ambulance. Hank, the male EMT, returned to the interior of Johnny's to have a look at Charles' eyes and to wait for the other ambulance while Julie attended Shelly. The orange-haired lady leaned down from her stool at a nearby bandit, where she had never ceased to jam coins into the machine. "Rena stabbed him, you know," she mumbled into Hank's ear. "Ricky tried to choke her to death and she stuck him good with that fancy, little, knife of hers."

Hank stared at her in shock. "But there is no blood, no wound," he said. Charles cleared his throat to get the man's attention and then made a crazy, spinning, motion with his finger at his ear. Hank smiled and nodded in understanding. The orange-haired lady continued her gambling without skipping a beat.

Soon, the second ambulance arrived to remove Ricky's body from Lame Johnny's. "He doesn't have any family that I know of," Charles explained to the new EMTs. "If no one claims him, Lame Johnny's will assume the costs of his burial." After the body had been removed, Charles noticed a slender, polished, white, object lying on the floor where Ricky had first landed. He stooped to pick up the curious object and was startled at what he had found. He held a tiny finger bone, white as ivory. "Must have been some sick good luck charm of Ricky's that fell out of his pocket," he said to himself. Days later, at Rena's funeral, he stepped to the iron border fence on Mount Moriah and gently pushed the finger bone beneath the turf. Perhaps in some manner, it would be rejoined with its owner.

* * *

Charles declined all of the urns of various styles and prices that the crematorium had to offer for Ricky's remains. Instead, he found a terra cotta piggy bank of the classic style in a small ceramics store in the neighboring town of Lead. After sealing the slot in Porky's back with candle wax, he took the piggy to the crematorium director and instructed him to pour Ricky's ashes into the larger hole beneath the vessel's curly tail and then to stuff in the cork provided. In answer to the director's inquisitive expression, he explained, "Money always held a great attraction for Ricky and his kind. I felt this would be a more appropriate receptacle for him to rest comfortably in."

When Charles received the piggy full of Ricky from the crematorium, he took the next day off from managing Lame Johnny's Casino. Packing the terra cotta pig and a few other essentials into a day pack, he left Deadwood early in the morning. He hiked high up into the Black Hills, to a place where only the most solitary trekkers go. In a dark hollow on the very top of a pathless mountain, a vertical shaft penetrated a wide flat plate of the blue-black bedrock of the peak. Stunted, twisted, ancient, trees surrounded the natural bowl, shielding the unique setting from the prying eyes of general tourism.

Charles set his day pack on the ground and pulled out the ceramic piggy bank containing Ricky's ashes. Without ceremony customary to the disposal of the dead, he strolled to the rim of the shaft and hurled the pig down into the depths. Far below, he heard the sound of exploding pottery. After a few seconds had passed, a small puff of ashes spiraled up toward the top of the shaft. "Whoof!" Charles blew the ash spiral back down into the shaft with a fierce heave of disdainful breath. "Sandman huh, you're nothing but ashes now," he sneered. Returning to his pack, he rummaged around for a moment until he found a small, glass, bottle of clear liquid. "A priest friend suggested that I dump a little holy water onto your grave to help you settle in," he spoke to the shaft opening as he uncorked the bottle and sprinkled the sacred liquid in. A faint hissing and sputtering sound rose from the bottom of the shaft, followed by the clink and shattering of glass as the bottle struck the rocks below. Charles reached down again to rifle through the contents of the pack gingerly. Dynamite was hard to come by in that day and age, but Charles lived in an old mining town, with lots of friends with special access to substances of an explosive persuasion. He lifted a small bundle of seven sticks of dynamite from the pack. "Another friend suggested this would be a better way to seal up a dangerous pit. Being a rather lapsed Methodist myself, I have a tendency to put more faith in this second choice," he said to the hole. Fishing a gold cigarette lighter from his pocket, he struck a flame to the fuse and tossed the bundle down the shaft. Lickity-split, he snatched up his pack and sprinted up the rim of the bowl and leaped over the edge. A great rumble and roar shook the mountain top, nearly tipping Charles off his feet as he hop-frogged down the steep mountain side. He turned quickly to see if any large boulders were falling from the sky or rolling down the mountain after him. Only a plume of dust rose from the crater above him. The gentle summer breeze soon dissipated it into a thin, unnoticeable, haze across the dark, pine, forest. "A perfect burial," Charles said to himself and resumed his leisurely trek off of the lonely mountain.

Charles had to replace the slot machine that Rena had played before she had died. She had completely used it up - bearings were worn out - electrical circuits had shorted and burned. A shiny new machine took its place within eight hours. A few days later, Charles called in the slot machine serviceman and handed him a small, brass, plate. "Please screw this plate fast somewhere unobtrusive inside the service compartment of that new machine," he directed.

The serviceman looked at the plate quizzically. "Ricky? Isn't that the name of that creepy character who died in here a few days ago? None of my business, but why would you put his name on a new machine?" he asked.

"I am enacting a new policy for Lame Johnny's. If an employee passes on while working here, I will name a machine after him or her. Having the name on the machine will be kind of like he was still working here," Charles explained with a secretive smile. The workman did as he requested.

Charles had no intention of naming his machines after deceased employees. Instead, with every pull on the new machine's handle, he intended to imagine Ricky - forever compelled to carry big, heavy, boulders in an endless effort to fill up the miles of forgotten mine tunnels, deep beneath the streets of Deadwood. The new machine's jingle would have a particular, musical, sweetness to the casino owner's ears whenever a coin dropped into its slot.

TOM SNIFFTY
THE CHIMNEY SWIFTY

Nicholas Bradley the Third crept quietly down the cellar stairs and peered around the old, wooden, support post at the bottom. His query was kneeling in front of the ancient furnace. The old man had removed some metal panels from the furnace and had placed them to one side. Nicholas knew the man was old because he had spotted the man's bald head and white whiskers when the man had knocked on the front door. Alerted by the knocking, Nicky had spied down from his bedroom window. He had been pretending to be sick so that he would not have to go to school.

Nicky was in the First Grade. He was in the First Grade for the second year in a row. Mommy just could not understand why he hadn't passed First Grade last year. She knew that he certainly wasn't stupid. No, no, he was terribly bright - probably too bright for the mundane lessons of First Grade. Having to learn stuff bored little Nicky. That was why he misbehaved so much. Poor Nicky was sick a lot too, so he missed quite a few days of school. He probably missed one day out of every week.

Phys Ed was scheduled that day, so Nicholas had begun to feel ill immediately after eating his Cocoa Puffs for breakfast that morning. Phys Ed always made him sick. Besides, it was the day after Halloween, and Halloween had occurred on a Sunday, and kids should always get a day off of school for Halloween.

His sitter, Old Phyllis, had answered the front door to let the heating serviceman in. The serviceman had removed his hat when he had greeted Old Phyllis and that was when Nicholas had seen that he was bald and that he wore a soot-stained, white, beard. Nicky always felt much better around Ten O'clock because that was when Old Phyllis stretched out on the sofa to snore herself to sleep. The serviceman's arrival had delayed her nap for a few minutes while she had shown him the way to the cellar, but she had soon sprawled out again and turned on her soap operas. Nicky could hardly wait to see what the old guy was up to. As soon as Phyllis had started her wheezing, snorting, racket from the couch, Nicky had begun his stalk to the cellar.

Only the man's fat hinny protruded from the cabinet at the bottom of the furnace. The pale, puffy, tops of the serviceman's behind squished up out of his pants, revealing his butt crack. Nicky clamped his hand over his mouth to stifle a snicker. His hand smelled like the M&Ms that he had eaten earlier that morning while he had waited for Old Phyllis to fall asleep. He would have to eat some more of the candy as soon as he was finished with this funny, old, man. A spider crawled across the bottom step where Nicky crouched. Pinching the spider up by one leg, Nicky padded silently in his stockinged feet over behind the serviceman and dropped the Granddaddy Longlegs into the exposed, dark, crevasse.

"Woohaa!" shouted the serviceman, followed by "Son of a bitch!" when he slammed his head into the top of the metal cabinet that he was working in.

Nicholas jumped back to the second step, giggling like the silliest girl in his class, as the serviceman tried to back out of the furnace with one finger poked into the crack of his butt, trying to subdue the beastly spider. When Mister Squiggly had been turned into Mr. Smudge, the serviceman sat down with his back against the furnace and rubbed the back of his head. Nicky expected the man to come storming after him at any moment, but the man only sat where he was and studied the boy.

"Did you bump your noggin?" Nicky asked coyly.

"Yes, young man, I did. Something crawled into the seat of my britches when I was very busy doing an important job," the serviceman replied.

"My pet spider wanted to see where you put your pencil so you won't loose it," Nicky said smartly.

"I'm afraid your spider has a bigger head-ache than I do, and his is permanent."

"I'll get another," Nicky said.

"Maybe your old spider's big brother will crawl out of this chimney to replace the one you have lost. Maybe he won't be so friendly," the serviceman said with a slight smile.

"Aint nothin' up that chimney but soot," Nicky snapped back. "Say, what's your name, Mister?"

"Wouldn't you like to know!" the serviceman snapped back just as quickly.

Nicky laughed. "Well Mr. Wouldn'tyouliketoknow," he asked, "Just what do you think you're doing to our heater?"

"It's called a furnace and I am going to tighten the belt on the blower and grease the bearings, if you must know, Mr. Big Nose."

Nicky stepped down from the stairs to get a little closer.

"How do you do that?" he asked.

"Well get over here where you can see," the man said. "You might as well learn something at home this morning, seeing as how you obviously didn't want to go to school." He handed Nicky a big flashlight, saying, "Here, point this light into that metal box down there."

Nicky did as he was told for once. The light illuminated a large metal object that resembled a flattened snail's shell lying on its back. A finned wheel was encased within the snail's shell.

"That looks like the wheel that my hamster plays on in his cage," Nicholas observed.

"Very good!" said Mr. Wouldn'tyouliketoknow, "It's called a squirrel cage and the entire thing is called the blower. Now hand me that screwdriver with the red handle from my tool pouch and I'll take out a couple of screws so that I can pull the whole thing out of the cabinet."

Nicolas liked all of the shiny tools in their special pockets in the tool pouch. He handed the red handled screwdriver to Mr. Wouldn'tyouliketoknow and, when the serviceman ducked his head back into the metal blower cabinet, Nicky pulled another screwdriver out of the tool pouch and stuffed it into the waistband of his pajama bottoms. After removing the locking screws, the serviceman pulled the blower assembly out of the cabinet, on its support rails. Nicky crawled in closer to see what was going on. Behind the blower loomed a dark cavern. Nicky stuck his head into the cavern and discovered a tunnel leading off to the left.

"Better get your head outa there!" Mr. Wouldn'tyou growled.

"Why? What's in there?" Nicky asked. "Where does it go?"

"It goes clear to China and there's nothing in there that you would want."

In defiance, Nicky crawled in a little deeper. "Maybe Mommy has hidden some of my Christmas presents in here. I can't find any of them anywhere else in this house and I've looked everywhere," he said.

"Santa Claus brings Christmas presents to all good children. So I guess that leaves you out! Now get the hell out of there!" Wouldn'tyou snarled as he tugged harshly on one of Nicky's legs.

Nicky scrambled out of the metal cabinet. "Santa Claus is a lie. Mommy says there is no such thing and that *she* buys all of my presents," he said matter-of-factly.

The serviceman wrestled the blower back onto its rails and slid it into place. "Santa is magical," he said curtly as he replaced the locking screws.

"Mommy says there isn't any magic left in the world. She says that Daddy used to promise her magical things and they all turned out to be lies. She says that she will never lie to me, especially about silly things like Santa Clause."

"Maybe your momma needs a new papa," mumbled the serviceman, half to himself.

Nicky piped up, "Oh she has a boyfriend, but I don't like him much. His hands are rough and he has a funny looking finger."

"Nothing wrong with rough hands," said Wouldn'tyou, "They are a sign of a hard worker."

He handed the red-handled screwdriver back to Nicky. Nicky noticed that his hands were much rougher than his Mommy's boyfriend's were. Nicky began to wonder about the tunnel that led away from the bottom of the furnace. He doubted that it led to China. When he had crawled down into the ditch that the men that had been working on the street in front of the house had dug, they had also told him the ditch was going to China. Mommy told him people always said that about holes in the ground because China was located on the other side of the Earth. Perhaps if Nicky could catch the neighbor's kitty, Fruffy, he could stuff it into the tunnel and wait to see where the cat came out. Nicky had used Fruffy for so many experiments by now that she was getting very had to catch.

"Nicholas Bradley! Where have you snuck off too?" screeched Old Phyllis from the top of the cellar stairs.

Nicholas ignored her calling.

"You better get up there," Wouldn'tyou advised.

Nicky ignored him too.

"He's down here stealing things," Mr. Wouldn'tyoulike-toknow bellowed up the stairs.

Nicky jumped to his feet and scrambled up the stairs, clutching his pilfered screwdriver carefully through his pajama bottoms.

* * *

Stillness enveloped the Bradley house as Nicholas slid silently out of his bed to creep over to his toy box. Lifting the painted, wooden, lid, he reached deep down into the bottom among the cluttered pile of video games to pull out his stash of Halloween candy. Selecting a couple of Snickers Bars, he quickly unwrapped them and stuffed them into his mouth. The chocolate made him thirsty, so he decided to pad out into the kitchen for a glass of milk. Of course he couldn't bother with a glass; he drank directly from the carton. A liter bottle of orange soda captured his interest instead of the milk. Orange soda soon dribbled down from his chin to puddle on the linoleum floor. He rubbed it out of sight with his stockinged foot.

A muffled knocking emanated from the basement beneath his feet to freeze him in his tracks. Then he relaxed, realizing the noise was probably only Fruffy down there, searching for a mouse. Suddenly, Nicholas remembered his plan to send Fruffy through the ductwork tunnel at the bottom of the furnace. Now would be his best opportunity! But he would need his screwdriver. He retrieved it quickly from his sock drawer in his bedroom. From past experience, he knew that when he turned on the cellar light, Fruffy would hunker down wherever she was in hopes that he would not spot her - stupid cat. After hitting the light switch, Nicky charged down the cellar stairs, ready to pounce on the terrified kitty. No cat was visible anywhere in the dingy basement. The tapping sound resumed its insistent calling from the region of the furnace. Nicky padded over to the furnace.

"Damn furnace man!" he thought to himself, mimicking his mommy's voice, "He must have left something loose in there!"

The wind played murmuring tunes down the big tin flute of the chimney like whispers in church. Nicky leaned in to the small, rectangular, opening in the middle of the furnace and called up softly, "Who, whooooo are youuuuu?"

A scratchy, high-pitched, yet masculine, voice called out from the furnace, "Hi there, youngster! Hello! Hello! May I come in?"

Nicky stepped back quickly, but responded, "Where are you?"

"Lift the metal door and I'll come in," the voice said.

"What do you want?" Nicky asked suspiciously.

"Come on, open up. I've got a cat in a sack in here and it's crowded," urged the voice.

Nicky sprang to the furnace and began pulling at the cabinet door on the bottom.

"Not that door! Nobody comes in *that* door," demanded the hidden voice. "Lift up the top door and be careful. It has sharp edges."

Nicky pushed up on the edge of the metal panel above the blower box panel. When the panel moved upward an inch or two, four twiggy, black, fingers slithered over the edge and forced the door up off of its locking lugs. Again, Nicky sprang back. A soot-black character poured himself out of the top portion of the furnace, like smoke billowing downward. He turned back to the furnace to wrench a lumpy, squirming, green, sack out behind him. The strange figure stood tall and coarse hided as a hickory tree, but black as tamarack. He wore a pointed cap, stiff with soot like the rest of his garment. His boots were pointed, with steel toes that hooked downward. Nicky noticed that the heels also possessed backward-facing horseshoes of sharp-edged steel with little claws in the middle of the curve. He placed a finger on one side of his hawkish nose and blew out a cloud of soot, then repeated the action with the back of the same finger for the other nostril. He wiped the droplet of snot hanging from the end of his beak away with his sleeve.

Peering down at Nicky from eyes black as a midnight thunderstorm, he asked through glistening, white, teeth pointed as Fruffy's fangs, "What do they call you, boy?"

"You're the guest. You answer first," Nicky shot back as he pondered whether to run from the basement screaming for his mother or not.

"Fair enough," the creature answered, "I am Tom, Tom Sniffty the Chimney Swifty."

"What are you doing in our furnace?" Nicky blurted out.

"It's impolite of you not to introduce yourself after I have given you my name," Tom said with a curl at the corners of his wide mouth that allowed the incandescent light of the cellar's single bulb to glint off his long canines.

"My name is Nicholas Bradley the Third," Nicky responded with a defiance that he usually only deployed on his first grade teacher.

"Well you are a bold one, Nick," Tom retorted, "I'll give you that. I've got a brother named Nicholas. Some people call him a saint but I know he's a big phony. People think he brings presents at Christmas, but, most of the time, he is just snooping around and raiding their refrigerators - the fat slob."

Nicky repeated, "What are you doing here?"

"Actually, I work for the big faker," Tom Sniffty continued. "Old Santa Klutz can't get his fat rear-end down most chimneys or stove pipes these days, especially if the flue is clogged with soot. He used to be as agile as I am when we were kids, but not anymore, not after years of beer and pretzels every night. So now he pays me to clear the way down, or to find an alternate route into the house for him. I think he'll be slipping in the back door at a lot of places this year, including your house."

"We keep our doors locked at night. Besides, Mommy buys all my Christmas presents," Nicholas said.

"I usually snitch an extra key from houses like yours when I make my reconnaissance visit, or I practice picking the lock," Tom explained, stabbing one of his stiletto index fingers effortlessly into the mortar between the bricks of the cellar wall.

"What does reconnaissance mean?" Nicky asked.

Tom rolled his eyes upward in thought for a second. "Spying," he answered.

The sooty, green, bag wiggled a little where it slumped against the wall. Tom prodded it gruffly with his steel toe, "Settle down there, you!" he snarled.

"What are you going to do with Fruffy?" Nicky asked.

"I thought that I would shove him into the ductwork to see where he comes out in the house," Tom said slyly.

"I got a screwdriver!" Nicky volunteered, pulling the pilfered tool from the waistband of his pajama bottoms.

"Well now, how prepared you are! Just like a Boy Scout," Tom said as he snatched the shiny screwdriver away from Nicolas.

Nicky stood with his mouth wide open in objection, but Tom Sniffty was already stooped over, prying off the lower door of the furnace to remove the blower. Nicky decided to demand the return of his screwdriver later. He knelt down beside Tom to watch the twiggish creature's progress. Tom pulled a long, thin, green, candle from a concealed pocket in his sooty clothing and lighted it by some trick of snapping his sandpapery fingers.

"Here, hold this so I can see what I'm doing," he said, handing the strange candle to Nicky.

A sputtering, green, flame, more like a Fourth of July sparkler, burned from the candle's wick. Tom Sniffty wrenched the blower assembly out from the metal cabinet and peered into the darkness of the exposed tunnel.

He snatched up Nicky's arm by the wrist and dragged the candle into the entrance to the ductwork tunnel, hissing, "I see something. Gim'me more light!"

Nicky involuntarily followed the candle into the mouth of the tunnel. "What is it? What do you see?" he asked.

"It looks like a bundle of some kind, or a present," Tom said.

"I knew it! I knew Mommy hid my presents down here someplace! Do you see any more? I can't believe there is only one!" Nicolas exclaimed.

"I only see one, little, bundle, but maybe there are more farther in. Some people do hide their children's Christmas presents in places like this," Tom mussed. "Here, take the candle, crawl in there, and have a look."

Like a termite in a timber, Nicky squirmed past Tom Sniffty into the passage with the green candle. The silhouette of a package, wrapped with a ribbon and bow, could be glimpsed far down the tunnel. Nicky scrambled quickly down the passage to the present. Gripping the package between his knees and holding the candle in one hand, he tore at the plain, brown, wrapping, thinking to himself, "Pretty crappy wrapping job for Mommy's work."

"What is it?" called Tom from the blower cabinet.

"Just a minute!" Nicky snarled, "It's my present anyway; not yours!"

Suddenly, the box lid came off, revealing a big lump of black coal in the bottom of the box.

"Shit!" exclaimed Nicky, using a word that he knew was strictly forbidden, "This isn't very funny! Not funny at all!"

He looked up from his box, back down the tunnel toward Tom, just in time to see the Chimney Swifty shoving the blower back into place. "Hey!" Nicky shouted, as he began scrambling back toward the blower cabinet.

"My brother has good tools," Tom mumbled to himself as he screwed in the locking screws to the blower and slammed the cabinet door in place. "Now for a little of Cousin Jack's magic," he said to himself. He sucked up a great gulp of air, then exhaled a long, black, streamer of cloud that moved like a spidery shadow. The shadow crept up the stairs to find the household thermostat. Icy, spidery, fingers covered the thermostat like the hand of Death. Down in the basement, the furnace roared to life. Flames leaped from the burners above the blower cabinet and curled up into the bowels of the furnace. Some even curled out of the furnace as if trying to catch a victim to pull inside.

"In a minute," Tom said absently to the flames.

Meanwhile, inside the ductwork, Nicky had made his way to the blower at the end of the tunnel. He reached out to the squirrel cage, hoping to remove it from his path in some way. Tom laughed a hideous chuckle. The blower kicked on. Two of Nicky's fingers snipped off.

Screaming in pain, and clutching his injured hand under his other armpit, Nicky wiggled away from the whirling squirrel cage. "Let me out! I'm hurt!" he cried, over and over again, but no one could hear him beyond the howling blower. The green candle sputtered down the tunnel a short distance where he had flung it when he had lost his fingers. He crawled back to the green glow on his knees and one hand, then sat by the candle, sobbing and wailing. Eventually, the wailing subsided to whimpering as Nicky grew tired and the intense pain faded to a numb ache.

Something whispered far off down the tunnel; a voice murmured some indiscernible nursery rhyme. Nicholas stifled his whimpering and strained to hear.

"Spiders spin webs to catch a meal, webs work fine a wound to seal," sang the distant voice.

Nicky noticed some evil looking cobwebs dangling within reach in the corners of the ductwork, but he shuddered at the thought of pulling them down and wrapping them around his aching stubs.

Coming from the darkness behind Nicky's ear, the tinny voice became a snarl this time, "Use the webs to stop the red! Do it soon or you'll be DEAD!"

Nicky sprang from the looming voice, snatched the cobwebs, and wadded them onto his oozing stubs. The webs made the wounds sting severely and Nicky began to sob again. When his crying finally began to relent, he could hear the voice singing once more, far down the tunnel. The voice was sweet and soothing now.

"Bring your candle green and bright; and you'll be out before daylight," it cooed.

"I can't crawl all night," Nicky cried, "I'm too tired and I'm scared."

"In these tunnels live big rats. They are eaten by mad cats!" the voice recited.

Nicky heard a purring sound approaching from the direction of the furnace. The purring became a rumbling that Nicky could feel through the ductwork. Huge, yellow, feline, eyes glinted in the darkness.

"Crawl Nicky! Crawl!" demanded the voice, and Nicky crawled! He crawled for miles and hours, hours and miles. He crawled around corners right and left. He crawled up stairs and down slides. He grew tired and stopped to rest, but the eyes always followed. The monstrous cat would yowl a bloodthirsty cry that would freeze Nicky's blood and send him scurrying on after the insistent voice.

"Move your hands, Nicky; move your feet. I know that Kitty wants to eat," echoed back from the darkness far ahead.

Just as Nicky was about to give up, to lie down, and let the cat have him, light appeared faintly down the passage. Gathering his last ounce of strength, Nicky scuttled down the tunnel like an ant after sugar. As his head burst out of the tunnel exit, strong, black, spidery, hands snatched him under each armpit to swing him up into the glaring light.

"Rats in the cellar!" roared Tom Sniffty.

Tom spun Nicholas around in mid-air to face him. He was sitting on a huge, red satin, throne - much too wide for his narrow, bony, black, butt. Nicky looked down between his dangling feet, expecting to see a huge cat emerge from the tunnel mouth where it opened beneath the legs of the throne.

"Meooowww! Meooowww!" yowled Tom and his eyes glinted yellow. Then he laughed his hideous cackle.

Regaining his haughty attitude, Nicholas demanded, "Where am I? How did you get here? Why did you shut me in that nasty tunnel, you filthy spider man?"

"Spiderman is a silly cartoon, kid. I'm a Chimney Swifty and that is an entirely different cat," Tom corrected him tersely.

"Oh yeah? Then what about Mary Poppins, dancing on the roof tops, Chime Chiminey Cherrie, and all that Walt Disney stuff?" Nicky demanded.

"Daffy Dick Van Dyke never even met a real Chimney Swifty! But rest assured, someday soon, I'm going to pay that skinny, old, faker a visit to straighten him out on a few things," Tom growled.

"Who are you calling skinny? Your behind sure doesn't fit that chair you're in. Now where *am* I?" Nicky sassed back.

"This chair? This is Brother Santa's chair. He's out of town for awhile, so I'm using it while I direct his shop for him."

"So I guess that means I'm at the North Pole. I knew I had crawled a long way but I never would have guessed clear to the North Pole," Nicky exclaimed.

"This ain't the North Pole, kid, although it gets plenty cold enough in the winter here. This is China," Tom explained as he stood up from the throne, still holding Nicky suspended at arm's length. "Time to find you a seat that fits *your* behind. Time to put you to work. That's why you're here."

Nicky squirmed to get free and shouted, "I'm not working for you or anybody! You can't make me!"

Tom slammed him down into an empty chair beside a long worktable where other small people bent over various projects. "Shut up and pick up that paint brush!" he commanded.

Nicky stared at the people on either side of him. "These people are green! They're Elves! *They* know how to make toys and things. *I* am not an Elf!" he insisted.

"Oh yeah Smarty? Then what do you call this color?" Tom asked, snatching up Nicky's good hand to hold in front of the boy's face.

To his horror, Nicky saw that his own skin was indeed as green as a 7-UP bottle.

"Spent too much time under the light of the green candle. It happens to all of you on the journey," Tom mussed. "Now quit stalling and get to work."

Nicky lost his nerve and began to cry. "I can't work," he shouted through bitter tears, "I hurt my hand when you locked me under the furnace."

"Oh! I nearly forgot!" Tom exclaimed, "I saved your fingers for you – sort of. I went upstairs in your old house and searched under the heat registers - you know - those grate things in the floor where you hide things from your mother and Old Phyllis. Your fingers were thrown up through the furnace with the hot air where they landed in the upstairs heating ducts. I found them in the bathroom vent. Problem is, I travel by smoke. It's a lot faster than the tunnel system you came through. I had to throw your fingers onto the furnace burners so that they could travel with me." He opened a small, green, cloth, bag which he had pulled from his pocket and held it out so that Nicky could view the contents. "See," he said, "Nothing left but black ashes."

Nicky threw his head down on his arms on the tabletop and sobbed inconsolably.

"Oh all right! I'll fix it, Cry Baby," Tom snapped.

He pulled the bag wide open and spat into it. Rubbing the mess inside together, he yanked Nicky's injured hand out from under his head, jammed the open bag over the scabby stubs, and tied it on securely with the drawstrings.

"There!" he said, "Those will grow back in a few weeks if you leave that bag alone. It will stink some and itch a lot, but you'll get your fingers back. They will look more like blackened claws though than the little-boy fingers that you had before. Now hold the toys with the bad hand and paint with the other. When your hand heals, I'll start you at stitching sneakers," he said as he turned to walk away.

"I'll run away!" Nicky shouted after him. "I'll run outside and they will see that I'm not Chinese and they will send me back to America."

Tom laughed, "Everyone looks different from each other in China. No one pays any attention to the little, green, children who work here. No one cares how we treat you. Besides, this sweat shop brings in far too much money to China for the Chinese to wish to disturb it in any way."

"When Santa comes back, I'll tell him!" Nicky shouted.

"Santa chose this place, you little fool. He seldom comes here himself though, what with his homes all over the world. Right now, he might be at his ranch in Wyoming or his beach house in Tahiti. Who knows? *You* don't believe in him anyway," sneered Tom.

"My mommy will miss me! She will tell the police and they will find me. Even in China, they will find me!" Nicholas shouted in desperation.

"No, your mommy won't miss you, Nick. Fruffy wasn't in that bag that I brought into your cellar. I brought a replacement for you inside that sack. Another little boy had worked here a long, long, time. He slowly learned many things over the years and years that he spent working here in that very chair. He learned what fear, despair, and loneliness are. Most of all, he learned courtesy and grace. He learned not to be selfish, and to care about others. Ironically, he grew to look a lot like *you*. He had forgotten his old name after all those years so we called him Nicky. I stuffed him into your old bed, told him to behave himself, and, above all, to keep his mouth shut about us or I would come back to get him. Granted, he is still a little green and spindly, but you were supposed to be sick anyway. By the time he eats a little Thanksgiving turkey and absorbs some of the glow from all those Christmas lights, he will be as fat and pink as you ever were. In fact, he will most likely turn out a whole lot better looking. I know he'll be a lot better child to raise than you ever were. Your mommy will thank the Lord above for the change in you and never even suspect the changeling. I'm sure he will behave like a perfect angel, and, just to make certain, as the old song goes, Santa will be dropping by every Christmas Eve to see whether he *has* been naughty or nice," Tom Sniffty explained, "Yes, New Nicholas will be quite a fine Christmas present indeed! Now… GET TO WORK!"